FRIENDS LIKE US

SIÂN O'GORMAN

Boldwood

This edition first published in Great Britain in 2020 by Boldwood Books Ltd.

Copyright © Siân O'Gorman, 2016

Cover Design by Head Design Ltd

Cover photography: Shutterstock

Every effort has been made to obtain the necessary permissions with reference to copyright material, both illustrative and quoted. We apologise for any omissions in this respect and will be pleased to make the appropriate acknowledgements in any future edition.

A CIP catalogue record for this book is available from the British Library.

Paperback ISBN 978-1-80048-555-6

Large Print ISBN 978-1-80048-554-9

Ebook ISBN 978-1-80048-552-5

Kindle ISBN 978-1-80048-553-2

Boldwood Books Ltd
23 Bowerdean Street
London SW6 3TN
www.boldwoodbooks.com

For Ruby

1

MELISSA

Of course the crash was her fault. Melissa wasn't concentrating on the road when she whammed into the back of a Mercedes, as she was too busy having an out-of-body experience, thinking about herself; this woman who should have been all grown-up but was as unsorted as a tube of Smarties.

She was driving along the Grand Canal in Dublin, had just arrived back in the city after an unsuccessful weekend in Paris. It was a busy road at the best of times, filled with the usual battered and beaten up vehicles, the odd articulated lorry, the cyclists who only look up to raise two fingers to traffic that skims too close.

And there was Melissa in her orange Beetle thinking about Alistair and the fact he had just given her the old heave-ho. In the airport. After a weekend in Paris. So that was nice, wasn't it? At the age of thirty-eight, shouldn't she have achieved a little bit more, relationship wise?

But what was really bothering her wasn't just the fact that she had been dumped – again – but because she had persisted in pursuing a relationship which had, if she was entirely honest, lacked lustre from the very beginning.

I *should* have children, she thought, buckets of them. Mr Perfect in the corner, smiling, as one child smears Nutella on the sofa, while the other saws away tunelessly on a violin. Isn't that what women should have? Isn't that what we're told life should look like?

But there was no getting away from it; Melissa had had a truly *terrible* weekend, the *least* romantic since her school leavers' do when Tony Tierney puked all over her dress and she walked home crying and covered in vomit. However, being an imaginative type, she preferred to think the weekend's failure was because poor old Alistair had been under the weather and not at his sparkling best. But, come to think of it, she had never seen him at his sparkling best. Maybe he didn't have one.

Flu, Alistair had muttered darkly – and kept re-tucking his scarf, sniffling and snuffling throughout the weekend. She had managed to steer him away from Molly Malone's near the Champs Elysée and instead they ate in a restaurant in the Marais. However, he complained about the steak (too bloody), refused to be amused by the grumpiness of the waiters and blew his nose in the napkin. Crimes on the lower end of the scale and ones Melissa had been certainly determined to overlook.

She remained stoic. Remember Stalingrad, she had kept thinking. It was colder then, surely, and they were hungrier. But although she may not have been *actually* freezing her arse off in a Russian winter in 1943 and fearing for her life, those soldiers at least didn't have to put up with the snufflings of Alistair. Amazingly, he was able to reach out for his pint of lager and shiveringly bring the vessel to his blue lips. Undeterred, she threw back the red wine and the whole weekend became not a romantic cliché but an alcoholic blur.

You can't have it all, she had thought, consoling herself. And it is *Paris*; he's ill and no one can help that. Maybe she just had to try harder, be funnier, nicer, attractiver. With a little helping of Florence Nightingale on the side.

Okay, so it may not have been a success but even if he was a slight hypochondriac, she hadn't *actually expected him to finish with her. At the airport*. They were heading through arrivals, both pulling their little wheelie cases, him still snuffling and she smiling winningly, hoping he would say he had had a lovely time, but instead there was silence from Alistair. Well, apart from the sniffing and the sneezing.

'How are you feeling now?' she said, trying to prompt a response. 'Glad to be home?'

'Going to go straight to bed,' he mumbled. 'Sleep this thing off.' She wondered if he was confusing a hangover with flu. Whatever it was, he was in Garbo-mode.

'Good idea,' she said, masking devastation. 'You do that.' An awkward silence hung in the frozen air. And then she realised her smile was full of hope and desperation but she knew how transparently pathetic she was so instead tried to look frowny and concerned. And, crucially, grown-up.

'Melissa... listen.' He dropped his voice. 'Listen, um...' A taxi had pulled up... it was as if he had actually planned the swift getaway.

She realised, finally, that he was going to finish with her and that his shortcomings were in fact hers and that she was the unlovable one. Please say something nice to me, she inwardly pleaded. Just *want* me again. Just like me. Please *like* me.

'Melissa, it was a fun weekend.' (It hadn't been. They both knew that.) 'But I... I don't really feel able to have anything serious at the moment. I'm so sorry...'

She was motionless, heart thumping now, blood coursing around her brain, sirens going off. She was being dumped. You'd think she would have got used to it by now. Searing pain that soon numbed to a throb, the pulsations of which were a reminder of her own essential unloveableness. This was how her life was meant to be, a catalogue of failed flings.

'Melissa, are you okay?' He was looking around now for the taxi.

'Of course,' she said. 'Totally. I agree, I'm so glad you said it. I've really enjoyed our time together.'

He looked hugely relieved. 'Thanks. I mean you are great and everything but you know...' Ah, there it was, the taxi! He swung his case into its open boot.

'I know.' She smiled again, this time to show what an incredible sport she was.

She waved bravely as the taxi sped off. Was that him waving from the window? She couldn't quite see. And had he promised the driver extra to vroom away as though on a heist? Regardless, she was left alone.

This was how it always played out: the ascent as she was desired, and then the drop, an ignominious free-fall through the air. However attractive she was, she was no girlfriend material. Not the marrying kind; she was too weird, too needy, bordering on neurotic. It never took long, usually around three months for them to realise... and Alistair had got out in a record-breaking two months.

There was nothing else she could do except to recover her little orange Beetle from the car park and start driving home, allowing the shame and humiliation to embed itself. No one knows, she thought, as tears streamed down her face, no one knows who I am. I am nothing, no one, worthless.

Other people found relationships easy but Melissa found them torturous. It was always full-on and then over. Keeping her deep unloveableness a secret was taking a strain.

Never again, she thought. No more. A life of spinsterhood loomed. Well, anything had to be better than watching a man blow his nose on a napkin.

And now, here she was, wending her weary, woeful way home along the Grand Canal and about to crash into a Mercedes.

A swan flapping its wings gave her a jolt, granting Melissa a look in his beaky, beady face, as if to say, *who do you thing ye are? Gallivanting again? Well, you've only yourself to blame.*

She saw the bumper of the Mercedes whizz towards her; the swan having a good gawp. 'You were right!' she wanted to shout. 'You were right. I do have only myself to blame. It's all my fault. All of this. Everything!'

In the very short journey from uncrashed to crashed, she heard the screeching of her own brakes (her body had gone into action, as least it wasn't letting her down), and then the terrible crunch, the breaking of glass and the sound of her head hitting the steering wheel. A nice Mercedes, she imagined, would have air bags. An old Beetle wouldn't. And didn't.

Her head against the wheel, Melissa wondered what to do before she heard voices and someone trying to help her out. She staggered, stunned and blinking, out of the car, resting on the arm of an old man, who in different circumstances, would have been leaning on her.

'Terrible traffic,' he was saying. 'There's always accidents along the canal. Too many cars. I always walk into town this way and I say to meself that it's a miracle there aren't more prangs or pile-ups. That's what I always say.'

He led her to the wall alongside the canal. Bloody hell, she thought. Jesus Christ. I've just been in an accident. The dizziness was beginning to clear and she looked around. Her head was hurting but she was, she realised, still alive.

'Now, love, are you all right? No broken bones?' said the man. 'Everything in perfect working order?'

'Just a broken heart,' she said, unable to resist the temptation of the drama.

The old man laughed. 'Oh, now,' he said. 'Lovely woman like you. Surely not?'

She managed to smile so as not to scare him off entirely. She put her hand to her head and felt it carefully. A huge lump was forming underneath, bubbling Vesuvius-like. But it was her car she was most worried about. She noticed two men had managed to push it up onto the pavement, its bonnet buckled and forced open, bumper hanging off.

And people – passers-by, good Samaritans? – were helping the Mercedes driver out of the other car, a blonde woman, expensive highlights glinting in the rare late-afternoon winter sunlight.

Oh God, Melissa knew this type. Better just hand over her life savings to pay for the dent in the back of the Mercedes. Although it looked perfect, well *perfect enough*, apart from that teeny-tiny-titchy *scrape*. The woman looked perfect enough too, with her swishy blonde hair. Melissa looked away, still shaky and not quite ready to face the inevitable confrontation, and began rifling in her bag for her phone. She wanted to call Cormac. He'd be nice to her.

She was aware of the woman coming towards her and Melissa braced herself. 'I'm so sorry,' she blurted out, looking up into the sun. 'It was all my fault. I just wasn't concentrating.'

The other woman was open-mouthed, 'Melissa!' She was laughing now. 'Oh sweet Jesus, Melissa!'

'Steph! Oh my God, Steph!'

It *was* Steph, looking exactly the same since they'd last seen each other. Blonder, perhaps, her straight hair in a long bob, her face the same, just slightly older, perhaps, minimal make-up. Polished, groomed, she was working the glorious trinity of the jeans-Converse-Breton just like any other thirty-something mother, but on her, it was smarter, newer, *and expensive*.

Melissa managed to stand up and the two hugged each other for so long it turned into a kind of dance as they began to rock together. The crowd gave a cheer and there was even a round of applause.

Steph, her old, old, old friend. How sweet the vagaries of life. Who said that? Someone, anyway. Oh. She felt strange and had to sit down again.

Once upon a time, Melissa and Steph were inseparable. School friends and then friends into their twenties when something happened – life? – and they drifted. Like a swan on the old canal, especially the type of swan who predicted bad luck... or in this case, maybe the swan was a signifier of good luck. Drifting back into each other's lives again. Or rather *crashing* back in.

'I don't believe it!' Melissa said. 'We haven't seen each other in years and then this happens.'

'Of all the backsides in all the world, you had to run into mine.' Steph was still smiling and Melissa grinned back, but she felt embarrassed. Here was Steph, all gleamy and glowy, and there was she, dusty and dishevelled. She pushed her hand through her brown hair that refused to either lie straight or curl. She was wearing an outfit (skirt and ankle boots) that had been meant for Paris, but now, in Dublin, seemed over the top and ridiculous. She'd plastered herself in make-up too, full foundation, the works, and she felt like a drag queen that hadn't mastered the act of dressing like a woman.

But Steph was still smiling, seemingly not noticing or caring that her old friend was a mess.

'So, what do we do now?' Melissa asked. 'You know about this...' she gestured to their cars. She actually wanted to get herself home and changed and into something more like her. She was feeling a bit ridiculous in her Parisienne non-chic and, she was thinking that maybe they could meet up again later, once she had her jeans and trainers on again. But Steph didn't seem to notice what she was wearing and was too busy thinking about sorting out the car situation which, Melissa had to agree, was the more pertinent of the tasks.

'Well, I think mine is driveable,' said Steph. 'But we can always get yours towed. We'll get it sorted.'

And Steph did, even though the accident was technically Melissa's fault, Steph took charge and phoned a garage to arrange for them to pick up the Beetle while the crowd, slightly disappointed that there wasn't any blood or more carnage, dispersed, leaving them alone.

'You're white as a sheet, Mel,' Steph said. 'And you're shaking.'

Melissa could feel her teeth chattering as though she was Bugs Bunny eating an invisible carrot. She suddenly felt terrible, as if she was going to be sick.

'I think Melissa, that we'd better get you to hospital,' said Steph. 'Get you checked out.'

Melissa began to shake her head, no, which, she soon realised, was exactly the wrong thing to do.

'Come on, we'll go down to Vincent's... to A&E, just to be on the safe side.'

Melissa could only nod and allowed Steph to lead her to the car. She lay back in the seats and immediately felt better. It had to be admitted, what the Beetle gained in cuteness and character, it lacked in the comfort department that the Mercedes had in spades.

They pulled out into the traffic and made their slow progress along the canal. Melissa looked at Steph as she indicated and smiled at the drivers who let them out. She hadn't changed at all, same old Steph. One of life's good people, the kind of person you wanted on your side.

'I've just had a thought!' said Steph suddenly. 'Eilis!'

'Oh my God, yes!' They both laughed. 'Imagine!' said Melissa. 'She could be there, you know?' Eilis was their old school friend, part of their tribe of three. She was a consultant, as far as they knew, at the A&E in Vincent's hospital. 'Ouch!' Melissa pressed both her hands to her head. 'Shouldn't have laughed. That hurts. Major headache.'

'You poor thing,' said Steph, glancing over. 'You must have given it a huge whack. I hope they test you for whiplash too.'

'I hope they won't think I'm wasting their time,' said Melissa. 'You know, when they have really ill people to deal with.'

'You are meant to go to A&E after a car crash,' said Steph. 'You could be walking around with a head injury otherwise. No, of course we are not wasting their time.' There was silence between them for a moment.

'Are you... are you still in contact?' Steph said. 'You know, friends? With Eilis?' For a moment, Steph looked so vulnerable, so easy to hurt; it was a look that Melissa had never seen before. It's true, she realised slowly, people don't *stay* the same, even if they look the same and behave the same. Life always, always changes us. Something had happened to Steph which had made her insecure, or scared. It was hard to tell but Melissa had never seen that look in her eyes before. She was always so together, so happy. And then she had married Rick and she disappeared into wifedom and motherhood, as so many do. Melissa had been sad about it but she had her own life, other friends. It had seemed a natural parting. Melissa was single – still! – and marrieds socialise with other marrieds, and singles with their own kind and never the twain, et cetera.

'It's just that I lost contact with Eilis,' Steph was saying, 'as well as you, but you two probably still hang out...?'

'Not for a long time,' said Melissa. 'Not for ages. Years. D'you think she still works there?'

'I don't know... we can ask.' Steph was looking normal, again, almost relieved. She glanced over at her. 'It's good to see you, Mel.'

'It's good to see you too.' It was, it really was. 'So how is everyone? Rick? Rachel?'

She waited for Steph to say that they were fine, everything was wonderful, Rick grand, work going well, and Rachel was brilliant, or what mothers usually say about their lovely children. But instead there was silence. Melissa looked over and saw tears rolling down Steph's face.

'Steph?' she asked.

'Don't mind me. Must be shock. God, accidents always take it out of you.' She wiped her eyes with the sleeve of her cashmere cardigan. 'Stephanie!' said Steph to herself. 'Stop crying!' She tried to laugh. 'I think I just need a cup of tea. Six sugars. That kind of thing. They're fine, though, Rick and Rachel, before you worry. Both hale and hearty.'

Melissa was suddenly aware that something was wrong with Steph and after having to deal with her own mother all her life, she was highly sensitised to other people's moods, their inner feelings. It's partly what made her such a good journalist but also it made life difficult because you couldn't shake others off, their emotions were always so tangible to Melissa.

'By the way, you make it sound like you have lots of accidents,' said Melissa, trying to make her laugh, bring some light into the car again and give her space to recover herself.

They parked in the car park and began to walk to A&E.

'I feel silly now,' said Melissa. 'I'm sure I'm all right. No brain damage.' She was looking carefully at Steph, who still hadn't really stopped crying, her eyes still filling up with tears. What was *wrong* with her? 'Well, apart from the usual.' But Steph didn't seem to be listening, she was miles away.

They went straight to reception and found two seats in the waiting area.

'Steph,' said Melissa. 'I'm so sorry to have caused all this trouble. You know, the accident. And now I'm taking up all your time, having to sit here for hours...'

'But Melissa,' said Steph, still tearful, 'I've nothing else to be doing... and I've thought about contacting you so many times over the last ten years... or however long it's been... and then it gets too long and then you feel awkward and then you don't think that the person would want to see you and then you literally bump into me. If I was a cosmic person, which as you know I'm not, but if I was, then I would say that you were meant to crash into me.'

'Or maybe it was just an accident.'

'Or maybe it was just an accident. A lucky accident.'

They grinned at each other and Steph took a huge breath. 'Right, I think I'm myself again. Let's see if I can get a cup of tea for us out of the machine. Keep your expectations low.' They sat together, comfortably, chatting away, drinking tea, and it could have been ten years ago, twenty years ago, that old easiness between them had returned. It had just been dormant, ready to spring into life again.

Back home, later that evening, concussion dealt with by machine-tea, Melissa dialled Cormac, her go-to person, her fail-safe, never-let-you-down, best friend.

'Busy?' she said, trying not to sound plaintive. 'Fancy some company?'

'Who are you suggesting?' He sounded suspicious. 'Myself and Rolo are about to sit down to watch Supervet. So, it'd better be good.' Rolo was his spaniel; bouncier than a squash ball and sweeter, believed Melissa, than an actual Rolo.

'Me?' she said.

'Really?' Cormac sounded exaggeratedly surprised. 'I thought you and Basil were currently shagging on the top of the Eiffel Tower.' He paused. 'You're *not*, are you?'

Basil was his deliberately-wrong name for Alistair. He always did this with all of Melissa's flings, pretended not to know their name.

'*Alistair*.' They had been through this routine many times since Melissa began seeing the afore-mentioned. 'And no, we are not *currently* shagging up the Eiffel Tower.' This time it was Melissa who paused. 'It's too cold.'

'Amateurs,' said Cormac. 'Why do I keep forgetting his name? Maybe it's because he is just so *forgettable*.'

'Anyway, we're not seeing each other anymore,' she said airily.

'Come round,' he said, suddenly. 'Kettle is going on now and I am tearing open the Mr Kiplings with my teeth.' There was a rustling sound and the phone went dead.

2

STEPH

They had been in the same class since they were twelve... and as the rest of the girls formed twosomes, threesomes, and foursomes, they too found their own group. They complemented each other, they were all easy to be with and there were never the fallings-out, the promiscuity that infected the others in their year. They were all only children, as well, which gave them a different feeling, they needed each other; in a way, they were surrogate sisters.

Steph was always quietly sure of herself. Life, she believed was going to be all right. Her own parents were normal, which is more than she would have said at the time for most of the girls at the Abbey. Nuala and Joe, her parents, never let her down, did anything embarrassing, were just perpetually loving and permanently kind. She knew, even then, how lucky she was.

For Eilis, it had been different, not so easy. Her mother was ill while they were at school, for all of their teenage years, she was dying, Eilis her carer. Eilis was quiet, hard-working and never quite let on how difficult it was for her watching her mother fading away. Steph always believed that she and Melissa gave Eilis her few chances to be a normal teenager.

And Melissa? Who knew what had been going on there, at Beach Court, but it was obvious that Melissa just wanted to get away from it as much as possible, hiding it all with her cleverness and her wit.

Eilis hadn't been on duty that evening they had turned up in A&E, but they scribbled a note, making the woman, Theresa, behind the desk, give it to her.

'Tell her it's us,' said Melissa, who was acting almost giddy after the accident. 'I think sense has either been knocked in or out of me.'

It was another doctor who checked Melissa out, performing all the tests: the biro-following trick, the walking in a straight line, touching her nose with her finger. Steph and Melissa were nearly in hysterics by the end and Steph had (almost) been sorry when Melissa was pronounced perfectly well and they would go their separate ways again.

But the Beetle hadn't fared quite so well. Steph called the garage and was told it would have to stay in for a whole week. Steph said her insurance would cover it.

'Isn't that illegal?' asked Melissa. 'Lying about whose fault the accident was.'

'But perhaps it was me,' insisted Steph. 'I was on my phone, I wasn't concentrating, you know, stopping and starting in the traffic. Let me, please Melissa?' she said. 'Rick's just had some obscene bonus. Divorce. It's very lucrative.'

'Lawyers...' Melissa shook her head.

'I know... I know...' said Steph. 'It's not like they are saving lives...'

'Just tidying them up,' said Melissa.

'Life's great de-clutterers, lawyers.' Steph shrugged. 'So, as a result, I can pay. And I would like to, please?'

She always felt a bit guilty about Rick's money, his obscene pay-check which she felt she didn't deserve. She wanted to earn her own money, not spend his. They weren't a team, he wasn't earning on behalf of them, and if she felt she could pay for Melissa, it made her feel a bit better about it all, at least the money was helping someone else. It also explained the large cheques Steph wrote to various homeless charities and women's refuges.

She was thinking about Melissa, the following day, when she was tidying up, putting things back in their rightful places, cushions, remotes, glasses, mugs, books. The detritus of a home. But it wasn't really a home, was it? Not for her. Hopefully, it was for Rachel, but not for Steph. A home is somewhere you feel safe, but Steph was living with a bully, a man who was quick to anger and who wasn't afraid to push her around. Literally.

When she was pregnant with Rachel, he grabbed her arm behind her back. She'd been reading a pregnancy book at the time and was engrossed in thoughts of maternal love and wondering how to get babies to sleep and hadn't heard what he had said. So, when she felt him twist her arm, she was too surprised and shocked to react and it was over so quickly that the next morning, she wondered if it had actually happened. Although, he brought her breakfast in bed... which was quite unlike him.

'Bit drunk last night,' he said, standing there, in the doorway, tray in both hands. She wondered if he was trying to apologise.

If only she had done something about it then, gone to her parents, refused to live with someone like that. So she had often thought over the years, in a way, *she* was to blame. There was nothing stopping her from leaving, really, was there? But she had chosen not to, and now this was the bed she had made for herself, her own doing and therefore she couldn't complain.

And this is how she lived her life: walking on broken glass.

Even with Rachel, she couldn't say the right thing any longer. Everything caused Rachel, who was now sixteen-going-on-stroppy, to bite her head off. And there was nothing left that she was good at, nothing. Once she might have thought she was a good mother, but that talent had fallen by the wayside. And she used to be a good friend, was she able to at least be that?

But having seen Melissa again, she felt a lift in her heart. Normally, she felt so leaden, so weighed down, as though there was an actual physical pressure on her shoulders, but today she walked a little taller, a little brighter, feeling, weirdly, a little less alone. Steph felt good; she could almost remember the person she once was, the person she was before she met Rick, before she got married. Almost.

Her parents made marriage look so easy, they were a real team. Nuala was the ideas-person, the one holding the reins, and Joe was happy to be along for the ride, one which had now lasted forty-three years.

Whatever Nuala pursued, Joe would be there, her cheerful companion in life, and now on all the retiree trips they seemed to go on – to gardens across the country with the 'Grey Green-fingers', to France for the 'Francophiles over Fifty' group and to the mountains, on the first Sunday of every month, with the Wicklow Wanderers.

Behind every great woman was a man like Joe. It was he who made sure that the book for Nuala's reading group was put aside for her in the library. It was he who took the Dart into town to buy the Prussian Blue from the art shop now she had taken up oil painting. And, even now, he made her a cup of tea, put two shortbreads on a saucer and a flower plucked freshly from the garden into a vase and carried them to her at seven a.m. (He'd only ever missed one day that Steph could remember – when Nuala had gone into hospital to have her gall bladder removed. That day, instead, he had made a flask and transported the entire ritual.)

Steph never failed to marvel at how two people could be so right for each other, and silently and lovingly cursed them for making it look so easy, especially when it was so hard for Steph and Rick.

Rick loved Rachel, of course he did, but it was obvious he no longer loved Steph. If he ever did. And she hadn't loved him for years, there was something mean about him, a darkness and a *rage*, which made life a daily trial.

He had always done exactly what he wanted. He worked, he drank, he socialised, he *womanised*. And she had long suspected that something was going on with Miriam, her next-door neighbour and (former) friend. Miriam was always friendly, always flirtatious, but then, imperceptibly, something changed. There were the little things, like quick glances between Miriam and Rick, or sometimes it was the fact that they didn't look at each other at all. And suddenly it was all rather *perceptible*.

She had no proof, nothing. Except she knew it. If she accused him, he would only call her mad and she would look such a fool. But she knew it, she did! Being the weak person she thought she was though, Steph continued socializing with Miriam and her husband, Hugh, smiling when required, and running the house and looking after Rachel. Inside, she was wallowing in failure instead of going mad and all-Edward Scissorhandsy on his suits. And while Rick sprang up the career ladder, Steph felt she had nothing to show for her life. She used to be ambitious, the girl most likely, until life upended everything and she had achieved absolutely nothing.

And why, oh why, did she have to lose it in front of Melissa yesterday? She normally kept all her feelings buttoned up, but it was just seeing Melissa again, just being around her and remembering the girls they used to be, and the tears just came and wouldn't stop. And Melissa was her usual brilliant self, allowing her to cry and being utterly normal and unfreaked out about it.

And what about Eilis? Would she get the note, would she call? Steph had left both their mobile numbers, asking if Eilis would meet them next week. There was something Steph was hoping to rope Melissa and Eilis into and it was something that might bond them together again.

One of the old nuns at school had called her name when she was dropping Rachel off at school earlier. Sister Attracta, unbelievably still alive and now some kind of honorary nun, wafted around the Abbey looking increasingly wizened but rejuvenated by her the task of organizing each year's reunion. 'Stephanie Sheridan,' she'd called, using Steph's maiden name (another thing, apart from her independence, that she shouldn't have relinquished). 'I wonder, my dear, if you would like to help with this year's reunion. It is your twentieth.'

Normally, Steph would have run a mile from such an event, but Sister Attracta had ways of making you agree. The big night wasn't until December and was to be held in the Shelbourne Hotel, which was a far cry from their leaving do which was held in the school hall, draughty and miserable, with the nuns beadily managing the consumption of orange squash. Steph remembered having a bottle of vodka confiscated and so the orange squash had remained unadulterated.

Would Steph be able to look after all the invitations? asked Sister Attracta in a tone that would not countenance a negative response. *All* she had to do was track down each of the one hundred or so girls in their year and invite them to revisit their school days and their past.

Steph immediately thought of Melissa and Eilis. *She* would if *they* would. She was going to ask them when they met next week, and this, she had begun to think, begun to hope, was a way of them being the way they were, the three of them against the world, a gang. She hoped they would say yes, she didn't know what she would do if they didn't want things to be the same. She hadn't realised how much she had missed them, and she hadn't realised how much she needed them.

Tidying some newspapers, she found Rick's mobile, left over from last night. She was amazed he would leave this hanging around. He normally had the thing permanently in his hand or pocket. Quickly, she dropped it on to the rug and, aided by a sharp kick, its new home was among the dark and the dust. Steph had been engaging in this subtle form of domestic terrorism for quite some time now. It was strangely satisfying.

And then, she spotted Rick's keys on the hall table. Would hiding them be too much? Probably. Don't push it, Steph, she thought. Keys could be tucked behind a cushion or slipped into a drawer another day. The phone was enough for now and she didn't want Rick suspecting he was living with a domestic terrorist, he might get angry and that really defeated the feeling of satisfaction.

She looked at herself in the mirror. This is me, she thought. I'm thirty-eight and what do I have to show for nearly four decades on this planet? What exactly have I *done*? Except turn into a wreaker of domestic acts of terror. The temptation to cackle maniacally was overwhelming. The secret, she realised, was staying on the right side of madness. But she was like a beginner, wobbling on the tightrope.

She heard a beep from his phone from beneath the sofa. She paused, in mid-air, and suddenly she knew she had to see what that text was. Normally, she would never check his messages but she was feeling slightly reckless, the old Steph wouldn't have been afraid of anything and after seeing Melissa again, she could feel something of her younger and more daring self stir.

She fished it out and looked at the screen. Immediately, she wished her younger self had stayed where she was.

Missing you.

And the name of the sender? Angeline. His junior from work.

She scrolled back from the text and read as many as she could, her heart beating wildly, trying to take it all in.

They went back months and months as far as she could tell. Texts from Angeline saying she missed him, texts from Rick saying he wanted her. Arrangements to meet, times and venues, hotel rooms, bars and restaurants, passion, sex, desire. It was all there, an affair in text form.

If she was a braver woman, she thought, she would smash Rick's collection of horrible crystal whiskey glasses or flush his phone down the toilet. But she wasn't brave, not anymore, she was scared of what he would do. Even if she held the moral high ground she never, never, had the upper hand. He was always in charge and in control.

And Steph had met Angeline... how old could she be? Not thirty, anyway. Could she be mid-twenties? Twenty-five? What an utter bastard Rick was.

Managing to keep her anger on simmer, she dropped the phone back under the sofa. And, suddenly, she thought of something else, something else she needed to know. On the sideboard, in the hall, were letters from the credit card company. Normally, she left them to Rick, but this time she opened the envelope and scanned the rows and rows of transactions.

She spotted her own transactions: Rachel's new school coat, Steph's facial, paying for Melissa's car. And then something caught her eye.

Netaporter – €365.

She had often looked at the website, imagining outfits she might wear if she had dates to go on or weekends away. But her life never demanded a cocktail dress, and she had no idea that Rick had heard of the website. He certainly didn't buy her anything expensive and glamorous. Rick had never bought *her* anything like that. It was dated last month. And then more, a few days later, all in London. Selfridges. And the Wolseley, a Claridges bar bill and a room in The Connaught. They came to thousands and thousands of pounds. And she remembered that one of the texts specifically mentioned the bar in Claridges.

She checked the dates; the weekend he went to London to meet clients. But if that was a business trip, she was Rumpole of the Bailey. She then had a thought and went on Facebook and searched for Angeline Barrow. Birthdate? Last month. So it was a birthday weekend away. It had to be. Angeline was 29 years old. Steph shook her head. What was he thinking? Steph felt disempowered, dehumanised, worthless. Someone else was worth his time, his energy and she was nothing. She should have been used to it, but each time she was faced with his utter disregard for her and their family life, it was a new shock, a fresh wound.

Somehow she managed to get her coat, bag and keys and drive to the Dundrum shopping centre, and she did what she always did when subtle domestic terrorism did not quell her feelings of utter powerlessness. She went shoplifting. It was far more soothing than eating cakes, she thought, or drinking alcohol. The high was so much higher.

3

EILIS

Aching feet, damp patches under her arms and, sticky-up hair. For an A&E consultant, this was what was called getting off lightly, the mere physical manifestations of a night shift and it didn't do you much good to dwell too long on the emotional toll. Eilis McCarthy knew dwelling on anything didn't get you anywhere. She was half-way through a night shift and it was 4am but in the parallel universe of hospital life, the time didn't matter, you didn't care. It was a case of getting to the end, whenever and wherever that was.

But in all these years, the nightmarish whirl of a shift on the A&E ward never ceased in its power to shock. And then, suddenly, like some terrifying fairground ride, it was over and you would be deposited on terra normal, legs shaking and eyes blinking in the sunlight, the throb of it all jingling and jangling in your brain.

And all those patients, the old, the dying, the strokes, the beaten-up women, the bizarre domestic accidents – all those *stories* – they didn't just float off and disappear. You couldn't just forget about them and carry on with your day. Well, Eilis couldn't, anyway.

She would go home and try to do some gardening or gaze in the fridge for something to eat or be brushing her teeth and then she would realise she had totally stopped, frozen at the memory of the person who, just hours earlier, was fighting for life. They were men and women at their lowest, at their most vulnerable. Helpless, inadequately clothed, often alone, and Eilis would have stitched them up, made assessments, talked to them, soothed them, dispensed drugs, and then she was expected to just walk away. And then there were those who didn't make it, the ones who couldn't be soothed and medicalised back to full health, the ones who they couldn't help, couldn't save. It was them, the ones who had lost the fight, that were the worst, those were the faces that most haunted her waking moment.

Maybe she should have gone in for paediatrics. But that was heart-breaking, too, wasn't it? Worse, maybe. Or... maybe she should never have done medicine. But it was all her mother wanted for her.

The kettle in the little kitchen of the staff room in A&E was a slow-boiler and even if you tried not to watch it impatiently, it still took ages. But she persisted as she was suddenly desperate for the comfort of a hot mug of tea and a proper read of the note she had skimmed. And maybe a biscuit. Eilis rooted around in the tin hoping for one that wasn't soft or half-chewed.

She was thin and pale, the result of a diet of biscuits and not enough sleep. She was petite and pretty, her hair was cut pixie-style, but she spent most of her life avoiding mirrors so as not to be reminded of the dark circles under her eyes, and anyway, what could she do about it? Unlike practically every other workplace in the world, a hospital was one place where your physical appearance was of absolutely no consequence, thankfully.

The note had been written by Steph and Melissa. She had scanned it quickly, when Theresa had given it to her, but she wanted a chance to read it properly, to take it all in. The thought of Melissa and Steph – her friends! – made her feel that fresh air was being breathed into her life, something wonderful was there for her, if she wanted it.

And she did. She hadn't realised just how much until she saw Steph's handwriting. 'It's us,' the note had said. 'Here to see you. We miss you and want you to join us next week for drinks. Steph and Melissa.'

But what would they think of her? Would they see through her, realise how insular, how introverted she had become? And what would she say about Rob?

She and Rob had been together since they were first years... so twenty years ago now. But she wasn't sure if what she had with Rob was *normal*? They hadn't had sex since... since probably around the last time she had seen Steph and Melissa. No, that was taking it a bit far. But probably six months or so. Long enough anyway. Too long. When were you officially flatmates? What was the cut-off point? Six months? A year?

She and Rob were both doctors, so it was inevitable and entirely un-ironic that their relationship should be clinical. He was a consultant but had had the sense not to specialise in A&E, the front line. He was besuited and officed and led a far more civilised professional life than Eilis. He liked everything just so: his life, his home and his partner. He didn't go in for emotion or mess. Their small cottage was like something you might see in an interiors magazine, where if you left a mug on the table, it all felt wrong and weird. Their kitchen cupboards didn't even have handles, so you had to jab and stab at them, just to try and get them to open. Sometimes Eilis wondered just what was so wrong with handles. But these kind of things mattered to Rob... and it didn't really to her, so she went along with it.

Rob spent his evenings perched on their stylish but incongruously uncomfortable sofa. Supposedly a place to relax, it made you feel like you were waiting for your annual smear test. It wasn't what you wanted in a sofa; that much was sure. But Rob loved it and was happy to balance on its edge.

Their whole house was a bit like that, Eilis thought. Rob didn't even like cushions or rugs. The headboard on their bed had a piece of wood jutting out that caught Eilis on the back of the head. Every time. And even the tea towels were too nice to use. Eilis had her own secret supply of mugs that Rob said he *could not, would not* drink out of. If it didn't emanate from Scandinavia, then it wasn't worth having. He had also sharpened up his appearance lately but isn't that what happens when the forties loom, you either up your game or let things slide. He *was* more muscular these days and his hair was trendier. It was quite a shock when he came home with it, such a departure from the normal hair he had before... But he looked good. And very different from the Rob she had met all those years ago, when they were first years doing medicine in Trinity College.

He had dressed beyond his years in those days, blazer and smart trousers, hair cut in a style only a Granny would love. But now... he exuded that look of the lean, sporty type. Not the kind of man Eilis ever thought she would end up with and not the kind who she would have thought would have gone for her. But he had and there they were. A couple, uncoupled.

It didn't help that she felt surrounded by death. There was the hospital, of course, part of the job. Sometimes she felt like the last person left in the castle which was being besieged by faceless people with swords. She kept having to swing around and fight off the next one. But it was also her mother, who had died in her last year at school. She felt almost embarrassed that she was still, she felt, in grieving, even twenty years on. She still felt like that eighteen year old who lost her mother, she still carried the pain around carefully so as not to dislodge it. She couldn't, hadn't, told anyone about it as no one would understand her inability to move on.

But at least now she had Steph and Eilis... at least she had her friends back, after all that time. They hadn't given up on her.

She was desperate to phone Steph straight away, and say wild horses wouldn't keep her from meeting next week. She had missed the two of them as well and that making new friends like them had turned out to be impossible. She almost skipped out of the tea room, ready to get on with the shift and get home.

'Right, I need to talk to you.' A man in his early forties, wearing a checked shirt and sleeves rolled up, was marching straight up to her. Handsome, she couldn't help noticing. 'Yes,' she said, smiling warily.

'Are you a doctor?' He spoke angrily.

'Yes... but...'

'My mother has been waiting for more than eight hours. I just can't believe that this situation exists in this country. My mother... my mother is out there. Stroke... we think. Who knows? Not anyone in this bloody hospital! She's eighty-five, but no one has bothered to ask her that. No one has asked any questions yet because not a single doctor has examined her...'

'I'm sorry,' she said, thinking how worried he looked, wrung out. 'We are...'

'Listen,' he interrupted. 'I know you're up to your eyes, but when are you going to see her?'

'One of the nurses will have...'

'Do you think that is enough?' he said, speaking more quietly. 'Do you think that it is okay for an eighty-five-year-old woman to be left sitting on a plastic chair for eight hours? She's been given the once-over and that's all. Is it because she's old? Not worth saving? Are you all happy with that?'

'No... but... there's a system here...' She tried to speak kindly to him, to soothe, to calm.

He rolled his eyes. 'A system? There's a better system in any kindergarten. Bedlam this is. Proper bedlam.'

'I am sorry,' said Eilis. 'We are working as hard as we can.' This is the line that they all trotted out, something they have been told to use to keep anxious or angry relatives at bay while they get on with the job of looking after patients. But she was well aware of the flimsiness of the line, the lack of satisfaction it gave the relative who was only trying to help someone they loved. She thought of her own mother and how she would feel if she had been sitting on a chair for eight hours. 'We'll get to her as soon as possible. I promise.'

'Really?' He raised his eyebrow. For a moment, he looked away, his mouth taut with the pressure of the situation, the fight he was having to get his mother off a chair and into a bed.

'I'm sorry,' she said again. 'We will...'

He shook his head, as if to say he couldn't talk about it anymore and suddenly she was struck by him, this handsome man, with blue eyes, and she was struck by his humanity, his fight for his mother. She was touched and moved by him. And when he pushed his hair back, she noticed his hands; strong and tanned, even in this Irish winter. She was suddenly disarmed and didn't know what to say.

'I know it's not your fault,' he began and walked off back to the waiting room.

'We'll look after your mother, don't worry,' she managed to say.

Leaning against a trolley (thankfully patient-less) was Becca, one of the staff nurses, laughing with Bogdan, the porter.

'Everything all right, doctor?' called Bogdan.

'Jaysus, Eils,' said Becca. 'I thought he was going to have a coronary. In the right place, though, eh?'

Eilis didn't answer but instead walked to the nurses' station and took a moment to calm herself. 'Theresa,' she then said, 'there's a woman in the waiting area, she's eighty-five and she may have had a stroke. Could you check on why she hasn't been seen yet. Will you find out?'

'Certainly, doctor.'

Becca came up and sat down beside Theresa, swinging a 360 in the chair.

'Jaysus,' she said. 'I'd do him.'

'Bogdan?'

'No, that total ride. The one with the gorgeous ass. Mr Shouty.'

'Oh him?' Eilis dismissed it. She had a teenager with a broken leg who was just back from x-ray, a man who had been beaten up and needed stitches, and another man who had stumbled down the ladder of his loft and had fallen onto his back on his landing. She needed to assess him straight away.

'I wouldn't mind him shouting me into bed,' said Becca.

Bogdan overheard her. 'You've got to have more self-respect, Becca,' he said. 'Shouting is not good from man to woman.'

'It all depends,' shrieked Becca. 'If you get my meaning!'

Eilis left Becca laughing away and Bogdan shaking his head, puzzled. It was going to be a long night, she felt the note in her pocket, though, and remembered she had something, she had two friends who wanted to see her. And she felt something she hadn't felt in years: excitement.

4

THE GIRLS

Eilis called Steph the next morning and arrangements were made to meet. She had looked forward to the night all week, and had even bought herself a new top.

'Where're you off to?' he asked, not mentioning or noticing the top, the lipstick or the heeled boots. She noticed *him*, though. He wasn't in his usual off-duty clothes, he had his nice jeans and shirt on. Was he going out? That was the benefit of not having children, she thought. They could both go out and not have to mention it to the other.

'Meeting Steph and Melissa. Remember? I told you. We're meeting in the Shelbourne. Steph has a proposal.'

'Ah, yes, yes you did. Well, have a good time. And say hello from me.'

'Will do. So, what are your plans? You look like you're going out.'

'I was,' he said. 'You know, work night-out. But I don't know... I think I'll have a quiet night in,' he said. 'There's that programme on steam trains... so...'

Just then his phone beeped and he picked it up. Eilis took it as a cue to leave. They were like an old married couple, these days. Comfortable together. Unlike their sofa.

Sometimes Eilis wanted to buy something hideous and see how long it would take Rob to bin it or burn it or whatever he did with the aesthetic eyesores that inhabit most people's homes. Things would be disappeared, and nothing more would be said. Eilis toyed with buying a little jug, with a picture of the Parthenon on it, when they were in Greece last summer. Gloriously tacky, naff but nice. But she knew that its life, like that of a box of chocolates in a communal office, would be pitifully short if she brought it home, and instead brought back a bottle of Ouzo, a taste of the holiday.

And Eilis didn't *really* mind *too* much. He was the aesthete and she appreciated the fact that he was into *things* and the way they looked, far more than she did. Except, she did long for a sofa that did what it was meant to; something into which you could sink, something enveloping.

Rob was equally dedicated to his own wardrobe. He always dressed in purely navy or grey or black that he bought in the kind of posh men's shops which are always entirely empty of other customers and where the cost of jumpers is the price of a small family car, and the socks so luxurious you can't actually wear them.

But his style had rubbed off on her. A bit. Okay, a lot. She now dressed not unlike him in a muted colour palate which some might call stylish but she felt desperately boring, really, and middle-aged. But she *was* boring, she supposed, *and* middle-aged. Once upon a time she had a pair of red checked trousers and she didn't even consider that they might be garish or unflattering. She just wore them because she loved them. Who was that person, she often thought, the one who was so unselfconscious?

She took the winding train into town and arrived at the Horseshoe Bar in the Shelbourne, and ordered a gin and tonic and sat down to wait for Melissa and Steph, her old friends. The first large swig of her drink felt so good that she took another... and another. Her gin and tonic had slipped down like a log flume at a fun fair. She quickly ordered a second. She hadn't realised that she had been feeling so nervous, so she vowed to slow down and drink like a grown-up, not a nervous teenager on a first date.

* * *

Steph entered the Shelbourne hotel and went straight to the Ladies. There was a small bench in the room which she sat down on and tried to get herself together. She was still breathing hard after what had happened earlier. God knows how she had managed to get herself out of the house but she hadn't wanted to miss the evening with Eilis and Melissa, but she now realised she was in no fit state to socialise. She had to calm herself, get herself together. She had pushed the revelation of Rick and Angeline to the back of her mind, it was where she stuffed everything she couldn't think about. She was worried about what she would do if she decided to let any of it out.

Maybe she shouldn't have come, she thought, and why had she done such a thing? Imagine if it got back to Rachel? Or anyone she knew? Imagine if Fintan had told Miriam... the shame would be too much.

Earlier, she had been in Supervalu, picking up a few bits and pieces for dinner. And she saw they had their Easter eggs in. Already! She had her basket with milk and tea bags in and some of those juices Rachel liked when her eye spotted a Lindt gold bunny. And suddenly she knew she was going to steal it, and there was nothing she could do to stop herself.

Without looking around, with incredible sleight of hand, she slipped it into her handbag. And then she went to the till, hoping she looked normal, even though her insides were screaming with the surge of adrenaline, and calmly paid for the things in her basket.

She was just leaving when the manager, who she had known for years from being in and out of the shop, came up to her.

'Mrs Fitzpatrick,' he said, blushing beetroot. 'Have you forgotten anything?'

She managed to smile. 'No, Fintan, I don't think so... I have everything.' Does he know? she thought. Did he see? Why had she done it? Her heart was pounding, blood rushing to her head. Why had she done this again? What was possessing her to steal things, to slip things into her bag? She kept doing it and she couldn't shake the habit. The thought of being caught terrified and horrified her, but she kept doing it. And a Lindt bunny! The shame.

'I just wondered if you had,' he smiled, desperately, 'forgotten to pay for anything. In your bag, like. Just, you may have... forgotten.'

'What?!' she said. 'I don't think so, Fintan, but you can have a look.' She had no choice but to open her bag wide to expose the face of the bunny peering out. 'How did that get there? Oh dear, this is embarrassing. I have no idea...!'

'Oh no harm done, Mrs Fitzpatrick,' said Fintan, beginning to babble with the excruciating embarrassment of the situation. 'It happens to us all.

Me, I'm always forgetting things. I forgot to pick up Ciara from the crèche yesterday.'

'Oh, I don't know. I must be losing it,' laughed Steph. 'I am so sorry, Fintan.'

'Shall I put it through the till for you?'

'No, please don't. No, it's fine. I don't want it,' she said, smiling a weird crazed smile. 'If I did I would have paid for it! I'm in a bit of a hurry, anyway. Thanks for understanding!'

I can never go there again, she thought as she dashed out of the shop, leaving Fintan to replace the bunny on the shelf. And I am never stealing anything ever again.

She had gone about her day, but just as she was coming into town on the train to meet Melissa and Eilis, the shock kicked in. I can't let that happen again, she told herself. Why am I making my life so stressful? Why am I making things worse? Why can't I stop? And it's not as though I can't pay for it. Why the compulsion? She had taken things before and she didn't know how to stop. Suddenly an urge, an opportunity, would present itself and she seemed powerless to control it. Was it the need to feel powerful, to feel alive, to feel *something*?

And now she had to pretend to be the Steph everyone expected, the calm, assured grown-up Steph, with the lovely life and the lovely family. Plastering a smile on her face, she walked into the bar and spotted Eilis. She waved cheerily.

But when they pulled away from the hug, Eilis was sure she could see tears in Steph's eyes.

'Everything okay?' she asked.

'Of course,' said Steph laughing it away. 'Never better. Now, you are looking great! It's so wonderful to see you!'

Steph was wearing diamond earrings and a gold necklace. Rick must have bought them, Eilis thought. Rick was, what certain women (definitely not Eilis) might call, *quite the catch*. He had that look about him of the lascivious male, which some women found irresistible but Eilis had always found slightly creepy, not that she would ever admit such a thing to anyone. Steph looked the same, but her eyes were bloodshot and she looked a little tired.

'So, how are you?' Steph asked, setting herself down, and smiling as though everything was perfect.

'Great,' said Eilis. Great, just great. I didn't tell you on the phone but I'm living in Dalkey as well now,' she said, slightly sheepishly. 'We moved in a year ago. I meant to call you...'

'Don't worry, I understand... I get it. I'm the same. So busy. And... and we hadn't seen each other for so long.'

They looked at one another.

'It's good to see you Steph,' Eilis said.

'You too.' And it was, it really was good to see her. Just seeing that familiar face and Eilis' kind, gentle manner was soothing. Steph could feel her nerves being calmed just being there.

'I can't believe it's been ten years.'

'I know,' said Steph, sadly. 'Why did we let time pass?'

'I don't know. But it did. I have discovered,' said Eilis, 'that life gets more complicated as you grow older and it's harder to keep up with it all sometimes.'

'Yes,' agreed Steph. 'It is hard to keep up.' But where had the time gone? She had been busy with Rachel, of course, and then there was her utter confusion in trying to manage and normalise living with Rick. At first, she was stupefied by his behaviour and it took a great deal of her energy just trying to make everything okay. She had stopped that now and was living a half-life, living in the shadows.

'Why don't I call in, for a cup of tea sometime?'

'That would be brilliant.' Steph looked so delighted that Eilis wished she had made that call a year ago.

'When suits you?'

'Oh anytime, I'm always at home. It'd be great to see you and you can meet Rachel...' Steph brightened. 'Anyway, I have a proposal. I'll explain when Melissa gets here. But it involves helping out with our twentieth School Reunion.'

Eilis groaned. 'And I thought we both claimed to be so busy!'

'It won't be too much work. I promise! And it's a chance to have regular meet-ups,' she added, shyly. 'Anyway. It's all the fault of Sister Attracta... Oh look, there's Melissa!'

'Well, well, well!' Melissa called over as she walked towards them. 'Fancy meeting you two here!' They all hugged. Melissa had spent the day picking up the Beetle, meeting a dead-line, arguing with her boss about the edits and looking at her phone to see if Alistair had changed his mind. He hadn't. But she won the debate with Liam, her editor.

'I have missed you, Eils,' said Melissa. 'We're *not* going to lose each again, okay? Now I've found you both again, you won't be able to shake me off so easily. I'm like a terrier with a ball, these days.'

The other two laughed as they always had at Melissa, she was always the lighter one, the funnier one, the life and soul. It was so nice to see them, thought Steph, these two women, her two old friends.

'And,' continued Melissa, 'I just saw Rob as I was crossing St Stephen's Green. I'm sure it was him. Has he cut his hair really short, practically shaved?'

'Yes,' Eilis said. 'But he didn't say he was going out. But maybe...' Maybe he had gone out. But where, and why hadn't he mentioned it?

'Maybe it wasn't him... this guy looked a bit more built-up anyway...'

'Well... he has been going to the gym a lot, but I don't think it could have been him...'

They ordered a bottle of Prosecco and sat at the bar.

'So, we're thirty-eight. How did that happen?' Steph asked, smiling at them.

'I have no idea,' Melissa answered. 'It's a trick and someone is going to jump out from behind that curtain in a moment and tell us all we are really eighteen again. That's how I feel anyway.' She washed down a handful of roasted nuts with a large gulp of wine. 'Why do they serve this in such small glasses?' she wondered. 'The constant refilling is exhausting.'

'Anyway, I like being old. I have been waiting to be middle-aged my whole life. I am thinking of investing in a pair of elastic-waisted trousers,' said Steph, signalling to the bartender by waving the empty bottle.

She was far from stretchy trousers this evening; instead, she was wearing a little boucle jacket with her jeans. Her bag was buttery leather, handmade and Italian. Life was obviously going well, thought Eilis, still beautiful Steph. But there was something different about her. She looked different like her light, her glow, had gone. Was that age or something else?

There was Melissa, thought Steph. Her best friend, looking exactly the same as before. She was in jeans and trainers and smart jacket, her battered leather bag was full of notebooks, pens, which all tumbled out when she delved for her purse. Her brown hair had not changed since school; long, curly and defiantly un-styled. And her face was the same, thought Steph, slightly older, yes, but still that spark, that energy.

Meanwhile, Melissa looked at Eilis, her old friend, who, she was pleased to see was looking her usual cute self, Audrey Hepburnish. A bit peaky, though. She always had too many worries. Even when they were teenagers Melissa was aware that Eilis never had as much fun as the rest of them, permanently worried about something or other. Now it was work probably and all that dealing with life and death every day.

She smiled at Melissa, then, and Melissa could see the old Steph, the art history student Steph, the one who loved Botticelli and Bernini more than life itself, the one who had long hair that she would tie up into a loose bun and who wore kaftans which trailed along the filthy pavements.

'I just want to be comfortable,' Steph said. 'Is that too much to ask? Soft shoes, no bra and nice stretchy tracksuit bottoms all day long. Give up the pretence.'

'Pretence at what?' asked Eilis.

'Being normal.'

'I quite agree,' said Eilis. 'You should dig out your old kaftans, Steph.'

'Long gone, I'm afraid.'

'Well, I think it's time you bought some more.'

They all raised a glass.

'To comfort,' said Melissa.

'To slippers,' said Eilis. 'That's what I want to wear all the time.'

They all giggled a bit too loudly. The Prosecco was working and they drained their glasses and, more importantly, they were friends again. It really was that simple. But, thought Melissa, if only everything else in life was so easy, like relationships or stroppy bosses.

Steph thought of Rick and how much it had taken out of her, just trying to keep herself afloat in the marriage. That hadn't been simple. And Eilis thought of Rob and the hospital, and the how everything seemed so full-on, and that no one ever seemed to want to hear her, to listen to her. Except here, right now, with her friends. They were interested, they cared. She smiled at them and felt a deep love and affection for them.

'So, let's get the business out of the way,' said Steph. 'Melissa, I was telling Eilis that we have been asked to organise part of the school reunion.'

'I'm not going,' said Melissa. 'No way.' But it was clear she was ready to be persuaded as her protestations sounded half-hearted. 'My emotional scars from school still haven't healed.'

'Aw, come on. You have to. It'll be fun,' said Eilis, thinking that it was a chance to hang out with Steph and Melissa and revisit the old days. 'Fun-ish.'

'Well,' said Melissa. 'I want more than fun-ish. I think we deserve actual fun.'

'Well, then, it'll be fun. Forget the ish.'

Melissa looked sceptical. 'But the nuns,' she said. 'We'll have to meet the nuns again.'

'They can't hurt you now,' said Eilis, laughing. 'They are powerless over you. They are not going to slap you with a ruler on the back of your legs if your skirt is too short at this age.'

'I wouldn't be too sure,' said Melissa.

'You have to face your fears, Mel,' said Steph, joining the cajoling. 'Come on. We won't go, if you don't.'

'Okay, if you are hanging it on me, I'll go,' said Melissa, faux-reluctantly. 'I suppose there is the slight, vague possibility that it might be fun. But let's not get too rash. And what do you mean we have to organise it?'

'It's not much... I'll do most of it. It's not like I work or anything,' Steph laughed but looked slightly embarrassed. 'Anyway!' she said. 'The reunion is in December, just before Christmas. Sister Attracta has arranged it for here, in the Shelbourne. That's why I thought we'd meet here, in the bar.'

'Sister Attracta? Is she still there?' marvelled Melissa. 'She must be ancient.'

'Yes she is. But even more ancient. And even more wizened,' said Steph, looking around desperately for the waiter. 'Now, there is someone doing the decorations and all that malarkey.'

'Who's doing that?' said Eilis.

'Joanne Hanratty!'

'Big Jo!' Eilis laughed.

'The very one,' said Steph.

'I bumped into her at the hospital once, years ago now. Her little boy was ill. Only a small thing. But she was amazing. Had us all running around after her. Took total charge.'

'Sounds right,' said Steph. 'That woman is a powerhouse. Just back from Singapore, it seems. Big job in banking. Or something. And,' she continued, 'guess who's organizing the drinks and the food?'

The others shook their heads and shrugged.

'Paula O'Dowd. Or rather should I say *Paul*? I bumped into *him* in the village a few months ago. *He* recognised me.'

'No!' said Eilis.

'Jesus Christ. Paula! She kept that quiet. I mean, *he* did,' said Melissa.

'Yes, he has been transitioning for the last ten years. Told me, he should have done it while at school. Wasted years of his life. Says he wishes he'd been braver.'

'That would have gone down well with Sister Attracta and the rest of the Abbey,' said Eilis.

'Well,' said Melissa, raising her glass. 'Here's to Paul and being brave.'

'To being brave,' they echoed, smiling.

'So, as you can see we all have tales to tell. Some more interesting than others. So, all we have to do is get a list together, track people down and send out invites and gets responses.'

'Simps!' said Steph.

'Easy peasy.'

'So...' said Steph. 'Now the business side of the evening is out of the way... how's life, how's work going Melissa?'

'Still there, at the paper. Still typing away. Won the O'Brien prize last year... having a bit of a run of it at the moment. But we've got a new editor... Liam Connelly... and I don't think he's as keen on me as the judges of the O'Brien prize are. He's all about "the bottom line" and "entertainment". And I'm all about the story. But that doesn't sell papers, unfortunately.'

'So, what's going to happen?'

'Well, either he's right or I am. We'll have to wait and see,' she shrugged. 'So,' she changed the subject, 'Eilis, how's life at the hospital?'

Eilis had never been exactly voluble, she was quiet and reserved, not one to blather and blabber, and Steph and Melissa knew and respected this and never expected fully in-depth answers.

'Grand, you know. Busy, stressful. Not enough tea breaks. The usual. Nice patients and narky relatives.'

'Narky?' said Melissa.

'Well,' said Eilis, thinking of that man with the blue eyes who was so worried about his mother. 'I don't blame them, you know, if they are narky. And get annoyed.' She smiled. 'Actually, one sent me flowers.'

Steph and Melissa raised an eyebrow and shared a glance.

'Flowers?' said Melissa. 'That was nice.'

'Was there a card?' asked Steph. 'What did he say? Does he know you're kind of married?'

Eilis laughed. 'It's not like that at all... he was just saying sorry for shouting at me and to thank me for looking after his mother.'

'Well,' said Melissa. 'That sounds very nice, I must say. I can't remember the last time anyone did something like that for me. The closest I get to someone showing appreciation is Jimbo, who sits beside me, buying me a drink on a Friday night. But then forgetting his wallet.'

'What was his name?' said Steph.

'I don't know, I didn't ask and he didn't say on the card. He knew I would know who he was. To be honest,' she said, 'they were quite nice. The flowers. Not your normal posh roses or anything like that. More rustic, like they were from a very fancy florist or from a really amazing garden, all berries and viburnum. Really lovely, actually.' She smiled at the memory and Melissa and Steph caught each other's eye.

'You would notice them,' I suppose, 'you being green-fingered and all,' said Steph.

'What would Rob say if he knew you were being sent flowers?' teased Melissa.

'I don't think he would care,' said Eilis 'Anyway there was nothing romantic about it. He was just saying sorry.'

'Why had he shouted at you?'

'His mother hadn't been seen. Lovely woman, she was.' That evening on the ward, she had seen his mother as soon as she could, gave her every test going and asked one of the nurses to make her and the man a cup of tea. They both looked as though they needed one. 'It was a suspected stroke,' she continued, 'but in the end it wasn't. High blood pressure, dizziness, hadn't been taking her tablets. She's just old, you know. And he's worried... about losing her. Anyway... that's enough about work.' She changed the subject swiftly, deflecting all the attention away from her. 'How's Rachel, Steph?'

'A genius,' smiled Steph. 'Must take after her father. But she's good at everything... just a few teenager things going on. She's sixteen now.'

Melissa watched her two old friends. Two women she had known for a lifetime. She had missed them. Their lives were much more settled and grown up than hers. There was Eilis, still with Rob. A great guy. One of the best. He had swooped in just when Eilis could have crumbled after her mother died. And there was Steph, mother to Rachel, and still with Rick. He wasn't exactly lovely or easy, that was obvious, but they had made a home together. It always made Melissa slightly wistful – she had never found anyone crazy enough to want her back.

'Didn't you say you were back from Paris, Mel?' Steph asked, interrupting her thoughts. 'The day of the crash. I never even asked who you were with.'

Bloody Paris. Why had she said anything? 'Oh no one, not really. Just a guy... Alistair. It's nothing.' She waved it away, hoping there wouldn't be any follow-up questions. 'Anyway, it's Paris,' said Melissa, shrugging Gallicly and smiling enigmatically, as though she was the one to have finished with him, or that he was just some fling that she could take up or down whenever it suited her. 'It does all the work for you.'

'Well, you in Paris,' said Steph, 'and I'm off to Rome next month.'

'I'm not going anywhere until the summer,' said Eilis. 'Greece. I wish we were going right now. Bit of heat on my bones, ouzo in my veins.' She turned to Steph. 'Who are you going to Rome with? Just you and Rick?'

'Him and some of the gang. A rugby weekend. You know Miriam and Hugh... from next door? And some of their friends. It's going to be fun. And you know how much I love Rome. All that art, the churches. I can dust off my art history.' Except, she thought, I might as well have not bothered doing a degree. I can't remember the last time I went to a gallery. She vowed to sneak off, leave the rugby crowd behind, and get to the Pantheon, her favourite Roman church.

'Yes, yes, of course. That does sound nice...' said Eilis. 'That'll be lovely. Remember that summer in Rome, swanning about.'

'That was for the love of art,' said Steph laughing. 'And this is a love of rugby.'

'Oh dear,' said Melissa, pretending to be shocked. 'I didn't realise you had turned into one of those.'

'I'm not really,' said Steph, conspiratorially. 'I just have to pretend.'

'Marital harmony,' said Melissa. 'You probably have to pretend all sorts of things.' She laughed but she caught Steph's eye and saw again that look of something she couldn't quite figure out.

They have no idea how much I am dreading it, thought Steph. A weekend with your husband who doesn't speak to you, and a group of people you either don't know or don't like, and one of the woman you suspect you husband is sleeping with. Now, *that's* a weekend.

5

STEPH

Oh, the cafe of Brown Thomas was nice at ten o'clock in the morning, nice and quiet, it was practically a spiritual experience. It was definitely Dublin's smartest and most expensive shop, a place to dream of a better and nicer life.

Steph was sipping a cup of tea and spreading butter *and* jam onto her croissant. Pity, she thought, that you couldn't spend all your life eating butter and pastries, Irish Times propped against the pot, a respite from reality. I could live here, she mused. Like that man in that film who lived in an airport. Hide among the coats at closing time. Spritz perfume in the empty make-up hall, stroke the scarves and handle the shoes. Not a bad life... not a bad life at all.

Years ago, when Steph and Melissa house-shared on Baggot Street, life was full of possibilities. They could have been *anything*. Life stretched out endlessly, gloriously, deliciously. And then the options dried up. Why does no one warn you, tell you that there is a sell-by date on freedom? That life gets smaller as you get older?

At the time, marrying Rick hadn't seemed a life-depleting decision. She was pregnant, they were in love, she thought. What else was she going to do? She was twenty-two and felt ancient, as though she knew it all. And leaving that lovely job at the Edith Long Gallery didn't seem like such a big thing. She remembers Mrs Long's shock when she told her.

'Earn your own money, my darling.' Mrs Long had shaken her head.

'Don't rely on *a man*. Don't *ever* rely on a man.' She blew out her cigarette smoke.

Steph had laughed, actually laughed. 'It'll be grand,' she said, airily and dismissively. 'I might set up my own gallery one day. Or move to Paris. I just don't know.'

Steph still cringed at how naive she was... how wildly optimistic... how incredibly stupid.

'Well,' said Mrs Long, after a pause. 'Stay in touch with me and... Don't lose yourself. You never know...'

To all those with absolutely no idea whatsoever, Steph's life was *lovely*. There was the over-paid lawyer husband. Nice house. Life as a stay-at-home mother. What else could a woman ask for?

But pots of money do not equal happiness. No one actually believes that until they find themselves with spare money but not the things they actually want - love, companionship, respect - all of which are free. When your husband doesn't actually *speak* to you, when you sleep in the same bed as someone and you never touch, when you clean someone's clothes and stock the fridge and pile up newspapers and pick up socks and buy wine and that person, for whom all those tasks are done, can't be bothered to say thank you or ask how you actually are, when he is too busy with other women, when he is quick to anger and when the threat of his bulk, his superior muscle strength is always there, then the allure of the nice house etc wears pretty thin, pretty quickly.

If only she would go all crazy and pour away his vintage wine and put prawns in his briefcase or whatever, or CHUCK HIM OUT, she might feel better. But she hadn't so far and it didn't look as though she might anytime soon. So she was a pathetic weakling and this fact only made her feel worse. And what kind of role model was she to Rachel? A crap one, that's what.

She spread some more butter on her croissant and sunk her teeth into it.

'Steph!' A voice across the cafe. 'Steph!'

Oh Jesus. Miriam.

Frustratingly, she was looking particularly good this morning. Dressed, as usual, all in black, skinny jeans and towering boot things, blonde hair piled high and falling down and sexy flicky make-up. Not bad for a Wednesday morning. Dishevelled on Miriam looked sexy, but on Steph, it would have looked like crazy cat-lady. Miriam was sexier than Steph, she knew that. And in Rick's eyes, she was a fun person, loved a good flirt and a bottle or two of wine. She wasn't boring like Steph was. She could see the attraction. They deserved each other, but it didn't make the deception any easier to take.

She self-consciously pulled at her jacket, feeling immediately frumpy. Years ago, she used to wear ancient, battered leather jackets. Now, she was clothed in the vestments of one whose mojo has long since absconded. She had her hair done every six weeks, but she just didn't feel like herself. She didn't feel right... she was *uncomfortable* in her skin. She just wasn't *her*. At least those wafty kaftans she used to wear felt right. But Rick used to laugh at them, and there was that sense that he was slightly embarrassed by that bohemian side to her, and so she stopped wearing them and tried to be the good lawyer's wife.

Miriam weaved her way through the tables, armed with bags and Steph hid any murderous desires with a warm smile, and as they kissed hello, a waft of Miriam's perfume hit her nose, something deep and musky.

'Coffee... I *so* need one,' said Miriam. 'I am run off my feet. It is exhausting. Someone should ban communions. Sorcha's. Two weeks. You are coming, aren't you? Anyway, they are positively the worst thing ever. Who do I need to talk to? The Pope? Haw haw!' Miriam bared her gleaming teeth. 'No, but seriously,' she lowered her voice, 'he has no idea... the Pope, I mean... no fecking idea of the toll they take. I've had to cancel Body Pump with Paddy for the second time this week. And I said to the girls at the tennis club that I was sorry they would have to play the doubles match without me. I have. Too. Much. To. Do.'

Steph was trying to keep up with this onslaught but she was mostly just watching Miriam's mouth move, the lipstick and lip liner, the obligatory bleached teeth. She wished she was talking to Eilis or Melissa, a conversation of connection.

'So they were like so disappointed,' continued Miriam. 'I said, listen girls, you are just gonna have to do it without me and they all said they didn't know if they could.' She lifted a hand to summon the waitress. 'Okay,' continued Miriam, 'so they didn't win the semis, but I can't feel bad about that, can I? I am not God, I am not omnivorous. I can't be everywhere.'

Omniscient, corrected Steph in her head.

'So,' Miriam shrugged, 'we go down a point in the league. But I'm sorry, all right?' She laughed and fiddled with her up-down-do.

'Coffee!' Miriam called to the waitress. 'Skinny latte. Soya. Thanks, Petrina. You are an absolute angel.' She smiled winningly. 'Anyway, so this is my second...

Steph was trying to keep up. 'Second what?' Coffee? Coming? Affair with a married man?

'Second *communion*... and, I tell you, they have me *run* ragged. The dress, the shoes... and do you know, I cannot get the make-up artist to the house on Saturday. Alberto's fully booked. I am going to have to do it myself. And he's so good at the spray tan with that tent he has.'

'What?' Steph was utterly confused. 'Is Sorcha going to wear make-up and get a tan?' Sorcha was Miriam's youngest and only nine.

'Oh, she's fine... she's been sorted for months. I'm talking about *my* dress and *my* shoes. And Alberto always does my hair and make-up. I think Lucinda Coleman has him booked. Bitch. Haw haw. So, anyway,' she looked down at Steph's plate. 'You're having a coffee all on your ownsome?'

Oh Jesus. Make her go away. How could one woman do this to another, thought Steph. Was the sex that good? Not with Rick it couldn't be. She looked away and thought about just getting up and leaving Miriam mid-sentence. She may be sexy but she was exceptionally boring.

'And a *croissant* I see!' continued Miriam. 'Naughty-naughty!'

'Just a quiet moment, you know,' said Steph. Until you and your tedious stories interrupted me, she said internally. And by the way, Miriam, she wanted to say, your cleavage is too low. You look ridiculous. And stop sleeping with my husband, you woman of no morals. Or brain.

'You are brave!' said Miriam. '*And* butter? Throwing caution out the window?'

It's to the bloody wind, you fool! Steph shouted at her silently. 'Kind of.' Steph tried to smile now, knowing there was no way she could finish this French calorie-bomb with any enjoyment at all now. 'Would you like one?' she asked. 'To go with your... soya latte... thing?'

Miriam recoiled. She might as well have suggested eating a tarantula. 'It looks delicious but I just can't do carbs. I *so* wish I could, but my body won't allow it. You're lucky that you don't worry about keeping in shape. It's such a bore. But for someone like me, I've got to stay in the game. I mean, neither of us are getting any younger. But some of us are aging better than others.'

The croissant sat on the table between them as a symbol of all that was wrong in Steph's life. Fuck this, she thought. I'm going to eat that croissant, even if it is just a pathetic misguided attempt to show how different I am to this vain, passive-aggressive, boring, old cow. She defiantly began to spread on the Kerrygold in an extra thick mountainous mound.

'You've such a great appetite on you,' said Miriam. 'I wish I could eat like that. I really have to *mind* myself. I'm not like you...' She gazed sweetly at Steph who stared back maniacally while pushing some more croissant into her mouth. 'You eat what you want, never thinking of the consequences. You see I'm off *all* carbs. I'm alkaline these days. And, you know, I'm feeling *a-may-zing*. So much energy! You know, I just hop out of bed in the morning, ready for action. The girls at the club can't believe me. After a match, I'm always bouncing around wanting another game. Duracell, they call me. Isn't that funny?'

'Very,' said Steph, wondering how long Miriam and Rick had been sleeping together. Months? Could even be years. 'What's the opposite of Alkaline?'

'Um...' Miriam tried to think.

'Well, I'm on *that* diet,' said Steph, mouth full of croissant. 'Whatever it's called. The *Acid* diet?'

'I... er...' Miriam couldn't quite understand her through the croissant. 'I don't think that sounds good for you...'

The waitress came over and unsmilingly placed the coffee down beside her.

'Thanks, Petrina. You're amazing,' said Miriam before taking a slurp, getting lipstick all over the rim of the cup.

Steph desperately looked around for escape.

'So, anyway, that's why I'm here,' carried on Miriam, blithely. 'I'm sure you were wondering. I have been looking and looking and looking for the last two months for something to wear. Not a big ask, you would think. Wrong! A fucking big ask. Capital BIG. The biggest. So, today I get a phone-call from Lisa in Designer – talk about leaving it a bit late, Lisa, I said. Why couldn't you have saved me from a near fucking heart attack by calling last fucking week? But she said soooo sorry. They've only just come in. From Milan. She says that Donatella, *the* Donatella FYI, had only just managed to find the dress. So I'm like... okay. I'll have a look. I pretended to be all cool and everything but I am so excited. I mean, it's only Versace, isn't it. Haw haw! I need more of this.' She drank more coffee. 'So here I am. Little old me. And it's fab-u-lous. Worth waiting for. Can't wait to show you!'

Steph realised that if she endured one more nanosecond of this assault on her senses then she might combust. I've put up with her for years, she thought. And I haven't said anything. I've allowed us to be friends and I've allowed this situation to happen. No self-respecting woman would have put up with this. Why have I? Even if she isn't shagging my husband then I must get away from her for the sake of my sanity.

'By the way, you *are* coming, aren't you? You didn't respond to the RSVP... I know how busy you are with... with... you know... whatever. Anyway, it's at two p.m. But don't bother coming to the church bit – bore-issimo! We'll just see you at the house for the *real* event. Haw haw haw.' Miriam's epiglottis dangled like a condemned man (or woman).

'Yes, yes, sounds lovely,' said Steph, hating herself even more. And hating herself for suffering the witterings of the most life-sapping woman on earth. Jesus Christ alive. What had happened to Steph Sheridan, arts history graduate, confident, happy, surrounded by proper friends, people who liked her and weren't shagging her husband? And who was this joke in her place – Steph Fitzgerald cuckolded wife, fool of the century and general laughing stock?

Steph zoned out watching Miriam's mouth move frantically. She would have thought, she mused, that Rick would have better taste. Obviously not. She wondered about Angeline, and what Miriam would say if she knew about her. Did she think they were exclusive? Or was it possible to be exclusive if you were having an affair? A moral conundrum for the modern era.

'So,' Miriam was saying, 'Totally Cheffilly are doing the food – they did Hugh's fortieth. Remember? God, that pavlova was to die for. No gluten, you get me? Now, is pavlova alkaline?'

Steph shrugged. 'Not the foggiest,' she said, caring not one jot what the pavlova was (except delicious, of course).

'Anyway, I'll just have the teensiest crumb of it.'

'Of course.'

'So, let me tell you this, the nude Jimmy Choo just weren't right.'

Miriam was on to shoes now. I used to love art and culture. I once wrote essays on Giotto and Giacometti and Gaugin, and now I was listening to drivel about diets and shoes. 'So Lisa is ordering them from Jimmy himself. Such a sweet man. I met him in London last year. At his workshop. Not exactly Bond Street but full of a-may-zing shoes. My feet are so tiny, he says, like a bird's, apparently.'

'Bird's feet? Aren't they claws? Is that a good thing?' She high-fived herself in her head. Small victories had to be acknowledged.

'Totally, haw-haw, but you know what I mean.'

I ought to be ashamed of myself, thought Steph. Where's my pride, where's my fucking pride.

Steph watched Miriam quickly re-smear her lips with lipstick, smack them together, and gather her bags. 'Gotta go, you know,' said Miriam. 'Wish I could sit round all day drinking coffee like you but I am just *so* busy, right? But see you Saturday? And Rachel too. Aoife would *die* if she didn't come. And Ricky, too, of course!'

Ricky?! And she thought she could get away with having an affectionate nickname for my husband. Rick hated being called Ricky. He said once it's what his (weird and narcissistic) mother used to call him whenever she bothered to be around. Steph wondered if Miriam just used a pet name for him to annoy her, like they had something intimate between them. As though Steph hadn't a clue just *how* intimate. And Miriam was the one to bombard her and then walk away, leaving Steph feeling furious that she had allowed to be controlled by her.

She drifted into the handbag and scarves department and wound a soft and luxurious black cashmere scarf around her neck. Steph looked at herself in the mirror. It was beautiful. Expensive but beautiful. If she really wanted it, she could pay for it, using *Ricky's* money. But suddenly she was gripped with something else, she knew she was going to steal it. It was like she was possessed with this need, this desire, this urge. She had promised herself, over and over again, that she would stop this, not do it again, especially after the close-shave with Fintan and the chocolate bloody bunny. But the urge, whatever it was, was more powerful than she. Her whole body was filled with an energy which simultaneously empowered and frightened her, as though she was someone else, someone she wasn't in control of. She had promised herself she would stop, but each time she realised that it wasn't so easy.

She felt along the scarf for the security tag. None. Right, this shouldn't be too difficult. Leaving the scarf on, she casually checked out other scarves and more bags, fingering and feeling, drifting about dreamily as though she was any other woman on a browse. But, unlike all the other women, she left the shop with the black cashmere still around her neck.

Heart pounding, alarms screaming inside her head, she stepped into the street. Adrenaline pumping, she felt triumphant... but the feeling was frustratingly fleeting. In an instant, super-stealing powers dissipated and she was left standing on the street, a common criminal and she hated herself for it.

CORMAC

It was still a building site but one day – imminently, knuckle-bitingly soon – it was to be his and Walter's very own bakery. This mess of dust and cement would soon be the culmination of all his dreams. His *professional* dreams, anyway.

He thought of Melissa, and wished, as he always did, that she was with him. She'd say something to make him laugh and he would feel complete, happy, excited, as he always did when she was around. But he had a date that night with Erica, a set-up, a blind date, and he was feeling nervous and conflicted.

It was Melissa he wanted to be set up with, eating out with meeting for a drink, cinema-ing, not this Erica. Who, he suspected, would be high-maintenance and probably very scary.

He loved Melissa. She made him laugh, she fascinated and enthralled him. He loved her brokenness, her vulnerability, her strength. He loved her face and her body and her hands that he had to stop himself from grabbing, holding her and never letting go. Whenever they hugged, hello, goodbye, she felt small and soft and... and so incredibly gorgeous. She dominated his life, his thoughts, and he wanted her to be his and him to be hers. Ever undaunted, he had waited impatiently for her, hoping that one day she would change her mind, and there he would be, her knight in shiny shoes. Much as he tried, his ardour would not, damn it, wane, or dissipate or vaporize but instead had taken root. He might attempt a good prune but, within hours, he was back again, all aflame, like those relighting candles on birthday candles.

He was driven demented by her. Had been for years and years and years. Desperate to be the object of her affection, he was frustrated he was only allowed to be the nice best friend. But he was nearly forty and there comes a time when you have to admit defeat.

Cormac had started to wonder. Was this it? His life? Was this all he was destined for? I am, he thought, the empty crisp packet in man form, wafting unwanted along the street. I am a barnacle. A clinger-onner, a cling-on. Melissa would never love him or see him as anything more than the non-gay gay best friend. This second-best life was, he had thought, until now, good enough for him. But no longer. Erica was the answer to all his problems, the key to his freedom from this unrequited state.

He and Melissa had met years ago in University College Dublin, when life hung enticingly before them and responsibility stretched only as far as remembering to Sharpie your name on the hummus. He actually had a photograph from the very first day he saw her and he had given his camera to someone to snap them all. It was the beginning of term in their second year and Melissa, sitting on the grass outside the Arts Block, was wearing baggy men's pyjama bottoms, a holey jumper and black Doc Martens. And laughing. She looked so beautiful, so happy. He in contrast looked like a moody teenager (which he was desperately trying to be. He had to consciously not smile in photos and there is a decade of images of unsmiling Cormac. It had driven his mam, Meenie, mad.

And Cormac had been in love with Melissa since then. Properly in love, not just fancied-a-bit or found-attractive, but really and truly and desperately in love. He knew, logically that there were other woman in the world, but he didn't believe it, like conspiracy theorists or flat-earthers. He was afraid he would be trapped in this state of unrequited torture for the rest of his life, Cormac forever hankering after her and Melissa never knowing.

But she does know. Well, there was that time, embarrassingly, he happened to shout it out at the top of his voice. A particular mortification which still had the power to stop him in his tracks whenever the memory tunnelled its way to the surface.

A whole group of them had gone to Clare to hole up in a house for a weekend of windy walks, drunken late nights and hugely enjoyable pontificating. Bleary of eye and sick of stomach, Cormac and Melissa alone drove early on the Sunday morning to the Cliffs of Moher – probably the last place on earth one should go when unsteady and nauseous but she wanted to and he wasn't going to let her go alone. He'd go to Mars if she wanted to but luckily she's never expressed an interest so he was off the hook on that one.

They stepped out of the car and were immediately blown off their feet and couldn't stop laughing as they linked arms and huddled together, shuffling along the path, wobbling towards the terrible drop. They fell to their knees and pulled themselves, commando-like, towards the edge and peered over to the swirling, swirmy sight below them, seagulls surfing the waves of wind, like kamikaze pilots, brave, fearless and death-wished. But for humans, the fall, thousands of metres to the sea below, was horrifying.

Lying on their bellies, peering over the edge, being buffeted by the wind, they caught each other's hands, and for a moment he thought I am never going to let go, they are going to have to prise me off this hand, call the fire brigade or chip me off with a chisel. He felt like kissing it, kissing her.

'Yayhoooooooooo!' He shouted exuberantly into the wind.

Melissa grinned. 'Yoooooohooooo!' she countered, her voice slamming into the wind.

'Life... I love you!' she yelled, her voice this time carrying all the way to Boston. Cormac squeezed her hand again and looked at her, her beautiful brown eyes, her lopsided mouth, her freckly nose, her rosy cheeks. He couldn't help himself.

'And I love yoooouuuu!' He screamed it into the Atlantic wind.

Cormac had wished he could swallow his words back again, gobble them like a seagull, delete and rewind. He looked at her out of the corner of his eye, frozen in time and space. Fuck. Why had he said that? A seagull swooped past them, the tip of his wing almost brushing their noses.

Melissa was looking down to the sheer drop and the crashing sea below. He thought he felt her hand squeeze his a little tighter but he couldn't be sure. She turned and smiled. 'Ready to go back?' Cormac began to breathe again, thinking she hadn't heard him.

He nodded. But after they belly-shuffled back from the edge and got to their feet and when they were sitting in the quiet of the car, and before she started up the engine, she said: 'Don't love me, Cormac.' She played with her keyring. He remembers it, it was Snoopy and Woodstock hugging. 'Anyway,' she said. 'At least, not like that. Please.'

'I don't!' he laughed a little too hard. 'Not like *that*, okay? You know, like *friends*.'

She nodded. 'I need you, Cormac Cullen. I need you in my life. You're for keeps. Let's not ruin things. Ever.'

'That's what I meant! You fool.' He laughed it off. 'What did you think? That I was declaring my intensions? It'd be like incest anyway. We'd be arrested.'

How they laughed. Cormac's performance of his disgust of being physical with Melissa, the horror of her naked body next to his, kissing her lips, and touching her and sleeping with her, made them howl. It was convincing. So convincing the subject had never been returned to.

He should have been an actor but, instead, became a photographer, but after a decade or so, he decided that there was a limit to how many photographs you could take of children in pushchairs asleep at the end of the St Patrick's Day parade. So, somewhere along the way, he had discovered baking and instead dedicated his life to the joys of flour, eggs and butter.

After spending six months in Paris, learning the art of pastry, he and his friend Walter, a German whose bread knowledge and passion was impressive, bordering on the obsessive, had been planning their own bakery for years.

And this month, as finance was in place, the two had signed a lease on a modest premises in Dalkey, a small suburban village along the coast, with a little main street and a church at one end and a pub at the other.

There were to be ovens at the back and room for a coffee shop at the front. The only drawback for Cormac was the dawn starts.

But at the end of the day, it was only bread. Cormac wanted his life to be about more than just work, he wanted a partner. Well, he wanted Melissa.

But it was time for New Cormac. And New Cormac would not be pining and whining over Melissa, he was going to find a girlfriend. He had the blind-date tonight and although he knew he was still clinging onto Melissa, and that he wasn't ready to let go but tonight he would. He really would. But the thought was killing him.

This, he had decided, was his year to end it. He had to get on with his life, if he put his mind to it and showed a bit of backbone. He had the new business venture with Walter, so there was a new life just itching to get going but only if he had the balls to grab it.

And it was Walter, his business partner, who had handed him a life-raft. Or rather the name of the woman he was seeing tonight.

About a month ago, he'd met Walter in the building-site-bakery. He'd put down his take-out cappuccino from the supermarket.

'Disgusting,' he concluded.

'Ours will be better,' Cormac had said.

'Ours will be super-fucking much better,' said Walter, before their conversation turned to relationships. Walter had arrived straight from Bremen for a month's holiday in Connemara a decade before but had had his blond head turned by a red one, Nora's. And he was blessed with Nora, capable and brilliant, she was one of those women who was able to manage everything. Bremen was now a distant memory and he and Nora had five-year-old Axel, plus a brand-new baby due the week of the opening.

Walter had shrugged at the timing. 'We will cope,' he said, optimistically.

'Will Nora's Mam be looking after the baby?'

'A little. Or I'll have him in a sling with me.'

'You Germans!' teased Cormac. 'So modern!'

Walter shrugged. 'Why? Is it not normal? Should I not take care of my children?'

'Of course... I was joking.' Cormac looked at Walter who had balanced his chair on its back two legs. He was wobbling dangerously. 'You're a good team, you and Nora.'

Walter nodded, returning to earth. 'Every day I think that. Every day I look at this beautiful Irish woman and think how lucky I am.'

Walter took out his phone and showed Cormac a new picture of Nora and Axel grinning for the camera.

'They're gorgeous,' said Cormac, wistfully. Wife and children, a family, love. What more could any man want?

Walter nodded in agreement. 'I'm a lucky man. And what about you, my friend? Still pining? Like a puppy or a little child who has been forgotten by *Weinachtsmann*?'

'Who?'

'Father Claus. Whatever he's called.' Walter raised an eyebrow. 'How long have we known each other? Seven years?'

Cormac nodded. 'Our eyes met over sourdough.'

'Seven years! Seven years you've been obsessing over Melissa. It's too long, man. You need to let go and find someone who will want to be with you, sleep with you, be there in the morning, wave goodbye, say hello, kiss you... make love to you. Have babies with you.'

'No, I'm not pining. Anymore.' Cormac had felt a bit defensive. 'I admit I was but...' he paused and took a deep breath. 'It's time. Time I moved on.' For a moment, Cormac believed he was ready. He actually began to feel excited.

'Are you sure. Because you're wasting your life. You are no longer a young man...'

'Jesus, Walter. All right.' Cormac drank some of his putrid coffee. 'I know that... actually, it's something I've been thinking myself. I have to let go, to move on, to...'

'Good. Because, life is, as you all say, too small. Listen to me now, because we have an idea. A set-up, a fix-up... Nora's got a friend who works on some international bank. She's just back from New York – a banking exec person by day, a yoga teacher by weekend. Now, doesn't that sound intriguing?'

Did it? He supposed it did, but he wasn't filled with great enthusiasm.

Walter continued. 'Erica's her name. Something like that. Nora had the idea. She met her at some fundraising event and said as soon as she met this Erica person, she thought of you. Say the word and we can set something up. She is a very attractive woman – tall and stretchy, you know? She, apparently, is very conscious of her health. I thought that would suit you with your running and your swimming.'

'She sounds terrifying.' And totally unlike Melissa, he thought. Part of him was hoping that there might be a doppelganger out there, someone like Melissa but better, because she liked him back.

'Listen, my friend,' said Walter, all earnest and insistent. 'You should do this. In fact, I am going to order you to do it. You need some exercise of the different kind. You know what I'm saying? Huh?'

Cormac nodded. He did. He'd had girlfriends and lovers for years and years but none of them lit his fire. This time though, he was determined to just get on with it, with no comparisons with Melissa.

'Anyway,' Walter continued, 'Nora's told her all about you. Said you know about bread. We couldn't think of anything else, but it seemed to be enough. Men are few and far between when women get to a certain age so you should be taking full advantage of that, my man, get out there and enjoy your rarity factor.'

'Bread? Surely there's more to me than that?'

Walter shrugged as though there wasn't.

'Well, that makes me sound mad. And sad.'

Walter just raised one eyebrow. 'I think she said that bread was the devil, but Nora couldn't work out whether she was joshing or not.'

'Please let it be her wacky sense of humour.'

'She did ask if you were gay,' said Walter, 'however...'

'And what did you say?'

'I said, you may as well be.'

'*May as well be?*' Cormac spluttered.

Walter shrugged again. 'You are not, as they say, *getting much action...* you are wasting all that virile energy, your *männlichkeit.*'

'Okay. I take your point. My *männlichkeit* has been a bit on the quiet side lately.' He thought for a moment. 'Okay. Set me up with her,' said Cormac quickly. 'Why not? Jesus!'

'Seriously? You sure?'

'Fuck it. It's driving me crazy, all this. I've got to end it. Not that there's bloody well anything to end. I can't do this, the picking up, being nice, the listening to her heartbroken stories, being at the end of a phone whenever anything has gone wrong. I'm a doormat, that's all, a fucking doormat. It's time I faced it. I've realised that I can't be her friend anymore. No more *Herr* Nice Guy,' he said, for Walter's benefit.

His friend nodded, sensing Cormac's pain. 'It is time,' he said, seriously. 'I think you are making the right decision. I will organise it.'

Cormac shook himself. 'I'm ready. I am fucking ready.' He almost whooped in an embarrassing attempt of frat boy enthusiasm. He felt excited. Or was it fear. Who cares? At least it was something.

Come on, Cullen. Back in the game.

And he was meeting her tonight at the bar at one of the city's newest and swankiest hotels.

When he arrived, it seemed to be just one giant room with busy-looking people in serious-looking suits, loosening ties and ordering large amounts of expensive cocktails. He was wearing a shirt, one of his nicest. He had shaved extra carefully and was wearing his old jacket. He'd had it for years but, as far as he could tell, it still looked good. Well, good-ish, he thought, being generous.

He had looked at himself in the mirror earlier, while he was shaving. Jesus. Since when was he turning into his Dad? When exactly did he get old?

That was his first wobble. He briefly considered heading off to Glenstal and becoming a monk but, instead, forced himself out of the house, towards a life of non-celibacy. For that was why he was doing this awful, excruciating thing, wasn't it? To be *non-celibate* and all that signified, to move on from Melissa... to what? A family? A life? He didn't dare to think that far ahead. One foot in front of the other, one step at a time.

This hotel wasn't a Dublin he recognised. This was like being in New York or Los Angeles or Malaysia or someplace. He suddenly had a pang for Mulligan's where he and Melissa often met after work. He looked at the door (more a wall that moved) and wondered if he could make a run for it. Meeting Erica had been a bad idea. He wasn't ready for this, he wasn't a Tinder-using modern male. But standing people up, he knew, in any age and at any age, was not on. Or could he one drink and if she wasn't there, then maybe it was okay to leave?

He ordered a pint and tried to look busy or at least like someone who was not waiting for a stranger, in the hope of having a long and meaningful relationship, and studied the bar menu in great detail. He then stared around the room before considering getting out his phone and texting Melissa and telling her what he was doing... making her laugh, perhaps, or just being in contact. He felt suddenly so lonely, so dejected. The one person he loved, the one person he wanted in his life, was an impossibility.

He held his phone in his hand, looking at it. No. Put it away, Cullen. You are moving on.

Walter had said Erica was tall, with long brown hair. That sounds nice, he supposed. She had hair. That was good. And legs. Always useful.

He had nearly finished his pint. Could he go? Make a move? He had just slipped his phone in his pocket and was looking for money to pay for his drink when there was a tap on his shoulder.

'Cormac?'

Jesus Christ! He almost fell off the stool. It was as though Cindy Craw-ford, a crush from his teenage years, was standing in front of him.

'E-E-Erica?'

'Yeah.' She held out her hand. 'Pleased to meet you Cormac.' She smiled flirtatiously. She was looking at him up and down, appraising him as though he was a sheep at a mart. She smiled, he had obviously passed.

He took her hand and they shook. 'Can I get you anything?' he managed.

'Martini. Dirty. Extra olives.'

'If I say that, will they give us a drink?'

She laughed and shrugged. 'Try it and see.'

He motioned to the bartender. 'Martini. Dirty. Extra olives. Make it two.'

Within moments two fine-looking drinks appeared.

'I didn't know that these things could be concocted in this country,' he said, marvelling at it as though it was a museum exhibit. 'I thought that, maybe, meteorologically it was impossible. Too much water in the atmosphere. Or the fact that no olives grow here or that fancy drinks were banned by the Church in 1962 because they were deemed too exciting.'

To his surprise she laughed.

'Well,' she said, taking a sip. 'It's not 1962 any longer.'

'It's not?' he said. 'And there I was about to tell you about a brilliant new band called The Beatles.'

She smiled. 'Aren't you going to try it?'

'Okay. Are you sure I won't explode or get too excited?'

She raised an eyebrow. 'I can't guarantee you won't, no.'

Jesus. He was flirting. He liked this feeling. He could get used to it. He was back in the game.

He took a sip of the drink. 'Communion wine never tasted like this,' he said. 'We used to steal it after a service. I was an altar boy.' Why was he telling her this? He drank some more. 'This is good.'

'I know, right?' She was smiling. 'So, Cormac,' she said. 'Why don't you tell me about yourself, y'know? Like what you're into and stuff.'

'Yes, there's something I need to clarify,' he said. 'I know Walter said I was into bread. But that just makes me sound like a wheaten weirdo.'

She shrugged. 'So, maybe I like weirdos.'

'Yes, they have their place, I'll admit. And I am a weirdo in many ways. But there's more to my weirdness than just bread.'

'Glad to hear it because,' she leaned into his ear, 'I have a confession. I don't do wheat. I haven't eaten it in fifteen years.'

'No.' He was genuinely shocked.

'Do you think that might get in the way of us having fun together?' She flicked her hair and gave him what can only be described as the sexiest look he had ever been the recipient of. He took another gulp of Martini.

'No,' he said, raising one eyebrow and giving what he hoped was an equally sexy smile. 'No, I don't think so at all. I don't think bread needs to be an impediment whatsoever.'

'Well, that's good. I'm glad to hear it. Another Martini?'

'Yes please!' His voice came out a bit croaky, like it was breaking all over again, but thankfully she didn't seem to notice. This could be the most exciting night of my life, he thought. Oh my God, there could well be life beyond Melissa! He resisted the temptation to do a one-man conga round the bar or begin a Mexican wave fuelled by sheer enthusiasm for life. He threw a peanut into the air and caught it in his mouth.

I, he thought, am on fire!

7

MELISSA

Finally reunited with her Beetle, Melissa drove to her parent's house, a cul-de-sac called Beach Court, a place where life, unfortunately, had been anything but a beach.

Melissa had spent the day writing up a double-page feature, part of a series called Breadline Lives which she had been working on for the last three months. It told the stories of the women who live below the breadline and how they manage to keep going. It was an important piece, she believed, something the paper should be doing more of. She had been careful to give these women the dignity they deserved and tried to give a sense of who they were, that they weren't just poor, or under-educated or forgotten. They were deserving of respect and a far better hand than the one they had been dealt.

She finished it at about six and then knew she had to go and see her mother, whose birthday it was. The onerous task had been hanging over her all day. She wished she was knocking on Cormac's door instead. She would call him later and see if he would help lift her mood before the day was lost.

'Happy birthday, Mam.' Melissa stood there, smile on face, posh flowers in one hand, wondering if her mother was actually going to step aside and invite her in. There was always that feeling that her mother didn't actually want her there, but after a moment's hesitation, Mary stood aside and let her pass. Melissa had given up wondering why she didn't have a key, but she hadn't had one for years, the reason lost in the annals of time. But not having a key had its benefits, it meant she wasn't really a part of this family, part of her mother's life. It meant she could walk away and leave it all behind. She had realised over the years how much better that was for her sanity.

Automatically and surreptitiously, without even realizing she was doing it, she checked her mother's eyes for signs of drunkenness, listened to her voice for the slight slur and twitched her nose for the smell of fermented grape. Amazingly, her mother hadn't been drinking, which was always a relief, it made the ordeal ever so slightly more bearable. She could relax. Not a lot, but she could feel the tension lessen a little.

'I bought these for you,' she said, presenting the flowers.

'Right.' Her mother hesitated again, almost unsure of the correct protocol and behaviour, which was utterly bewildering to Melissa but she actually didn't know any other way. This was the way her mother was.

'They're flowers,' said Melissa helpfully. 'Freesias. Nice, aren't they?' she urged. Sometimes, she felt it was like trying to civilise someone who had never met other human beings before, like Tarzan. But Tarzan, she often thought would have been easier to get along with, a more amenable and predictable character altogether.

'Take them, Mam,' she said, 'they're for you. You're meant to take them.' Sometimes she had to spell normal behaviour out. Breathe. Just breathe, she told herself. This was a technique that enabled her to stay a good ten minutes longer sometimes. She loved her mother, she really did and she believed that deep down Mary loved her. They were mother and daughter, no one could take that away from them, but it was so hard sometimes just to be around her.

'Yes, very nice,' Mary said, eventually, and awkwardly. Already exhausted by the encounter, Melissa was reminded yet again how weird, depressing and tiring just being Mary's daughter was.

'Dad here?' she said.

'Garden.'

They walked through the house and out into the back. It was early spring and still chilly and her father, Gerry, was kneeling at a flower bed wearing an old cotton sun hat. Around him were pots of primulas and bulbs.

'Dad?'

'Melissa...' He tried to say something and gave up. Instead, Melissa bent down and quickly kissed him on the cheek as he tried to get up from weeding the flower bed. She could tell he was pleased to see her. He always was, in his very quiet way. They were close, she and her father, Gerry, but he was a man of very few words. He would try to speak but would soon stumble over words, losing confidence in the tumble. Mary was silent in a different way. She just didn't speak and her silences were deafening, frightening, in that they pervaded the whole house. It would have been better if she was a shouter. Melissa used to have her own transistor radio which she carried around the house when she was a teenager, just to have voices, music, anything, to lift the torpor.

'It's a bit cold,' Melissa said. 'And getting late.'

'Ah yes,' he said, standing up. 'Well, you know...' Her father loved everything Melissa did but he just never said as much. She knew it though. He knew how difficult Melissa found being there. He had tried to make this better for her by buying her treats such as a Nunch chocolate bar on his way from work on a Friday and leaving it in her coat pocket, or making sure she had a fiver in her purse 'just in case'. Melissa didn't know why he had stayed all those years, was it because he loved her mother, or was it because he loved Melissa. He was a kind and loyal man. They were both lucky to have him.

'Someone's been to the garden centre, I see,' she said.

'That's right.'

'What are you growing?'

'Bluebells, tulips and narcissi.'

'Nice.'

'Should be, should be.'

She looked across at her mother who was still holding the bloody freesias as though they were a bunch of weeds. Melissa watched her, this woman, who had given birth to her and named her and... what else? What had she to thank her for? This woman who had never got to grips with an alcohol addiction, who was still a total mess and although she wasn't drunk now, she would be later. She was still the same.

Her mother was small and grey now and really didn't have the same power she once wielded over Melissa, but it still shocked and surprised her when her mother was exactly the same each time she visited. Why, she would think, am I so naive that I think she will be different? Why do I never learn? This is as good as it will ever be... and that wasn't very good at all.

Her mother was a drinker; she would drink wine, whenever she could, most evenings and sometimes lunchtimes. She always drank alone as her father never touched a drop. He may have done once and maybe stopped to ensure there was at least one parent in the house. But Mary has been drinking since before Melissa's time. She doesn't remember her mother being anything but a drinker. She was more drinker than mother, that much was clear.

When Melissa was growing up it was gin, but she moved onto wine when every supermarket made it practically criminal not to put a bottle in your basket.

'I nearly forgot,' said Melissa. 'I have a present for you.' Melissa already wished she hadn't bothered.

'Another one?' Her mother's face pained at the thought of having to go through the performance twice.

'Presents are nice things,' said Melissa, losing patience. 'People normally *like* receiving them. Actually, in most cultures people are quite happy to have too many. Crazy, isn't it? Anyway,' she said, 'it's only small, not really a present. I saw it and thought you might like it. Here you go.' She passed over a paper bag.

'What is it?' Her mother took out the contents and stood there holding a jar.

'It's jam.'

What had seemed, when she had bought it, a useful, even charming, present now seemed totally rubbish. 'The jam is from Caviston's Delicatessen. It's posh. Rhubarb.'

'Jam. Right.'

'Yes, but nice jam. For your toast in the morning.' It's jam, she thought. Who doesn't like jam? Jam!

'Thank you Melissa. That's very nice of you.'

They chatted awkwardly for a few moments, her mother dangling the jam in one hand, the flowers in the other, her father standing there, trowel in hand, none of them knowing quite what to say.

'Well,' said Melissa finally. 'I should go.'

'You've only just got here...' said Gerry.

'I know, but I've work...' She knew they would never ask what she was doing and why she might have to work on a Saturday evening. So he nodded and patted her arm while Melissa kissed him goodbye. She felt bad leaving him in this house, in that atmosphere, when wine o'clock was nearing. She wished she could sort it out, make everything better for everyone but from painful experience, she knew she had to walk away.

'Bye Mam,' she said and walked out of the house to her car. As soon as she had shut the door behind her, she felt the utter relief of duty done. She was free again. She started the engine and was about to begin reversing the car when there was a tap on the window, it sounded like someone was knocking with a glass jar. It was her mother.

Open up, Mary mouthed. Open up.

Melissa wound the window down. A pot of jam was thrust in.

'You have it, Melissa. I won't eat it.'

'Mam I bought it for you,' said Melissa, fighting the urge to shout. 'And there's no need to say you won't eat it. You don't have to eat it but you also don't have to tell me you won't!'

'But it'll go to waste.'

'Grand, so. Waste it. It doesn't bloody matter!'

'Take it.'

'Jesus!' she took the jam and put it on the passenger seat and reversed off the driveway, resisting the temptation to lob the jam at the house like a grenade, pebble-dashing it with sticky red bloodiness. It slunk on the passenger seat, embarrassed to be so unwanted.

Text: 'Am eating jam with spoon. About to fall into sugar-fuelled coma. You know how I died. Tell Rolo I love him. Thanks for everything.'

There was no text back, however. And nothing all evening. Usually Cormac responded straightaway. That was one of the amazing things about him, his reliability. He still hadn't replied an hour later. Maybe he'd lost his phone? That was plausible, she supposed. Or maybe he'd had an accident and was fighting for his life in some hospital or in a coma. But somebody would have called her, surely. Or maybe he was out having fun. Could he be on a date? It was only a matter of time until he met someone else, though, she would think. Someone serious. He was undeniably attractive, not movie-star unreal but real-life *really* handsome. It was the combination of sexy greying hair, the slim build and broad shoulders. And then there was his smile, a sweet beautiful smile that spread over his face like a sunrise. And he was so un-moody, unlike all the other men she seemed to come across; he was always happy to see her. Cormac was one of those men who make you feel better about the world. One of those amazing, reliable, kind, amusing Brigadoon kind of men. The blue-moon types.

If he was gay, she often thought, it would make the whole thing easier or, at least, instantly more explicable to people.

She had decided very early on that she couldn't make herself vulnerable to him and risk losing him, like all the other men in her life. It would never have lasted between them, she believed, because very soon, he would have got fed up with her and walk away. That's been the pattern of her life so far so why would it be any different with him? And they would never have had this wonderful friendship. This way, it was perfect. This way, she could be her best self and never lose him. It had worked – kind of – for years.

But she was aware it couldn't go on forever. Someone would come and take him away, some nice girl who loved Cormac, and she would have to watch while they skipped into the sunset with Rolo prancing about. And maybe they would ask Melissa to be godmother to one of their children and Melissa would have to get a cat or something, to stop her getting lonely.

But what if she wasn't nice? What if she was horrible? What if she banned Cormac from seeing her? What if they had to say goodbye after all? Melissa couldn't think about that. She was suddenly finding it hard to breathe. The thought of life without Cormac? Unthinkable.

8

EILIS

One morning, in an attempt to shed all memory of the night shift at the hospital, Eilis found herself handing over her credit card to buy a tree. A lilac tree.

It had been the usual blur and buzz of trying to move patients from the waiting area, to being seen, and either home or a bed. Nothing had moved as fast or efficiently as she would have liked. She thought of that man, the guy who had sent the flowers, the one who had shouted out of sheer frustration as his mother was sat on a plastic chair. She wondered how they both were. She often thought of people, once they had moved on, and how they were getting on. And she imagined all of them, living nice normal lives, away from the hospital, their brief brush with it over and nearly forgotten.

Rob was at work, one of the main benefits of his specialism was that he hadn't done a nightshift since his training. But this morning, when she tried to sleep away the nightshift, she couldn't so instead of lying there thinking she got up, pulled on her old cord trousers and her wellies and went out into the garden. Spring was beginning to peak out, the garden gently rumbling into life on this morning. As she stood there, surveying her tiny plot, she could feel herself being woken up.

She took a moment, standing in the sunshine, to text Steph.

When can I come and see you?

She had been thinking about her and wondering if everything was as it seemed. There was something about Steph, something slightly shaky about her, she wasn't the same as she used to be. And it was a chance to see Rachel again. Steph was always the coolest and the calmest of the three of them, but not anymore. Her energy was different, she acted the same, but Eilis couldn't help thinking that there was something wrong.

Gardening was Eilis' therapy. It was something she did on her own, entirely without Rob, it was her space, her thing. And if the insides of the cottage were a homage to all things modern, the garden, on the outside, was a hymn to all things traditional. She had honeysuckles and roses, she had lupins and foxgloves, she had climbers and ramblers, she fought duels with slugs, snails and greenfly and she put food down for birds and would let ladybirds crawl over her hands. If she didn't have this garden, she often thought, she would have gone quite mad.

Mam would have liked this, she would often think, as she was kneeling down digging away. And she would imagine her mother sitting on a chair nearby in the early-spring sunshine, the two of them chatting every now and then. But she couldn't think about that because it made her too sad, so she would shake the thought away and carry on weeding.

A lilac tree, she thought. That was the answer. A lilac tree! She suddenly couldn't think of anything else. She would plant it just there by the fence and she imagined it in full bloom, and she thought of the blossoms she would pick every year in early summer.

She'd been driving past a new gardening shop in Sandycove, just down the road, for some time now and she wondered if it was time to try it out. According to the small swinging sign by the front door, it was called O'Malley's Garden. And one thing she had discovered, second only to gardening on the soothing the soul stakes, was a good potter in a gardening shop, a surveillance of secateurs and seeds, a pondering of pots and plants. And God knows, she needed soothing. O'Malley's Garden was on the corner of the row of shops in Sandycove. There was a yard to one side, filled with plants and pots, and inside were all the seeds and gloves and trowels and kneeling pads and various trinkets and treasures that only the green-fingered would love, such as a large and impressive display on bug and disease repellents. She stood inside for a moment, thinking how lovely it was; her perfect place. Some women liked the posh stores, she liked gardening shops. She settled in for a long and leisurely browse.

Eventually, she found a lilac tree outside and shifted it to the cash desk, and waited her turn to be served. It was probably on the big side but she had thought that maybe she could half-roll it, half-shuffle it back to her car, get it in somehow and she'd worry about the getting it out of the car when she got home. Rob wasn't the gardening type, even if he was around. She was used to yanking things around, wrestling with trees and bags of compost.

'Going far?' She jumped as the girl behind the desk spoke.

'Um...' Eilis was hidden by the tree.

The girl sized Eilis up. 'I'll get some help for you.' She obviously thought that a small woman like Eilis wasn't able to carry a huge tree on her shoulders... And she'd be right. The girl shouted in the general direction to the back of the shop. 'Muscles!'

A man appeared. Tall, broad and handsome and wearing a checked shirt rolled up to his elbows, his face stubbly, slightly salt and peppery, with dark hair curling around his ears. He reminded her of someone...

And then she recognised him. That man from the hospital, the one who sent the flowers. Mr Blue Eyes, or Mr Shouty as Becca had called him. Suddenly, Eilis felt incredibly embarrassed and tried to shrink even tinier. For one, brief mad moment, she imagined she could hide behind the tree like someone in a cartoon but, petite as she was, she couldn't get quite enough cover.

Eilis peered at him through the leaves. My God, she thought. He certainly is handsome. Better than she remembered at the hospital. But then again, A&E wasn't the place which showed people in their best light, she should know; the fuzzy, buzzing electric lights of the hospital, sucked the light out of everything. He was laughing.

'Muscles?' he said. 'Me? Who do you think I am? And doesn't my brain get a mention?' He raised an eyebrow.

'If you had one, it would. As it is, we're just being kind to you. Care in the community, you know, dear brother. Now, would you be so kind as to help this lady to the car with her beautiful lilac tree.'

Eilis couldn't take her eyes off him. He was more the kind of gorgeous that you thought was long gone with Clark Gable or the rise of the New Man. Who was it he reminded her of... Poldark! That's the one.

And then he looked up and Eilis found herself frozen to the ground. And then she saw that he was blushing.

'It's you,' he said, slowly, surprised, a smile now edging its way across his lips.

'Yes, it's me,' she said.

'You know each other?' said the girl.

'Yes,' he said, at the same time as Eilis shook her head.

'No,' she said.

'Which is it?' said the girl, intrigued.

'Well,' he said. 'You know that night when Mam had to go to hospital?'

'When I was in Cork?'

'Yes, well,' he paused. 'And we had a bit of a wait in A&E...' he broke off to glance at Eilis. 'Well, I was a little on edge and I took my frustration out on this poor woman. She was the doctor on duty... in the middle of, I presume, an extremely stressful shift...' He looked at Eilis. 'I'm sorry. No excuse. I was out of order and I am sorry for making your difficult job worse.'

'That's okay,' said Eilis. 'We get it. Don't worry. It happens all the time.' She was gripping her tree and squashing the leaves under her sweaty palm.

'Well, I'm really sorry... I was just... you know.'

'It's okay,' she said gently. 'It's fine.'

He was looking at her intently.

'Thank you,' he said. 'What can I do to show I'm sorry?'

'Well, you sent the flowers, so that was enough. Thank you, they were lovely.'

'I'll have to think of something else,' he said, looking at her. 'I was really out of order.'

'You can carry it to the car, that's what you can do,' said his sister. 'You're a pillock. We now have official confirmation.' But she was laughing. 'Please ignore my brother,' she said to Eilis. 'Once an arse, always an arse. And thank you for looking after our Mam.'

As she was speaking, the Poldark-alike had moved around the counter towards Eilis. He took the tree from her and for a moment his hand was on hers and she felt suddenly that something was happening, and it felt dangerous and exciting and that she was alive. Jesus. She tried to breathe.

He hoisted it easily and they began to walk towards the car, about ten metres away.

'Just there,' she said. 'Thanks so much.'

Poldark placed it down while she searched for her keys and, as she fumbled around, she couldn't help noticing his hands, the very opposite of Rob's smooth doctor hands, she thought. These were calloused working hands, made for grabbing and carrying. How could *hands* be attractive? she thought. Hands! For God's sake. She felt hot... early menopause, she wondered, or a mid-life crisis or just generally crazed. What was wrong with her? She wasn't normally so flushed and blushed.

She could see chest hair poking out of the top of his shirt and found herself thinking of his hands grabbing her and him kissing her all over her body and what his body must look like under his clothes...

He held out his hand. 'Charlie O'Malley.'

'Eilis McCarthy.'

They shook hands. His felt rough to the touch, nothing soft about those hands. She wanted to hold onto them and never let go. But thankfully she managed to loosen her grip just before it got too weird.

'Will you be okay when you get home?' he asked, speaking gently. 'Do you have help the other end?' He was looking at her with his amazing eyes. He looked like he really cared. Would it be too much to ask him to come home with her? To help her, of course.

She was going quite, quite mad.

'Grand, I'll be grand... don't you worry,' she said, sounding not grand at all and rather addled. He was looking at her as though she was a curiosity. Which of course she was. A sex-starved female who was latching on to the first gorgeous, visible man.

'How's your mother?' she managed. 'Is she totally recovered?'

'Oh...' for a moment, she saw something flash across his face. Sorrow or fear. 'Well, I don't know... but you're very good to ask.'

'But is she okay?'

'Yes, I think so, but it's just hard to see her so old. She is in her eighties now, but she was the best mother, ever, *is* the best mother ever. We're just very fond of her. She's just not in the best health...' he paused. 'The thought of losing her scares me, if I'm honest.' He looked at Eilis. 'Sorry, it's not something I talk about very often but you were there. You looked after her.'

'I understand,' she said.

'You wish they would last forever, don't you? Is your mam in good health?'

'Not really.' Eilis paused. 'She passed away. Years and years ago, when I was eighteen.'

'Oh my God, I'm so sorry.'

'That's okay.' She almost laughed. 'Sorry,' she said, looking at his appalled face. 'You weren't to know.'

'You were so young,' he said, searching her face for signs of how she was feeling.

'I know...' But that's the thing, she wanted to say, that's exactly it, I can't seem to move on. I can't stop feeling like it has just happened. I can't stop feeling like that eighteen-year-old whose mother has just died. 'So, anyway,' she said, 'thanks so much and say hi to your mam.'

There was something about him that made her want to stay and talk to him, something that drew you in. She didn't want to leave but she could hardly just hang around like a lemon. She turned reluctantly to get into her car.

'We give classes, you know,' he said, suddenly. 'On tree care. On loads of gardening-related things. Why don't you come to one? They're free.' He stopped.

She looked at him, into his handsome face, his dark eyebrows, his blue eyes and she realised that she had to see him again.

'So, maybe you'll come?' he said. 'The classes. Gardening... you know. All sorts. They're really popular. We've got a little gang now. They are all really nice. Come next Saturday. It starts at five. And if you can't come this Saturday, it's every Saturday, Now, spring is here, it's going to be weekly.'

'Are you giving them?' Shut up, she told herself. You are acting like you will only go if he is there. Which may have been the truth but he did *not* need to know that.

'Mainly my sister, Kate. She is the real gardening genius. I'm just the man about the shop.' He nodded in the direction of the shop. 'We've both been gardening for years, but I set up the business a year ago and Kate helps out whenever she can. She's a horticulture lecturer at the Botanic Gardens. I'm the brawn. She's the brain.'

'You're the muscles.' She involuntarily glanced at his broad shoulders, his height, his arms, his torso. Oh God, he noticed her. She was like a sad old woman, desperate for male attention. She looked away.

'Yeah...' he said, running his fingers through his hair, as though suddenly self-conscious. 'You could say that. I'm just here to lug things round.'

'What were you doing before?' she found herself asking, as way of keeping him there as long as she could.

'Law. But lost the will to live eventually. I went into it for my dad... to make him proud, but then one day I thought, he's still going to be proud of me even if I am not a lawyer.'

'Really? And is he?'

'Well, he's passed away now,' he smiled to show that it was okay, 'but I am 100 per cent positive that he would be. I wish I'd done it years ago.'

'I went into medicine to make my Mam proud,' she said, wondering why she was telling him this. She never spoke about her mother but there was something about him that made it seem like the most natural thing in the world.

'And did it?'

'No, she died before I even went to college but she would have been. I'm sure of it. Her daughter, a doctor! I often think of her when I am on my way to work, what would she say now? She would have told everyone about me.' She couldn't stop talking! Just close your mouth, it's not that hard.

'I'm sure she would,' he said, looking at her, smiling gently at her.

'It's quite humbling, thinking of that pride and then me just being me, nothing to be proud of, really. Anyway,' she said, realizing that there was only so long she could keep the poor man captive. 'I should go. Let you get back...'

'Okay.' He hesitated. It was him that seemed reluctant, or was she imagining it?

'So, see you around,' she said, casually. 'I might see you at the class.' Might? *Definitely*. 'Well, thanks so much for your help.'

'No problem at all.' He was still looking at her. 'Glad to be of use. See you.'

'Yes, see you.' As he walked away, she allowed herself to watch him walk back to the shop. She had never seen anyone so... so happy. He was tall, tanned, muscular... and happy. Is happiness so rare, she thought, that it's *obvious* when someone looks it?

She got into her car and pulled away onto the road, winding down the window and desperately trying to focus on the journey home. She thought of Charlie giving up his job and following his dream. But I don't have a dream, she thought, I've never had a dream except trying to fulfil other people's.

Those hands... the sexiest hands she had ever seen. She wondered, apart from carrying trees, what else he could do with them. She opened the window and made herself think of other things, mundane things. But she couldn't think of anything, except Charlie.

She tuned in the radio. Born To Run came on and she sang at the top of voice.

We've gotta get out while we're young... cos tramps like us, baby we're were born to run.

She had conveniently forgotten all about Rob and, for the entire drive home, she no longer felt unsettled or unhappy, she felt *alive*.

Baby, we were born to run... tramps like us, baby we were born to run.

9

STEPH

Communion day dawned bright and blue. Steph had spied the vans arriving at next door's since eight o'clock that morning. Totally Cheffilly had two vans, and then there was the hire crowd with the glasses and the plates. From the off-licence van there materialised boxes and boxes of wine and trays and trays of beer.

Rick came downstairs.

'Everything all right?' she asked, trying to make an effort, hoping he was in one of his friendlier moods.

He didn't answer her, just grunted, it was as though she hadn't spoken. She felt suddenly foolish, as she often did, always on the back foot. And then Rachel joined them, they obviously had been midway through a conversation. 'But why won't you, Dad. Hugh comes on Fridays.'

'But Hugh doesn't work like I do,' he said. 'Hugh's a pussy.'

'Dad!'

'What?' he said, laughing. 'He is! Public relations. No wonder he can take Fridays off to watch schoolgirls play hockey.'

'Dad, please. Come on, just once.'

Come on, Rick, urged Steph, say yes, say yes to your lovely daughter that you will go and watch her play hockey. Rachel knew Steph would jump at the chance to cheer her on, but Rachel had her eyes on the bigger prize; her father's support and approval. But he was a busy man, busy giving others his approval.

'Sweetheart,' said Rick. 'I would love to, there is nothing more I would like than to stand on the side of a freezing pitch on a Friday afternoon, in March, and watch you play hockey.' He was teasing her, they all knew, but it was tinged by his harsh sense of humour.

Rachel punched him on the arm. 'Loser,' she said. Steph was always impressed at Rachel's confidence around him, something she herself had never mastered, but she was also sad about how he always got away with being the kind of dad who lets you down.

'Listen, Rachel, I'm busy. I have clients. I get paid to be in meetings... that's how we can afford to buy you nice clothes and whatever else it is you girls are into.'

'Dad,' said Rachel, looking at him straight in the eye. 'Did your dad watch you play rugby or football...?'

'Rugby,' he said quickly.

'Did your Dad see you play rugby when you were at school?'

'No,' admitted Rick.

'And would you have wanted him to?' Rachel had him now. Steph's admiration for her only child reached its zenith.

'Yes,' admitted Rick.

'Well, then.'

He smiled at her and raised his hands in surrender. 'Look, I'll see what I can do. Okay?'

Rachel shrugged. 'Just let me know when you can squeeze me in. But remember, when you are old and wrinkly and in a care home, I may or may not choose to visit.'

He laughed and Rachel swept out of the room, point made and scored.

He turned to look at Steph. 'I think,' he said, 'that we may have another lawyer on our hands. Chip off the old block, if you ask me.'

Steph didn't mention Rachel's love of art history and her brilliant English essays, that she too might have a claim on her daughter. But she smiled and said nothing.

'I just have to go and see Mam and Dad,' she said. 'See how they are getting on.'

'Send them my best wishes,' he said, faux-gallantly. He could, if he wanted, play the role of caring husband but most of the time he couldn't even be bothered to act.

Steph's parents lived just up the road, in the house she grew up in.

'Mum? Dad?' She couldn't hear the radio. Usually its job was to blast out news all day long but today it was quiet. What was wrong? 'Everything alright?' she called.

'In here,' she heard her mother call out. 'Kitchen.'

She walked through the hall, the little table with the letters and both sets of keys, the picture of Steph on her graduation day on the wall, Steph and Rick on their wedding day, Rachel as a baby and a picture of Steph and Rachel taken in the back garden, when Rachel was ten, their arms around each other, so easily and naturally. There they are, in the photo, as though nothing could break them, and now that bond seems to be broken.

Steph may have had her own house, shared with Rick and Rachel, but she still thought of her parents' house as her real home. It made her realise that she hadn't properly moved out and on, emotionally she had never quite flown the nest. If things had been better with Rick, then maybe she wouldn't feel like this. But her house was no safe haven and her childhood home was where she could be the old Steph, the confident relaxed Steph. She felt fulfilled and fortified by each visit.

'In the kitchen.' Her father's voice sounded strange. She walked quickly through the house and was met by the sight of her dad, Joe, sitting on his armchair, looking pensively through the French doors at something (a blade of grass? a leaf?) in the garden, while her mother, Nuala, sat on a campstool dabbing paint on a canvas.

'I can't talk,' he said, trying not to move his mouth. 'I am posing and have been told not to move a muscle.'

'Okay...' said Steph, whispering, relieved to see it was just another of her parent's many activities. 'Genius at work.' She tiptoed dramatically to the work surface and put down some peppermint creams, some scones and some lemon curd she had bought at a school fundraiser, and a copy of the Irish Times.

Her mother laid down her brush; the spell was broken.

'Hello Stephanie,' she said, smiling brightly, genuinely delighted to see her daughter. 'How lovely to see you. Is that elevenses?'

'Even Picasso would have breaks for tea,' said Steph, slipping back into her role as important member of this family. Here, she had status. Here, she was important. 'Although his was probably a glass of absinthe. Nothing *pedestrian* and ordinary for him.'

'Pedestrian? Tea?' Joe was standing up, stretching his back. 'Heresy!

Drink of the Gods, tea is. I bet Pablo only drank absinthe because he thought he had to. All part of the look, you see. That and the stripy T-shirts. He probably drank tea when no one was looking. And wore a nice plain cardigan. Not unlike this one, I would imagine.'

'Perhaps,' said Steph, laughing. 'You and he share a certain swagger.'

Joe nodded sagely.

'Let's put the kettle on, so. Pablo here needs a cup of tea. As do I,' said Nuala. 'What do you think, Stephanie? You're the art expert in the family.'

Steph coloured. 'Was, not anymore,' she said. 'Now... let's have a good look at it. Hmmm. Well, I think it's brilliant, Mam.' And it was. For an amateur. And if you didn't know it was meant to be an *actual* person.

'More blue, I think,' said Nuala. 'On the nose.' She reached out for her paintbrush to add a dab.

'The nose?' Steph's dad, Joe pretended to be indignant. 'My nose is many things. But blue it is not.'

'It's art, dad,' said Steph. 'Mam's in her blue period. And you can't come between an artist and her vision. And if Monet here thinks your nose is blue, then blue it is.'

'Exactly,' said Monet, dabbing some blue on the canvas. 'There. Just... like... that.' She looked up. 'Your nose *is* blue, anyway. Have a look in the mirror.'

Joe made a sound like hmmphffftt.

'And you've really caught the perpetually vacant stare in Dad's eyes,' said Steph.

Both her parents laughed. The two of them always found the amusing side to any situation. In fact, whenever anything bad happened, Joe would always say: 'Right, when can we see the funny side to this?' And eventually, with most things, they would.

'Are you finished with me, Maestro?' Joe was still stretching. 'My legs are stiff as a board.'

'You okay, Dad? I'll put on the kettle.' Steph stood up, pleased to have something to do.

'No, no, I'll do it.' He waved her down. 'You sit there and talk to your mother. It's been ages since we've seen you.' He hobbled to the kettle, exaggerating the effort.

'It's only been a week!'

'That's ages when you get to my ancient-ness.' He smiled at Steph. 'One of these nice-looking scones?'

'Definitely.'

Nuala had moved to the small sofa and patted the seat beside her, inviting Steph to sit down.

'Now, how is our lovely granddaughter? What has she been up to?' Nuala said.

'Um...' Steph racked her brain. 'She's got a test... and coursework to hand in. Geography.'

'Oh yes, I texted her to say Good Luck. And I wanted to know if she had the next series of The Wire. We finished series four last night. It's very good, isn't it, Joe.'

'Very good,' he agreed. 'Haven't a clue what's going on, but very good all the same.'

'And I wanted to make sure she was wearing a coat. There's a terrible wind.' She took out her phone and started scrolling through. 'It's great, the old mobile, because you can ring anytime and everyone is always in. Here... where is her last text?' Nuala peered at the screen. 'Thanks Granny, she says. That's all. But three exclamation marks. Those things are fierce handy.'

'Well,' said Steph. 'At least she is talking – or texting – to someone. I feel invisible at the moment.'

'Teenagers, that's all,' said Nuala, trying to be kind. 'You were the same.'

'I was? I don't think so.'

'Remember, Joe?' Nuala called over. 'We had a few slammed doors in this house, didn't we? The odd moody silence?'

Joe nodded. 'I think I recall a bit of stomping around, too,' he said.

'It's just teenagers,' said Nuala. 'She's fine with us... children are like that with their mothers. It's just growing up. Give it two years and she'll come back to you.'

'Two years!' But Steph couldn't shake the feeling that Rachel's antipathy was something more, related to something deeper than just hormones and the fact that it seemed aimed more at her than anyone else. 'Anyway...' she said, changing the subject. 'How are you two?'

'You know us... rubbing along...' And they began to talk about their week, both completing each other's sentences, finding the same things amusing, two lives utterly in harmony.

Steph had only seen her parents argue once; it involved the neighbour's cat and their dog, John-Paul, and the fact that Nuala kept feeding
the cat which drove John-Paul mad. The dog was long gone and the argument practically forgotten. However, sometimes, Joe might mention, 'Do
you remember that cat from next door?' and the two of them would laugh
conspiratorially.

After John-Paul's sad demise, the two had wondered about getting a
new dog. 'We're too old.' Joe had said, resigned, when they finally came to
the decision not to replace him. 'We would slow the poor thingeen down.
Dogs need young and frolicky owners...'

They may have been dog-less but they had each other and they would
walk together to the cafe on Killiney Hill every morning for a cup of tea
and fresh air, taking treats to surreptitiously feed to the motley crew of
dogs tied up outside. Then, they would go inside and say a cheery hello to
all the dog-owners, pretending they had not just been giving their dogs a
feast outside, and order a cuppa and a slice of lemon drizzle. To share.

Nuala and Joe had met at an ice cream stall in Dingle, in Nuala's home
county of Kerry. She had been cycling the treacherous Connor Pass with
her friends when she met Joe, who was down from Dublin with friends on
a hot bank holiday weekend, and they began a conversation which showed
no sign of petering out. Married within three months, they set up home in
Killiney, where Joe had begun work for the Civil Service and they'd been
each other's best friend and husband and wife ever since.

'So what about you? Any news?' her mother asked.

'Not really...' Steph tried to conjure something up. 'Um...'

'What about Rick? Still working hard?'

'Yes. All the time. He's never home.' She and Nuala exchanged the
briefest of looks, the kind that happened every so often, and the kind that
convinced Steph that Nuala understood everything: about her and Rick,
how he could be physically abusive to her, about how unhappy she was,
about how fake her life was.

And she couldn't swear on it, but there was something, unspoken,
unarticulated in the air whenever Steph – casually – mentioned Miriam.
She sensed that Nuala knew about Miriam too. She didn't know how, but
mothers did have a sixth sense when it came to their daughters. Still, she
longed to just blurt it out, but Nuala, being a discreet woman, always aware
of the dignity of others, would never poke or prod or probe. It was Steph's

secret to keep and there must be a good reason why she wasn't telling them.

Joe who was now shuffling over with the peppermint creams. 'Is it too early for one of these?' he said, already sucking on one.

'Definitely not,' said Nuala. 'It's never too early.' She slipped one out of the box proffered by Joe. 'Peppermint cream, Stephanie?'

'I will, why not?'

'I'm going again.' Joe slipped another into his mouth. 'Cholesterol be damned. This is living on the wild side, hey?'

After her second cup of tea, it was nearly time to go and start getting ready for the Communion so she said goodbye, wishing she could stay with them, not having to face her real life. She stood up, feeling her visit was all too brief and as she nosed her car down the hill back into Dalkey, she was gripped with her usual anxiety, the familiar tightening in her belly and by the time she was putting her own key in the lock, her stomach was as knotty as Miss Havisham's hair.

At two thirty, once they had knocked on Miriam and Hugh's front door, Steph and Rick and Rachel all immediately went their separate ways; Rick to the kitchen to grab a beer before joining the other guys in the sitting room where a rugby match was blaring, Rachel upstairs with Aoife, Steph hovering in the hall, wondering what to do, who to latch onto?

She spotted Miriam and for the splittest of seconds they looked at each other, before Miriam smiled at her and gave an annoying little wave, as though they were great pals. Which, of course, they were, weren't they?

Rick walked past Miriam, bottle of beer in his hand, just about to duck in to the TV room. 'Ricky!' said Miriam, using her annoying name for him. 'Aren't you going to say hello?'

He kissed her on the cheek, in a friendly, neighbourly way, but then whispered something in her ear which made Miriam laugh and slap him, flirtatiously. And she looked up again at Steph, and this time Steph looked away, shame suffusing her. She realised that being here, she couldn't hide behind the façade of a marriage. There was no pretending anymore.

Wine, she thought. Where's the bloody wine?

She found it in the kitchen and swiftly grabbed a glass, filled it to almost teetering, and gulped a big, long drink, allowing the alcohol to be quickly absorbed by every corpuscle in her body. Finally she felt able to face this awful party.

Sorcha, the Communion girl, was running through the house closely followed by a troupe of shrieking friends. Everywhere, adults were helping themselves to brimming glasses of white wine or fishing for cans in a barrel.

A waiter proffered a prawn-thing. Steph took two and a napkin, with her wine glass in the other hand, she munched miserably, sipping her wine and feeling utterly out of place.

Two women joined her, the charity case. 'We were just remarking on your beautiful scarf,' one said kindly. 'Cashmere?'

'Yes, yes, it is.' It was her stolen one.

'There's nothing quite like it, is there?' said the other one, smiling.

'No. No there isn't,' said Steph. She introduced herself, holding out her hand and desperately changing the subject.

'I'm Gillian and this is Valerie. We're friends of Miriam's from Pilates.'

'I'm her neighbour. That way.' Steph nodded her head in the direction of her house. She thought of her house, only yards away, and how quiet it would be now, and peaceful. She wished she was there, on her own, drinking tea and listening to a play on the radio. She took another sip of wine. The small talk continued: schools, houses, encounters with Bono. The usual chit-chat.

Valerie was talking about her daughter who, now she was sixteen, had disappeared into a whirlwind of school, socializing and sport.

Steph suddenly caught sight of Rachel, in a gang of girls, smiling and laughing. She caught Rachel's eye and waved but Rachel looked away. She loved being a mother, but it just wasn't as simple as it used to be.

'Do you miss her?' Steph wondered. 'You know, when they're not little girls anymore?'

'Miss her? God no, she's off doing her own thing. I was exactly the same. They barely need us now – we're just cash machines. And the twins are worse.' She turned to Steph.

'How many do you have?'

'Just the one.'

'Well, that makes it much easier.'

'Yes, yes I suppose it does,' Steph agreed mechanically. She and Rick never did have a second child. By the time Rachel was born and Steph might have been ready for another, they didn't try. Steph knew she didn't want another with Rick. He was too unpredictable. And he scared her.

But beautiful Rachel was enough for her. She loved it just being the two of them, she and Rachel, mother and daughter. There was something so special in just having one. She remembered so vividly dropping Rachel off to junior infants all those years ago. And, as they neared the playground, Steph's stomach would begin to flutter, at the thought she and Rachel were going to have to leave each other. For three hours. It sounded so silly now, but they were so bonded, she couldn't imagine them having separate lives.

And neither could Rachel, then. She would sob so hard that Steph would have to physically pass her over to the teacher and walk away. She remembered that feeling inside, like she had just given up her heart.

But Rachel's journey to independence had begun, and one day, Rachel turned her face to Steph's, tiny rosebud lips pursed, and kissed her goodbye. And that was it. No tears, no hanging on. Sometimes, Steph would give anything to be back in that playground for one moment, for one second, to feel those little lips on hers again.

She spent the party talking to people, some of them she knew, others for the first time. Later, at about nine, she was just wondering if she could leave when Rachel placed herself in front of her.

'I'm going to stay here tonight.'

'Did Miriam say it was okay?'

'Yeah, 'course.'

'Who's staying over?'

'Just me. Aoife and I are going to watch a film and get a pizza.'

'Okay. I'll just check with Miriam.'

'SHE SAID IT WAS FINE OR DID YOU NOT HEAR ME?' Rachel glared at Steph and a few people glanced over. Even above the noise of the party, they could hear her tone of voice. Steph let it go. She would just talk to Miriam herself.

'Okay, sweetheart,' said Steph. She longed to smooth her hair back but feared a swiped hand and a scowlier scowl.

'Mum, your eyes are funny. I think you've had too much to drink,' said Rachel, before disappearing back into the giggling mass of teenage girls and away from the room. There was no defence and Steph just had to pretend to laugh it off in front of the other guests when all she wanted was to smooth everything, make she and Rachel close again.

She went into the living room where the rugby match was now over and someone had put on music, it was Madness, 'Welcome to the House of Fun'. Steph laughed inwardly at the ironic choice of music. Hugh was there, talking and laughing with friends.

'Where's Miriam?' she asked him.

'Try outside,' he said. 'I think she said she was going for a smoke.'

'Thanks.'

'You alright?' he asked. 'Got everything? Drink, food?'

'Everything's perfect, Hugh. Thanks,' she said. 'Great party.'

She headed outside. It was dusk. The evening was cool. The doors of the house were all open and the cat dashed past her, racing from one adventure to another.

She heard sounds coming from around the back of the garage, hidden by a trellis of jasmine. The smokers? She walked towards them. But it wasn't anyone smoking but instead a couple in the throes of drunken love-making. Kissing wildly, passionately, deeply, desperately. The man with his hands up the woman's skirt, his trousers undone, his mouth covering hers. Her hair was out of place, the shoes, those beautiful, ridiculously expensive shoes, sinking into the mud. Her skirt pushed right up to her thighs, his groin thrust into hers.

Rick and Miriam.

Steph stood there, frozen in the late-spring air. She watched while her husband and neighbour consumed each other, grabbing and grinding, panting and pawing.

She staggered backwards in the dark, accidentally kicking over a pot of dead geraniums. Hiding behind the trellis, her heart desperately trying to escape from her chest.

The lovers had stopped what they were doing and were now absolutely silent.

She heard Rick's voice say, 'It's nothing,' in that posh drawl of his. 'As you were.'

And they both laughed and the horrible sounds started up again. Steph crept away, as though she was the guilty one, as though she had something to hide.

She found the gap in the hedge between the two houses and walked across her lawn, her own heels sinking into the grass, like wading through jelly. Once inside, the sounds of music and laughing and singing from next door faded as she leaned against her worktop, breathing fast and heavy;

she felt as though she was going to be physically sick. The wine didn't help. Maybe Rachel was right, she had drunk too much, but what was the alternative? Spend the afternoon at the worst party ever, stone cold sober? That was impossible.

What she had witnessed was passion. Desire. Something that Steph hadn't given or felt for Rick for years. She almost felt sorry for them, out there, like teenagers, hiding from everyone. And she felt jealous... not of Rick. Miriam and Angeline could have him. But that they had desire and passion. It was something, wasn't it? It counted for something.

10

MELISSA

Her mother had a secret, she been convinced of it for ever now. It wasn't the drinking; that was anything but clandestine in their house; it was just something they never talked about. No, there was something else, something missing, stories never to be told or heard. Nothing about Mary's life before marriage, dances, games or friends, ever found its way to Melissa's ear. 'Ancient history' was used to brush aside Melissa's inquisitiveness or 'don't remember'. When her mother wasn't drinking and when she was in her sober periods, Melissa would ask questions, trying to make the most of her mam's rare lucid periods.

'Did you have a beehive?' she asked once, when she was about ten years old.

'A what?'

'A beehive. You know, your hair.' Melissa already was beginning to wish she hadn't asked.

'Never you mind,' she was told. 'Never you mind.' It was always never you mind, or she was met with outright silence.

'Did you have a boyfriend before Dad?' she asked when she was older, wildly curious now about her mother and the person she might have been before her. The look which flashed across her mother's face seemed pure anger. But there was something else tucked in there; hidden, a secret, but Melissa had glimpsed it. She needed to know what it was.

Parts of the house were out of bounds. Certain drawers and cupboards

('Leave it alone, Melissa, you're always meddling!') in her parent's bedroom. When she was a child and her mother was downstairs, Melissa would take advantage and creep in and peer round, hoping that secrets would be revealed just by being in the room. On the top of the wardrobe was an old white suitcase – small, rounded, with a clasp at the top. And locked. It haunted her.

'But what's in it?' she persevered, suddenly desperate to know. She was only ten or eleven but she showed signs of being a journalist even then.

'Nothing, it's empty.'

'Can I have it then?' Melissa thought it would be perfect for carrying around her books.

'No!' her mother snapped. 'Leave it be. It's mine, so leave it alone!'

Years later, when she was about fifteen, alone in the house, she began rooting around with the precision of a detective, looking for clues, for answers. In her mother's underwear drawer, she found a small key. She took it out, fingering it in the light from the window, immediately knowing what it was for.

She pulled a chair from the landing over to the wardrobe and reached up, knocking the suitcase off the top, so it bounced off her head and shoulder, releasing a smoke bomb of dust. She scrambled to her feet and, fingers trembling, turned the key, and lifted the lid.

Nothing. Empty. Well, empty-ish. Just some of her old baby clothes, a little knitted cardigan, a teddy bear and a few other bits and pieces. Normal enough. No great secrets. Nothing to see. Except that until then, she had never regarded her mother as particularly sentimental. Other mothers, Melissa had noticed, placed photos on walls, pinned paintings to cork boards, displayed clay disasters proudly on mantelpieces. Mary didn't even bother ordering Melissa's school photos but although she still smiled for the camera, she became quickly aware of the utter futility of the exercise.

But after finding the suitcase, Melissa felt exuberantly pleased. If her mother had kept this stuff and was so possessive about it, then she did love her, in her own, unique way. She was like all those other mothers; Melissa was – gloriously, wondrously, rapturously *loved*.

When her mother returned that day, Melissa was on her best behaviour, making tea, and had the house pin-neat, anxious to return this newly discovered sentimentality. But her mother didn't respond to Melissa's love-lorn advances and, eventually, the suitcase on top of the wardrobe lost its power and Melissa was left with the very clear impression that she was lower down on her mother's priorities. She did love drink though, that was clear.

But nothing could shake the feeling that she was to blame. If, somehow, she had been a better daughter, her mother wouldn't have drunk. If she had been more beautiful, cleverer, better behaved, whatever, all would have been well. There must be something about her that made her impossible to love.

When she was little, she would watch The Little House on the Prairie and marvel at Ma; so nice, so kind and so smiley. She would have loved to have had a mother who smiled at her, instead of being dead behind the eyes and nothing Melissa ever did made her mother act like she was a good daughter, a good person, someone worthy of love.

Once she moved out and into the flat on Baggot Street with Steph, in their third year at university, life became much easier and Melissa began to breathe more deeply. But she wondered if she would ever feel normal. Being normal seemed effortless for the rest of the world. For her, it was a daily struggle to just try and get on with her life, to pretend to everyone that she was normal and not just hiding a mass of insecurities and feelings of unworthiness. She did quite well most of time. It helped having Cormac around. He always made her feel good and thankfully later on, she was meeting Cormac. He had called her and asked her to call in to have a look at the shop.

'Hello stranger!' she had said when she picked up.

He laughed but sounded slightly sheepish. It had been ten days since she had spoken to him but there had been texts, so she knew he hadn't died or anything. He'd just been busy with his new shop. There was a lot to do. She wondered though if it was just the bakery that was keeping him. She had a niggling feeling that it was something – someone – else.

'What's going on?' she said. 'Don't tell me you've fallen in love?' She was teasing him but she wanted to know. She braced herself for the answer.

'No,' he said, to her relief, 'nothing like that. Just busy with the bakery. Actually that's why I'm calling. The painters are in... come on... I need your beady eye. You can advise me on colours... and, whatever you say...'

'You'll do the opposite?'

'Totally.' Cormac laughed, sounding normal again. She felt a lift in her spirit. He was back, the Mel and Cormac show was back on the road.

'I think that's very wise,' she said. 'Very wise indeed.'

'No, seriously. Come and have a look at it.'

'I would love to.'

They drove along the coast, through Dun Laoghaire with all the day trippers and swimmers and ice-cream eaters, zipping along until they got to Dalkey and the two of them, Rolo lolloping beside them, cut through past the library and onto Church Street.

'Here it is.'

They stood outside a boarded-up shop.

'What do you think, Rolo? Will you like living in a bakery?' Melissa pretended to listen to the dog. 'What's that? Oh bad news, Cormac, he says he'd prefer a butchers'. Oh dear. Poor Rolo. He's going to be disappointed.'

It was between the newsagents and the supermarket and a big sign stated. 'The Daily Bread opens here soon. We look forward to baking your morning loaf.'

'Corny?' asked Cormac.

'Totally. But nice. I like it.' She smiled at Cormac who shrugged. He looked nervous. 'How are you feeling?'

'Like it's Christmas and although I *know* Santa isn't coming, I'm still hopeful he might.'

Melissa nodded. She got it. 'It'll be amazing. I know it. You've got all those commercial contracts, and all the ladies will be popping in to take a look at the new hunky bread man in the midst. You can just appear covered in flour and grunt and they will all love it.'

'Now *that* excites me. A non-speaking role in the fantasies of red-blooded females. I'm not scared one bit.'

'You're well able for them.'

Although he looked wrecked from all the hours he was putting in getting the shop up and his daily running, he was looking good. Well, he always did but she found herself studying him. She noticed the hairs on his forearms were golden, his skin brown. And then she realised she wanted to touch him. Not in the normal way, the hugs, the playful swipes, but to reach out to touch him, as though to see if he was real.

I must be going mad, she thought. Maybe it's because we haven't seen much of each other lately. She tried to keep the conversation going but she was distracted by a slight musky smell off him. And what about his jaw... his broad shoulders and, of course, the most attractive thing about him of all: the way he was perfectly comfortable with himself. And so completely happy. She'd always loved him, but she was struck that there was something more, something deeper. She *loved* him. Oh no. This was going to ruin everything.

11

CORMAC

He and Walter had agonised for weeks over the name of the shop until he had gone for The Daily Bread. They had toyed with Bread Box (too plain), even just Bread! (as though it was a musical). For one mad five minutes, Cormac actually considered Body of Christ, but luckily Walter reminded him that no one would buy bread from a shop that reminded people of communion sessions. Especially in Ireland.

So The Daily Bread it was to be. And now there was only six weeks until he moved into the flat above and rose before dawn to begin making his sourdoughs, his boules, his baguettes, his cottage loaves. He felt sick with nerves and excitement.

But there was one person he wanted to soothe him, to reassure him that everything was going to be okay, and that was Melissa. He had been trying to resist calling her and instead had been spending all his spare moments with Erica. They'd been our five whole times, to a restaurant (her choice), to the cinema (his), to a historical walk of Dublin of the Georgian buildings (Erica's idea), to a vegan café which was surprisingly delicious and to his for a meal cooked by him. It had been an unqualified success and it was true what they say about the quickest way to a woman's heart was through her stomach. She stayed the night and everything was most satisfactory and enjoyable. They were starting to think of themselves as boyfriend and girlfriend.

But she wasn't *quite* Melissa and one day he cracked and picked up his phone. And now here she was, standing, silently, absorbing the whole scene. He saw her look at him, and she looked shocked, or maybe it was something else that he couldn't work out.

'Are you all right?' he asked.

'Fine, fine,' she said. 'Now, let me have a good look around.'

They walked round the back and had a look around. Cormac pointed out where the baking part was going to be, where the front counter was, which would have high stools, where the coffee machine would be, where the sofa for lounging would go. Rolo was sniffing around.

'Well?' he ventured. 'What do you really think?'

She looked up. 'You know something Cormac Cullen. I think it is amazing. You are making your dream come true and not many of us actually manage to do that. And the world needs bread. As Marie Antoinette realised to her peril.'

'True,' he said.

'And Rolo is very proud. Aren't you Rolo? We're both proud.' We can't wait to critique your baps.'

'Critique my baps!' He laughed.

'What's wrong with baps? It wasn't rye sourdough you were reared on, Mr Cullen. You'd have been happy with a bap five years ago. Bread snob.'

He laughed again and looked around at his little shop, happy she was there, sharing this exciting time in his life with him. He'd wanted to bring Melissa here first, before he brought Erica. She was still the most important person in the world to him. A hard habit to break. Wasn't that a song? And he really should tell her about Erica, before he didn't and then it got too weird. 'I... I...' he began.

'Yes?' She looked at him hopefully. Was he trying to tell her something?

'Nothing,' he said, suddenly feeling awkward. He didn't trust himself to tell her without showing his true feelings. Any one normal would just say it but he was convinced that she would guess that Erica was just a foil while he moved on from loving Melissa. 'I forgot what I was going to say. Come on, let's get some fresh air,' he said. 'Now I'm to be living in the suburbs, I may do as the suburbans do... and start walking the pier.'

'Oh God,' said Melissa, 'to think I got away from South County Dublin and you are *choosing* to come back.'

'It's nice, okay? I'm too old to live in town, these days. I want a gentler pace of life. And Rolo's going to love it.'

'You'll be buying a cagoule and wearing pleather slippers next.'

'You obviously haven't seen me relaxing at home, lately. Anyway, don't all natives walk the pier?'

'It's the law. I haven't done it in years.'

'Well then? Coming?'

'Only if we get an ice cream afterwards? Or is whippy ice cream too uncool for you. Does it need to be *gelato?*'

'Not if a flake is involved.'

'Now you're talking. Rolo? Walk?'

They chatted the whole way along the pier and later queued for ice creams. They sat on a wall by the sea. Melissa was busily pushing her flake inside her cone and then licking the top to seal the hole.

'Jesus!' Melissa's 99 had collapsed and it was melting through the bottom of the cone.

'Why don't you just lick it like a normal person?'

'Because that would be weird. You cannot veer from anything but consuming it like you did when you were seven. I wouldn't trust anyone who ate 99s neatly.'

Rolo was in full attention mode. At any moment, there was going to be ice cream on the ground and he was ready. And Cormac was watching Melissa out of the corner of his eye.

He was loving every second of being with Melissa. It was like binge-eating the night before a diet. He wasn't quite ready to give up sugar yet, but he knew he had to. This shop was the beginning of his new life and he knew his old life, slavishly loving Melissa, his unreciprocated love affair, was over. He had no choice. It was as though the universe had decided for him. He looked away. A surge of sadness welling up. He felt his heart was breaking. The thought of not sharing a 99 with her was like a death to him. Yes, I am pathetic, he thought.

But it wasn't right to do this to Erica. It was going well. She was so different to Melissa. She was cool, impressive and nice. She might be on the slightly extreme end of faddy (she only consumed what Aztecs and yogis ate) but he was beginning to realise that it *was* good to meet people who could teach you things. And Erica was teaching him that not everyone thinks a bag of cheese and onion crisps is something to be savoured. In fact, it was to be scorned.

But for now, he was hanging out with Melissa, his guilty pleasure. Soon to be consigned to history.

They were saying goodbye – a long goodbye.

12

EILIS

It was early morning and recently on her way home from night shifts, Eilis had begun detouring through Sandycove and past O'Malley's Garden. It was still closed, shutters down, but this morning just as she skimmed past, she saw Charlie unlocking the front door and waving to a passer-by. He was dressed in an old wax jacket, heavy boots and trousers which had seen better days. He couldn't have looked more opposite to Rob. And she realised that she couldn't stop thinking of him, that the only thing that stopped her from jumping out of the car, letting it career into a wall, and running over to him, begging him to take her on as an apprentice or slave or whatever, was that some vestiges of dignity remained.

He is settling in for a nice day at work, she thought, and I am just driving home feeling as though I have been in some kind of medieval stocks with cabbages been thrown at me. She realised the metaphor wasn't quite an adequate description of a night shift in A&E but with her brain only half functioning it was the best she could do. Despite the fact that all she wanted to do was stop and pretend she needed a pelargonium or a pergola or whatever, just to see him and talk to him again, she made herself drive on.

Home at last, slightly disappointed that her sensible self was so in evident that she had driven on past the shop without talking to Charlie, but if she could just survive the battle with the remote-controlled kettle

(Rob's idea of a sensible household gadget) and make herself a cup of tea, all might not be so lost.

'Hi!' she called out. 'I'm home.'

She heard Rob's voice make a muffled response and when she walked into the living room a scented candle was burning away on the mantelpiece.

'Morning,' he said. 'How'd things go?' Suit on, briefcase in hand, ready for his day as consultant cardiologist. And she thought immediately of Charlie, and how different he was to Rob in every way. She felt guilty and mean. 'I'm not going to be home tonight,' he said. 'I'm going out, with work. And I think I'll stay in town... taxis are just too expensive.'

'Yeah, good idea,' she said. He'd been doing this a lot lately, going out and staying out. Another woman might have thought he was having an affair, but she was sure he wasn't. You didn't want to be coming home to the outer suburbs of Dublin, all that way, and paying thirty euro in a taxi. But more than that was the fact Rob just wasn't into sex; it had never been a big part of their relationship. In fact, it barely had a walk-on role. And certainly never a *hands-on* part so surely he wouldn't be looking elsewhere for it.

Long ago, she stopped longing for him to change. Now, she knew, it was just the way he was. She used to wish he'd grab her, pull her to him, kiss her, *desire* her. In the early days, they had been so young, she hadn't quite known what to do and he seemed as clueless as she. And of course, she was still grieving for her mother. She thought both elements would get better... she assumed they would. But neither had. The grief was still there and the sex... well, it never really got going.

Rob didn't seem to worry about the lack of physical contact. And how do you talk about something like that without seeming strange or over-sexed? And if Rob was okay about it, then maybe she should be too. She consoled herself with the fact that they had a deep friendship, companionship. Which was more than others had, wasn't it? And maybe it made life easier... look what happened to the lonely and sex-starved. It didn't end well for Anna Karenina, did it? And what about Emma Bovary?

But... it might have been nice... and now she was thinking of Charlie all the time. I am obviously sex-starved, she thought, otherwise why am I fantasizing about a man I don't know? Maybe it was biological, maybe my clock is ticking, time running out. How many years had she left? Who knew but she'd hung around for too long to think that she had many left to waste.

She *had* wanted a child but Rob wasn't interested. 'We're enough,' he had said once, years ago. 'You and me. And we're busy... and we want weekends away.' And she had agreed because she thought he might be right and children weren't everything, but she had the sneaking feeling that perhaps they might be. Sometimes, she would see a mother, teeth gritted in determination, attempting to manoeuvre a pushchair through a shop door or pretending their child wasn't screaming as they were trying to buy milk, or seeing women standing on the side of the football pitch in the frozen wind and sleet, cheering on their child... and she would think, I would like that. I would like to be the one for that child; the one who carries you when you cry, who stands in the cold for you, the person who thinks of you all the time. Rain or shine. And they'd never even had many of those promised weekends away. Just the annual two weeks in Greece.

Rob went over and blew out a candle which was burning on the windowsill.

'That's a gorgeous smell,' she said, focussing on him and trying to be normal. 'The candle.'

'Vetiver and amber,' he said. 'Good for mornings... uplifting and energizing.'

'It's very nice, anyway. Better than the whiff of hospital.'

'Eau de disinfectant. I don't think Jo Malone does that one.' Rob laughed at his own joke.

'Whoever *he* is,' said Eilis, but Rob didn't laugh back.

'Right... so. I'm off.' But he didn't move, she caught him looking at her. Wistful, sad, sorry. And then it was gone, and he was back to Rob again, calm and slightly cross. 'Dinner's in the fridge. You can microwave it later for lunch.'

'Thanks so much. You're amazing.' And he was amazing at so many things. He was a great doctor, she knew that. He was smart and intelligent and kind and thoughtful. A brilliant cook. He had a great eye for design and a passion for architecture. But she had begun to wonder if all these amazing things were the kind of things she wanted. 'What is it?' she wondered.

'Chicken and barley.'

She desisted in asking him if that was another candle. 'Great. Can't wait.'

'Scatter some of the parsley over it.'

'Will do.' Secretly she was thinking that all she wanted was a slice of toast and jam. What's wrong with me? she thought. This kind of thing you couldn't just take for granted, not nice meals and scented candles. Other people arrived home to chaos, to shouting, to someone sitting in a vest and drinking beer. Not Rob, always so immaculately dressed.

But she didn't want immaculate. She wanted passion. And this house, so perfect and so sterile. She needed something more. Was it any surprise that she did so much gardening? She liked getting her hands dirty, to feel the soil, to watch things grow. This happened in the garden, things were alive. And when things died, it was okay. You got over it.

13

STEPH

Steph was browsing in a designer shop. She was still reeling from spying Miriam and Rick in the garden the other night, but she hadn't told anyone, she had kept it to herself. She could have confronted Rick, she could have knocked on Miriam's door, but she hadn't and she knew she wouldn't.

She had come here because she didn't know what else to do... she didn't really want to be around anyone, not feeling so jittery.

She picked up a small yellow purse. It was lovely, the colour was bright and gorgeous, the leather soft and supple. She wondered if she needed a purse. No, the one she had was fine. But she found herself unzipping and checking for a security tag.

Nothing.

She suddenly felt the surge of adrenaline, heart pumping; she was going to take it. She didn't need the purse, in fact, if she had walked away right now she would never have thought of it again. She could have bought ten of them, if she wanted. She could have bought anything in the shop and made no dent in the family finances. But it made no difference, she wasn't going to buy it, she was going to steal it.

Holding the purse casually in her hand, she continued her browsing and when she pulled out a jacket to take a better look, she slipped it into her bag.

She had managed to turn her jitters into full-on seismic shocks, a way of masking the pain inside, a way of creating even more drama. She had no idea. All she knew was that she had to stop but she couldn't. She tried on more jackets, took her time and then, ever so nonchalantly, walked toward the doors, her insides about to explode. She felt like one of the Great Escapers... she was nearly in Switzerland. Come on.

'Excuse me, Madam.' A man's voice. She turned around.

'Would I be able to check your bag, please?' He was a large man, dressed in perfectly ordinary clothes.

This was it. Game over.

She had no choice but to follow the man to the back of the shop, heart thumping, pulse at her temple banging against her head. Steph looked straight ahead, just in case she saw anyone she knew. A fleeting thought: imagine if Miriam saw her. Would she laugh and point in horror?

She thought of Rachel and the shame she would bring on her, the girl with the mother who is a shoplifter. And her parents, they would never imagine in a million years that this was how low their daughter had sunk.

Her face was scalded, her stomach desecrated. The man brought her into a room with no windows and a table with a few dirty paper cups. There was a smell of the dead about the room. This was a far cry from the glitz of the shops. This is serious, she thought. There was no getting out of this. She couldn't just pretend to be forgetful or scatty like she had with Fintan. This is it. The beginning of the end. The architect of my own demise. And it's all my fault.

And what was going to happen? Court, prison? What would Rachel say then?

Prison? Who would have thought that her life would end in prison? The shame would be stratospheric. She couldn't put Nuala and Joe through that. They wouldn't be visiting, bringing grapes to see her. No, that's hospital. What did people bring to prison? God only knew.

'Why would you like to check my bag?' she asked, quavering but trying to remain dignified.

'I think you may have put an item into your bag that you have not yet paid for, Madam.' He looked at her, right into her eyes.

'Really?' she managed. 'I don't think so.'

'Well, may I check?'

She slid her bag towards him on the table, as accepting of her fate as Anne Boleyn on the scaffold. It was to be. Prison awaited. Her life over.

'May I?' he said.

She nodded, tears brimming in her eyes.

He poked around. And then poked around some more. The bag wasn't that big. What was the problem?

'I can't see anything there,' he said, finally. 'I must have been mistaken.'

'Oh...' she was unsure what to do.

'I am terribly sorry, Madam. Will you accept my apologies?'

'Yes, yes of course.' She couldn't believe it. Trembling they walked out of the room. She had no idea what had happened but she just wanted to get away.

'We've had terrible problems with shoplifters, you see,' he explained, all chummy and matey now. 'They are the bane of my lives. And sometimes I get a little trigger-happy.'

'You mean you shoot them?' Her voice was shaking.

'Just a turn of phrase,' he laughed. He bent down to whisper in her ear. 'I would though,' he hissed. 'I fucking would. Those little feckers. I would blast their fucking little heads off.' His eyes were bulging and his teeth gritted in a most alarming way. 'Now you madam, you don't look like the type to pilfer, to pinch things. You wouldn't do anything so low-down as that, would you?'

Steph shook her head hard. 'Absolutely not!'

'You are free to go.' He swept his arms out into a princely gesture and she walked towards freedom once more. This time, chastened and appalled. I must never, ever steal again, she repeated. I can't do this, I can't live like this. It's going to get me in trouble. Think of Rachel, she hissed to herself, think of Rachel if you can't think of yourself.

By the jackets, she noticed something on the ground. The canary yellow purse was lying on the floor. She hadn't managed to drop it in to her bag. This was a sign. She was ready to re-find God, anything. She would never steal again. She had been given a second chance.

I am sorry for everything, she atoned. I promise, never again. Thank you for this chance. I have been weak and stupid but I promise I will sort this – sort me – out. I just don't know how yet. I just don't know how.

14

THE GIRLS

This time, Melissa had invited them around to her tiny flat in Portobello for a take-away curry and wine.

Steph thought twice about coming. She was still trying to recover herself after the incident in the shop... and seeing Miriam and Rick in the garden. Images of them kept flashing into her mind, all the time. She knew she looked and acted normal, but inside she was shaking, permanently. And then after the shop-lifting near-miss, she wasn't quite sure how she was managing to get out of bed every day. Surely someone must see she was a zombie and on the brink of craziness, but no one seemed to notice. It's a nightmare, she thought, this lack of control. She was petrified about what was going to happen next. She was so determined to turn over a new leaf, to start again but even if she got the shoplifting under control, there was still Miriam and Rick to worry about.

She sat down next to Eilis on Melissa's sofa.

'This is nice,' said Eilis, 'really comfortable. I could fall asleep on it.'

'Sometimes I do... and that's never a good idea,' said Melissa. 'Here have a poppadom... Steph?'

She took one. 'The flat is gorgeous,' she said. Tiny, she thought, compared to her house in Dalkey, but perfect for her and Rachel. She imagined living somewhere like this, her own place, just her and Rachel, not just a tiny corner of it and never having to flinch when she heard the key in the door. She could have all her things around, make it her own. Being single looked so easy.

She looked around at the pictures on the wall, the framed posters from different plays Melissa had seen over the years, a photograph of herself and Cormac.

'Cormac looks particularly handsome in that one,' said Steph. 'Is he getting more attractive or am I imagining it?'

'No, you're not imagining it, it's true,' said Melissa. 'I'm like his Dorian Grey portrait. I'm getting older and he is getting younger. Very, very annoying.' They all laughed. Melissa looked at the photo. The two of them were on a boat in France, one of the holidays they had taken together. The sun was glinting off the sea, the two of them, their arms around each other. They'd given Cormac's expensive Nikon to the sweetest old lady to take the photograph. She remembered his whispering, into her ear, 'That's the last time we'll see that camera.' And she giggled just as the shutter closed. And she remembered his arm around her and the feeling she had when he took it away, the emptiness she felt when it wasn't there and how natural it was with his arm around her, their bodies pressed together. The photo is there, her laughing, him grinning. She loves it. It's them in a nutshell. She took him for granted all these years and it is suddenly dawning on her that maybe she made a mistake. By keeping him at arm's length she might have wasted too much time, that life was for living and taking risks but her fear of failure had meant she would never know what it was like to have that arm over her shoulders, to hear him laugh at one of her jokes or to hold his hand or eat an ice cream on the pier ever again.

'By the way, Steph,' she said, changing the subject before she thought too much about it, 'I passed Mrs Long's gallery on Molesworth Street and thought of you. Remember her?'

'Of course! How could I forget? She was wonderful. I should have stayed there. It was such a lovely job.'

'And then Rick would always come and drag you off somewhere...' said Eilis.

'Yes... that's a long time ago,' she said, smiling her fake smile, as though she was adrift in happy memories. That was when she was in love with Rick, when she thought life was going to be easy. Ha! 'Shall we eat first and then start making the lists,' she said, 'I've got some invitations from the designer – it's a guy in the paper – for you to look at? We can email them to everyone.'

However brilliant Steph might have thought her acting was, Melissa was again receiving the message loud and clear that all was not right. She had never seen her quite so tense before, her jaw clenched and shoulders hunched.

When Steph first met Rick, Melissa was witness to the whole thing. But even then, Melissa had found him rather intimidating, had always wondered what Steph saw in him. He was just so... so Alpha. *So bloody male*. He had never had much to say to her and Eilis and, initially, Steph was torn, living two separate social lives. But that soon becomes exhausting and when your husband doesn't particularly like your friends, then you have to choose.

Melissa had turned up to some of their parties. She did it for Steph, and tried to mingle and mix and meet everyone, but she felt like a sore thumb. Rick was bloody terrifying, and those friends of theirs were quite, quite mad, especially that Miriam. She had always wondered how Steph, who was so normal, stood it all. But then, Melissa really didn't understand how marriages worked.

She herself had lied so blatantly about her miserable time in Paris. And Steph obviously telling porkies about her life being okay. She looked over at Eilis... she never really spoke about anything either... Here we are, she thought, such old friends and yet we lie to each other, as though we don't trust the others.

How could you be friends without full-disclosure? Suddenly, she was possessed with the need to tell the truth. She was exhausted by living in the shadows, scared that someone might actually know the truth about her, that things weren't perfect in Melissa-land.

'Listen, I've got something to say. It's my Mam...' Here we go, she thought, warts and all, here I am. 'Well, she's not like other mothers...'

Eilis and Steph exchanged glances. They knew what she was going to say.

'My mother... Mam, is an... an alcoholic. And it's the hardest thing in the world. It's had the most awful effect on me and I need to tell you so I can start to deal with it.'

Melissa looked at them, feeling vulnerable, exposed. She willed them to understand. She wished she hadn't said anything. She hated this feeling of being so alone. Steph was the first to put her arms out and hug her and then Eilis joined in.

'We know,' she said. 'We've known for years. You poor thing... you poor, poor thing. Why don't you start at the beginning?'

And Melissa did and told them everything.

15

STEPH

At home, the next day, Steph felt all the feelings, disappointment, rage, sadness, begin to spark again, but instead, Stepford Wife-style, she popped in the dishwasher tablet and turned it on. She even practised her fake smile when she was on her own but it was beginning to hurt her cheeks and her eyes, she had noticed, had a crazed hollow look. She looked not quite real, like a waxwork. Exhibit A: unhappy wife.

Poor Melissa! She had been so brave to say what she had. She couldn't stop thinking about her. At least, they could now talk about it. That would help, surely?

She wondered if she too would ever be able to express how lonely she was, how certain she was that her husband was a bully and an adulterer and how fearful that she may have lost Rachel. She didn't think she could ever say it out loud. If people knew the truth, it would make her failure official. Eilis was on her way round for a cup of tea, they were neighbours after all and Melissa lived in town, and she had to look normal and definitely not unhappy.

When Steph and Rick moved into the house on Kish Road, Rachel was only three. The cracks in their marriage were already crevasses but they had a young child and Steph didn't dwell on them. The problem, she thought now, was that there hadn't been proper love, real love there in the first place. And they would never have got married if she wasn't pregnant.

The family next door seemed just like them. There was Miriam and

Hugh and their three-year-old daughter Aoife, and a few years later, little Sorcha arrived. It suited everyone when the families began spending weekends together, and even holidays. There were dinner parties, joint children's parties with huge bobbing bouncy castles and bottles of fizzy orange. It took the bare look off an unsuccessful marriage. But now, of course, there was the not inconsiderable and rather inconsiderate matter that Rick was sleeping with Miriam. And Angeline. And... there were most likely to be more. There had to be. And then there was the bullying, the anger, the ignoring, the total disinterest in her life. It ground you down all of that, until you begun to lose sight of who you really were.

There was a ring of the doorbell.

'Eilis! Come on in. Kettle's on.' They hugged hello. 'It's so nice to see a friendly face,' Steph said. 'Come in...' she led the way to the kitchen.

Steph noticed Eilis looking around, the old dresser she found at an auction, an armchair with a flattened cushion on it and a rug. A book titled Finding Your Spark was spread open on the arm.

'The house looks nice,' Eilis said. 'You know, cosy.'

'Does it?' Steph laughed. 'It's messy, though. I never seem to win against the clutter. I'd love a minimal space, a blank canvas.'

'Well, that's what I've got. Rob's choice. Everything is hard and poky. I was thinking of buying a chair, just for me, something soft, but no one is allowed to sit in it but me. Like yours.' Steph wondered if all was well with Eilis. Didn't she have a choice about the furnishings?

'Well,' she said. 'Rick's got his study, Rachel's got her bedroom and I've got the kitchen. Well, one chair.'

'Everyone needs a chair.'

'A chair of one's own. You can do lots of things in a chair. Reading, thinking...'

'Exactly. So will you come round and see our uncosy cottage? It's Rob's vision, everything Danish and designer. Even his egg cup. I've got my garden, though. My oasis.'

'These things are important... egg cups and... and tea towels.' They laughed.

'Our kettle has –' Eilis dropped to a stage-whisper '– a remote control.'

'Wow.' Steph was feeling so much better that she had a friend in her house, it gave her a greater feeling of possession, of ownership, having Eilis around and hearing about her life. She put down a pot of tea and two large mugs. 'Now that's serious. Why on earth would you want that?'

'And I'm always losing it. There's always a frantic search for it before I can even have a cup of tea!' They laughed.

'You should buy your own, to be beside Rob's. And while he's still trying to find the remote, you could be sipping your tea. He'll soon realise that normal kettles are fine. Rick has pretty firm ideas of things too,' Steph said. 'He actually chose this kitchen. Though God knows why as he's never here. But he wanted the double burner and the ice-maker. And the wine fridge, too.'

'That's considerate,' said Eilis. 'A nice full wine fridge.'

'I would prefer it,' said Steph, 'if we had a chocolate fridge. You know, to make sure chocolate was kept at the perfect temperature.'

'There's a business idea in there somewhere,' said Eilis.

'Somewhere!'

Steph would have loved to talk about Rick, what was really going on. Not just skimming the surface. She realised that this hinting that all was not well was desperate, hoping someone might see the truth and know the pain she was in. She was so lonely, she longed to open up to someone. She was just about to say something, to admit all was not going well when they heard Rachel from upstairs.

'Mum! Muuuuu-um!'

'Yes darling?' She dashed out of the kitchen to attend the emergency. An angry face at the top of the stairs: Rachel, furious, incandescent.

'Have you been *tidying* my room again?'

'Just straightened up a few things, picked up your clothes, collected some mugs, that sort of thing. I found mould – *mould* – inside those mugs.' Steph tried to sound confident, but inside, her chest was constricted. A permanent fixture. She couldn't remember the last time she breathed freely. She had even given up her weekly yoga class as she would lie there supine with nothing to do in the quiet except think about how unhappy she was. It became embarrassing, pretending she wasn't crying.

'They are my mugs. Okay?'

'Technically, they belong to the family,' said Steph, immediately wishing she hadn't. Teenage wrath was, she was learning, best avoided. Brilliant, she thought, your parenting is brilliant.

Rachel death-stared at her. 'Just leave everything. It's my room. Okay?

And *now* I can't find anything and NOW I'm going to be late. And IT'S YOUR FAULT.'

Should Steph shout back? No, she wasn't much good at shouting. Try and argue and reason her point? Maybe she shouldn't have tidied up. It was interfering, but then again things had to be cleaned. She just didn't know. She glanced at Eilis who was pretending not to hear anything, just gazing out of the window.

'I'm just trying to get everything ready for the weekend. Getting your stuff together? You're staying with Granny and Granddad. While we're in Rome. Okay? And Rachel?'

'What?'

'Do you want to meet Eilis... you haven't seen her since you were tiny.'

There was no answer.

Steph went back into the kitchen, smiling in an embarrassed way at Eilis. 'Teenagers!'

And then there was a sound of feet on the stairs and then into the room came Rachel.

'Oh darling, there you are.' Steph was beaming now, genuine delight and pride. 'This is Eilis... you have heard me talk about her so many times. She lives in Dalkey now. Again. She grew up in the village. I was up on the hill.'

Rachel shook hands. 'Pleased to meet you,' she said.

'So you're in Fifth Year now,' said Eilis.

'Yeah...'

'And how's it going?'

'Fine, lots of work. But you know...' Rachel smiled at Eilis and Steph saw that the sweet girl was still there, just well hidden.

'What's for dinner?' Rachel said, turning to her mother.

'Pasta!' Steph made it sound like it was something new and exciting.

Rachel groaned. 'Not again. We're not Italians!'

'I know that,' said Steph, rolling her eyes at Eilis, who was smiling at the two of them. 'I thought you liked it.' She turned to Eilis. 'Who doesn't like pasta?'

'Me,' said Rachel. 'It's fine. Don't worry about me. I'll have toast or something later.' And she headed out of the kitchen.

'Nice to meet you, Rachel,' called Eilis.

'You too,' said Rachel.

'It's just that...' Steph began. Too late. Rachel had disappeared upstairs and slammed the door and Steph was left standing there uselessly. For a brief beautiful moment, she remembered the little girl who used to hold her hand and would leave love notes on her pillow. It was so clear, so real and then like a bubble it began to float away.

'So!' said Steph, when it was just the two of them again. 'Family life!'

'Yeah, it's all go, isn't it?'

'And we've got Rome this weekend,' said Steph, smiling that false smile. 'So that's going to be fun.'

'Yes,' Eilis said. 'I forgot about that. Remember you spent that summer in Rome, didn't you? And I was so jealous because I had to work in that hospital in Cork. I was almost dead by the end, but you came back glowing with life and calling everyone 'bella' and saying 'ciao' all the time!'

Steph laughed. 'I can only apologise for my pretentious insensitivity. Oh, but we had such a ball. It was myself and Pippa and Eileen. No money, surviving on pizza.'

'But I thought you weren't Italian?' They laughed again.

'I keep trying to be, don't I?' said Steph. 'When will I ever learn?'

They chatted for ages about the old days, about the new days, about Eilis' job, about Steph's mam and dad and then, finally, Eilis stood up to go. 'I'll leave you to it. Making that pasta.'

'Maybe I'll try to be Spanish. Paella or something.'

'But you like Italy, don't you?'

'Always have done.'

'So carry on being Italian. Don't change. And come and see me in Uncosy Cottage next time. Text me when you are back from Rome. Please?' She hugged her goodbye. 'Take care, won't you. Enjoy Rome.'

'I will!' said Steph smiling. 'Thanks for coming round.'

'Look after yourself, won't you,' Eilis said again.

'Don't worry about me. Ciao!' They laughed again, but when she finally closed the door on Eilis, Steph thought she was going to cry.

Music was coming from Rachel's room. Once it was very clear she and Rick were not going to be happy together, Rachel had been Steph's only chance – for love... joy... purpose. And so it was into Rachel that she poured all the tiny tendernesses of a mother's passion; the singing and giggling together, the incessant chatting about nothing, the playing. She moved her hand, trying to remember what Rachel's little fingers felt. There was nothing there. Now, she was mother to a sixteen-year-old who had perfected the art of the scowl and the door slam and seemed so *angry* at her. Steph had no idea how to get it all back.

I want to matter, she thought. I want to matter. *I want to mean something to someone.*

A whole life stretched ahead of her. How was she going to fill it all? There were years of it to go. And Rome to deal with.

And pasta to boil.

16

MELISSA

Jimbo was dunking his custard cream. He was Melissa's desk-mate at the *Standard*, in the features department.

He threw over the packet of biscuits. 'Lunch?'

'Normal people eat sandwiches,' she said, putting down her phone, which she had looked at for the millionth time. She hadn't heard from Cormac for days now, since the ice cream on the pier in Dun Laoghaire. What was going on? Had he tired of her too, like Alistair, like all the others? Not Cormac as well. No, he couldn't, because he was Cormac and Cormac didn't do things like that. You could rely on Cormac and that was the whole point of Cormac and her, wasn't it? It was something steady, something she could depend on. Take the passion out and you had the perfect relationship.

'Aye,' said Jimbo, 'but no one ever said I was normal.'

'Nor am I,' she said, taking one. 'Thank you! I didn't know they still made these.'

'You know, Melissa...'

'What's that, Jimbo? You're looking serious. Should I be scared?'

'Aye, you should. Because I don't say this very often...'

'What?'

'And I shouldn't say it. As a member of the League of Men, a not-always-proud member of that ancient and august club... I shouldn't say what I'm about to say...'

'What? Spit it out?'

'That some men are wankers.' He looked at her.

Melissa laughed. 'Are you including yourself in that?'

'Maybe.' He shrugged. 'It's just that they are. Wankers. Some of them.'

'I knew that, but thanks anyway.' God, was she so transparent that Jimbo knew what was going on? That she had been dumped again and had fallen in love with her best friend, despite years and years of protesting she felt nothing, she now realised that she felt something very deep indeed. But was it rebound, that's what she was trying to wrestle with. Feeling vulnerable? Fall in love with your male best friend!

Or had she been fooling herself all these years that the one thing, the best thing, was right under her very nose. She felt scared. This was not what she planned, they were meant to be happy as friends for ever and ever. Not this.

'I'll take it on board,' she said, smiling smoothly. 'Thanks Jimbo.'

'You're welcome. I like being earth-shattering.'

'You should give a Ted Talk. It'd go viral.'

'I should, aye.' He dipped his biscuit and sucked noisily on it while looking pensively, perhaps dreaming of auditoria, ovations, fame. Maybe a self-help book? 'Avoiding wankers and other horrors. That's the title.'

'Perfect.'

They heard a raised voice and rolled their eyes at each other.

'Talking of which...' said Jimbo.

Liam Connelly was shouting, something he enjoyed immensely. As features editor of the Irish Standard, he was never silent for long and relished the sound of his own voice, liberally articulating freely and loudly his thoughts, feelings, itches and twitches. He loved a good shout and his voice carried easily from the partition walls of his corner office, echoing down the corridors of the Standard.

At his first staff meeting, six months ago, he announced that there were going to be changes. Unpopular ones, he added darkly and ominously. Lost readers would have to be unscattered, scooped up, won back, and he had set to the task with vim, verve and vigour, which mainly consisted, as far as Melissa could see, of meting out a series of bollockings.

She noticed Jimbo was looking at her.

'Yes?' she said.

'Weren't you off to Paris?' he said. 'You never divulged the gory details.'

'That? That was ages ago now.' Don't remind me, she thought. She hadn't heard from Alistair since that humiliating day he dumped her. It wasn't Alistair's fault, though. It was hers. She had been too needy and who would want that? She thought instead of Cormac, wondering what he was doing. He was being distant again. She glanced at her phone to see if he had texted.

'And was it, is it... um...' he searched for the right word. 'Fun?'

'Paris?'

'Aye. Paris. City of romance, the beret, the boulevard and the baguette. Fancy-pants central. Am I right?' He drank some of his tea.

'You've obviously never been.' She looked at him curiously. 'You're not thinking of going, are you?'

'Never,' he said, shaking his head. 'Sounds too insipid for me, too flowery. I don't think my stomach could take it. All that smoochy stuff.' He took another biscuit. 'Give me Berlin. Or Madrid. Stockholm. Proper cities, so they are. Not soppy, with moony honeymooners and torrents of tourists, too afraid to lose the rest of the group just in case they accidentally have an adventure.'

Melissa realised that this was his way of trying to be nice to her, making conversation, he'd obviously noticed she wasn't herself. Before Paris she had been quite giddy, almost excited and now she was quieter. But he had picked up on something, that much was obvious. Was she that transparent? Did she wear her feelings on her shirt like a badge for everyone to see? She and Jimbo didn't do much sharing of their lives away from the office and normally spent their time when not typing away, engaged in mindless banter. It certainly helped the time pass. And now she felt as though they were moving from banter to something else. She quickly brought the conversation back to the light and the frivolous.

'I can just imagine you in Paris,' she said. 'Reading Sartre in a cafe... trying to order an Ulster Fry in a Belfast accent.'

'A croissant just isn't breakfast.' He dunked his biscuit into his tea.

'And nor is a custard cream,' she said. 'You've got to stop substituting biscuits for meals.'

He shrugged. 'You'd be surprised. So... good was it?'

'Paris? Of course. It's *Paris*. It's never not amazing!' She beamed at him convincingly. 'It's bad manners not to drink red wine in copious quantities in Paris, apparently,' she said. 'So, not to cause a diplomatic incident, I imbibed a great deal. I told you, you would like it.'

Jimbo's eyebrows rose approvingly. 'Aye. That sounds right up my *rue*.'

'Jimbo!' It was Liam, shouting across the office.

'I am to be today's bollockee, it would seem,' he said.

'Good luck!' said Melissa, giving him a thumbs up.

He returned twenty minutes later.

'Cock. He's a cock,' he said, returning. 'A tool of the highest order, so he is.'

Melissa laughed. 'What was the problem?'

'My story...' Jimbo sat himself down and pulled his chair up to hers. 'You know the interview with Mary Oliver – the one whose husband...'

Melissa nodded. 'The vest and pants man.' She was referring to a politician who was once caught in just his underwear, dazed and confused, in the rose garden of a posh golfing hotel.

'Exactly. Anyway, well, she's gone to the Express. She rang me last night – all upset – but she said that they turned up on her doorstep and she did the story – she didn't realise the fucking meaning of the word "exclusive". So she told the Express about dubious pleasures of life with Mr Undies and how she is now happier and in her prime et cetera-et cetera-blah-blah-blah-cliché-cliché.'

He leaned back on his chair and took the last custard cream. 'So, the story's gone – through no fault of mine by the fucking way – but Mr Cock-man over there thinks it is.' He jerked his head in the direction of Liam's office.

Melissa tried deflection. 'Just forget it...'

'I don't know why I bother. All this saving-the-world, Pulitzer-winning journalism is exhausting.' Jimbo was warming to his theme of career anni-hilation. 'I'm done. I'm going to give Liam what he wants. Banality.'

Melissa was used to Jimbo's rants. They were often at his own expense and her job was to soothe and bolster when needed but her phone beeped and she dived for it. Cormac! At last! 'Sorry Jimbo... been waiting for this,' she said, as though it was an important work missive.

Cinema?

· · ·

They always went to see a film every week but they hadn't for at least a month.

The new Bond was out. 'Yesh pleash,' she texted back.

Text back: 'Sean Connery is long gone.'

There's a new Bond? When did all this happen?

While you were shagging that idiot in Paris. Probably.

Devashtated.

Life and its general crapness was put in its place by Cormac. Nothing seemed too bad when he was around. He even got her jokes. Weak, admittedly, though they were.

STEPH

She looked out of the tiny window of the aeroplane which was circling over Ciampino. I shouldn't have come, she thought. A Rome *rugby* weekend. It was some kind of evil oxymoron. They'd caught the six a.m. flight from Dublin and the whole plane was quiet, everyone trying to work out what madness had caused them to book a flight which meant they had to be at the airport at 4.30 a.m.

But Steph was thinking of Rachel. The previous evening, she had brought her up to stay with her parents and she'd watched how different Rachel was with them, just the way she used to be with Steph.

Nuala scootched up on the sofa for Rachel to sit down. Most unusually, Nuala was wearing a pair of tracksuit bottoms, far from her usual attire. 'I'm far more comfortable like this, Stephanie,' she explained. 'I should have bought a pair of these years ago.' Her mother looked tired, but Nuala brushed aside all concern. 'Just been overdoing the walking, haven't I Joe?' she said. 'Now, Rachel, love, are you all set? Have you got all your bits and pieces?'

Joe had got a classic comedy, Tootsie, out from the library and had bought popping corn for the occasion. 'It's either Tootsie,' said Joe. 'Or...' he peered at the box set. 'Or Borgen. It's meant to be very good. It's Norwegian, I think. What do you think, Rachel? I met Paul Stafford in the library and he said it was "must-see TV", which sounds like a recommendation. And, after all, we are now Europeans.'

'Grandad, we have been for some time...' said Rachel, smiling at him.

'And, I never miss the Eurovision,' he said.

'But that's because,' said Rachel laughing, 'you are always convinced Ireland will win.'

'And why wouldn't we? Haven't we won it loads of times before? I have no idea why we are still not winning. They should just ask Johnny Logan to enter. We'd walk it.'

'By the way,' said Rachel, pretending to lecture him, 'Borgen is Danish.'

'Isn't that what I said? Lovely bacon too. So are we on? Tootsie or Borgen?'

'I don't know,' said Rachel, turning to Steph. 'What do you think, Mum?'

What was this? Was she actually asking Steph her opinion? Surely some mistake.

'Well,' she said, giving the matter some serious thought. 'Tootsie *is* very funny... you do have the whole weekend – two nights.'

'Okay...' Rachel was actually thinking about what Steph had said. This was nothing short of a miracle. 'What about Borgen now... and then Tootsie later to recover?

'Well,' said Nuala. 'I'm on... as long as you explain things to me when it gets complicated. Is that a deal, Rachel?'

Rachel put up her hand for a high five which Nuala met like a professional. Steph watched as her daughter pulled some of Nuala's rug around her. The two of them looked happy, snuggled together, she wished she was under that rug with them.

'It's like Downton Abbey in this house,' Joe said, pushing the footstool under both Rachel and Nuala's legs. 'Are Madams ready for their popcorn and chocolates?'

'Oh, I think so, what do you think, Rachel?' said Nuala.

'Yes, Granddad, we're ready!' Nuala and Rachel giggled together and for a moment Steph lingered, not wanting to leave. She really wanted to say that she would miss them but it seemed unnecessarily dramatic.

'Take care, please?' She hugged her mother. 'Don't get up.' Nuala did look very tired and drawn. 'See you Sunday afternoon?'

'*You* take care. And don't be taking any nonsense from anyone.' Steph knew exactly what she meant. Nuala had long guessed that all was not right with Steph and Rick.

Rachel didn't stand up to hug Steph, so Steph leaned over and kissed her on the cheek.

'Bye sweetheart, I love you,' said Steph.

'Bye Mum,' she said. Teenagers don't say that they love their mums, so don't expect it, Steph told herself. The most important thing is that Rachel is happy. She looked back to see Rachel offering Nuala a Minstrel.

And now she was in Rome, sitting beside her husband, and an arm-length from the woman he was sleeping with, but her heart was back in Dublin. They were taxi-ing to the terminal. She looked out of the small round window of the plane. Steph had no idea why she was there, what made her so weak that she clung pathetically, to this fake life, her fake husband, her fake marriage. We are all lying to ourselves, Steph thought, that it is okay to have a disappointing life as long as no one knows about it. And Steph was the biggest phoney of all. From the outside, her life seemed lovely but in reality she was being humiliated, laughed at by her husband and her friend. What was worse, Steph was letting them do it. And here she was in Rome, sucking it up.

When you are young, thought Steph, it's so easy to change your life. You can suddenly move flat, meet a new group of friends, you can decide on a radical lifestyle change and become a vegan or be a Goth for a few weeks. You make choices and decisions all the time, you can change your mind as quickly as you made it up. It's all so easy. Things go wrong and you just do something else but with age, it's not so easy to change direction. You get stuck. Which was how Steph felt right now.

'Coming?'

It was Rick, standing up, waiting for her. He didn't make eye contact, he never did. He tolerated her and she never had managed to lose the fluttering fear when she was around him.

'Coming.' Steph gathered her things. 'Sorry,' she said to him.

They began the aeroplane-exit shuffle. There were six of them together: Steph and Rick, Miriam and Hugh, and Theresa and Harry, Hugh's partner at work. They seemed nice, thought Steph. But when you meet someone for the first time at dawn, you don't ever get a clear impression.

Miriam looked over Hugh's shoulder and back at Steph. What actors we are, Steph thought, flashing an Oscar-winning smile. But there was something in the air. Danger. Why, she thought, exactly had Miriam arranged this trip? Was she playing some kind of game? What was going on?

And she had to act the dutiful, happy wife as well. It was the first time Steph and Rick had been together for a long time. They lived together, slept in the same bed, ate food at the same table, but it never failed to surprise Steph how impersonal the intimate could be. Living with someone and not speaking, seeing someone naked and never noticing.

And now, they were away together in Rome. She felt suddenly awfully awkward.

The noisy, bantering group took a taxi to their hotel and then the couples split up, each twosome making their way to their rooms. She and Rick busied themselves opening suitcases.

'Nice room,' tried Steph.

Rick nodded back. 'Yeah... nice room.'

'Pity about the weather.'

'Yeah... it'll be a wet match.'

'Muddy...'

'Muddy, right.'

That was more than she had got from him for years, so Rome was obviously working its very special magic.

'So... what is everyone doing?' Steph was not part of the organizing committee for this weekend. It was clear her role was tag-along, and it was all too obvious that Rick didn't want her along.

'The match is at five,' he said. 'It's lunchtime. They are all going for something to eat. That,' he paused, 'suit you?'

'Yeah, I suppose so.'

'Miriam knows Rome. She says there's a place by the Spanish Steps.'

'What's it called?'

'O'Donoghues.'

O'Donoghues?

'Is it a pub?'

'Yeah...'

'An *Irish* pub?'

'Well, it's a restaurant as well,' he said. 'Not just a pub. Anything wrong?' He was taunting her, willing her to show her pretentious side, her arty side, to remind her just how out of place she was on a rugby weekend.

'No... yes, we're in *Rome*?' She couldn't help it. This was the city she loved, a city of incredible art and culture and of history. And they were going to *an Irish pub*? Just give up, Steph, her inner voice counselled. Just go with it. You have made a massive mistake just being here. Just get through it. Survive.

'So?' he said, with a sneer. 'We're not here to see the Sistine Cathedral, you know? No sightseeing or paintings.' With one word, he dismissed who she was. 'We are here for a rugby match.'

'You're right... you're right.' Get through this. 'Sounds perfect.'

She looked out of the hotel window at the tiny street below, the yellow stone, the people hurrying about, and the sound of the church bells. It brought back the two months she'd spent in the city as an art history student when they stayed in a hostel so grotty Steph was sure they would get bed bugs. They didn't. Another wonderful miracle of that summer.

She and her friends, Pippa and Eileen, were totally penniless but filled with coltish excitement and swarmed the city soaking up the art, the atmosphere, the life. They starved all day and then at six o'clock would buy a slice of pizza, which they ate sitting on the fountain in Piazza Santa Maria Novella, watching the tourists, the street performers, the kids playing football. An everlasting summer in the eternal city. They did have one indulgence every day. After the pizza, they would wander over to the Campo de' Fiori and buy from Nico's, the best gelateria in the city.

She felt transformed when she returned to Ireland. But it all dissipated. And real-life, grown-up life kicked in and, the following autumn, she got the job in Mrs Long's gallery and later that year she met Rick.

Last thing she'd heard was that Pippa was in London and Eileen had disappeared with a musician somewhere. Last seen in Spiddal carrying a bodhrán. At his precise moment, she would love to disappear with a man with a bodhrán. And that's not something you wish for every day.

Steph watched Rick as he pulled something out of his suitcase and disappeared into the bathroom. He reappeared, hair lightly gelled, his broad shoulders jumpered and jacketed, his jaw set, full-on Alpha mode, as though she didn't already know who was boss.

O'Donoghues was absolutely fine. If you didn't try to remember you were in Rome. Harry and Theresa were very nice and Steph spent most of her time chatting to them, Rick with Hugh and Miriam. She often wondered about Hugh. He was a nice guy, as far as Steph could tell, wildly indulgent of his wife's flirtatiousness, but he seemed utterly in the dark by how far she'd taken it. He also seemed to like Rick, almost looking up to him. Rick was like the popular boy in school, Hugh wanting to be just like him. But what would he say if he knew the truth that his so-called friend was sleeping with his wife?

Steph thought of all that art out there, scattered around the city, but she quashed her inner art history student. Instead, she tried to focus on why exactly she was there. She was still trying to pretend to the world that she and Rick were a happily married couple doing married couple-y things. The pretence was exhausting.

Everyone began drinking heavily and, when it was time for the match, God only knows how they got to the stadium, all of them several sheets to the wind. Steph spent the match with one eye on the pitch and the other on Miriam, laughing away, the life and soul of the group. She'd even managed to make a green rugby jersey look sexy, having had it taken in at all the right places. The fact that Ireland won by sixty-two points just made everyone even more jubilant and want to hit the bar even harder. Steph tried to look as thrilled at the rest of them.

Back in the centre of Rome, they piled into a bar, full of green shirts, and Steph ordered a large glass of red wine. She could feel it going straight to her head. Rick was talking and laughing loudly – he looked happy. Far removed from the distant, chilly aggression he exhibited just for her, Hugh and Miriam laughing at his jokes. She felt tired, broken, self-esteem in tatters at her feet, her life a categorical failure. After the horror of the communion and now they were rubbing her face in it. It was as though being here in Rome was ramping up Miriam's excitement levels somewhat. She was flirting and laughing, lapping up Hugh and Rick's attention.

Steph was getting drunk and she knew it but she couldn't just *stand* there anymore and take it. 'Excuse me a moment,' she said sweetly to Theresa and Harry. She stood up and walked over to Rick, standing in front of him. The gang stopped and looked at her. 'Rick?'

He looked up, his eyes hooded. He raised an eyebrow. 'Yeah?' He was pretty far gone too.

'Rick, I want to go home.' Scene-making wasn't usually her thing but adrenaline and alcohol had taken over.

'Home?' He laughed. 'It's a bloody long way to go home. I don't think the night bus comes this far.' He looked at the group to receive a snicker of approval. There were a few awkward smiles but Miriam had her game face on, concerned. She knew where the line was. She was not going to laugh blatantly at Steph.

'No,' she said. 'No, the hotel.' You are still my husband, she thought. You still owe me this much.

'The hotel?' He actually laughed. 'Stephanie, *love*,' (this was a term of *en-sneerment*) 'we're on fucking holiday – we are in Italy. Weekend away.' She could see his nostril hairs and the sweat glistening on his forehead. 'We are – *sweetheart* – having a good time. You should try it sometime.'

No one was laughing now. Everyone could feel the tension, the anger between them.

'I don't feel well.' Steph could feel her knees give way slightly as she tried to brazen it out, the wind in her sails having dropped dramatically. She was in the doldrums, and didn't know what her next move would be. She wished she hadn't said anything, she wanted fresh air and to be anywhere but here.

'Well, I feel fucking fantastic,' he said. 'And if you want to go back to the hotel, I will see you later. Much later. Right?'

'Please?' Oh my God, she was begging him. Stop it, Steph, stop it, she implored herself. You are making a holy show of yourself... She didn't listen. 'Rick. Come with me. Please?'

'Steph,' he smiled an unfriendly smile. 'Either get yourself another drink or go back to the hotel. I'm staying here.'

He shook his head at the gang, almost rolling his eyes. They smiled slightly awkwardly at him. No one knew quite what to do. She saw Theresa smiling at her, trying to encourage her to come and sit with them again, but she'd had enough. Harry patted the seat between them.

For a moment, she stood there, wondering what to do, what her next move should be. The room was spinning and the noise of the shouting and roaring became unbearable.

But Steph was defeated and there was no way back. It took me *this* long to realise it, she thought, but I lost this battle years ago. Why didn't I move on and move out long ago? And now I'm stuck. This is what my life looks like. It stretched into the future, unchangingly, unhappily forever.

She stood there, unsteadily, but Rick took charge. 'I think, *sweetheart,* it might be a good idea for you to go back to the hotel.' He smiled at her.

'Okay,' she said. 'I will.'

She got her bag and coat, nodded at Harry and Theresa and glanced at Miriam who had a look of fake-concern on her face.

'See you later,' she mouthed. Steph ignored her.

And that was it. There was nothing to do but walk out, leaving them all behind. It took her a while to get her bearings and she began to walk in the direction of the hotel. And then she heard someone calling her name.

Hugh.

'Are you all right?' he said.

'Yes, yes of course,' she said. 'Just too much to drink.'

'You're not the only one,' he said. 'We've all had too much to drink. Come on, I'll walk you back.'

When they got to the hotel, they stood there. She wondered if Hugh knew about Miriam and Rick, but he didn't, she was sure of it. He was a nice guy. Why would Miriam and Rick do this to him? He didn't deserve this deception either. And what about Aoife, their daughter? Did no one think of collateral damage?

'Okay, then,' she said, 'thanks for getting me here safely.'

'It's no problem,' he said. 'But Rick should have done it, though. Walked you home.'

'Well,' she said, not knowing what to say. Of course her husband should be the one making sure she was safe, but for so many reasons, Rick wasn't her husband, not in the true sense, not in any important way. 'Thanks again.'

'You look after yourself, okay?' he said.

'I will.'

And Hugh stood there until she had woken up the concierge and was safely inside the hotel.

The next morning, she woke early. Rick asleep beside her. At least he isn't with Miriam, she thought, grateful for the smallest and most minuscule of mercies, horribly aware it should never be something any wife should be thankful for. Stumbling to the bathroom, she looked at the woman in the mirror, make-up was smeared across her face like a clown gone bad.

What to do, how to recover? Was it even possible? Was this her life now, the shamed woman, the outcast? Should she make a badge? 'Don't talk to me. I am mad. I've been a fool and I've lost control and I have no idea how to get it back.' It would have to be quite a big badge, then.

She showered and dressed and left Rick's sleeping corpse on the bed. He wouldn't know or care where she had gone, he'd just be sleeping off his hangover until it was time to go to the airport but she knew exactly where she was headed. To a little cafe on the Piazza della Rotonda facing the Pantheon. She and her friends from all those years ago would gather there first thing, for strong espressos into which they would sink sugar lumps, turning it into something they could just about drink. And it hadn't changed. Everything seemed the same, she could have been twenty all over again.

Except... except everything was different, with her at least.

A couple were sitting there under the awning, laughing and spooning the froth from their coffee into each other's mouths. Honeymooners. Steph warmed her hands around her cappuccino and ignored them.

She texted Rachel.

Ciao Bella! Hope all is well and the three of you are having a lovely time.

She stopped. And thought of Rachel and how she was the only person who really mattered in all this, and how strong her feelings were for her, a mother's love. The most powerful bond of all.

I miss you. I love you xxxx.

She sent it off.

She left the cafe and the lovebirds behind and went across to the Pantheon before doing some quick souvenir shopping for Rachel and whoever else would like a present from Rome. There was a service going on. She sat down on the edge of a pew, listening to the Latin Mass, hoping for a sign from God? An answer? Absolution? Forgiveness?

Finally, she began to cry. Great tears rolled down her face. For what? Self-pity? Shame? Because her life – once so promising, so much fun – hadn't turned out the way she believed, was so sure, it would. Because she was scared.

She crept out of the pew, desperately trying not to show her face. The rain was pouring down through the giant oculus, the perfect circular hole in the roof. She watched as it splashed onto the marble floor and drained away. She looked up to the sky. She had fucked her life up royally.

She turned to go, tears blinding her, and as she walked towards the vast doors, she slipped – in a totally un-metaphorical way. It was a puddle which caused her downfall and she landed spread-eagled, inelegantly.

There was no more devout pilgrim that day, lying prostrate before God, but perhaps more in humiliation than true devotion.

She didn't even properly thank the elderly woman who helped her up, instead, she was just desperate to get out of there, to forget the whole sorry weekend. Determined that it wouldn't sully her previous memory of the city. Don't let this define you, something inside her insisted. This doesn't have to be your story. This is not the end. But she didn't believe herself.

And she'd thought being caught for shoplifting was rock bottom. Surely this is it, surely life can't get any lower?

18

EILIS

Back in Dublin, Eilis was thinking about Steph and how she was getting on in Rome. She hadn't been looking forward to it, she could tell, however much she'd said she was. She had looked apprehensive, bordering on scared. Eilis hoped everything had gone well.

On the surface, she thought, Steph seemed to have it all. But all things, all possessions, were meaningless, unless you had love. And it was very clear that Steph lacked love and was pining for it. She was reduced to one small armchair in her large house, it was as though she had no power and was merely incidental rather than the central force of the family, the home.

I wouldn't mind some love as well, she thought, someone to put their arms around me and tell me they love me. That person should have been Rob. But she didn't want his arms around her, or at least when she imagined it, it wasn't *him* embracing her. It was Charlie. He was infiltrating her thoughts and she would just think about his face, happy and smiling, his checked shirts, which were well-worn and well-loved, and those gardening hands. She had managed to avoid driving past the shop or bumping into him. She was determined that she was going to stop behaving like a hormonal teen and focus on her and Rob. But for this night, anyway, she was on her own as Rob had texted to say he was staying in town again for the night. She took full advantage and ate toast and jam in bed, watching something or other on television.

He returned home the following morning, at around ten a.m., just as she was in the garden, planting her sweet peas.

'Good night?' She stood up, unsure quite what else to say. There was something different about him, or it was as if the atmosphere was charged in a new way. What was wrong?

'It was all right, yeah, fine.' He seemed unable to meet her eyes or act normally, but maybe she was imagining it. I am paranoid, she thought. 'So, what happened?'

'Are you going to give me an inquisition?' he snapped. 'I thought we didn't do that? I thought we weren't that kind of couple?'

'We're not, whatever *that* kind of couple is. I'm just asking if you had a good night.' She was looking at him but he still wouldn't meet her eye. Was he alright? What was going on? She had the feeling something had changed, something in their relationship had shifted but she couldn't quite work out what it was.

'I'm going in... you're...' He stopped. 'Just don't be one of those women.'

'What?' She was caught off-guard. He never spoke to her like this.

'You know...'

'I don't know. What do you mean by that?' She looked him, bewildered. This wasn't him.

'A nag.'

'A nag?' She was flummoxed. What was wrong with him? He never spoke to her like this.

'There was a tone to your voice.' He turned to go.

'A tone?'

'An accusatory tone. A *nagging* tone.'

'I was just asking...' she tried to change the atmosphere, but she knew she sounded desperate. 'Anyway, it doesn't matter. Do you want a cup of tea or something?'

'No, I think I'm going to have a sleep.' He began walking to the house.

Eilis knelt down and began digging again but stopped to wipe away her tears. But by lunchtime, normal Rob was back. He reappeared, showered, shaved, in clean shorts and T-shirt.

'Sorry about earlier,' he said, kissing her on the top of her head. 'Just hung-over, you know...'

'That's okay...' she smiled at him, relieved, trying to make the aberration a distant memory and move on to a better and more loving future, the way it was meant to be.

'You look good,' she said, noticing his T-shirt, slim cut, showing off the body he had developed since his fitness regime kicked off last year. He was a good-looking man, with a great body. Yet she couldn't help thinking of Charlie. She felt a heat around Charlie that she had never felt with Rob, or for him. That was the difference. 'You know, your muscles. That trainer is obviously good.' She laughed, slightly awkwardly.

'Thanks.' He looked pleased. 'Not too built up?'

'You look good...' She didn't really know what to say so she changed the subject. 'Would you like a Greek salad? I bought feta in the market, and some olives. Get us in the mood for the holiday?'

'Sounds good to me.' He put his hands around her waist. He hadn't done this spontaneous display of affection for months... years even. They were an old unmarried couple, weren't they? They were normal. 'You smell nice...' he nuzzled into her neck. But it felt forced and unnatural.

'Just my new shower gel... coconut, I think.'

But he stepped back, suddenly, as though recoiling. What was wrong? An undiagnosed nut allergy? Nuzzling aborted. 'Everything okay?' she asked, suddenly worried and embarrassed. 'Anything wrong?'

'Fine, fine,' he said, smoothly, making her feel as though she had imagined his repulsion. 'Greek salad sounds perfect.' He began laying the table. 'Have we got any oregano?' He looked his usual self; unruffled, in control.

'I'll go and pick some.' Eilis left the room and headed into the garden to her herb patch, glad for the fresh air. What the fuck was happening? Was she so repulsive? Why wasn't he interested in her physically? She wasn't unattractive, she knew that, she made an effort, she wasn't hideous and Rob liked her, she knew that, he just didn't want to sleep with her. Beside her, yes. With her, no. It was starting to make her feel that it was her fault, that it was something wrong with her. She couldn't work it out and she couldn't talk to him about it because in the past, every time she had tried to broach the physical side of their relationship, he had swept her concerns aside, reassured her she was beautiful and claimed tiredness, stress or getting old. He was thirty-eight for God's sake. Look at Julio Iglesias. He was still going.

What about Charlie. Was she repulsive to him – and all other men? But what was the point of wondering about Charlie, it was utterly impractical to think about him. She had to focus on her relationship with Rob, work on it... make it better. Charlie wasn't going to help matters.

But he might. He might help, her inner voice urged. He might, but you'll probably never know.

* * *

Steph had returned from Rome, armed with a cushion for Eilis. It was soft and squishy and made from the softest wool. Eilis lifted off the tissue paper to reveal it. She held it to her face, rubbing it to her cheek, in her kitchen when Steph had called round for a cup of tea. 'Heaven,' she said. 'Like a cloud.' She hugged Steph. 'Exactly what I wanted.'

'I saw it and thought of you. Italian goat's wool, apparently. I bought one for Melissa too, although she already has too many cushions. But you can never have enough, I suppose.'

'Or, as Rob would say, one is too many. Where am I to hide it? Rob destroys anything comfortable.' She meant it as a joke but she knew that Steph understood that there was more than an element of truth in what she was saying. You only had to look around Uncosy Cottage to see that cushions were verboten.

'Could you keep it in a cupboard and only take it out when he's not around?'

'I'll have to. I'll push a wardrobe against the door of a secret room which is full of all my blankets and rugs and cushions. And a really nice armchair and posters of Morten Haarket.'

'Sounds like my kind of room.'

They laughed. 'Sit down... I was going to say make yourself comfortable, but I realise that is impossible.'

Steph looked around. 'It's really nice,' said. 'Very cool. I like the plywood finish. You don't get that in ordinary kitchen shops.'

'Rob sourced in in Stockholm,' said Eilis. 'It's grown on me, I have to say. But I would like a dresser like you, Steph, one I could put jugs and plates on...'

'And all the household letters and junk.'

'Exactly,' laughed Eilis, loving the idea of the fact that it was the little bits of clutter which made a home a home.

She made tea – managing to find the remote control on top of the fridge – put some biscuits on a tray and the two sat at the kitchen table, Eilis on her new cushion.

'I am comfortable,' she said, 'I am liking this strange feeling very much.'

'Where's Rob?' asked Steph. 'Working?'

'Out, I think,' said Eilis, who was thinking about how little she saw of Rob these days. They hadn't spoken about what happened when they tried to touch and she hadn't known what to say. Everything seemed fine on the surface but inside she had so many questions for him, about them, and either he wasn't around for her to ask or she just felt too awkward to ask him outright about why he didn't want to be intimate with her. 'Out with friends. He didn't really say where. He's become quite sociable in his middle-age. I'm the opposite. I'm just going to have a quiet evening.' She spoke brightly enough, as if his going out and being out was utterly fine with her. Which it was... usually... if he wasn't so distant. She couldn't put her finger on it, but there was a feeling that it was all going to come to a head soon.

'Me too,' said Steph. 'I like Saturdays in on my own, I've decided. It's like the whole world is out having fun and I'm doing something secret.'

'Staying in?' said Eilis. She noticed that Steph looked tired after the weekend, she could see it around her eyes and she looked as though she wasn't quite present, as though her mind was elsewhere.

'It's the new going out.'

'Well, let's hope no one else will discover it or then we'll have to go out.'

'The new staying in?' said Steph.

They laughed.

'And...' Eilis wondered how to broach the subject. 'How was Rome?'

'Lovely, I'll tell you all about it another time.' Steph gave a tight smile as if she didn't want to talk about it. 'So,' she said, changing the subject, 'Rob's a party animal?'

'Well, I don't know if I would put it like that, but he seems to have a nice group of friends and he likes to see them. I don't keep him prisoner... he's free to do as he pleases. And he does,' she laughed. 'He does exactly as he pleases.'

'And is that all right with you?'

'Yes, of course!' Rob was the last thing on her mind, instead, she was thinking of Charlie, again... his amazing hands, his eyes and the light stubble on his face. She liked Rob being out, it gave her more time on her own to think about the things she wanted to think about. And she had started to think about Charlie a bit more and had even driven slowly past the shop, half-terrified she would be spotted, and half-excited she might see him. She knew she should just park and go in, like any sane and normal woman and she would, she would, as soon normality and sanity decided to return. 'Sorry, Steph, what was that?'

'I said I liked the picture of your mother. She looks beautiful.'

Eilis looked over to the tiny framed picture of Brigid. 'Yeah,' she said. 'Yes, she does.' And she immediately felt that tightening in her stomach, the loss, the pang, the ache. Brigid had been old when she had Eilis and young when she died. I wish you'd got it the other way round, Mam, thought Eilis. I wish we'd got more time together.

Brigid had left Galway as a young girl, leaving behind a family, the farm, and her friends. She cried all the way to Dublin, the neighbour she got the lift with pretending not to notice, and began her career on her knees, scrubbing steps of large and lovely red-brick houses.

She was quiet, reliable, good at her job and, as those qualities were noticed, and she rose – literally and figuratively – from the scullery to become a housekeeper for a Mrs Willoughby of Ailsbury Road. She stayed there long beyond her marriage to Dermot, himself a blow-in from Glenamaddy and the two moved to the cottage in Dalkey. Living there, Brigid used to say, was like being on holiday every day and, after taking the bus home from Mrs Willoughby's, Brigid would make tea for herself and Dermot and then they would take evening walks up to the quarry and over Killiney Hill, breathing in the sea air, clearing out their lungs after the city smog.

Finally, after the longest wait, she became pregnant and handed in her notice to Mrs Willoughby. She was forty-one, ancient by all accounts, and was rewarded with the birth of a little girl, called Eilis after Brigid's own mother.

Eilis has no memories of her dad, except a few hazy, disconnected images. One: a man giving her tea to drink out of a saucer. And two: when her mother led her by the hand up some steps to the hospital. She thought, or remembered it as going to heaven, and there was Jesus with some sweets which she took.

When Dermot never came home, it was just Brigid and Eilis, and once

Eilis was in school, Brigid went back to work. Not to Mrs Willoughby's but back to the raw red hands of scrubbing and cleaning, with no nice dress to wear but a pink house coat, where no one said hello to her and instead would walk past her, as though she was invisible.

At night, her knees would be calloused, her feet throbbing and she would rub Vaseline into her hands, but once everything was cleared away, the two of them would settle down to read their library books. Brigid would read aloud and then, as Eilis grew older, she would read to Brigid. It was a cast of thousands: Miss Marple, Lord Peter Wimsey, Dracula, Jane Eyre, Lucy Honeychurch, Cait and Baba all took up temporary residence. The only other sound in the house was the clock in the hall, ticking. It had been a wedding present from Mrs Willoughby, and every night, before they went to bed, Brigid would wind it. Sometimes, even now, Eilis can still hear its heavy, clear tick.

Brigid had motor neurone disease, whatever that was – a lingering death sentence was all they knew it to be. She was unable to work, and they lived on hand-outs, charity, benefits. Eilis suggested that she left school – she was fifteen at that point – and got a job. Her mother wouldn't hear of it.

'You're staying in school and you are going to university.' Brigid would say it every evening when she got home as Eilis got older, and so Eilis no longer spent the evenings reading aloud but studying, with Brigid barely breathing so as not to disturb her.

On Christmas Day of Eilis' Leaving Cert year, Eilis cooked a chicken and a few potatoes and opened a box of Quality Street. They sat there, smiling at each other and watching television, both pretending this was normal. Neither of them said very much because the truth was unspeakable; her mum wasn't getting better, she was getting worse. She was going to die.

By New Year's Eve, Brigid's decline was rapid. Steph and Melissa were heading to a house party and had begged her to come out with them. Instead, just after eleven, Eilis put her mother to bed, pillows around her, readied for another sleepless, pointless night.

'Eilis? You are...' Brigid began. She was breathing with difficulty.

'Mam, don't speak. Don't tire yourself.'

'Eilis. Listen to me, now. I am so glad, so glad for you. You have been the golden light in my life.'

'Mam...' Eilis didn't know what to say.

'Please, please hear me.' Her mother was desperate to breathe, she was wheezing and gasping for air. She struggled on. 'I did something... something right, somewhere, to have you, my lovely girl.'

Eilis began to cry. 'I love you, mum.'

'I'm sorry, Eilis, I'm sorry to leave you. I wish I could stay.' Bridget tried to swallow.

'Don't Mam...'

'And watch... and watch you grow up.'

'Me too...' Tears fell onto the bed. They were holding hands. 'I don't want you to go.' The futility of the situation, of their powerlessness over life and death was so stark. They had no choice. Her mother had no control over when she died. No one did. Eilis wanted to rage against it. She wanted to shout and to scream and to get someone to do something. But no one could.

'But you, you be happy. That's what I want. Happy. Not for anyone else, not for me, not anyone, but for you. Promise me?' Eilis remembered being surprised at the strength in her mother as she gripped her daughter's smooth hand. But it was to be the last time they held each other's hand, the last time they spoke. Eilis still thinks about it and wishes she knew and wonders would she have said anything different, anything more?

'I will. I promise,' she did say. 'Now, go to sleep. I love you.'

'I'll miss you.'

Eilis couldn't speak. That night, as distant fireworks banged in the night, her mother slipped away, with Eilis sitting on a chair by the bed. She does know what she would say if she had a second chance of saying goodbye to her mother and that is this: thank you for everything, you were enough for me. You gave me all your love and that was enough.

But after her mother's passing, it was just her in the house. The doctor was in and out, the funeral directors came, the neighbour's all rallied round but there was no one to bring a cup of tea in bed before school and the house was utterly silent. It took her ages to work out what was different and then she remembered she hadn't wound the clock in the hall. It had stopped, as though the world had stopped. And for Eilis it had.

After the funeral, and once everyone had gone home, she remembered her promise to her mum and breathed in, picked up her bag and went back to school. She was eighteen. God knows, how she had managed to get

on with her life, going to medical school, all that training, the competitive-
ness, the exhaustion, the exams... it was all going to be worth it, wasn't it
though?

She didn't have much to show for the world... except for me, thought
Eilis. Except for me.

'Yes,' she said to Steph. 'She was such a beautiful person.'

Later, after Steph had gone home, she went into her bedroom and took
out Brigid's old cardigan. 'Where did it all go wrong?' she wondered. She
had worked so hard, done everything right, hadn't asked for too much or
too little from Rob, and yet she was nearly 40 and was no closer to having
the kind of relationship she had always imagined she would have, something fulfilling and deep and wonderful. She and Rob were close but not
close enough. She was aware she was only living half a life but she wasn't
sure how or why. Her mother was so wise, she would have known what she
should do.

Eilis had arrived at university, traumatised. She had buried her mother,
sat her Leaving Cert, and moved into a flat in town, all in the space of six
months. She had not cried once.

She remembered looking around at all the other first-years in the
Walton lecture theatre; the shiny-haired, fresh-faced, expensively clothed
Gods-in-waiting. Not one of them looked like her. They were glossy and
confident.

She'd thought of Melissa and Steph, over in UCD, wishing she was
with them. They had begun the week before and were already full of
stories of parties and clubs and new friends.

And here she was facing into a six-year course. She didn't know where
she was going to find the energy for it all. She pulled the door open, ready
to flee. And then she saw a boy, sitting by the wall, his hair was bushy, his
jacket too big and too old for him. He glanced at her and he raised his
eyebrows. Just that. And it was enough for her to think, to know, she wasn't
alone. She turned around and walked up the steps and found a seat and
sat down. She watched this boy after that. He would sit by himself, all the
time. She didn't quite have the courage to speak to him.

His name was Robert – this was before he called himself Rob. He was
up from the country and entirely opposite to all the other lads who all
seemed to know each other from various schools. Over the years, she felt
protective of him in the way that he was determined to remake himself,

mould himself into something he wasn't quite. His ambition was impressive, and who was she to judge. His accent was moderated, family history subtly modified.

But when she first met him he was green around the ears, a farmer's son straight off the bus from Ennis. They spoke for the first time one evening when she was in the library, working. She was aware of someone standing beside her. She looked up.

'Eilis?'

'Yes.' It was the first time anyone from her class had bothered talking to her in the four weeks since term began.

'I'm Robert. Rob. Howya.' Already she could see his hair had been cut since day one and the blazer swapped for a cord jacket.

'I know.' She didn't know what else to say. His hands felt slightly clammy, but she liked the feel of him, strong. He had kind eyes, she remembered. They were the things that drew her to him.

'So... how're you getting on?' he said. 'How's the essay going?'

'Yes, I handed it in this morning. Have you done yours?'

'Just finished.' He put up both thumbs. 'It was a killer. So, what are you working on now? Don't you ever take a break?'

She shrugged. 'It's relentless. I just find that if I read ahead, I can just about understand what is going on. Otherwise, it would all be a bit much.'

It was the first time she had opened up to anyone about how hard it all was. No one knew quite how much work it had taken to get there. And it seemed that everyone else on the course found it so easy.

'It's tough, isn't it?' said Rob.

She nodded. 'I feel so stupid all the time... like I shouldn't be here. I wish I was at UCD. Doing arts.'

He raised his eyebrows. 'Arts? But, sure, that's not a course. It's a hobby.'

She laughed. 'My friends are doing it. They sound like they are having fun...'

'I rest my case,' he said, smiling.

'Did many come up from your school?'

'Not a soul,' he said. 'So I can't leave. Because,' he spoke slowly, 'my mother would kill me. The shame. She'd prefer me dead than a failed medical student.'

They laughed, knowing that it was a hair-breadth from exaggeration.

'Mine too.' It just came out, but Eilis was so desperate to show Rob that he wasn't alone that she momentarily forgot her mother was dead.

'They're all the same. Mothers.'

She nodded. 'But mine's... mine's...'

He waited, curious.

'Mine's dead.'

'Dead?' He almost laughed from surprise. 'When?'

'In May.'

'May just gone?' His mouth fell open.

She nodded and bit her lip.

'And I thought my exams were hard work.' He stared at her. Eilis wished she hadn't said anything. It always made people embarrassed, telling them.

'Well?' He changed the subject much to her relief. 'What about something to eat. Medical students need to eat. Keep our strength up.' He spoke in the voice of an old Irish Mammy and Eilis laughed. 'You on?'

'Okay.' It was the first time since she had started at college that someone had reached out to her. She grabbed on.

They found a tiny vegetarian restaurant on Suffolk Street that did beans and rice, along with a glass of unspeakable wine for the princely sum of three pounds.

'It's terrifying,' she confessed. 'Everything. The work, the lecturers, the others, the fact that I don't fit in. The fact I don't have nice, swishy hair, which seems like a prerequisite to being on this course – male or female.'

Rob laughed. 'And I haven't told anyone yet, but I have never played rugby in my life and I have no plans to take it up. I keep grunting in the manner of a rugby player. When they find out, I will,' he paused dramatically, 'be asked to leave.'

'The Mammy!'

'Scandalised!' He drained the last of his horrible wine.

'We just have to get through it...' She trailed off.

'Well,' he looked at her thoughtfully, 'maybe we could... help each other. We have six more years of this. Maybe we could be a support group of two? What do you think?'

'I'd like that.' She spoke carefully and quietly. She felt something inside her dislodge as the pain she had been carrying around her seemed to react to his lifeline. 'So... I'll be your friend and you'll be mine.'

He held out his hand. 'Deal?'

'Deal.' They shook on it.

'Another glass of this wojus wine?'

'Why not?'

They clinked and drank to themselves. 'To happiness... may it be ours.'

And that was then, when she thought that maybe Rob would help her through life. And that maybe she might help him. But here she was, nearly forty, and things hadn't gone quite to plan.

'What shall I do, Mam?' She brought the cardigan to her face, hoping there was a trace of her mother left. It just smelled of old cardigan. 'What shall I do?'

She sat there, on the bed, with the cardigan pressed to her face, tears dampening it. Eventually, she slipped it over her shoulders and buttoned it up and went back downstairs. She missed her mother so much. But it was crazy. Wasn't time meant to heal? Weren't you meant to feel okay about someone's death after a few years; sad but philosophical? Bearing up, keeping on keeping on? She wondered how she could move on but she seemed stuck.

19

THE GIRLS

The next task on the reunion-reunioners was to find addresses for the girls, now women, who were in their year at school. The school had given old records of parent's addresses but, after twenty years, no one thought it was going to be easy.

The friends met in a wine bar in town.

'Let's split the names up and we can start contacting them. Is that all right?' said Steph, seeming quite normal.

'I've got an idea,' said Melissa. She took out a pair of tiny nail scissors from her bag and started cutting the list into three. 'That's for you, Steph... and there's yours Eilis. And this is mine. Done. Let's contact them all when we can. Right, business part of the evening sorted. Let's relax and enjoy ourselves.'

Steph collared the waiter and ordered a glass of red wine. He asked her what type. 'Just red is fine,' she smiled. '*Large*, please.' She looked back at the other two who were watching her closely.

Eilis and Melissa glanced at each other. 'It's medicinal,' Steph explained. 'Heart and stuff. Red wine is good for you. You should know that, Eilis.' The waiter returned and placed a huge glass of wine in front of her. She had begun to rely on the medicinal qualities of wine too much she realised, knowing that she would have to knock the extra glasses on the head very soon. But just this one glass would sort her out, change the fluttery feeling inside her to something warmer, more soothing.

'No one needs that much medicine,' said Eilis. 'Unless you are a whale.'

'Everything all right, Steph?' said Melissa.

'Never better!' she announced smiling manically. She picked up the glass like a priest with a chalice and drank deeply. 'And now,' she said grasping it with both hands, 'even better than better.'

Finally, she put the empty glass down.

'Now I feel human,' she announced. 'And I don't need anymore. I'm fine now. Just took the edge off a few... things.' She drank some water. 'Melissa, how has your week been? Eilis, any news to report?'

The two of them had been sitting there silently watching her. They shook their heads.

'Have *you* anything to report, Steph?' asked Melissa, suspiciously. 'How was Rome?'

'Great... Rome was... you know, umm...' What to say? It was a nightmare and I am mortified beyond what a normal person could stand. And I have to leave my husband, but I am not sure how that will happen or if I can actually do it. She had kept out of Rick's way since returning from Rome and ducked back into the house whenever she had heard Miriam's front door opening. She was living the life of a fugitive. In her own house. It was crazy.

'It was... beautiful,' she said. 'Apart from the rain.'

The only light in the entire weekend was when she went to collect Rachel from her parent's house. Box sets had been watched and Rachel was now an expert in various card games and Nuala was teaching her granddaughter to knit and the two were surrounded by wool and patterns, Joe snoozing in the armchair. Nuala looked tired, though, paler than usual. She just needed a few walks on the Wicklow Hills thought Steph, get some colour in her cheeks. Would do us all good, she said to herself, wondering if she was too young to join the Wanderers.

'So... how was Rome?' asked Nuala, getting up with difficulty so that Rachel helped pull her up, and giving Joe a shake.

'Oh it was lovely... all the gang. Miriam and Hugh, of course. Buckets of wine. You know, the usual.' She beamed at them. The smile of the convicted. A woman facing the executioner's axe. A look passed between Nuala and Joe, fleeting and almost imperceptible, but Steph caught it.

Nuala made her a pot of tea and Steph could feel herself trembling as she handed out the spoils of the trip – a purse for Rachel from a scary designer, which she'd had to converse in broken Italian to buy. Rachel loved it, she could tell, but her daughter just said, 'Oh, thanks Mum.' And for Nuala, she had bought a pink silk scarf, from a less scary shop, one she was allowed to go in and actually touch the merchandise. And for Joe? She had gone into a shop which sold clothes for the clergy and had bought him a pair of bright red cardinal socks. He was delighted. He was so easy to buy for, always pleased with everything.

'I'll wear these to Mass,' he said. 'When we next go.'

'And when is that going to be?' asked Nuala.

'Ah, you know... sometime. Or maybe I'll wear them now.' He put them on and walked around in his socks, wiggling his toes, so everyone had to keep admiring them.

'Ready to go, Rach?' said Steph, standing up, eventually. 'I don't think I can say how good those socks look once more.'

'Already?' said Nuala. 'But we've got used to having Rachel here...'

'It's nicer living here than home,' said Rachel.

Steph wondered if she was serious. Rachel seemed happy enough at home, it was Steph she had the problem with.

'But now you can play bridge,' said Nuala. 'You can teach all your friends. That's what we used to do when I was young, get together for bridge.'

Rachel looked sceptical.

'I can play with you sometime, if you like,' offered Steph. 'Granny taught me when I was young.'

'Yeah... maybe.' Rachel was off-hand and Steph longed to reach out and hold her close and to ask her what was going on in that teenage brain of her and explain that adults didn't always get it right and that Rachel was loved, deeply loved for who she was and the young woman she was growing into.

She became aware that Melissa and Eilis had been trying to get her attention.

'Steph, what's going on? Are you okay?' asked Eilis. 'You're miles away.'

'Not hungry,' said Steph, trying to smile. 'Just drinky.' She picked up her wine glass and took a large sip and immediately wished she hadn't. The wine suddenly reminded her of Rome and so she picked up her water glass. 'You know, she said, I think I'll stick to water. I think I've gone off wine.'

Eilis and Melissa again exchanged a glance. What was going on?

The waiter returned with their food, Caesar salad for Steph, posh burger for Melissa and tuna steak for Eilis.

'You know?' said Steph. 'Wine isn't all it's cracked up to be.'

'Really?' said Eilis, smiling but wondering what Steph was hinting at. 'And I thought it was the great social lubricant. That we wouldn't be able to even talk to people without a couple of glasses on board.'

'I just drank too much in Rome,' said Steph. 'It's nice for a few and then... you know...' She drifted off.

'Was Rome okay?' said Eilis.

'Rome was Rome,' she said. 'We all just drank too much.'

Melissa and Eilis waited for her to say more but it was clear that Steph didn't want to continue.

'This looks good,' said Melissa and set about trying to eat the burger with a knife and fork. 'I give up,' she said, 'would anyone mind if I...?'

Steph and Eilis shook their heads and Melissa picked the burger up with two hands and began to eat. 'I am starving,' she said. 'I am finding food a great comfort these days.' She thought of Cormac and wondered where he was and what he was doing. She felt adrift without him. She had texted him and phoned him but he never answered these days. It was clear that he wasn't just busy, she was being cold-shouldered. Had she said something to make him recede like this, after so many years of being so close? Had he picked up on her feelings for him? Was he awkward and did he think the best way to let her down was to drop her like a stone?

Steph took one mouthful of her salad and put down her fork. 'You can have mine, if you like,' she said to Melissa. 'I'm not feeling too great.' She smiled as if to say that everything was all right. 'I'll be fine, just slightly under the weather.'

'Steph, what's wrong?' said Melissa. 'Tell us. Please. Is something going on? Did something happen in Rome?' After unburdening herself about her own mother, she really wanted Steph to do the same. She felt so much better reaching out to her friends and sharing a problem which she had carried around all her life, she wanted them to feel they could do the same.

And then, in an instant, the Cheshire cat grin faded and tears filled Steph's eyes.

'Everything's fine,' she said. 'Everything's fine.'

'It's not, is it?' persisted Eilis. 'Come on, you can tell us. That's what we're here for.'

And Steph looked up at them, defeated. 'You're right, everything's not fine. Everything's awful. And I don't know what to do.'

'Go on...' urged Melissa gently.

'Rick is... Rick is sleeping with Miriam. I saw them... doing it,' she said, tearfully. 'At the communion. In the garden.'

Melissa and Eilis were open-mouthed.

'Jesus!' said Melissa.

'Are you sure?' Eilis said.

'Yeah,' said Steph. 'I'm sure. I wish I wasn't, but I'm very sure indeed.'

Melissa had reached over and grasped Steph's hand. Eilis took the other, shaking her head in shock.

'That's awful,' she soothed. 'Jesus! That must have been terrible.' She looked at Eilis and mouthed 'Bastard'. Eilis nodded grimly.

Steph was really crying now. 'Oh, don't be nice to me, it'll make it worse.' She looked around to see if anyone in the restaurant had noticed. 'It's been going on for ages, years actually, and I was just trying to pretend it wasn't happening at all and now... I can't really.' She lowered her voice. 'You're the only ones who know. Don't tell anyone.'

They both shook their heads. 'We won't.'

'And he's horrible to me, too. I'm sure I'm awful to live with and everything but he's not a nice person to live with. Not nice at all.'

Eilis and Melissa looked at each other.

'In what ways is he not nice?' said Eilis.

'Oh, he gets angry and he shouts at me. He's just got this layer of aggression all the time, ready to spill over. And it's only ever directed at me. No one else. Not Miriam. Or Angeline.'

'There's another one?' said Melissa.

Steph nodded. 'Work colleague. 29.'

'Has he ever hit you,' said Eilis. 'Has he ever hurt you?'

'A couple of times,' said Steph. 'Not badly but just pushing me around.'

'You need to get out of there,' said Eilis.

'We can help you,' said Melissa.

'I know. And I will. I'm going to get my shit together. I promise. I just need a bit more time. I'm not in danger or anything just need to try and decide how to do this.'

'What about Rachel?' said Melissa. 'Is he nice to Rachel?'

'Yeah, he is,' Steph said. 'In his own way. She is angry at me and not him so much. I don't know why.'

'Mothers and daughters,' said Melissa. 'So close. It's a more complicated relationship.'

'I suppose, I don't know. But she wants him to go to watch her play hockey but she never asks me.'

'But could that be one way of her reaching out to him?' said Eilis. 'He's hard to get close to and this is it?'

'I suppose, but he's the one having an affair, not me, I'm the one who's there for her and who wants to spend time with her. '

'You'll sort it out, I promise,' said Melissa. 'She's only sixteen.' Melissa hoped it would work out for Steph and Rachel, that they would find their way back to each other again. She remembered how much she longed for her own mother aged sixteen, except in her case it was her mother rejecting her. And she was determined that Steph would move out and away from Rick. She wondered if they could move in with her for a bit. That could work. The three of them together could sort this one out.

'And,' continued Steph, dabbing her eyes with a napkin, 'this thing with Angeline. He's having an affair with an affair.'

'Who does that?' said Melissa. 'Jesus!'

Steph nodded. 'And I thought she was nice. I've met her at the Partners' Partners' Party.'

'Was that,' said Eilis, 'what it was actually called? Someone went a bit alliteration crazy.'

'An alliterative arse,' said Melissa.

They all laughed, even Steph. 'But,' she continued, 'Angeline was lovely. Now I know why. She just wanted to see what I was like.'

'What a cow,' said Melissa. 'Conniving, cunning cow. Shall I stop with the alliteration now?'

'I found texts,' said Steph. 'She seems to be in love with him.'

'Fool,' said Eilis, 'she's a fool. And so's Miriam.'

'A fecking, flipping fool,' said Melissa. 'Sorry,' she said, 'it just came out.'

'But I am too, aren't I?' said Steph. 'I am just in this terrible mess which I can't get out of. I keep doing the most destructive things...'

'Like what?' said Eilis.

'Like... oh I don't know, like things I shouldn't do...' She couldn't mention the shoplifting, it was too shameful. She was feeling a big enough failure in front of her friends already and they were being so nice to her. She didn't know if she deserved such kindness. 'I just can't help myself. I can't quite focus enough on anything to move on. I don't know how to change things. It's been like this for years and years and I keep going round and round and round. I'm going mad.'

'No, you're not,' said Eilis, 'it might feel like it, but this is what life feels like. It's not easy to live and be normal. Things always happen and you've just got to get through them. And you will. You'll get through this.'

'Yes,' said Melissa, 'you will, Steph. You're strong, you're brilliant. You'll get through it.'

'But I don't know what the future *looks* like,' said Steph. 'I don't know how it is going to end. If I knew, it might make it easier. I don't want to be with him but don't know how I am going to move on. I have no plan at the moment. I've only just realised that I don't have to be like this for the rest of my life.'

'But no one knows, none of us know what is going to happen,' said Eilis. 'We just have to keep going, you know?'

'You have us, Steph, doesn't she Eils?' said Melissa. 'We're here for you, whenever you need us.'

'I suppose I'm scared,' said Steph. 'You know, the future... that things might get worse.'

'They might, but then it will be okay, that's the way life works,' said Eilis, wishing fervently that she was able to apply such wisdom to herself.

'We are all scared,' said Melissa. 'Life is bloody terrifying.'

Eilis agreed. 'Yeah, it's super scary just being out there. What's going to happen next? I keep waiting for my nice life to start, but it never does, you know where everything is calm and there are no nasty surprises.'

'Or nice surprises,' said Melissa. 'Just no surprises at all. Just everything mapped out and non-scary.'

'But that would,' said Steph, 'be boring.' Eilis and Melissa had actually succeeded in making her feel a tiny bit better, already she felt a little lighter, a dab happier. 'You're not shocked?' she said. 'Everyone thinks my life's perfect...'

'Who thinks that?' said Eilis.

'Everyone... everyone.'

'Do they?' said Melissa. 'Really, though?'

'Maybe they don't. Maybe that's something I've put on it myself, that I had to make everything wonderful, but I have never been able to. I can't seem to make everyone happy.'

'Is that your job?' said Melissa.

'My Mam and Dad made it seem so simple. Happiness wasn't something we had to work on in our family, but I can't seem to get it going in our house. No wonder Rachel hates me.'

'She doesn't hate you,' said Eilis. 'You're her mam.'

'You'll work it out,' said Melissa. 'I know you will.'

'And then there's Rick,' said Steph. 'He's so angry with me.'

'Maybe... maybe it's not you he's angry with,' suggested Melissa.

'Who then?'

'Himself?'

Steph shrugged. 'Perhaps, who knows? Whoever it is, he's not a very happy person. Well, he's definitely happier with other people. Like Angeline or bloody Miriam.'

'I can't believe you're not angrier,' said Melissa. 'I'd be throwing things around. Using his cereal bowl as the cat's toilet or giving his suits away to charity. Or,' she was on a roll now, 'or tattooing his forehead with the word Bastard. Isn't that what you are meant to do in these circumstances?'

'But they don't have a cat,' said Eilis. 'So, not all of those are applicable.'

'True. Scrap idea number one, then,' said Melissa.

'Yeah, you'd think you would,' said Steph. 'But that's not exactly what happens in real life. I just feel numb and powerless and not able to actually move things forward.'

'But you will move forward, you will move on,' said Eilis. 'You're just not a drama queen, like other people. You don't cause scenes and force things to move faster than they would naturally.'

'So, what are you going to do?'

'I don't know, I can't see a way out,' Steph said. 'I can't imagine a different kind of life.' But having opened up, she was starting to realise that a new life, a new direction didn't seem so impossible.

'Should I order more drinks or cake,' said Melissa. 'Eilis, what are the doctor's orders?'

Steph laughed. 'Well, I'm not a doctor, but I prescribe conversation... talking... all of us, to each other.'

'Okay,' said Eilis and Melissa. 'Okay. It's a deal.'

'And as a fully qualified medical doctor, for this evening, I prescribe dessert.'

'At last,' said Melissa. 'I've been eyeing up the crème caramel that's just arrived at the table over there. Anyone else?'

'The chocolate tart for me,' said Steph. 'With ice cream. And extra cream. I think I need it.' Her appetite was coming back, she noticed, so that was good.

'Make that two,' said Eilis.

And they sealed the deal with sugar.

20

MELISSA

Her father had phoned her, which was unheard of, asking her to come over. She knocked and waited for her mother to appear behind the glass door.

'Dad?' He *never* answered the door. She looked at him suspiciously. 'Everything all right? What's going on?' She gave him a kiss on the cheek.

He shrugged, not knowing quite what to say. 'Your mother... um...'

'My mother what?'

'A letter. She's had... a letter.'

'A letter? Saying what?' Wondering what it was all about, she walked past him into the house. At the kitchen table sat her mother, still in her dressing gown, a mug of tea in front of her. She didn't look up.

Here we go again. Melissa looked around for empty bottles, and checked her mother's face for signs of drinking. She didn't see any.

'I made her a cup of tea,' said her father. 'But she won't drink it.'

'Mam?' Melissa scraped out one of the wooden chairs from the kitchen table and sat down. 'You okay?' There was no response. 'Mam? What's going on?'

Melissa exchanged looks with her dad. He looked wide-eyed.

Her mother spoke. 'I had a letter...' she started and then stopped.

'A letter?' Melissa prompted. 'Go on...' She tried to look encouragingly and kindly at her mother, but she was feeling furious with her. All the drama, all this bloody drama, all the time. 'Do you want to tell me?' Melissa managed to speak gently in her journalist's voice.

Silence. It was pointless wondering why they couldn't do life like a normal family, such as have a simple conversation. They never had been able to. Instead, everything had to be so complicated.

'Was the letter from the doctor's or from the hospital?'

Her mother shook her head.

'Mam, are you ill?'

The slight shake of the head again.

'Right, so you are fine. So what was this letter?'

There was no movement.

Melissa turned to her father, who was standing in the doorway. She shot him a look as if to say why did you make me come here for this?

'I can't speak,' said Mary. 'I can't say it.'

'You can't say? Or you don't want to say?' Melissa felt enraged, like so many times before. She was being shut out again. 'Do you know?' she shot at her dad, accusingly. 'Has she told you?'

He said nothing, looking his usual stricken self. This wasn't his fault, she knew that. Her mother always seemed to be at the centre of everything, all the dramas, all the crises.

Melissa softened, for his sake and realised that she would have to revert to type, let's pretend everything is normal and nice. There wouldn't be any great revelations here today.

'Okay, then,' she said, 'I'll make a fresh pot of tea. Maybe it's your tea-making skills. Maybe that's why Mam's not drinking it?' She put on a funny voice, letting him know she wasn't annoyed at him and she was sorry. 'Did you warm the pot?'

Her father smiled shyly and shook his head.

'Ah, that's where you went wrong. You see? I'll show you.' She took out clean mugs and found the teabags. She set a fresh cup of tea in front of her mother.

'There you go.'

She handed her father one. 'Now, look at this. It's a good cup of tea. I should be charging you for this, you know, for tea lessons.' She smiled at him and took out a packet of pink wafers she had found in the cupboard. She bought them when she visited months ago. They were untouched and unwrapped. 'Biscuit? I wonder what the sell-by date is.' She turned it over.

'I knew it! September 1973. No wonder they taste stale. Ah, they'll do for me!' She took one out and winked at her father.

Melissa sat there for half an hour, chatting away, in a meaningless soliloquy, making zero progress on the contents of the letter. But eventually, she couldn't do it any longer, her performance had left her totally drained. She was sucked dry. She knew it was time to leave. And she had eaten all the pink wafers. There was a very big chance that she would never find out the contents of the letter and she had already spent her life with so many unanswered questions. This was just another one of those. She would be left wondering and wondering about her mother for the rest of her life and she just had to accept it.

Sitting in the car, she wanted the one person who she knew would make everything seem so much better. She texted Cormac.

Can I come round? Need to vent.

She wondered would he see her... she felt nervous and she didn't expect a response but she couldn't give up on him even if he had on her. But the next moment, she had a text back.

Yes, I'm at home. Call in.

Happy and almost giddy with relief, she turned on the radio and sang all the way to his. He may have been distancing himself lately, and perhaps if it was because he had noticed that she was acting weird around him, all she had to do was stop that and then maybe everything would be okay.

21

CORMAC

Finally, he was going to have to finish things with Melissa once and for all. He'd been dithering for too long now and it would have to be done with the conviction of Robespierre. No pussy-footing. His indecision hadn't done him any good.

Not that there was anything to finish, but he had to... what was he going to do? End the non-relationship? Dump his non-girlfriend? Walk away from the person he loved most in the world who he shouldn't love? The person he was only supposed to love totally and utterly and depressingly platonically.

When his phone rang, he always, *always* hoped it was her. Arranging to meet her somewhere and seeing her hand shoot up in a wave, her face in a huge grin. Or taking ages and ages to buy her Christmas present and wishing he could just give it to her even though there were still weeks to go. Or talking and talking and laughing and laughing while sitting on the sofa, her feet touching him, the heat of her body making him itch with desire. But he had to commit to his new life. And Melissa was holding him back, from a fresh start, the bakery, seeing his other friends... Erica? That was going well. She was fun, sexy, a breath of fresh air. Maybe not funny like Melissa was, but that wasn't everything, was it? The most important thing was that Erica was into him. So it was time to say goodbye to Melissa.

* * *

As soon as Cormac answered the door, Rolo jumped up into Melissa's arms. 'Hello sweetheart!' she said. 'I've missed you too!' She stroked and kissed him on the head. 'I need a cup of tea,' she said, putting Rolo down and facing Cormac. 'I've just been at my mother's house and let's just say it was a trial of epic proportions. The Hague has got nothing on Beach Court.'

He was filling the kettle and not looking at her, but she was acting slightly jumpy, like she didn't know whether to sit or to stand, or to talk or to listen.

'And work is a nightmare,' she was saying. 'Liam is being a total pain in the arse. Everything is more tabloid, as you know, and I think I am going to have start writing quizzes and articles such as My Dog Is Too Fat for the Flap or, more likely, My Parrot Beats Me At Mastermind. He's not a fan of Breadline Lives, even though questions were asked in parliament the other day. And, you'll never believe this...'

'I can't do this anymore,' he said suddenly, 'I'm sorry, Melissa.'

'Do what? Make the tea?'

'I can't. I just... I just...' He suddenly realised that this was going to be harder than he had thought. He saw Melissa's eyes swim with confusion. He stumbled on. 'I just can't be your friend anymore, listening to your problems. It's just not working for me. It's all about you.'

She began talking, fast. 'It doesn't have to be. I am so sorry if I have always been rambling on about me all the time. I am so incredibly sorry. Cormac, please.'

He stood up, as though he needed to get away from her, as though suddenly drained by this friendship.

'Listen, Melissa, I'm about to open the bakery – this is my dream. It is stressful, exhilarating, amazing and the most frightening thing I have ever done in my life. And I need to look after myself, put me first from now on. I can't be there to mop up after your next crisis, okay?'

He looked away. He couldn't bear the tears in her eyes.

'Cormac...' she began. 'We can be friends, can't we? It's all a bit dramatic, isn't it? Have you been at the teen fiction again? Or watching Hollyoaks?'

'Sorry Melissa. Listen, will you go? Erica's coming round. We're driving to Dun Laoghaire for an ice cream.'

'Eric?'

'*Erica.*'

'Who's Erica? Why didn't you tell me about *Erica*?'

'My girlfriend.' This was as hard as he thought it was going to be. He was hurting her. He was like all the other stupid men who had been in her life. He was the one who was meant to make everything alright and yet he was a bad as all those losers. 'Me and Erica, well, we've been seeing each other for a couple of months now, and it's going well.'

Melissa stood up and put Rolo on the ground. 'Well, I'm really pleased for you. That's great.' She walked to the front door. 'See you Cormac. I'm sorry I've been so selfish.'

'Yeah,' he said, not making eye contact. 'See you.' I am such a coward, he thought.

'Bye Rolo,' she said and walked away.

He closed the door and stood there, not moving, hearing her footsteps recede. He looked down at his hand and noticed it was trembling.

Melissa, he thought. Oh Melissa. I'm going to miss you so much.

22

MELISSA

Oh, Jesus Christ.

Without opening her eyes Melissa realised the horror of where she found herself. Jimbo's bed. And worse, she was naked.

She desperately tried to piece together last night. Drinks, yes, lots and lots of drinks. Did she start to cry or was that Jimbo? Probably both. Jesus, she really couldn't remember much more than that. Did he say something? That he really, *really* liked her? Oh bloody hell.

The sheets didn't smell especially clean, not like her own at home. She wished, wished, *wished*, she was back there, teleported home, or better still, just back to yesterday and she could make sure the whole thing would never happen.

Leaving Cormac's, and walking out in the bright sunlight, she had felt devastated. From the moment she had seen him again, she was so pleased, so thrilled to be in his orbit again. She'd had that lovely, delicious feeling again, that she wanted to touch him, to be able to... kiss him. She looked at his mouth as he spoke, his lips moving, and could feel this sensation of being drawn towards him. I love him, she had thought. I love him. I want him. But then he mentioned something about a girl named Erica. And then everything started swimming and she can't really remember the rest. He mentioned he didn't want to be friends anymore, like they were schoolchildren, and so of course she had to leave straight away and did she even say goodbye? She couldn't remember. She had got back into her car and cried until a few people noticed her and she went home and realised that there was nothing comforting to eat apart from that jar of rhubarb jam so she had a spoon of that and it tasted disgusting. Her mother had been right. It hadn't been a good present

She knew one thing, very clearly. She was never drinking again. Yes, they all say that, but she was determined. Not one drop, ever again. There was – she hadn't quite admitted it before – but there was a propensity for her to drink too much. She had never thought she could be like her mother, but drink got the better of her far more than she was comfortable with. It was something she would have to manage far more assiduously. She had a tendency to use drink as a way of softening life's blows. She wasn't going to do it anymore. When did she call Jimbo to go for a few drinks? When she realised that a spoonful of rhubarb jam wasn't going to quite cut it in the soothing stakes.

She closed her eyes again. Melissa. Will you never learn? Jimbo? Of all people! Now, that's going to make working together a breeze, isn't it? She opened one eye to a slit. Yes, there he was: Jimbo, large as life and snoring away. Life was shit enough as it was, without this happening, and it was all her fault and all so avoidable.

Was there a chance that she could sneak out? Maybe he was so drunk last night that he wouldn't remember? It was worth a chance. She began to peel back the duvet cover.

The bed creaked, so she moved even slower and began inching in increments so small that a snail would find the going slow. Come on, easy does it. Get out of here alive.

Her feet touched the floor. Yee-es! That's it, now get yourself upright. Brilliant, she was out of the bed. Now, clothes. She looked around for them... scattered in a hideous paper chase around Jimbo's flat. Socks, jeans, T-shirt, knickers, bra... coat, bag, phone still inside, thank God.

After leaving Cormac's, she had called Jimbo to see if he was about. He'd suggested a drink... which had turned into multiples. She had felt a little better initially but now things had definitely taken a downward turn.

Right, she tiptoed, to the door. She turned the latch... quiet, quiet, that's it. Nearly out...

'Where're ye going?'

Melissa screamed. 'Jimbo!'

He stood there naked except for an old towel, tied around his waist.

Why, why, why, had she allowed this to happen? Who makes such a stupid mistake at the age of thirty-eight? If she was twenty, it might be considered necessary, even sensible to sleep with a friend. But this wasn't what grown-ups did. Next, she'd be off drinking Buckfast and eating cereal for dinner. Two not altogether unattractive propositions, it had to be said.

'I'm so sorry, I mean, you know, it's just there's something I've got to do... and I've got to get there...' she realised her head was throbbing.

'Slipping off without saying goodbye?' He was looking at her, emotionless. She knew it was bad form. They were colleagues. He wasn't just some randomer.

'Well, yes.'

'It might have been better if you had said you were going.'

'Yes, but you were asleep. I didn't want to disturb...'

'You okay?' he said.

She smiled as much as her headache would allow. 'Of course! You?'

'You know...'

'Listen, Jimbo. I'm really sorry about last night. I don't know what happened. You know, I was so drunk. You know me, useless around drink.' She was speaking rapidly, panicky. 'I'll see you... I'll see you later, at work. Thanks Jimbo. Take care.' Melissa gave a cheery false smile and disappeared to the other side of the front door. The relief was enormous.

Melissa walked home, buying a coffee and a muffin on the way. She stopped off in a chemist for some headache tablets and sat on one of the benches along the boardwalk of the canal.

Why had she allowed such a thing to happen? What was wrong with her? She used to feel amazing, invincible. But now? Now, she was making mistakes left right and centre. Terrible, awful mistakes. And work was now ruined as a result. How could she face Jimbo ever again? She was good at something, all right, she thought, as she downed her coffee, which did little to alleviate the sense of death and decay, she was very good at fucking things up.

23

STEPH

Steph went upstairs to Rachel's room and gently pushed the door... no one there. She looked around at all of Rachel's things; posters on the wall, her books, and her dressing gown hung on the back of the door, make-up on her desk, boots and shoes in a heap, Pinky the rabbit (old and one-eared) lying pensively on the bed. And, on her bedside table, was what looked like a diary. She didn't know Rachel was keeping one.

'Rachel Fitzpatrick' was written in careful teenage hand. She looked at the first page, not meaning to read it... but she couldn't stop.

Had a laugh with Aoife, Caz and Siobhan in the afternoon yesterday. Went to Fundaland and met up with Barry and his friends. He let me wear his hat and scarf because it was so freezing. He's so nice. Came home at four.

Mum was out and the house was empty. Everything was quiet except when Aoif and I went to my room, we heard a noise. We thought we were being burgled or something. We went onto the landing – Aoif holding my hockey stick in her hand.

And Dad came out of his bedroom. Trying to look normal and claiming to have had a sleep. It was obvious he was lying because he was smiling and looked weird.

He gave myself and Aoif some money to get a pizza. Basically, he was trying to get us out of the house.

So, we did, but we hid behind a car to see if we could solve the mystery.

No one came out. So, Dad was telling the truth and is just ACTUALLY weird. Or there's a dead body in there.

Aoif reckons dead body.

Jesus. What was going on? Was Rick actually sleeping with Miriam in the house?

Steph scanned a few pages, found a new entry. She recognised the date – Rick's birthday. They had had a few people over to dinner.

Rachel wrote:

I went downstairs to get some Coke out of the fridge and more crisps. When I passed the downstairs toilet, Miriam came out pulling down her skirt. She tried to pretend everything was normal but then a moment later Dad came out of the toilet too. I just know something was going on. Like they were having it off or something. And then I knew what had happened before, when Dad was being so weird. Miriam must have left by the back door. Dad, the twat, just pretended everything was normal. And then Mrs Head in the Sand herself came out and was all nice as pie. Anyone would think I was an eejit.

Steph scanned forward a few pages.

February 7th. Some of the girls know about my dad and Miriam and they've started saying things. I told them they were liars and they don't know anything. And then I got into a fight...

'Interesting reading, mum?' Rachel was standing at the door of her bedroom, face incandescent.

Steph nearly fell off the bed.

'Rach! I was just... tidying up and then I just glanced at the book. Your diary, is it? I didn't read it. I've only just come in here.'

Rachel just stood there, looking at her. Steph gabbled away. 'I was just trying to find something. My scarf... remember you borrowed it?'

Rachel raised one of her eyebrows. 'Really, Mother?' Her voice was icy.

Steph had to give her daughter credit. 'Is that the best you can do? Why don't you admit it? You were snooping, weren't you? You were spying on me. Find out anything?' She was like a Bond villain.

'Well, actually...'

'You are pathetic, Mum.' Rachel unleashed her anger. 'A total and utter weakling, that's what you are. You have no idea what is going on in this fucking house, so you resort to reading your own daughter's diary to find out. Other mothers know what's going on. They know what their kids – and their husbands – are up to. But not you. No, no. You have your fingers in your ears, always trying to get people to like you. But they don't, you know. Your husband doesn't like you. Miriam doesn't like you. They are just laughing at you behind your back. And you are letting them.'

'Rachel...'

'Yes, fucking Miriam. She and Dad are sleeping together, by the way. And everyone knows except you. Aoife knows, I know... the whole bloody street knows, everyone in school knows, and I am a laughing stock. It is so humiliating! You are too busy worrying whether I have eaten a fucking bowl of cereal for breakfast than the fact that your husband is sleeping with your friend. You... you... you moron!'

'I'm sorry Rach. I... um, I did know about it, but I hadn't quite worked out what to do and I was just buying some time.'

'While they have been *fucking* each other, Mother, you have been poncing about and being useless. A normal woman would have thrown their husband out, but not you – doormat!' Rachel had started crying. 'And now you read my fucking diary. As if I have anything else. I don't have a fucking family. And now I don't have any fucking privacy.'

Steph felt pathetic and weak. I must be such a disappointment to Rachel, she thought. 'I'm really sorry Rach,' she said. 'I thought I was doing the best thing.'

'A proper mother would be strong, you know? Not like you.' She began to sob now. Steph went over to her. She put her arms around Rachel. 'I'm so, so sorry, my darling girl. My darling girl.'

'I hate you Mum,' said Rachel. 'I really, really hate you.' But she let Steph smooth her hair and shush in her ear.

'But I really, really love you, though, so maybe it cancels it out,' said Steph. She sat beside Rachel, waiting for the sobs to calm down. 'You're right,' she said, speaking gently. 'I have been weak, but these things aren't easy to sort out. You can't – you don't just make decisions and then act on them... there's a lot to think about. There's you... the house, everything... We will get through this. I just don't know what the future looks like. I wish I did. But that's really scary and I wanted to be sure I was doing the right thing. For you. You love Dad and it's hard to make a decision to break up the family.'

'Yeah, he's my dad and everything,' said Rachel, 'but I would prefer not to live in this chaos.'

It was chaos, their home, that's where she had failed the most, adding to the chaos. Why hadn't she protected Rachel better? How could she have let her be burdened by all this? Eventually, Rachel stopped crying.

'I'm sorry you had to go through this,' Steph said, gently, holding her hand. 'About Dad and... Miriam.' And Angeline. And all the other lucky girls in Rick's sight. Ugh. He was truly disgusting.

'Why didn't you do anything about it?' Rachel was looking furious again. 'You could have stopped it. You should have stopped it. You can't let Miriam do this to you. She's just a stupid cow. I hate her.'

'Sometimes adults behave badly, do stupid things. You don't suddenly become wise and all-knowing when you get to eighteen.'

'I hate him too. And I hate you.'

'You know, sweetheart, I don't blame you. I don't blame you one bit.' She looked at Rachel's lovely face, tear-stained and angry. 'I'm sorry,' she said. 'I'm so, so sorry. It's not easy, you know, it's not easy being grown-up,' Steph said. 'I'm doing my best and I know I've let you down and I am so, so sorry. Listen, I wish I had all the answers, but there's no bloody manual for what to do when your husband starts having an affair with the neighbour.'

Rachel had stopped crying, she was listening. 'There should be,' she said.

'Yeah, there should be. But unfortunately there isn't.'

And then Rachel suddenly stood up. 'I don't want to hear any more,' she said. 'You know, Mum, it's crap being me. Do you realise that? It's crap being the girl whose father is sleeping with Aoife's mother. It's embarrassing having such pathetic parents.'

And she walked out of the house, slamming the door.

And finally Steph felt rage at Rick for doing this. For putting Rachel through this, for embarrassing her. He never thought of the consequences, the impact his actions had on others. She needed to get a few things together. Like what? Her passport, her driver's licence, bank details, all the things that would enable her to leave. She kept them in a box file, in Rick's study. He didn't lock it, but he knew she'd never poke around but now she went in to retrieve cheque books and medical cards from the box file. She needed to get them into her possession. She didn't know how relations were going to go.

Over by the window of the study, there was a large desk, laptop and a photograph of Rachel as a baby. There was also a picture of Rick and his father, the rather scary Richard Fitzpatrick, on Rick's graduation day. They were standing side by side, slightly awkwardly, Rick's strange mother on the other side. She'd always believed that they didn't think she was quite good enough for Rick. They would have loved Miriam, though. Right up their street. She grabbed the box file and went to leave but under the blotter was an envelope sticking out. Should she open it? Was this in the realm of acceptable snooping? Or was it a divorceable offence. Go ahead, punk. Divorce me.

It was from the head of chambers.

...Come to our attention... unprofessional behaviour... allegations of miscon- duct which contravenes office policy... relationship with colleague... Angeline Barrow's contract is terminated with immediate effect... you are on a warning. Any transgressions... such behaviour and your employment will cease...

Good God.

So he and Angeline had been discovered. And she had been sacked. Surely it should have been Rick who should be sacked. But he had been a given a stay of execution. How utterly humiliating. For everyone.

And there was Rachel getting into fights because of this. She felt the hairs on the back of her neck prickle. No way could this go any further. It had to stop now.

Rick's life was a mess and for too long he had dragged her down. She had to start getting back on her feet and getting her and Rachel far, far away.

24

MELISSA

When she walked into the office on Monday morning, the first person Melissa spotted was Jimbo. Oh God, she groaned, willing herself or him to dissipate, Star Trek style.

He was talking to a young woman but something was decidedly different because, in all the years she had known him, Jimbo, normally bored-looking and slightly stoned, was practically animated. Even his beard looked perkier. Who even knew beards could do such a thing? What had Jimbo, a man so afraid of showing his emotions that he covered his face with a ridiculously large beard, so interested?

'Jimbo,' she said, when she got to her desk, smiling as though everything was fine, pulling off her woolly gloves and unwinding her scarf. Inside she was dying.

'Ah! Murphy,' he said, perfectly normally as though their last encounter wasn't of the naked kind. 'Meet our latest inmate, ahem, I mean fresh-faced recruit.' The young woman laughed. Melissa tried to bat away images of Jimbo in the altogether, his white chest and sticky-out ribs, the inadequate loin cloth of a towel.

Jimbo continued. 'She arrives this morning full of hope and optimism; by the afternoon, her dreams will be thwarted, ideals twisted, desired mutilated and thrown back at her feet. Her wish to help others and to fight the evil forces of capitalism pushed screaming down the toilet bowl of life. In short, innocence transformed into foul, fetid faeces of disappointment and the slow, dawning realization that we are powerless, that we journalists can do nothing except what our small-brained and tiny-testicled editors tell us to do, who in turn are governed by managers who march to one tune only, that of the Great God, Commerce.'

Good old Jimbo. He was his usual smart-arse self. She almost loved him for it.

'Ignore this idiot and his melange of metaphor,' she said. 'Thanks for the effort, Jimbo. And so early in the morning. Congratulations. Your oration was wasted on me as I was too busy wondering how a person can carry so much hair on their chin. It's amazing you can actually lift your head. Fair play to you on that one. Neck. Of. Steel.' Melissa turned to the girl. 'I'm Melissa. Welcome,' she smiled. 'Jimbo just hasn't been able to laugh since he believed Jacob's changed the recipe for fig rolls.'

'They have! They're not the same!' Jimbo said. 'I'll get to the bottom of it! I will!'

The girl was laughing. 'I'm Louise McArthur, Lulu.' She grasped Melissa's hand with both of hers and shook it. 'It's an honour to meet you, Ms Murphy...'

'Call me Melissa...'

'Thank you.' Lulu smiled. 'Um, Melissa? I must tell you, but I did an entire dissertation on the art of the feature writer. I used your work as my case study, to illustrate the authorial voice, the role of the woman's voice in newspapers to filter world events, and specifically your distinct ability to create a sense of safety for readers.'

'Jesus. Steady on...' Jimbo began.

Lulu continued. 'What you say about the world, and this is what I surmised, whether you are talking to a celebrity, or politician or writing about health issues for women, people trust you and believe you. Like Oprah, I suggested, or the pope.'

Melissa didn't know what to say. 'The pope, you say... that's...'

'I mean, you didn't win the O'Brien Prize five years in a row for nothing...'

'Six.'

'Wow!' exclaimed Lulu.

'Well, one year I shared it with Caitriona Brannigan from the Times... so...'

'Her nemesis,' explained Jimbo.

Melissa ignore him. 'So, technically six.'

'But *actually* five,' said Jimbo.

'Six, of course,' said Lulu, 'my mistake. Anyway, it's a real honour to meet you.'

'And it's very nice to meet you, Lulu. Did you pass? You know, your dissertation?'

'Yes, I received a double first and have just been in the States – at the Columbia School of Journalism. And now I'm... here!'

Melissa fully expected her to do a twirl.

'I have been reading your work since I was fifteen...'

'That long? I don't know if I've been writing that long...'

'It's not long, really,' Lulu assured her. 'I'm twenty-five.'

'That young?'

Lulu laughed again and Melissa and Jimbo exchanged eyebrow raises. And then Lulu suddenly stopped and looked deadly serious. 'The thing is, I want to be you.'

'Me? You want to be me?'

'Yes! You, if you don't mind. Well not exactly *you*. You but me, if you see what I mean? Would you mind?' Lulu held up her phone and smiled at the camera and had tweeted it before Melissa knew what was happening, but she could see that in the photo she was open-mouthed and double-chinned. And those were definitely the remnants of her breakfast on her jumper. And why on earth would this fresh-faced 25-year-old want to be her when she could be *anyone*?

'Thanks so much! I know we are going to be so close. Mentor!' Lulu put her hand out for a fist bump. Melissa bumped back, awkwardly. She could see Jimbo was laughing. Behind his beard.

Lulu was looking at her phone. 'Right, I've got a meeting with Mr Connelly in eight minutes. He's asked me to bring a few ideas. I have forty-five. Is that enough?' She looked worried.

'No, I think you have enough. Doesn't she, Jimbo?'

'Aye, she does that,' he said, nodding. 'Definitely enough. I haven't had an idea since 1986.'

'And that was when you devised a plan to make a mobile out of Hula Hoops so you could eat crisps while you worked.'

'Aye. Must see if that patent has expired...'

Lulu clearly wasn't quite sure if they were joking or not. 'Excuse me a moment... see you in a while...' She disappeared.

Melissa and Jimbo just looked at each other.

'Mentor?' Melissa looked perplexed. 'Moi?'

'Mental more like.'

'Are all young people like that these days? Is that normal? I suddenly feel like I need a sit down,' said Melissa. 'And my slippers. Maybe a nice watch of afternoon telly, like Countdown. And a mug of Ovaltine.'

'That, my dear,' said Jimbo, 'is the new generation. They are like a relentless robot army – shinier, newer, sleeker than us. We're over. We may as well go home.'

'I feel useless all of a sudden,' she said.

'Actually I feel the opposite. I need to rig up my Hula Hoop mobile... I had forgotten just how good my ideas used to be...'

'Jimbo?'

'Aye?'

'I'm sorry.' The sight of Jimbo naked kept interrupting her waking thoughts, like newsflashes. She could only imagine Jimbo suffered the same mortification.

He looked at her. 'It's grand,' he said. And that was it. They were moving on. 'Let's have a custard cream, shall we?' he said. 'I can't work on an empty stomach.'

Later, things were so normal that they went for a quick drink and a moan in their usual seats in Fallon's. Melissa was on the sparkling water – she had decided that a clear head was what she needed after what had happened with Jimbo - which made going to the pub an ordeal rather than a pleasure, removing the very point of a pub. She made the best of it by ordering crisps, which slightly enlivened and elevated the occasion.

They were moaning together – always a shared pleasure – about Liam and the direction towards tabloid populism. But, perhaps, higher circulation. This weekend's paper was not leading with Melissa's story but something by a freelancer. A mea culpa of a minor pop star who slept with his make-up artist while his wife gave birth in hospital. The manager had decided that he should say how difficult he had found fame, how stressed he was after the loss of his labradoodle who had been run over by the drummer in the band. It was the usual career-saving pointless exercise that meant little or nothing to anyone except the popstar, the wife and the dog.

Melissa was failing in her attempt to be magnanimous, but she was really furious. She usually led the weekend features section, as she was, after all, chief features writer, and the Saturday issue was their department's most important day. She pushed a handful of crisps into her mouth.

'These count as one of your five a day, don't they Jimbo?' she asked.

'Aye, if they're cheese and onion. It's the onion that makes them healthy.'

They shared the packet, like an old married couple eating chips at the seaside, licking their fingers.

'Another one of those... whatever it is. Is it even a drink?' Jimbo pointed at her glass, the lone lemon looking as appropriately desultory.

'Yes, Jimbo, water is a drink. You can have it all on its own as well. It's not just a mixer for whiskey, you know?'

Jimbo pulled a face as if to say, 'I have no idea what you are saying', and stood up to get a round in. A voice interrupted.

'I'll get them. My pleasure for the hardest working writers in Ireland.' They looked up. Liam was standing there, smiling his infuriating smile. 'G&T for you, Melissa? Pint, Jimbo?'

'She's on the water. The bubbly kind,' said Jimbo.

'Melissa!' Liam pretended to be shocked. 'And you a journalist. What is the world coming to? They'll be asking for your NUJ card back next.'

They reluctantly shifted up in their seats to make room for him, annoyed that their moaning session was at an end. Liam returned with the drinks balanced in his large hands, packets of bacon fries in his teeth.

'Not still sulking are you? Surely you are loftier than that?' he asked Melissa. 'Or maybe not?'

She scowled unprofessionally. 'It's a good story. It should have been the lead.'

He looked at her and... shrugged. 'It's all right. I mean, it's not Watergate. It's not even Pat the Hat.' The latter was last month's big scoop, broken by the Evening Express, their rival newspaper. It had involved a senior politician who had a penchant both for headwear and young men while extolling the primacy of the heterosexual home.

'Maybe not. But it still deserves Page One.' Melissa began to doubt herself. Maybe it wasn't that good. Maybe her story about a couple who had been denied council housing because of complaints on the estate wasn't such a good story. Maybe she was losing her touch. She didn't know what to say.

'Melissa...' he grinned at her, showing that he knew he was annoying her, 'I like you. I think you are a great girl...'

'A great *girl*?' She raised an eyebrow. She knew he was goading her, but she was too exhausted to resist the bait.

'Woman, then. And you, Jimbo...'

'A great man?'

'I am sure you are, Jimbo. I'm sure you are. You're mother, I imagine, would be the first to concur.'

'I wouldn't be too sure of that,' said Jimbo.

'But...?' said Melissa.

'But?' Liam took a long soak from his pint glass.

'But what?' said Melissa. 'I'm great, Jimbo's great, the paper's great. We're all fecking great. But where's the but?'

'But...' he said, 'we are not selling papers. The point of our very existence is to sell papers, but we are failing at that quite spectacularly. And we are not selling them. Our circulation is going down. And so, my dears, things have to change. Which I know no one likes and no one finds easy.' He was smiling at them. He wanted them to understand that this world they were in was changing and they had to find a way of changing with it. 'We need to increase our on-line presence and stories about people on the breadline are not click-bait.'

'We know that,' said Melissa. 'But you place so much emphasis – too much I would say - on entertainment and not the important things...'

'What?' Liam was laughing now. 'Is it the fact I'm from the West of Ireland and not the posher parts of Dublin, like the rest of the media mafia?' He shrugged again, looking distinctly unbothered.

'I'm from Belfast,' said Jimbo. 'There's nothing fancy about Belfast.'

'Well, here's to us outsiders,' said Liam, clinking his pint to Jimbo's. 'Here's to Belfast.'

'No... it's not that, it's...' Melissa tried to get the conversation back on track but struggled to explain herself.

'Melissa, listen to me.' Liam put down his pint. 'This paper is fecked. This country is fecked, if you hadn't realised. And if you have been working all fecking week doing a shitty job and then on Saturday, your glorious day of leisure, your paper of choice, decides you should read about people with even shittier lives than you, then that's a bit fecking depressing, don't you think?'

'No...' But she didn't sound convinced. 'I...'

'Well, believe me it is. It's pretty fecking depressing to read about the hovels that some people are forced to live in, and their crappy lives. It may be important, we all know that. We know we should be reading about people on the breadline, but we don't actually want to. And that's why we are not only haemorrhaging readers, my dear bleeding heart liberal, we, as a newspaper are barely alive. We are on life-fecking-support. People, after five wrecking, horrible days of cleaning toilets, driving buses, or being shouted at by pricks like me, they want a bit of... what do you fancy folk here in Dublin 4 call it... is it razzmatazz? A bit of fun, a bit of enter-fecking-tainment. Is that too much to ask?'

'No.' Her voice was quiet.

'You nice Dublin 4 girls, you don't know what it's like to throw a shovel on your back and break your bollocks for some bollocks on a building site, do you?'

'No.'

'Well I do, and the last thing I would want to read about is fecking lesbians. I don't care about their rights, not here, not on this paper. It's called escapism. And that's what we want – it's what we need – in the paper if we are to survive. I mean, for feck's sake, hardly anyone reads fecking newspapers anymore and they certainly don't want to read anything serious. We'll do it, but it's not our lead.'

He took a long drink of his pint. He put it down and smiled broadly at them. 'Just had to get that off my chest,' he said. 'Feel better now.'

'So glad for you,' said Melissa. 'So what do you want me to write about? What do you think would get people so amazingly excited that they would actually get off their arses and buy the fucking paper?'

'Oh I don't know. Just not fecking lesbians! Anything but lesbians... you're obsessed with them! Every fecking copy has a lesbian in it...'

'They don't! Jesus! Anyway...'

He wasn't listening but he was smiling. 'Now, here's an idea. What about going off and having a fecking vajazzle – or whatever it's called – and telling everyone about it.' He laughed at his own brilliance while Melissa perfected her most withering of looks. Jimbo took a large slurp of his pint.

'I'm a journalist. Not a... a... an idiot,' she said.

'Yes... but, and this bit is crucial, people would read it. It's called enter-taining people.'

'So what *are* we leading with? What's this idea of Lulu's?'

'Lulu's done a piece on sexting.'

'Sexting?'

'You know, when you send a photograph of your genitalia to someone and they forward it on to all their friends and it ends up on Facebook and you lose your job. It's all the rage. That never happened to you, Melissa?'

'No. No it hasn't.'

'Jimbo?'

'Not lately,' Jimbo admitted. 'But I'm hoping I won't have too long a wait. I don't want to deprive the world of my magnificent tackle.'

Liam laughed loudly but Melissa squirmed in her seat. She didn't want to be reminded of Jimbo's tackle and she didn't recall anything particularly magnificent about it.

'People will read it, Melissa,' said Liam, appealing to her. 'It has every-thing: lurid, funny, and gossipy. *You* would fucking read it! And by Sunday it'll be yesterday's entertainment and the world moves on. People work hard, Melissa, let's just give them a bit of fun. Is that too much to ask?' He did big puppy-dog eyes. 'Please?'

'Liam, you're wrong. People need the serious stuff, the important things...'

'Yes, but not if you want readers. Bring me something fun, Melissa. Just don't make it about lesbians.'

Melissa finished her water. 'Gentlemen, if you'd excuse me. I will see you in the morning but I think I'm going home. And by the way, Liam, I'm not from fecking D4.'

'So where are ye from?'

'Glenageary!'

He laughed. 'Same thing! Same thing!' he hooted.

25

EILIS

In the bed at the hospital was Mrs O'Malley, Charlie's mother. Oh dear, Eilis thought. I hope she's okay. Poor Charlie. He'd be so worried. She suddenly was desperate that he might be there with her and looked around but no handsome head lurked anywhere.

'Mrs O'Malley? You're back again?' Eilis smiled at the small and frail figure on the bed, a sheet pulled over her, her handbag on the chair beside her. She'd just been seen by Mr Kapil and was now waiting for tests.

'I can't keep away it seems.'

'No, we have that effect on people... we're the place to be.'

The old woman tried to smile.

'So...' said Eilis, reading the notes, 'you fell again. We're going to have to do something about that. We'll have to have a special bed for you.'

'I know, dear. Sorry to be such a nuisance.'

'Not at all... we just want to make sure you are all right. You lie there and we'll take care of you.'

Eilis examined her, checking her eyes, holding her hand. 'You're freezing,' she said. 'We need to get you an extra blanket.'

'Do you know...?' The old woman spoke so quietly that Eilis leaned in to hear her. 'Do you know...? I was just thinking of politics...'

'You were? Why on earth?' Eilis almost laughed.

'You see...' Mrs O'Malley was almost whispering. 'My father said never to trust the other side. We were Labour, you see, through and through.'

She smiled and nodded at Eilis, suddenly animated. 'And I didn't. I didn't. Even when the man I had agreed to marry was revealed to be from the other side.' She smiled at the memory. 'He had lied to me. Would you believe it? Lied for months, knowing I wouldn't have anything to do with the likes of him. I thought he was one of us. Until the day he confessed all.'

'And what did you say?'

'I was shocked. Of all things! I had no idea what I was going to tell Daddy. I couldn't go through with it. We were in Howth for the day, taking a walk on the hill. And he looked at me, his face as white as his Sunday shirt, the colour all at his feet. I said, no I couldn't and no I wouldn't. I told him never to call on me again. And I walked away.'

'And you left him there?'

'Yes. We had been courting for sixteen months and we'd had a fine old time of it. He was handsome, and tall, a beautiful dancer. So light on his feet he was. We loved dancing together. Hours and hours we would dance. But he was one of *them*. I walked all the way to the train station to take me back to town, and I was crying. Tears rolling down my face. And I found a seat. And just... just as the train to Connolly was pulling away, a man sat down beside me and put a bunch of heather on my lap. Picked from the hill.'

'It was him?' A nurse stood behind Eilis trying to get her attention. She had the sense of this whole hospital, the accidents, the emergencies, the pressure all taking place outside this curtain. She resisted the pull... just for a moment, she would listen to someone, take the time. 'He followed you?'

'We were married the following week,' said Mrs O'Malley. 'I always said we were a mixed couple. We agreed on everything except politics. It was a happy forty-two years. My Sean. He passed ten years ago.'

'You were lucky.'

'I was. Sean was a good man. Even though it took me six years to tell Daddy he wasn't Labour and it took him another six years to come round. He did though and the two were great pals.'

'And you had two children,' Eilis prompted.

'We didn't think we would,' Mrs O'Malley admitted. 'We thought that maybe God had other plans for us. Anyway we had each other. And then, our darling Kate was born. And her brother a year later. Sean was a wonderful father. Perhaps you remember my son, Charles. He was with me last time. Kate, you see, was in Cork. But Charles was there that night.'

'Yes, yes, I do remember him. I bumped into him in his shop. I was buying a tree. Is he...' she tried to be as casual as possible. 'Is he coming in to see you?'

'I think Kate will be calling in for me,' said Mrs O'Malley. 'I'm ready to die, doctor. Join my Sean. I've been long enough without him. I'm ready.'

'Please don't say such things,' objected Eilis. 'You are going nowhere. Your family would obviously be lost without you. You are going to be fine.' She smiled, trying to show that she meant what she said and that they weren't just white lies. 'I'll be back later to check on you, Mrs O'Malley.' She turned to Becca who was just passing. 'Becca, is there any chance you could get Mrs O'Malley a cup of tea?' It was the least they could do.

'Consider it sorted,' said Becca.

And then Eilis saw him. Walking down the ward with a bunch of flowers was Charlie.

'There's my son,' said Mrs O'Malley, sounding surprised.

He saw her and came over. 'Mam? Are you okay? What happened? You fell again. Was it the path outside the house? I knew I should have swept up the leaves.'

'Hush now,' she said. 'I'm alright. Just ask this nice doctor here.'

Charlie looked at Eilis then, who was standing there, wondering if she should go or stay. What would normal protocol be? Stay and have a quick chat or run away and risk being thought of as weird and rude.

'Hello,' he said, smiling at her. 'We're making a habit of this, aren't we?'

'You and me?' she said.

'Well, that as well but my mam and me. Hospitals. I swear none of us have ever been in and out of hospitals before this year and now we're regulars. Aren't we Mam?'

'I thought Kate was coming,' said Mrs O'Malley.

'We just thought it was easier if I came,' he said, looking sideways at Eilis. 'Kate's so busy and I just thought it made more sense for me to... you know...' he smiled, blushing slightly, 'so I'm here.'

'And I'm being looked after by the kindest doctor,' said Mrs O'Malley. 'She says I'm ready to go home, as soon as possible.'

'Well, maybe tomorrow. We just want to keep an eye on you,' said Eilis. 'I'll ask Mr Kapil and see what he thinks you should do. He's waiting for test results.' She could sense Charlie close to her and she was trying to focus on what she was saying.

'So, how are you feeling, Mam?' he said.

'Grand, thank you Charles.'

Eilis looked up at Charlie and their eyes locked in together, like two strong magnets finding each other. She felt this force surge through her body, her whole being charged with a sense of rightness, that something strange and profound and wonderful was happening and as though she had known him all her life, she felt she knew everything about him. He was looking at her as though he felt it too. She looked away, breaking the connection.

'I don't know who to give these flowers to,' she heard him say to his mother. 'You or the doctor? For looking after you.'

'Yes, do give them to her, Charles,' said Mrs O'Malley. 'This lovely young woman, here. So young *and* a doctor, isn't it wonderful? In my youth, I would never have dreamed of such a thing. None of us would.'

'Yes, but Mam, you did other things,' said Charlie, taking her hand. 'Like your garden, your beautiful garden.'

Mrs O'Malley smiled. 'I wish I could still do what I used to do with it. But my hands...' she held up her un-held hand which was bent with arthritis. 'It's not so easy these days.'

'You should have seen it, Eilis,' he said. He looked straight at her and again the electric charge between them was so strong, she could have boiled a little. A remotely controlled kettle at that.

She forced herself to look back at him, desperately trying to seem normal and casual but she was feeling overwhelmed.

'It was filled with colour, all year round. Nothing ever died when Mam was around, all her plants grew just for her. We had an apple orchard, and a rose garden and a greenhouse where we grew melons.'

'Hush, Charles,' said Mrs O'Malley. 'You're making it sound like it was a stately home.'

'Every inch had something growing. It was such a beautiful place to grow up in. Kate and I loved it. We used to have an open day for the neighbours and people would pay fifty pence to come in and all the money went to the homeless. One year, we made 650 pounds. And everyone had a taste of melon. It was the talk of the neighbourhood for years.'

Mrs O'Malley was laughing. She shook her head at Eilis. 'That's the way he remembers it but it wasn't always like that. There was the time when the birds got into the greenhouse and ate all the grapes on the vine or when the storm blew down the apple trees.'

Eilis looked up and she saw Charlie was watching her.

'Will you take them?' he said, holding out the flowers. 'For you. From me.'

'No, you've already given me flowers.'

'Please? I grew them myself.' He smiled at her. 'In *my* greenhouse.' And he winked at his mother and Eilis found herself smiling back and blushing. This was ridiculous. She felt as though she was skipping through the pages of a Mills & Boon novel... and she was starting to enjoy it.

'I can't,' she said. 'I'm sure your mother would enjoy them and the other patients.'

He stood up and put the flowers into the vase on the bedside cabinet. 'I'll give these to you so, Mam. It's seems that Dr Eilis is too important for flowers.'

He was teasing her, she knew, but she protested. 'I didn't say that, I meant...'

'Well, maybe Charles, you could give her some flowers again. What do you think of that? When she's not working.'

'I could,' he said. 'I very well could.'

'Doctor,' said Mrs O'Malley, 'Do you have a young man in your life?'

'Um...'

'Because my son is in need of a young lady. He never seems to find anyone special.'

'Mam!' Now Charlie was blushing.

'I'm only trying to help, Charles,' she said, blithely. 'Aren't you always saying how you would love to meet someone really special? And you're really special and it would be nice if you met someone who deserves you.'

'Mam, please...' He looked at Eilis. 'I am so sorry.' He turned back to his Mam. 'Let's talk about something else, okay? How are you? Feeling better?'

'But aren't you always saying that all the girls you meet aren't into the things you are?'

'Mam. Let's move on.'

'Anyway, I'd better go,' said Eilis, not wanting to leave but realizing she had to. She found herself imagining her and Charlie together, she had been enjoying this fantasy of the two of them. 'Get on with things. You'll get your results soon but I'll ask Mr Kapil about them as well. Bye, then.' She began walking away.

'What? I'm only trying to help, put in a good word,' she heard Charlie's mother say.

Later, he was waiting for her at the nurses' station. She had just finished with another patient and was checking to see what was next on her list.

'I'm so sorry about earlier,' he said. 'I hope my mother didn't embarrass you.'

'Not at all,' she said. 'I think it's nice. She loves you.'

'And thanks for looking after her. It means the world to me. She means the world to me and Kate.'

'I know, I can tell. We'll do our very best.' She turned to go, not knowing what else to say.

'The gardening class,' he said. 'Will you come? Saturdays at five p.m.'

'Okay,' she said, turning around. 'I might see you there.'

He was standing there, smiling, looking so handsome and gorgeous and sexy. She didn't dare make eye contact but she longed to look at him and feel that connection again.

'Flowers,' he called to her. 'I owe you flowers.'

She knew she wasn't going to go to the gardening classes because she couldn't, could she? She had a boyfriend and you didn't go round fancying other men when you did. She had to work on her and Rob. It wasn't over yet and maybe they would get through this sticky patch, if that's what it was. She was committed to him. And she was going to see it through. But flowers would have been nice.

26

THE GIRLS

Plans for the reunion were still going on. Steph had a notebook and was crossing off jobs done and writing jobs to do.

'Is this something we should be doing?' asked Melissa. 'You know a reunion. Forcing people to see each other who, if they wanted to see each other, would have stayed in contact.'

They were eating burritos in a Mexican place that Melissa knew. They were the oldest people there by a good two decades.

'You make a very good point,' said Eilis. 'Are we manufacturing fun? And isn't fun something that cannot by its very nature be manufactured. Because then you take the fun out of the fun.'

'You're getting philosophical, now, Eilis,' said Steph. 'And I don't think Sister Attracta and the Reunion Committee do philosophy.' She pushed away her burrito.

'Not eating that?' said Melissa.

'Not hungry,' said Steph. 'Just can't eat lately.'

'We'll share it, so,' said Melissa. 'Food is the only thing keeping me going these days.'

'What do you mean?'

'Well, Liam is being his usual annoying self and I just don't think there's a place for me at the paper. I don't fit in. I am trying but the paper keeps moving further and further away from me, and I can't keep up.'

'Could you leave?' said Steph. 'Go somewhere you're appreciated?'

'I don't know. Jobs aren't leaves.'

'What?'

'They don't grow on trees.'

'What about freelance?' suggested Eilis. 'Could that work?'

'What work from home all day?' said Melissa. 'Make cups of tea and not have to ever see Liam's face every again? Sounds awful.'

'So, what about it?'

'I don't think I'm brave enough,' said Melissa. 'I like the safety of an office, the security of my little desk and not having to make decisions about paying tax or looking for work. I don't think I am brave enough to be out there, like starting my own business or anything.'

She thought immediately of Cormac and wondered how he and the bakery was going. It would be opening day soon and he must be busy and excited. She was hating life without him. It was as though her right arm had been cut off. She missed him more than she could ever have imagined. She woke up every morning with a feeling that something was missing, that there was something wrong and it took her a few moment to realise what it was. And she had to go through that feeling that he had said those things to her, that he didn't want her anymore. And she began each day feeling crushed.

'I can see you running a business, Mel,' said Eilis, 'all in charge and your own boss. Like being a freelancer or something.'

'Really?' Melissa was pleased that she would have so much faith in her.

'Yeah, you'd be brilliant. You'd be in charge of you.'

'I'd like that,' said Melissa, smiling. 'I'd like that very much.'

'Better than being trapped in a hospital,' said Eilis. 'But how do you change your life? Get out of the groove you're in? Jump ship? I sometimes think that there's no point in changing anything. You just have to stick with what you know.'

'I like the thought of jumping ship,' said Steph. 'And adventures, sailing away...'

'Into the sunset,' said Melissa. Her and Cormac, sipping pina coladas and laughing.

'Sounds amazing,' echoed Eilis, thinking of Charlie, the two of them diving into the warm water. The fantasy of swimming in warm water with Rob simply didn't have the same appeal. She had to find a way of falling back in love with Rob before she got too caught up in this silly fantasy of

Charlie. But the way they had looked at her in the hospital, that intensity had been so strong that she could still feel it, it was still there, that power of connection.

Steph, meanwhile, was thinking of Rachel and how much pain she and Rick had caused her.

'I'm going to get one of these burritos to take home,' she said. 'For Rachel. She could have it tomorrow for her lunch. She'd love it.'

But a burrito wasn't going to be quite enough to make things better. She was going to have to do better than a tortilla wrap.

27

MELISSA

Mary was sitting on the armchair in the kitchen by the patio doors, looking out at the pots of lobelia that Gerry had planted. Melissa felt her throat seize up. And she thought she was going to cry, she wasn't quite sure why: was it Cormac, work? General existential angst? What?

Without Cormac to talk to, Melissa felt totally alone. She needed Cormac to help her make sense of the world, Mary's mysterious letter, everything that was happening to her at work, even the Jimbo thing. She would have loved to tell him about it, but that would be so wrong. In a previous life, she might have. No wonder he was so sick of her. Erica, she hoped, was worthy of him.

Seeing her mother brought a rush of emotion, the helplessness of it all, the wasted life, the unhappiness. A sadness that was too deep, too embedded to be relieved by a half-hearted yoga class once a week or even sinking a bottle of red. Thankfully, she had some Minstrels in her bag.

'How are you feeling, Mam? Better?' she encouraged. 'Worse? Same? Okay to middling?'

'Better than when?'

'You know... last time. The letter... you never told me what it was about.'

'No,' said Mary. 'I didn't.'

'So...?' Melissa could feel her heart beating.

Her mother shrugged, a resigned drop of her shoulders.

'Right...' Melissa didn't know what to say, becoming frustrated. She tried a different tack. 'Shall I make you a cup of tea?' she said, thinking that maybe the softly-softly approach was the better idea.

'If you want one.'

'I do.' She began to fill the kettle.

She poured the Minstrels into a bowl and laid the tea tray between them on the sofa. As Melissa sat down, she realised she was going to cry. She poured the tea and stretched out her eyes, trying not to give in to the tears forcing their way out.

'Mam?'

'Yes?'

'So, what's going on... what is it you can't tell me?'

Her mother looked at her and sucked air in sharply. 'I should have told you years ago... for God knows I had nothing to be ashamed of. I know that now.'

Melissa didn't twitch a muscle. Her mother had opened up to her and she was afraid that if she made any sudden moves, the spell might be broken.

'I died a long time ago,' her mother carried on. 'Before you were born. Does that make sense?' Melissa didn't feel able to shake her head. 'I've been alive all this time wishing I wasn't.'

'What?' She ventured. 'What do you mean?'

'It was in 1968. Life was over before anything had had a chance to begin.'

Melissa stared at her. 'What do you mean?'

'They took my baby.'

'Me?'

'Not you, my other baby,' she said, trying to keep her voice steady. 'My first. They took my baby from my arms. They took my daughter, my little girl, and left me to die.' She stopped to try and cough away the emotion.

Melissa looked at her mother, eyes wide with shock.

'You had a daughter? Before me? Another girl?'

'Yes, I had a daughter. I thought she was dead. I never thought we would meet again. But she wants to. She's alive.'

For the first time ever, there was a light behind Mary's eyes. She looked alive. Melissa felt the world was shifting. Her mother looked happy, excited. And she felt jealous. Somebody else was making her happy.

And she had a sister. It was all too much. Her hands shook as she reached for a handful of Minstrels and crammed them into her mouth. It's all I have these days, she thought, bloody Minstrels.

He mother carried on speaking. 'She wrote to me. She wants to meet. I don't know what to do. I have never been so terrified in my whole life. I can't breathe.'

'Jesus Christ, Mam, you might have said something. Why didn't you tell me years ago... it might have...?' She didn't say anymore.

It might have helped, is what she was going to say. It might have helped me.

'Once she was mine,' said Mary. 'And then she was not. She was taken from me. My baby, my daughter, was taken from me. A little girl, she was small, tiny, in my arms, and seeing her, holding her, I didn't care about anything. Nothing. Not what had happened? Not what was ahead of me, with this girl, I was free. Tara Rose I called, her. A beautiful name, don't you think?' Melissa nodded. 'But the Sisters didn't like it. Called her Frances...' Her mother's voice trailed off.

'And the father... who's her father?'

'No one.'

'No one?'

'No one worth remembering.'

'Right. Okay.' Melissa tiptoed gently through the conversation, she was desperate not to scare or startle her mother back into silence. So many questions were vying to be asked and so many feelings were fighting for primacy but she kept everything under control and remained as calm as she could. 'And you were alone and pregnant...'

'Yes.'

'How old were you?'

'Seventeen.'

'Jesus.'

'You see, I gave her away. I said I didn't want her. I told the nuns that I didn't want her. And so they took her. It was my fault.'

'How old was she when you... gave her away?'

'Six days.'

'Tiny...'

Her mother nodded. 'Yes, tiny, so tiny. I thought that I would feel relief that it was all over. I wanted them to take her and I thought it would be like it was all over, that it had never happened.'

'But...?'

'But, it was though my heart was broken. Like I was broken. I gave myself away that day. I broke myself.'

'You couldn't get her back?'

'Where would I go? I had nowhere. My mother wouldn't take me back with a baby.'

'And the baby's father?'

'He's nothing. I was alone.'

'Mam, were you *raped*?' she asked, worrying about her mother, that young girl she was, with no one to look after her. She hoped she would say no, she wasn't. That it some boy she was in love with and they didn't know what they were doing.

But her mother said nothing.

'Were you?'

'I suppose that's the word nowadays. I didn't know what was going on.'

Oh no, that was exactly what she hoped had not happened. Her mother. Defenceless, alone and raped. 'Who was it?' Melissa felt sick at the revelation.

'A friend of my father's,' said Mary, quietly. 'A big, foul-smelling friend of my father's. His breath. I will never forget the smell of his breath...'

'Oh my God. I am so sorry.'

'He's dead now,' she said, bitterly. 'What's the point of being sorry?'

'And the baby... Tara Rose... my sister... She's written to you?'

'Yes, she wants to meet me. But she's going to know that I drink... that I can only drink... it's the only thing I've ever been good at.'

'You haven't cared about me knowing that.' She knew she sounded angry and she was immediately sorry that she had brought her own feelings into this. 'Sorry, Mam,' she said. 'Sorry.'

Her mother stopped. She looked at Melissa.

'No,' she said. I'm sorry. *I'm* sorry I wasn't able to stop.'

Melissa didn't say anything. She didn't know what to feel about this Tara Rose. The person who had caused so much upset and loneliness for her mother. It wasn't Tara Rose's fault, obviously, but if she didn't exist, her mother might have been different and Melissa's life would have been so different, happier, perhaps. 'I don't understand why you never told me... all those years. It might have helped me, understand why you drank. It was pretty lonely having an alcoholic for a mother.' This was the very first time they had ever spoken about her mother's drinking but Mary said nothing and Melissa realised that she had probably got more out of her mother on this subject that she was every likely to.

'Mam... this baby. Tara Rose...'

'She's called Frances now, Frankie she calls herself.' Her mother's voice sounded cracked and strange, as though she was unused to speaking.

'This Frankie, then... how do you... how do you feel about her?'

Mary looked at Melissa straight in the eye.

'Like I've been living without my soul. They took my soul that day. They took away my ability to live.'

'But I'm your daughter too! Don't you every think about me? Haven't you ever thought about what it's been like for me? Living with you? Your silences? Your depressions? Never any affection, or pride in me. You've been a nightmare! A fucking nightmare!' That's it, she thought, sitting back, slightly shocked and slightly ashamed at her outburst, but that's it, I've finished with her forever, I've tried to make her love me, to want me, but I've never been good enough. I can never be Tara Rose and she's the one Mam wants. She felt a stillness in the air, as though all the life had been sucked out. She waited for her mother to respond.

'I'm sorry.' Her mother was suddenly crying, the cold façade that Melissa had been used to for years and years was gone, and she was faced with a mother she had never seen before. A woman who had been through almost unimaginable trial and had coped as well - or as badly - as she had.

'For what? What are you sorry for?'

'For everything. For you. For you being landed with me as a mother. Look at me. This life, who I am. I did it all badly. You, your father... Tara Rose, Frankie... I've let you all down, Melissa.' Mary wiped her eyes with her sleeve and tried to breathe. 'Oh God...' she wailed.

Melissa watched her and wished she could put her arms around her. She noticed her father had come in from the garden and was standing outside the back door, listening to them.

She wished everything had been different, that her mother hadn't gone through that terrible time, that Tara Rose hadn't been taken away, that her mother hadn't turned to the comfort of alcohol. It had been a waste of so much.

'No one can blame you,' she said. 'You did all you could. You weren't looked after, you weren't minded.'

'I shouldn't have... I shouldn't have drunk. I shouldn't drink now. I shouldn't...'

'But you did. You do.'

'Yes, I did. I do.'

'I want to stop.' Her mother, her old lined face, her cool grey eyes still filled with tears. 'But I don't know if I can. I don't want to.' She looked terrified, real fear was etched on her face. 'It's the last thing I want to do. I don't want to stop. But I can't die being this... this person.'

'Why didn't you tell me about the baby, about Tara Rose?'

'I didn't know what to say. I thought if I didn't say it, it wouldn't be true.'

'Did you think about it?'

'Every day. Every day. It would hit me the moment I opened my eyes in the morning and I would close them at night thinking about her.'

'And me? Did you ever think of me?'

'Of course I did.'

'Could have fooled me.'

'I wish it was different. I wish I had been different for you. You deserved that. A mother who wasn't broken and battered and weak like me, someone else. Anyone else.'

'You are my mother. You're all I had. All I have.' Melissa began to cry again. 'You're it, for me. I don't get to choose.' She felt a pair of small, cool hands take hers.

'I'm sorry, Melissa, I'm sorry.'

They sat there for a moment holding hands – which didn't feel quite as awkward as Melissa might have predicted – until eventually they pulled away.

'You're all I have, Mam.'

'And you are my Melissa, who deserves so much more than she was given.'

'*Your* Melissa?' My Melissa. The phrase, so simple so loving, but never said before.

'Yes, my Melissa. This wonderful girl, this strong, wonderful girl.'

'You, Melissa, helped me survive. If it wasn't for you, I would not be here.'

This was more than Melissa had ever heard from her mother. The closest to I Love You they had ever come. The intensity was too much for both of them.

'Fucking hell. Jesus. What a pair we are. No wonder dad is hiding.' She and her mother exchanged a small smile. 'By the way, how much does he know?'

'He knew back then. I told him before we got married.'

'Right. God. So everyone but me knew everything.'

'No, he didn't know... everything. Not about me. I don't think I knew it then either.'

'What?' Melissa was confused.

'I told him about the baby. He didn't mind about the baby. About Tara Rose. But he didn't know about me. What I was. Who I was.'

'What do you mean? The fact that you're...'

'A drinker.'

Melissa was silenced for a moment. Her mother had never mentioned it before. 'Mam, can I ask? When did you start drinking?'

Immediately Mary looked down, and began twisting her wedding ring around her finger, her eyes not able to meet Melissa's. Eventually she spoke: 'The night the baby was gone. I was in shock and I was given a drink of brandy. Sister Bernadine it was, who came and found me. In the scullery, crying my heart out, screaming, and she gave me a drink of this. I remember it going down, this warmth, this numbing feeling. I felt better. I felt I could cope. I remember thinking, why haven't I done this before?'

'Right.' Melissa stood up. 'I think we need another cup of tea, don't you?'

'I'm going to stop, you know. I'm going to stop drinking.'

'Good for you, Mam. Good for you.'

And at that moment, Melissa didn't care why her mother decided to get help but she was just glad that her mother had finally taken it on herself to try and beat this and maybe one good thing may come out of all of this.

'Dad?' she called. He shuffled in.

'Yes, Melissa, love?' He was worried about her, she could tell.

'Are you okay?' she said. 'Would you like a hug?'

And she went over and hugged him because Mary wasn't huggable in any way and Melissa needed one.

'You're our star,' he father, whispered in her ear. 'Our little star.'

She pulled away and saw tears in his eyes.

'Our shining star,' he said again.

'Thanks Dad,' she said. 'I'm going to put the kettle on and we are all going to have a cup of tea. Right Mam?'

'Yes, Melissa,' said Mary, who had found a packet of tissues in the drawer and was wiping her eyes. 'A nice cup of tea.'

Bloody hell. Life was one continuous drama. It just didn't stop, thought Melissa. What's next? Pestilence, plague?

'Penguin?' said her father, who had been rummaging around in the cupboard.

28

STEPH

As she turned the key in her parents' door, Steph could hear barking. Nuala and Joe were in the kitchen. With a Jack Russell.

'Who's this?' Steph reached down and stroked the little dog. He was slightly whiskery around the jaw, his brown eyes looking up at her.

'Dingle. Meet your new brother,' said Nuala, as Steph rolled her eyes like a teenager. 'He's the latest member of the Sheridan clan. We found him at the shelter. We couldn't leave him there, could we, Joe? He's an orphan.'

'An orphan?' said Steph.

'No parents. Does he, Joe?'

Joe shook his head. 'So we,' he said, 'are his new mam and dad.'

'Should I feel put out?' asked Steph, picking him up and letting him lick her face. 'Although he's a lot friendlier and nicer than I am.'

'You may not be a licker and a wagger but you have your own considerable charms, Stephanie.' And then Nuala lowered her voice. 'You're still our favourite child,' she said, covering Dingle's ears.

'I've always wanted a brother, anyway,' laughed Steph. 'I'm no longer an only child. At last you got round to it. But I thought you said no more dogs... what happened?'

'Ah... we talked about it and it was hard after John-Paul passed away. But we thought it would be good for us – get us out of the house. And who could resist this little fella?'

Steph looked down at Dingle, wagging his stubby tail. His eyes were those of someone who had escaped a terrible fate, and he was now in a place of greater safety.

'We've just been on a walk, exercising our new son,' said Joe. Nuala laughed and went over to put the kettle on.

'Now, what we all need is some tea,' said Nuala. 'And some more of those cherry bakewells. From Marks and Spencer they are. You'd know it, too. Dingle loves them.'

Steph kneeled down and stroked Dingle. He looked up at her and licked her face. She thought she might cry into the little dog's fur. Not a good start to a brand-new sibling relationship.

After pouring her heart out to Melissa and Eilis, Steph felt better. Still emotionally battered and bruised but a tiny bit soothed, nonetheless. But talking about Rick and telling them the truth of her marriage had made it all more real, and therefore finding a solution was even more pressing. Especially as she had to protect Rachel who hadn't been as immune to their problems she had hoped.

'And how's our lovely Rachel?' said Nuala, as though reading her thoughts.

'Grand, so.' Oh God, poor Rachel. No wonder she was so angry. She had every right to feel utter disdain for me, thought Steph.

But as Nuala poured out the tea, Steph noticed her hand was shaking. Joe noticed too and, without saying a word, took the tea pot from her.

'What's wrong?' said Steph.

'Nothing's wrong, why'd you ask?' said Nuala, glancing at Joe.

Now, her dad's hand wobbled and he began pouring tea onto the tray and the tea pot lid rattled.

'Something's wrong, isn't it? Tell me.' Steph looked at her mother. 'Mam?'

'Well,' said Nuala, looking at Joe, who put down the pot and covered her hand with his. They looked at each other. Dingle was on his own cushion on the seat next to her. 'Jesus! Mam. Dad. Tell me?'

'We do have some news. But we've decided it's absolutely nothing to worry about. Nothing to be upset about because I have a slight health issue, but,' she smiled a slightly false smile, 'everything is fine – or rather everything is going to be completely and utterly fine.' She spoke in a rush. 'That's what we think, isn't it Joe?'

'Dad?'

'Well...' he began. His face was white.

Nuala turned to Steph. 'I'll say it. Well,' she smiled, 'I've had some tests.'

'What?'

'I've had a bit of pain, discomfort, really. For some time. Since last year. That's why I've discovered tracksuit bottoms. Nice and comfortable.'

'Last year!' said Steph.

Nuala continued, 'Nothing to worry about, I thought. So I didn't. But then Joe here – always worrying about me – insisted I go to see Dr Finucane. And he was marvellous. Sent me into Vincent's straight away.'

'Vincent's *hospital*?' Steph was appalled. She had never known before what it was like for blood to run cold. It was like the cold tap was turned on and her whole body was suddenly chilled.

'Oh, it's lovely now. They've got a brand new entrance area. All very nice. Like being in America, or some place. And a shop that sells pens and things.'

'Yes, yes,' Steph was feeling panicky and irritated. 'But what is it?'

'It's... cancer. But noth...'

'Cancer! Jesus Christ! Mam!' She had noticed Nuala was tired but isn't everyone? It was horrible seeing Joe and Nuala getting older but she never thought they would get ill. They had been so healthy, so fit, never drank or smoked. Losing them was years away, she had never even countenanced that it might be sooner than she thought. Losing her mother? It was unthinkable.

'But I'm under a Mr Sidney Rose – isn't that a wonderful name? Sidney Rose. "Mrs Sheridan," he said, "I can't promise anything, but I am going to do my very best." And you can tell he will. Lovely hands he has. Hasn't he, Joe?'

Steph started to cry. 'What sort of cancer?' Maybe it was the kind that was curable, the easy kind. Was there such a thing?

'Cervical.' Nuala was smiling at her, desperately trying to show her that this was going to be okay. 'I'm getting the best treatment and Mr Rose says they have caught it early.' She got up and put her arms around Steph and tried to soothe her. 'We'll come through this, you'll see.' Steph realised that she should be the one comforting Nuala. 'Yes, yes,' she said, 'we will. You will,' she sobbed, trying to stop.

And then Nuala began to cry too and the two women cried in each other's arms. 'I am so sorry, loveen, I'm so sorry. It'll be fine, it will. It'll be fine. We'll get through this.'

They pulled apart and Steph looked over at Joe, who had tears falling down his face. She took her father's hand and squeezed it. Nuala smoothed back Steph's hair and wiped away her tears with her thumb.

She spoke softly. 'Come on, come now. It's just chemotherapy.'

'*Just chemotherapy*?' Steph found her voice. How to deal with this? Be brave? Presume the best? Battle, fight? Wield swords and syringes? Believe in the power of doctors and nurses and modern healthcare? 'Oh Mam!' She felt as though she was a child again and desperately looking to her mother for reassurance.

'Now, don't you be worrying about me, loveen.' Nuala held Steph's hand, their fingers curling around each other's, like they used to when Steph was tiny. 'Mr Rose, we don't call him Sidney, Mr Rose is the best in the business, isn't he Joe?'

They looked up at Joe who was leaning against the kitchen table. The colour had drained out of his face. Poor dad, thought Steph. Poor mam and poor dad.

'Well, that's what another one of his patients told me. Margaret she is and she's some months into her treatment. We've met twice now in his waiting room. Lovely woman. From West Cork. Ballydehob. Been in Dublin for years.'

'But cervical cancer. It's not... you don't... you can't...' Steph was lost for words.

'Let's just see shall we? We have to be positive.'

'Okay,' she said, trying to be calm. 'We have to just get on with this. This time next year, we will laugh about it. Won't we, Dad?'

Joe tried to arrange his face into something normal but terror was all he could show.

'Anyway, I feel like I'm in some sort of club, don't I Joe? You know, after Mary got it and then Nancy, and it was awful but they all got through it – and their hair grew back and everything.'

'This is a club you don't want to join, Mum.'

'I'm in it now, though, and we'll make the best of it.'

29

EILIS

Eilis looked at the clock. It was nearly time for the gardening club... Didn't Charlie say they had them every Saturday at five? It was quarter-to already.

Rob had left earlier, telling her he was going out with his friends, and this was after she had bought some food for them to share. It was only salmon and potatoes but she thought they could eat it in front of the television and have a night in. Together.

Right, she thought, if you not going to try, then I'm not either. There comes a time in life when going to a gardening club is the craziest thing you can do. And, she thought, not without regret, I have reached that time. Bring it on.

Her heart started thudding in her chest, as desire, adrenaline and excitement kicked in, it was beating so loudly she thought it might be audible without a stethoscope. She applied lipstick and pulled on her tightest jeans. I am officially mad, she thought, looking in the mirror. I can't help myself. She wiped the lipstick off and felt a little better, a little more like herself, although a supercharged version.

She drove to Sandycove like a woman possessed. This is wrong, she thought. She should go home. Yes, that's exactly what she should do. She should concentrate on getting her relationship back on track with Rob. Maybe they could go and see someone, therapy of some sort.

However, despite what her mind was saying, her body had other plans for her. It seemed determined to lust after a man who wore checked shirts, whose hair was unfamiliar with grooming products and had proper man-hands (big strong things, ideal for tugging roots out of the ground and who knew what else). And was able to separate his gerbera from his geraniums. It was surprisingly and refreshingly attractive.

I am succumbing to madness, she thought, as she parked close to the shop. Was it too late to go home and wait for Rob and never complain about the kettle again and try harder? That was it, she just had to try harder and then things would be better, they would slot into place. But she didn't turn around. Madness, it would appear, had never felt so good.

At O'Malley's Garden, about twenty people had gathered in the shop, sitting on garden chairs and benches that had been pushed together. Some had notebooks, others had plants in their hands, diseased specimens from their own gardens, cuttings to give others. It was like a secret world, a conference, where the like-minded met behind closed doors. Eilis felt like she belonged. There wasn't that air of mania that surrounded the rest of her life. She wanted to be part of this crew.

She looked around for Charlie, but she couldn't see him. He'd said that Kate did the talks so there was no certainty that he would be here so her turning up on the off chance of seeing him just proved what a fool she was. Had she chosen to come the one night he wasn't here? She saw his sister at the front of the shop chatting to some people and then she moved to the front of the seats and cleared her throat. Eilis sat down towards the back, now suddenly feeling stupid. What was she thinking, coming here? If Rob could see her now, joining retirees in gardening club, he would have a field day. He wasn't a fan of getting his hands dirty, anyway. He may have grown up on a farm but he had left that behind long ago.

Kate had moved to the table in front of the chairs and was tapping a trowel against a bucket for silence. 'Thanks for coming to the Gardening Club, everyone,' she said. 'The meetings are going really well. We are becoming quite a community now. We have our own Facebook page... which I know most of you are on. And our stall in the market on Sundays will be starting this week, so please come down... And we have our field trip to Mount Usher Gardens coming up... so anyone else interested, see me... but before we begin, let's have some refreshments... now, where's that brother of mine?'

And there he was. Charlie. He had a tray of glasses, a plate with biscuits on it, and a bottle of something. Just seeing him made her feel that she had made exactly the right decision coming along.

'Just before we get started,' he said, smiling at everyone. 'My own elderflower cordial. I just want everyone to try it and see what they think.'

And then Charlie spotted Eilis and stopped for a moment, his whole face lit up. 'And we have a new member, it seems,' he said. 'Eilis is joining us tonight and hopefully for longer.' He looked at her again, a smile playing broadly on his face, but his eyes had that intensity of connection and she felt it spread throughout her body, from heart, to brain, to the tips of her fingers. He didn't break eye-contact. 'She's a very good gardener and an excellent doctor,' he said, looking right at her. He was smiling but there was an intensity about him that made her feel simultaneously embarrassed and thrilled to her very core.

Twenty grey-haired heads peered around at her, all smiling. There were a few 'you're very welcomes' and a couple of 'good to meet yous'.

Charlie smiled at her and then began passing out the glasses.

'And he makes his own Elderflower cordial as well!' said an older woman in a loud voice. 'Could he be any more perfect?'

Everyone in the room laughed.

'Thank you Rosemary,' he said. 'But taste it first. It might not be any good.'

'I'm sure it will,' said another woman. 'I tasted your sloe gin at the last class and it was delicious.'

'Thanks Pauline,' he said. 'I'll have more of that soon. I'm also trying strawberry champagne this year. We'll have a taste of that in a few weeks.'

'Champagne!' said Pauline. 'I haven't had it since my wedding. 1971 it was.'

'I've got a damson tree, Charlie,' said Rosemary. 'I'll pick you some for damson gin.'

Charlie, noticed Eilis, seemed to have quite the following. She watched the clamoring for Charlie and his tray and suddenly her excitement leaked away. She felt like a waif he had picked up. He was nice to everyone; she wasn't special like she had dared to hope. She must have imagined everything. She felt like a balloon from a party a week ago. I'm just a sad, sex-starved woman in need of a little male attention. Only I believed that he might like me too. How stupid I am, she thought. He just thinks of me as another member of his coterie. She stood up, ready to sneak out.

'You're not going, are you?' A deep, low voice. Charlie!

'I think I've got to go... you know, things to do...'

'But you're here now? Stay for a little bit anyway.' He was looking at her, intently. Those blue eyes. Jesus. She stopped breathing for what seemed like minutes. She must be officially dead, she thought, and if her lungs didn't kick in again soon, she might need medical attention. Another of one of life's little ironies. Was she imagining it? Was it real?

'One for you?' He offered a glass to Eilis. 'I hope you like it. The elder-flower is from a tree in my mother's garden. It's in full bloom now.'

And... breathe. Great. Lungs working. She returned the gaze. She might just stay after all. She realised that she didn't have a choice in the matter. Her body was preventing her from behaving sensibly.

'Look,' he said. 'I'll have a sip. Just to prove it isn't poisonous.' He took a swig from his own glass. 'No, look, still alive.'

He gave her a glass. 'Slainte,' he said.

'Slainte,' she returned, feeling as though if she looked into those eyes any longer, she might be rendered to stone. She sipped. It *was* delicious. She looked up. He was smiling at her. 'It's gorgeous,' she said. 'So sweet...'

'I know,' he said. 'I can't quite believe it myself. It just turned out really well. It doesn't always. Often, the concoctions I make are undrinkable. But this is nice, which is why I brought it round for the gang this evening. I am now fantasizing about becoming a cordial billionaire. Don't encourage me.'

She laughed a little too long, a little too hard. But it was intoxicating to talk to him. She felt a bit giddy and light-headed. And totally unlike her usual self. She didn't laugh like this, or feel like this usually. She normally felt weighted down or serious. This was different. What was it? Happiness?

'Every day is like Saturday now,' he said. 'Giving up my nine-to-five was the best thing I ever did. And now I am free to make elderflower cordial and hang around with interesting people.' He looked at her. 'I'm not waiting all week for the glories of a weekend. Every day is like Saturday now.'

'That sounds wonderful,' she said. 'You're lucky.'

He shrugged. 'I don't know about that...' he said. 'But sometimes I *feel* lucky.' He laughed.

'I'm a coward, though,' she said. 'I couldn't give up my job. However much I wanted to. The thought of it just being me scares me.' And for a moment, their eyes locked again and she felt that charge between them. It was like she had been electrocuted.

'Really?' he said, looking serious. 'Something tells me that there is nothing cowardly about you at all. You have an aura of strength.'

It was quite the nicest thing anyone had ever said about her and she took a moment to let his words sink in, to enjoy the compliment. Charlie, she realised, was one of life's listeners and asked questions and nodded along, as if he was actually interested. It was unusual and lovely.

'So why gardening? When did you get the bug?' he said.

'My first house,' she said. 'It had a tiny yard and I began growing things and they *grew*! It was most surprising.' He laughed again. And then Eilis told him how gardening kept her sane; being in her little plot, tying up her roses, planting out seedlings was an antidote to the madness of her working life.

'So, you'd prefer to be fighting off black spot and destroying slugs...' he said.

'No, it's not that. I love being a doctor,' she said. 'I love helping people. Or I did. God, I feel awful saying that. It's not that I hate helping people, I just don't want to anymore. Or I want to take a break, I just don't know. I have become aware...' she stopped, searching for the right words. 'I'm just aware of my limits, how little, we mere mortals, us doctors, can do. And once you realise that, it's terrifying. Like stage fright. Or like you are on a tightrope and you look down and see the drop. You just think I can't do this. I'm going to fall.'

I'm babbling now, she thought. Babbling like a mad woman. A nice man asks a few questions, seems to listen intently as if what she had to say *mattered*, and I open up. What will I tell him next? The details of my menstrual cycle? In spite of herself, she carried on talking.

'Most doctors don't allow themselves to look down, to see the drop,' she said. 'But I did and now... now I don't even trust myself anymore.' She could almost feel her voice beginning to break. Why do I always make a show of myself? I'm going to be blubbing in a moment. Don't be nice to me, she was thinking, don't be nice or I will be a bawling mess. She took a slurp of the elderflower cordial.

'Compassion fatigue,' he said. 'That's what it's called, isn't it? God, you doctors are amazing. Jesus. What you guys do. Dealing with all that, day in day out. No wonder you're tired of it.'

'I am,' she was nodding now, grateful he understood. Being tired of caring was something that you couldn't tell other people, certainly not other doctors. She had never admitted this to anyone, not even Rob. 'I *am* tired of it. Oh I don't know.'

'I know it won't solve your problem,' he said, passing the plate to her. 'But have one of these,' he said. 'A cheese straw. To go with the cordial. It's the best I can do at short notice. Sorry.'

'They'll help, I'm sure' she said, taking one. 'Did you make these as well?'

'From a packet,' he said. 'Cheese straws might be a bit of a stretch for me.'

'They're delicious.' She held out her glass. They clinked.

'And here's to you,' he said. 'Here's to you being brave... doctors and nurses. I take my hat off to you.'

They looked at each other. It was a look of recognition, deep recognition, a connection as though he was really *seeing* her. She had no other way of describing it. Strangely, she thought she was going to cry, she could feel this surge of emotion spread across her body. She had found someone who understood her, and it felt amazing. Whatever happened, this was enough. She was happy knowing one person on the planet was like her. After a lifetime of feeling like an outcast, she knew she wasn't alone.

'Fruit trees, people.' Kate was standing up in front of the rather motley crew, tapping the bucket again with the trowel. 'How to grow fruit trees...'

And then, as she moved to sit down, Charlie whispered in her ear: 'Join us in the pub afterwards. Gogginses, across the road. We all go. It's become quite a tradition.'

She sat down, and tried to listen to the talk but her mind was pounding with so many thoughts. Mainly of Charlie. She kept glancing at him. The straight nose, the hair curling over his ear, the way he tried to get comfortable on the small metal chair.

Once, he looked around and caught her eye and smiled at her. It was the sweetest smile she had ever seen. Am I fantasizing? Am I projecting? She smiled idiotically back. Stop being such a fool, she thought. And stop being such a coward and deal with your life. I'm not going to the pub, she thought. No way.

No, I am going, just for one. I'm driving so I won't stay long. I'll just be sociable for once.

No, I'll go home. Nice early night. And it was decided. She wasn't going. She was almost disappointed with how grown-up and sensible she was, but it was the right thing to do.

But as soon as the talk was over, she found herself walking with the others to the pub across the road. I'm just a pawn, she thought, a pawn in an evil game my body is playing with me. Surely this proves I'm not normal? I have no control over my body. But for once, she didn't care. She was going to the pub. Caution was being thrown to the wind.

But in the pub, Charlie was talking to Pauline and Rosemary and some of the others. He had waved at her, but she found herself cornered by George, probably the nicest man in the whole wide world but who had a tendency to go on a bit. And we all have that problem sometimes, thought Eilis, thinking of her recent babbling, so I can't complain.

'So that must have been in '85 or '86,' George was saying. 'And it wasn't the first time. And not the last, I can tell you. You see it gets hold of you, and destroys everything in its path. It's not letting go. Once it gets its claws into you, you may as well give up.' He shook his head, caught up in his terrifying memories.

'That's awful, George,' said Eilis, feeling his pain.

'I nearly lost everything, I did,' he said, emotion in his voice. 'Nothing was untouched by it. I must have sweated for months and months. In the end, I had to use chemicals. It was the only way.'

For a moment, Eilis allowed herself to imagine George, who must have been in his eighties, as an Arnold Schwarzenegger-type, muscles and napalm. He took a sip of his half-pint.

'So, George,' she said. 'Did the chemical warfare work?'

'It came back again,' he said, his eyes taking on a hardness, a determination. 'And this time, it could tell I meant business.'

'What did you do?'

He looked around, making sure no one was listening.

'Fire,' he said. 'I burnt the little bugger.'

'Wow, that's serious.' She was impressed. 'Did it work?'

'Too right it did. Haven't had a problem with Japanese knotweed since. My Maureen called me Sam for years afterwards. You know, Fireman Sam. It did make us laugh. Fireman George,' he chuckled.

Eilis glanced over at Charlie and caught him looking back. He held up a hand to wave and beckoned her to join them. But she felt foolish and silly, hankering after someone who was effectively a stranger. She should go home.

She said goodbye to George, wishing him well in his one-man campaign to rid the planet of Japanese knotweed and slipped out, not even looking back at Charlie. Life isn't meant to be fun and games and fancying people and thinking about their hands and what is underneath their shirts... she stopped herself again, vowing to stay clear of the garden shop.

Anyway, it was only weeks to go until she and Rob were going to Greece, returning to the place they went to last year. Good food, sunshine, the Aegean. Last year had worked well; they had got into a routine where Rob would run in the early morning while Eilis went to the market and then they spent the days reading, sunning themselves and eating. R&R would make a very nice changed from A&E; even if she had the feeling she might have a better time with Charlie than with Rob.

She drove away from O'Malley's Garden and didn't look back.

30

STEPH

Steph was at home, looking at the Sean McSweeney painting Mrs Long had given her on her last day working at the gallery, before she, pregnant and fuelled by the self-belief of youth, married Rick. Steph loved the painting so much when it hung in the gallery and had stood for ages and ages staring at it, and soaking it up that, eventually, Mrs Long said she couldn't stand her 'mooning' anymore and presented it to her when Steph brought her the last cup of Lapsang she would every make for her.

She cried when she opened it. The sea was glinting in the background, a field of yellow lilies to the fore. It was a painting which expressed freedom, or a shimmering and wonderful world. And that's how everything seemed in those days, excitement just to be alive. Looking at it now, the shimmering light of the Sligo bogs, the sea beyond, she was reminded how reckless and careless she had been with her freedom.

Mrs Long didn't come to the wedding. She was on her annual pilgrimage to Florence which Steph was relieved about. At least, she wouldn't have Mrs Long and her disapproving eyebrows watch her walk up the aisle.

'All right?' whispered Joe. They were standing at the back of the church, on her wedding day, everyone craning to get a look at her in that ridiculous dress.

'Yes, Dad...'

'You know,' he spoke, urgently, 'are you sure? Because if you aren't, we can just walk away.' He smiled gently, his eyes reaching hers, locking in. This was her last chance. She could, she knew, just walk away. She could... But she didn't.

Once they were married, the hints she had about Rick became real. When Rachel was about two, Rick said something to her and she didn't answer. She remembered it so clearly because Rachel had a cough and couldn't sleep and Steph had been to the doctor's. And then Rick asked her a question and Steph didn't really hear him, she was so busy thinking about Rachel. She had heard him but it hadn't registered he had spoken. It was so hard to explain, but whatever it was, she hadn't answered him.

'Steph!' The shout made her jump. 'You never fucking listen, do you!' He had been drinking a glass of whiskey and he threw it full whack against the wall. It splashed over everything, including Steph, and bits of glass ricocheted through the air. It was a miracle that she wasn't hurt.

'Now,' he said. 'Now, look what you made me do. Listen,' he hissed. 'Just listen in future.'

He poured himself another glass and walked out, leaving Steph to clear everything up with shaking hands, before rushing in to see if Rachel was alright. And the next day, the excuses: tired, stressed at work, bit too much to drink.

'Yes, yes,' she said. 'Totally fine. Don't worry.' But inside she was thinking he was mad. People didn't behave like that, did they? And yet it carried on. There could be months and months between an episode, even years, but then there it would be.

And he was still doing it. She had never got used to it. The shaking never got any less.

She was lost in thought, and still staring at the painting when she heard Rachel coming downstairs. It was time to tell her about Nuala, she couldn't keep it from her any longer. She had been dreading telling her but she wanted to at least not keep this a secret, however painful it was, however much she wanted to protect Rachel. Full disclosure was the only way. She'd already let Rachel down enough.

'Good morning, sweetheart. Would you like some juice? I've got pancakes.'

'Not hungry,' said Rachel.

'Eat something, though. Please? Look, I've got those nice muffin things you like.'

'Don't bother, mum, I'm not hungry.' Rachel looked angrily at her mother. Things were still strained after Rachel caught her reading her diary. Steph had tried to apologise again but Rachel was still angry, the violation of her privacy was going to take a long time to get over.

'Come on, you've got time. We'll just have something together. There's something I want to talk to you about...'

'No.' Rachel swung around, ready to leave.

'Don't leave. Please don't leave,' Steph begged her. 'Let's not be like this.' She reached out to her, grabbing Rachel's shoulder, in an attempt to pull her back. Rachel grabbed her hand and pushed it away, almost disgusted. 'I need to talk to you.' Steph stopped. 'There's no right way of telling you this but... it's Granny... she's ill. Cancer. Cervical. I thought you should know.'

Rachel stopped, eyes horrified, staring at her mother.

'Of course I should know!' Rachel screamed at her. 'Or were you thinking of not telling me, like I am some non-person who doesn't deserve to be told things and all you stupid adults just keep fucking up their lives and expect me to deal with it.' And then she began to cry. 'Is she... is she dying?'

Steph hesitated. Nuala and Rachel had always been so close. 'I hope not,' she said simply. 'She's in really good hands and everyone is incredibly positive.'

Rachel headed to the front door.

'Where are you going?'

'Away from you!' Rachel shouted.

She could never get it right. She wished that Rachel would turn to her for comfort, would talk to her. They were both going to have to face this together. Instead Rachel turned to her grandparents.

An hour later, she received a text from Joe

Just to let you know that Rachel is with us. She's going to have a bite to eat and I'll drop her back later.

And when Rachel got home, she stayed in her room, refusing to come out. Steph knew she had to give her time.

In the end, Steph, needing fresh air and space to think, went out for a late-night walk, something she often did on her own, fresh summer air, the quiet of an evening when all the other people were at home, watching television, making dinner and spending time with their families. What went wrong here, thought Steph. Who's to blame? She knew she had to shoulder much of the blame; she was guilty of so many things. And she and Rick hadn't ever been right but they had brought Rachel into this mess and kept her there. Had that been fair? And now with Nuala so ill, she was threatened with the loss of the one person who Steph relied on, the one person who was always there unchanging, steady and loving. Without her, the world was a far lonelier place.

When she got home, she saw that Rachel's light was off, her curtains closed, but Rick appeared, eyes glittering, from his study, looking, Steph realised, worse for wear, and immediately she felt the cold-blooded fear. Wrong place, wrong time. If she had come home earlier, or even later, he might not have caught her.

'Steph?' he said.

She looked away and didn't answer. She had suddenly enough. Don't speak to me again, she thought, don't you speak to me again. She turned to face him, furious.

'Don't ignore me.'

'I wasn't... I...' Leave me alone, she thought. Just leave me alone.

'So,' he said. 'We should talk about Rome.' He was goading her, she knew it. He wanted an argument. He wanted to let off steam. 'What happened... what you did.' He laughed in her face.

'What did I do?' she said, taking the bait, now riled.

'You made a show of yourself and a show of me,' he said. She could smell his breath. 'Do you want to apologise?'

'No.' She knew she had been dragged into this argument and now wanted to get out. She didn't have the strength to get into this, with him, at this moment in her life. She wanted out. From everything. She looked down, not knowing what to do. Maybe she should just beg forgiveness and maybe, *maybe*, he would move on.

'What did you say?'

'I said I have nothing to aplogised for. You should say sorry to me.' Why did I say that, she thought. Just get away from him. She began to move for the door.

'Me? To you? *You*?' He laughed. 'You are nothing. Just a little stay-at-home. What exactly do you contribute? I think we should stop the pretence, don't you?'

'What pretence?'

'That you are a good mother, that you are such a good mother.' He laughed. 'We all know the truth. And the house! There are things everywhere. Your mess! Your shoes in the hall, bits on the work surface. I came home earlier and the house was a tip.'

'It wasn't,' she said, but wishing she had put away her shoes. But the house was always immaculate, she knew. He always did this, mentioned how good or bad a mother she was or talked about the state of the house. It was the latent or blatant misogynist in him. He was pathetic. You have no right to do this to me, she thought. She summoned her inner strength, raising herself up.

'You're sleeping with Miriam,' she hissed. 'And Angeline. And I am sure some other poor deluded woman who thinks you're the bee's knees.'

'So?' he said, giving her a death stare, not unlike the one Rachel was able to flash at times.

'So,' she said, faltering a moment, 'you shouldn't be. You're married.'

'To you, yes.' He came right up to her and pressed his face into hers. She could see the sweat glistening on his forehead. 'Waste of fucking space you are. No wonder I seek pleasure elsewhere. Any sane, red-blooded man would. You are a disappointment. And it's not just me who would say it.' He didn't laugh but stared at her, his face grimacing, looking at her as though she disgusted him, but she could smell the beer on his breath, see his high colour in his face.

She turned to go. Ignoring this verbal abuse was the only to handle it, wondering what else he would throw at her to keep her emotionally engaged in this dysfunctional marriage. But then she turned to him. '*Miriam*?' she said. 'For God's sake, Rick. She's our neighbour, the mother of our daughter's best friend. Are you so *desperate*? Are you so sad?'

For a moment, he looked shocked. She watched his face change from surprise to anger and then he shrugged. 'You're the one who's desperate,' he slurred. 'And you made the biggest show of yourself in Rome. Everyone was laughing at you. You stupid cow.' He stood right up against her to do what? Was he trying to intimidate her? Was he trying to show her that he could hurt her if he wanted to?

Steph took both his hands and pushed his shoulders away from her with as much force she could manage. He staggered back against the wall and then, suddenly, like a cobra, he was right in her face again. He grabbed her and thrust her full-force downwards so she hit herself against the corner of the radiator and landed sprawled on the floor.

'Don't you ever fucking touch me again, you little bitch,' he said. 'Just don't.'

And then he was gone, back into his study.

Never again, she vowed, as she stood up. Never again will he talk to me like that. She felt as though her whole marriage had been clouded by insanity and confusion and suddenly, beyond there was her future, one for her and Rachel, which was filled with clarity and sanity. It was within touching distance.

31

MELISSA

'How EU are you?' Melissa read out. 'What does that even mean?'

'Does drinking wine count?' said Jimbo. 'If it does, then I am. Very. And what's more, I don't care what country it comes from. That's how EU I am.'

'And, look, brilliantly, it tells you what character you are most like, depending on your answers: Amelie, Heidi or Fionnuala? Who the hell is Fionnuala? Is she a *thing*?'

'*Connemara Central*, you know, the Irish language version of The Wire? *Everyone* is watching it. Apart from you.' Jimbo shrugged nonchalantly. 'And me.'

'Jimbo, this is serious,' said Melissa. 'Answer the question. When going out on a date,' she read, 'do you a) wear Birkenstocks and drink beer, b) wear matching lingerie and order a glass of champagne, or c) feck what you wear and drink everyone under the table?'

'I don't.'

'What?'

'Go on dates. Whatever they are.'

If there was any residual awkwardness between them, they were both good at hiding it. They both behaved as though nothing had happened. Obviously, thought Melissa, they both valued their relationship as allies far more than dealing with an awkward sexual encounter.

'This is *hypothetical*,' said Melissa. 'It's meant to be fun. You should be enjoying yourself. Aren't you? Try again.'

'Hmmm.' Jimbo gave it real consideration. 'B?'

Melissa made a mark on the page. 'Question two. When,' she read on, 'on a night out do you a) go to see a strange experimental film in some dark and forgotten part of town, b) sip a glass of wine and get in bed by ten or c) find a lock-in and forget your own name? But how could you forget your own name,' said Melissa. 'It's written at the top, it's either Heidi, Amelie or Fionnuala. Oh, I'm taking this way too seriously.'

'What's wrong with you, anyway?' said Jimbo. 'Are you not impressed and joyous about our latest edition? Are you not celebrating this departure into the land of levity and brevity?'

'No,' she said. 'I'm not.' She was thinking about Cormac, really. On her way to work, she had bumped into Nora, Walter's wife. Nora massively pregnant was with little Axel bashing things with a small wooden sword. Small but deadly, as it turned out.

'So you've heard about the amazing Erica, then,' said Nora. 'The yoga queen.' Axel jabbed the sword into Melissa's calf. It may as well be my heart, she thought, dully.

'Yes,' she said, smiling through the pain. 'Wish I could do yoga but I never got the flexible gene.'

'Nor did I,' said Nora. 'I can't pick up anything from the floor. And it's not just this.' She pointed to her massive belly. 'This is just from eating,' she said. 'I've been mainlining cheese and onion for eight months now. I think the baby is going to come out with a bag of crisps in its hand. That's not going to go down well in hospital.'

'Just pretend they're organic. Then it's all right, isn't it?' Melissa said. 'So, this Erica, what exactly is amazing about her?' she said, casually.

'Well, she's kind of not of this planet. I know she's American and all that, but she just makes me feel all mortal and ordinary.'

'Wow.' Melissa didn't know what else to say.

'You'll like her,' said Nora. 'And Cormac seems happy.'

'That's great, that's really great.' Melissa was working hard to try and appear normal but she felt terrible. Was it too dramatic to feel as though her heart was being wrenched out and eaten by some monster?

'So, listen,' said Nora, 'what's new with you?'

Apart from no longer having a heart and lying here bleeding to death in the middle of town? Melissa shrugged, unable to think of anything that she could impart standing in the middle of Grafton Street, surrounded by buskers, shoppers, moving statues and being repeatedly jabbed by a tiny sword. 'Something will come to me, I promise,' she said, making a joke of her silence. 'Um...'

Nora laughed. 'I'm like that. By the way,' she said, 'will you come to our fortieth? Walt and I are having a joint one. You know, before the baby comes... there'll be cheese and onion crisps,' she added winningly. 'And cocktail sausages. I'll text you the details. But please come and you'll get to meet Erica.'

'I would love to meet Eric. I mean *Erica*,' said Melissa. 'I could show her a few of my yoga moves. It involves balancing a crisp on my nose and then letting it drop into my mouth. Takes years of practice *that* does. I had to go to India to learn it.'

They said goodbye, with Melissa promising to be there but not knowing if she would or could. After all, she and Cormac weren't friends, anymore, were they? They were officially over, even though they were never officially under.

She wandered along to work, deep in thought. Who was this Erica? She was lucky, that's who she was. She had Cormac and Melissa didn't. She was the one who received funny little texts from him during the day, went together to the cinema or ate ice creams on the pier. She missed him, so dreadfully.

She was struck by how selfish she had been. She had tried to section Cormac off and claim him as hers and no one else's. And it had worked for a time, but it hadn't been fair on him, keeping him close but not too close and now he had slipped his moorings. And he was right to do it, to get away from her. And he might be happy with this Erica. She might be the most wonderful person in the world and he might be ecstatically happy. Didn't she want that for Cormac?

Yes, she thought. I want him to be happy. Whoever this Erica is, then please let her be the most amazing woman on earth, that's what he deserves.

I wish it was me, she thought. I want to be his and I want him to be mine. I want to hold his hand, put my arms around him and feel his body close to mine. I want to love him, but I had my chance and I blew it. So, please, make Erica amazing. For Cormac, even if it broke Melissa's heart.

'Earth calling Smelissa!' It was Jimbo. 'Too dazzled by the brilliance of the new-look paper to connect with real human beings?'

She plugged back in and deployed the indignation button. 'You're a real human being?' she said, shocked. 'Is that right?'

Jimbo took a slurp of tea. 'I bet you did it, though.'

'What?'

'The quiz. I bet you completed the quiz.'

'Of course I fecking did! On Saturday. It was the first thing I did! But that's not the point.'

'And?'

'And what?'

He sighed patiently. 'And *just* how EU are you? Which are you?'

Melissa mumbled her reply. She had done it.

'What was that? I can't hear you.'

'Fionnuala.'

Jimbo laughed. 'I *knew* you'd been the Irish colleen. And there you pretend to be a woman of the world.'

'Melissa!' It was Liam, calling from across the office. 'A word, please!'

She rolled her eyes at Jimbo, walked over and knocked on the door.

'Come in! Come in! Sit yourself down.' Liam was in a particularly ebullient mood. 'So who are you?'

'Excuse me?'

'Heidi or Amelie? Which one?'

'What?' Melissa pretended to look utterly perplexed.

'The quiz! Our weekend splash! Our new fun-loving weekend paper!' He was laughing now he had seen through her bad acting.

'Neither.' Melissa spoke quietly. It was a bit bloody disappointing to be Fionnuala, whoever she was. She would, however, have been quite pleased to be Amelie, nice and French.

'You're Fionnuala?' laughed Liam. 'Ha! Dublin 4, my arse. You see, we've all got a bit of the West of Ireland in us, there's a bit of Connemara in you, I can tell.'

'It's hardly scientific, though, is it?'

'Exactly. That's the fecking point. It is what you might call a bit of fun.'

Melissa tried to look bored and began studying a picture on the wall. It was a framed yellowing page from the Farmer's Journal. The headline was: 'Cow gives birth to triplets'.

Liam followed her gaze. 'My dad,' he said. '1984 that was. We were famous.'

Melissa nodded. 'Triplets. Impressive. Did you name them?'

'Myself and my sister called then Keren, Siobhan and Sara.'

'Nice names.'

'Bananarama, you see.'

'I too was around for that golden age of music, you know.'

'We were fans, you see.'

'Obviously. And did your dad like the names?'

'No. But eventually he began calling them Keren, Siobhan and Sara. Persuasive we were, my sister and I.'

'I bet you were.' He hadn't called her in to talk about calf triplets, had he?

'She's worse than I am,' he said. 'In Silicon Valley now. Making millions with some start-up.' He shrugged. 'But I wouldn't swap grimy old Dublin for the sunshine of California for anything.'

'Really?'

'I'm lying, of course. I would sell my own mother for a bit of Californ-i-a.'

'Of course.'

'I've yet to receive the invitation. But it's imminent. I can feel it. It's in the post.'

'Don't hold your breath,' said Melissa. 'Anyway, you're the type that just goes lobster in the sun. You wouldn't blend in with the beautiful people.'

He pretended to look hurt. 'Melissa! Ouch.'

She rolled her eyes.

'So,' he said. 'Back to the quiz. Now, let's move on from last week's edition, diverting and fascinating as it was, there are some changes on the horizon.'

'More changes? What's next? Knitting patterns? Free relic of the True Cross for every reader? Cut out and wear mask of Colin Farrell on one side, the Pope on the other, depending on age and preferences?'

'Now, *those* are ideas,' said Liam. 'Why on earth don't you come up with good ideas like those at the editorial meetings, instead of all that worthy shite?'

Melissa threw her eyes to heaven and tutted while Liam, blithely, carried on. 'Now, I wanted to talk to you about the paper... and our direction.'

'Is this quiz where we are going?' asked Melissa. 'Okay, so I get your point about fun but it's not exactly *journalism*. What about my Breadline Lives? They are getting some amazing reactions. They are illuminating the real issues in this country.'

'Melissa, sweetheart, we work in a business. No one pays us to write worthy fucking articles that no one reads. Your last Breadline Life thing was, dare I say it, a little bit dull. Worthy, yes. Important, undoubtedly. Well-written, of course. But, let's face it? A fun read over the old cornflakes it maketh not.'

He ignored her eye-roll of irritation. 'Right! So, I have news. The feature section is reducing in size. We are going to be a tabloid pull-out every Saturday. There will be no room for worthiness on the paper, I'm afraid. I like your work and we want opinions and strong arguments. But I don't want any of that soft shite anymore. Well, not on the front page. Okay?'

'What exactly do you mean by *soft shite*?'

'We're changing, Melissa. We have to. Our circulation went down seven whole per cent last year, and the year before that, and the year before that. We are losing readers big time. This is serious. No one wants worthy stuff about hermaphrodites or multi-sexuals or whatever. But we do know what people do like and what they want to read; fun, gossip, food, cakes, what's on TV, who is shagging who, who has the fattest dog, who ate too many pies, who doesn't eat enough, that kind of thing.'

Melissa said nothing.

'So,' said Liam, 'I can see that you are overwhelmed by the brilliance of all this. So, are you in?'

'Or what? Out?' asked Melissa.

'Don't say anything now,' he said. 'But is this part of your future? Are you willing to change?'

'Do I have a deadline?'

'See, what I love about you, Melissa. You are a born journalist. Just mull it over, take your time. Try writing differently. Melissa, what about "Me and My Dog – celebs and their pooches".'

Melissa was speechless. 'Pooches?'

'What would you like to write about? What's this week's fascinator?'

'It's... it's about a woman...'

'Of course!' He punched the air.

'...who is suffering from mental health issues.'

'And?'

'She's deaf.'

'And that, my dear, is exactly why you won't be on page one of features this Saturday because no one wants to read about deaf, depressed, un-famous lesbians.'

'She's not a lesbian!'

'She, my dear, very probably is,' said Liam. 'I'll bet my house on it.'

'Jesus!'

'Yes?' He smiled maddeningly.

'I'm going!' Melissa pulled the door of his office in a half slam which she thought better of and caught her fingers in the handle.

She stood there. Oh My God, the man was an idiot. A total eejit. But from inside the office, Liam was whistling. Melissa could have sworn it was 'Robert De Niro's Waiting'.

32

EILIS

At last the holiday had arrived. Two weeks away, in the sun, just the two of them. Since the garden club, she had done quite well in banishing all her silly fantasies of Charlie from her head and instead dedicated herself to thinking lovingly of Rob, how good he was and how lucky she had been to have such a steadfast companion all these years. He may be spreading his wings and socializing more but then so was she, meeting up with Melissa and Steph, and her solitary gardening sessions. But just that morning her good intentions had slipped and she had driven past O'Malley's Garden, simultaneously peering out while trying to slide down in the seat. It was a miracle she wasn't arrested. Charlie was nowhere to be seen. A sign, she thought, a sign that I have been foolish in my fantasies. Right, she thought. Greece, here we come.

She spent the afternoon getting ready; washing, ironing, packing, loading up her Kindle. She allowed herself to feel excited. However, Rob was acting as if it wasn't happening, as though he had all the time in the world.

'Have you got everything ready, Rob?' she said. 'I can wash things for you. I need to put another load in.'

'I'll sort it later.' He sounded tetchy. But this was becoming normal. The middling of age, perhaps?

'I can't wait for the holiday,' she said, trying to get him to smile and soften. 'It's just what we need. A break from everything, from work and...'

'Yes,' he said shortly. 'It should be nice.'

'A bit of sun... and some good books, I can't wait.' She pointed to her tower of paperbacks. 'I can't remember the last time I read a whole book. I think I might have forgotten how to read.'

'No, I don't think you have, Eilis. People don't just forget how to read,' he said.

'I know, I was just joking...'

'Anyway,' he said. 'I'm going out. Have a good evening. And I'll see you...'

'Whenever.' It was early to go out, she thought, but he was a big boy, she wasn't in charge of him.

'Whenever, right!' he laughed.

'So, where're you going?' She wondered when he was going to pack. The flight was at two the next afternoon. She supposed he would still have time.

'Into town, with Michael. A last night before the holiday.'

'That sounds nice.'

'We all need friends. You have yours and I have mine.'

'Absolutely.' But, she thought, I don't see mine as much as you see yours.

'So... I'll be off.'

'Okay...' She leaned over to give him a kiss but it was awkward as he didn't realise she was going in for one and he put his arms up and they got into a bit of a tangle. It was like he was pushing her away.

They laughed. 'That went well, didn't it?' she said.

'I didn't know what you were doing.' Rob was smiling. 'Next time give me a warning.'

'Will do. I'll send you a text.' They laughed again.

Even though the kiss had gone very wrong, the warmth between them had returned a little bit. Eilis felt better, as though everything was okay again or had the promise to be. And they had Greece to go to... that would sort everything out. Holidays always did.

'Mam,' she said out loud to the photo in the kitchen, 'everything's going to be okay, isn't it?'

There was no answer.

'I wish you hadn't died, Mam,' Eilis. 'I wish you were here.'

The house was empty and quiet. Brigid was nowhere to be heard.

She had to stop thinking about her mother. She *had* to get over it. She wanted to live a life without the death of her mother always there.

'How do I say goodbye to you, Mam,' she spoke out loud again. 'How do I move on?'

Just let go... she thought she heard a voice. *Just let go.*

'But I can't let go. I don't want to let go. You're all I have.'

Just let go. Let go.

Rob didn't come home that night but reappeared at ten o'clock the next morning. She was getting anxious by then and was already wondering what to do when the police rang and said they had found his body.

She heard his key in the door and raced into the hall.

'Where have you been?' she demanded. 'We've got to be at the airport in two hours.'

He held up his hand to silence her. 'I'm not going,' he said.

'What?' She looked at him but he refused to make eye contact. 'What Rob? What are you trying to say?'

'I... I don't want to go on holiday.' He walked into the kitchen, with Eilis hot on his heels, heart thumping.

'Since when has someone not wanted to go on holiday? How is that even possible? What do you mean? You don't want to go? To Greece? With me? What's wrong? Is it me, you don't want to go with me?' She could hear herself beginning to screech.

'I'm sorry. I just can't go. I just can't.'

'Are you *serious*? I can't go on my own. I can't just go without you. People don't *do* that – what you are doing? What the actual fuck?'

'I'm sorry. But I can't. And I won't. Please believe me when I say I am sorry. I am really incredibly sorry, but I can't do this.'

'But we've paid for it. It's all paid for!' Stay calm, she thought, he's having a breakdown. *I'm* having a breakdown. 'Come on.' She modulated her voice, as though speaking to a nervous horse. 'We'll have a lovely time,' she pleaded. 'We will relax. You will eat nice food, swim in the sea, read some books. It's what you need. What we both need.'

'I can't.' He sounded final. 'Go on your own. But there's no way I'm going.' He walked out of the kitchen and a moment later, she heard the front door closing. He was gone.

Later, she emailed the owner of the villa and explained that, due to illness, they would not be able to travel. The owner was very sorry and she hoped that Rob would be feeling well again soon, but she was sure they understood but there was nothing she could do about returning their money.

Eilis spent the day watching the clock. We would be driving to the airport now, she thought. And parking. Now, we'd be checking in. And then going for a cup of tea. We'd be sitting on the plane, now, ready for take-off. I'd be reading and Rob would have his eye mask on, ear plugs in. And now we'd be getting off the plane, that first blast of heat after the chill of Ireland. But there was Eilis sat in an empty house.

Rob came home but didn't speak to her for the rest of the weekend. Granted he was barely around, but whenever Eilis tried to speak to him, he would simply say, 'I can't talk.'

She volleyed between fear for his mental health and raging hatred. It had better be a nervous breakdown, she thought, because if it was anything else, she might have to kill him. But without wrestling him to the ground lion/gazelle style, her options were limited. You can't make someone who very obviously doesn't want to talk, talk, and even though she was confused and hurt, she knew she couldn't force him to.

This is punishment, she thought. Punishment for even thinking of someone else. I deserve this horribleness.

Rob carried on his normal routine, he went into work as though nothing had happened, just cancelled his leave, patients were booked in by his secretary and he just carried on.

Meanwhile, Eilis stayed at home, scared to leave the house, in case anyone asked why she wasn't bobbing and bathing in the Aegean. Initially, she stayed indoors, trying to work out what had gone wrong, and then, eventually, ventured into the garden, wearing her mother's old cardigan and weeding her beds so beautifully, she would have won awards. She hadn't called Steph and Melissa, they assumed she was in Greece, she carried the shame and embarrassment alone.

On the day before she was meant to be returning to work, the weather was not gardening weather. It was summer in the rest of Europe, but Ireland, sentimentally, was clinging to winter. She got in the car and went for a drive, wondering what to do. The rain was coming down in sheets, she saw one old woman being blown off her feet as she walked across a zebra crossing, umbrellas were being forced inside out and down the rain came. She realised that she was close to Sandycove and close to O'Malley's Garden.

Slug pellets, she decided, were something she could not live without another moment. The lashing rain meant the streets were deserted and she parked and ran into the shop, the bell jangling, as she stood inside the door soaked through.

Charlie appeared from the back office, behind the till. She wished she hadn't given up on him, this, the gardening club. She didn't care if it was just a silly fantasy, it had sustained her. Real life was so rewarding.

'Eilis!' He looked delighted. 'We haven't seen you for a while. Have you been away?'

She hadn't told him about the holiday so she felt relieved that she didn't have to lie with him. 'No, no,' she said. 'Just working.'

He nodded, understandingly. 'What a day,' he said. 'It's not one for gardening.'

'No... but I needed a few things for the weekend. Slug pellets and... and...' You, she thought. Slug pellets and you. An exquisite juxtaposition. Never, in the history of love and romance had slug pellets played such an important role.

'I'll get them for you.' He went over the back of the shop and handed her a packet. 'These are the best. Organic.'

'Thanks.' She tried to look at the packet but she wasn't really thinking. He could have handed over a bag of sherbet lemons for all she cared.

'Anything else?'

'I can't think.' Her mind had gone blank.

'A cup of tea? I have the kettle on.' He motioned to the back of the shop to the little office.

'Okay,' she said, hesitating and wondering what she was doing.

He smiled, he looked so happy. And *she* felt happy being around him, he was a life-force, someone it was good to be around. It was the first time in two weeks that she had felt like this, not the constant dread that something had gone wrong, but there was the feeling that something was most definitely *right*.

'Take a seat,' he said, pointing at a little chair. Charlie began boiling a kettle and putting two teabags into mugs.

Eilis had no idea that offices could be such lovely places. There were old, faded cushions on the chairs; a vintage-looking lamp on a desk with a laptop, surrounded by papers. There were succulents in pots on the table and two pots of African violets. A small stove was glowing with burning logs. It was practically the nicest place she had ever been.

There were books and books on gardening. And on the wall, a signed photo of Monty Don and a framed poster of a quote.

Life is for daily adventures, cold ocean swims and
interesting conversations and deep kisses.

She read it out loud.

'Is that your creed?' she asked. 'Is that the rule you live your life by?'

He shrugged, slightly embarrassedly. 'Kind of. It's my "dance like no one is watching", I suppose.' He sighed. 'Ah, I don't know. It's a bit corny but I bought it years ago, when I was an idealistic student. And then, when I was giving up the law, I found it in a box in my Mam's house, and it kind of summed up what I was thinking... what I wanted. It's a bit cheesy.'

'I suppose one doesn't have an adventure *every* day,' she said. 'That might be asking a bit too much.'

'But,' he said, '*strange* things do happen every day, *interesting* things. You've just got to notice them, be alive to them.'

She thought about it. He was right. 'It's too easy to just get through your day, isn't it?' she said. 'You know, just getting from bedtime to bedtime.'

'I like strange things,' he said, smiling. 'And strange people. They are the best kind, the good strange. Normal-strange, if you know what I mean?'

She did. 'I'm strange-strange,' she said. 'I'm working towards normal-strange.'

'Me too,' he said, placing a mug in front of her. 'I'm hoping their normalness will rub off on me.'

She looked at him, the crinkles at his eyes, the greying hair, and the brown-freckly forearms. She wanted to reach over and touch him. She wanted to feel his skin against hers. She wanted to kiss him.

'What about the others?'

'What do you mean?' He took a big sup of tea and put his booted feet up on the spare chair and leaned back, smiling at her.

'The other parts of the quote. The ocean swims and interesting conversations...'

'Well, I'm a champion of *rambling* conversations,' he said. 'I don't know about interesting... you can be the judge of that...?'

Eilis raised her eyebrows and smiled at him.

'But,' he said, 'get me onto organic versus chemical gardening and I can go on for hours. Or Leinster rugby... now that's a subject I can bore even myself about.'

'And ocean swims?'

'No, but I swim in Seapoint every morning. Does the Irish Sea count? It's amazing. It feels incredible. Some of the gardening group go down there. George is a year-round swimmer... did you meet him?'

You have such a beautiful mouth, Eilis, was thinking. And such animated hands. She had meandered into thinking of the deep kisses part of the quote.

'George?' She was jolted back into the now. 'He's the one engaged in one-man combat with the Japanese knotweed, isn't he?'

'That's the man. He's great. Swims in the morning, goes home for breakfast with his wife – he makes her a boiled egg every morning and brings her a copy of the Times – and then works in the homeless shelter every day. Doing accounts for them and managing all the finances. He used to be an accountant, you see.'

'What a nice thing to do.'

'Total gent. He's definitely normal-strange, if you ask me, the best kind.' He stood up. 'Now, I think I have something nice to have with the tea.' He rummaged around and found a tin. 'Shortbread?'

'Yes, please.' She took one.

He balanced again on the back two legs of his chair, his hands behind his head.

'It's so cosy in here,' she said.

'Yeah,' he said. 'It's nice having you here.'

'It feels nice for me too,' she said, feeling all shy. It *was* nice, so nice to be there with him. She suddenly thought she wanted to tell him everything about herself, about her Mam, about Rob and about her job.

He almost read her mind. 'So, Ms McCarthy,' he said, 'tell me about the hospital and what is your plan for getting out.'

'Getting out? I hadn't thought of getting out,' she said. 'It's not an option. I've worked so hard to get there. I can't just give it up, it would be like the last twenty years were for nothing, a waste of time.'

He didn't say anything except look at her expectantly.

'I just can't. It's been such a struggle, such a slog to get here. I can't walk away.'

He still just looked at her.

'My patients,' she said, desperately, knowing that it was not her lone efforts keeping the people of Ireland from death's door. 'And... and... what else would I do?'

'We're here for a good time, don't you think?' he said. 'Not to make other people happy.'

'But it's for my Mam,' she said.

'But has it made you happy?'

'Well, there are moments, brief nanoseconds where you think you've made a difference but you never have time to dwell on it for very long. It's the mistakes, the problems, the times you *can't* help people, that's what you dwell on, those are the things that stay with you.'

He was listening, intently, to every word. 'It sounds tough. It sounds like you have to be superhuman.'

'You do... and I'm not.'

'You may not be superhuman, but I think you're a super human,' he said, smiling but a blush was spreading across his face.

She suddenly laughed with total pleasure at this sweet, childlike compliment. 'Thank you. I actually think that could be the second nicest thing anyone has ever said to me.'

'What was the first?' he said.

'You said I had an aura of strength,' she confessed. 'It's not true but it was nice to hear it.'

'There's a lot more where that came from,' he said, looking at her. He reached out his hand and felt for hers and for a few moments they sat like that, her small hand in his large rough one, feeling the heat and warmth from him, as though it was the most natural thing in the world. And then she looked at him and he was looking at her and there was that energy, that connection that was so strong, that the next moment they were on their feet, the table pushed to one side, his hands around her waist, and they were kissing, deeply, his leg pressed between her thighs. This was better than she had felt in a long, long time.

At last, they stopped, and noses touching, they looked into each other's eyes. 'I think,' he said huskily, 'that you are quite the superest human I've ever seen.' He stopped. 'And ever kissed.'

'I think you are superest too,' she said, ungrammatically but she didn't care, not even about Rob, wherever he was. 'I think you are quite amazing.'

'I've wanted to do this the since the first moment I set eyes on you...' he said.

'In the hospital?'

'Yes, totally. I know it wasn't the best first meeting and I'm sorry but I remember thinking how beautiful you were and how calm and kind you were, to both of us, Mam and me. And so I sent you the flowers because I couldn't stop thinking about you. And then when I saw you, standing behind that pink lilac tree, I thought you were the most gorgeous woman I had ever seen. And the sexiest.'

'Really?' She didn't quite believe him. No one ever said that to her. Rob wasn't one for effusive compliments.

'Oh my God, yes!' He laughed at her incredulity. 'Your face, the way you frown when you are thinking, your soul... it's like your goodness, the fact that you are such a good person, just shines through.'

'Good? I'm not good.' She meant this, other people were good. She saw it every day, the patients braving their illnesses with dignity, the nurses at the hospital who had the worst jobs to do but did it uncomplainingly, Steph living with that bully, Melissa and her mother. They were good people. She was just her.

'I think you are,' he said. 'And intelligent. And brave. It's all there. In your aura... but,' he continued, taking her face in both his hands, 'it makes me want to do this...'

He kissed her again and she had no idea that being kissed and kissing back could be so beautiful. And so passionate.

He pulled away hesitantly. 'I could do this forever,' he said. 'Maybe you might be amenable?' She felt herself forgetting to debate the merits of her goodness and losing herself in the moment.

'Have you done this before?' she whispered in his ear.

He laughed. 'No, I haven't made a habit of it, no. But I could with you.'

She was just about to agree when another terrible thought struck her. Even though she wasn't technically married, she felt as though she was committing adultery which, as far as her brain could work right then, was a prisonable offence. As awful as Rob was behaving, they were still, officially, as far she knew (and God knows she didn't know very much), a couple. Even if she had her doubts.

'I can't do this,' she said.

'I know,' he said, laughing again. 'It's unprofessional but... worth it.' He was smiling at her. It was so nice to be smiled at, properly smiled at, as though you are actually making someone happy. What a lovely feeling this was, but she couldn't... it wasn't right. 'Eilis,' he said, 'would you like to come to dinner tonight? I am cooking... I can pick you up and feed you and look after you and you don't have to do anything, just sit there and listen to me rambling on and then I can listen to you rambling on and then... then I can drop you home at any time you wish. Or you could... stay.'

Oh God. She almost said yes.

'I have a boyfriend,' she said, while watching his smile dissolve into confusion.

'I'd better go,' she mumbled. 'Thanks for the tea.' Grabbing her bag and coat, she stepped once again into the torrential rain.

33

STEPH

Balancing on the edge of a chair in Rachel's head teacher's office, nausea and anxiety having claimed permanent residence in her stomach, Steph looked warily at the formidable woman in front of her.

Earlier in the day, she had received the call asking her to come into discuss Rachel. Rachel? She had always done so well in school. Steph had never had to discuss her behaviour. Her blood had run cold.

'Mrs Fitzpatrick...' Mrs Doyle said.

'Call me Steph, please.' She was desperately trying to make the situation less formal and more manageable somehow.

'I wonder...' said the head teacher, 'if anything is going on at home.'

'At home?'

'Yes, at home.' Mrs Doyle gazed steadily back.

'Why... what's going on? Is Rachel in trouble?'

'No, not *trouble* as such...' Mrs Doyle stopped for a moment. 'But there has been a change in her behaviour which has caused her teachers to mention it to me. And I have spoken to Rachel myself and thought it wise to talk to you. I'm sorry your husband wasn't available.'

'Work, you know,' said Steph. 'But when you say change in behaviour... what do you mean?'

'There has been a sharp decrease in Rachel's performance levels. Her academic work has suffered. And of course, all teenagers have problems, hormonal, emotional, but this is something more... she seems... angry.'

'Angry?' And there was I thinking that everything could be contained within our four walls. How stupid of me, she thought.

'Yes. Is she angry at home?'

'Sometimes, yes,' Steph admitted. 'But it's normal, isn't it, for children, teenagers, to be angry with the world, isn't it?' But it's not normal for fathers to be sleeping with their neighbours and their mothers to bury their heads in the sand.

'She was embroiled in a fight, Steph. A few weeks ago. A physical, unpleasant fight. Hair pulling, scratching. With another girl. Not something I would have thought Rachel would ever have been involved in, would you agree?'

'Yes... but...'

'Did she tell you about it?'

'No...' she said. She obviously hadn't got that far in the diary. 'No, I didn't know.'

'Do you know why this might have happened?'

'Yes, I think so...' Steph felt her throat catch. Jesus, pull yourself together, don't cry.

Steph couldn't tell Mrs Doyle the truth. She couldn't say that Rachel knew that her parents' relationship was not just on the rocks, but that it had sunk.

'Well,' said Mrs Doyle. 'She has spoken to me. We talked at length yesterday.'

'Really?'

'Yes. One thing she told me was that things aren't good at home.'

'Right,' said Steph, miserably.

'She says you and your husband don't speak to each other.'

'We do... we...' Steph stopped. 'We do speak.' She looked helplessly at Mrs Doyle who eyeballed her calmly. Rachel was right, though, she and Rick didn't speak. They exchanged words, they *argued*, but they didn't *speak*.

'She said, and I quote, "it is horrible at home".' Mrs Doyle tried to smile kindly. 'I am only saying what she has told me, but I think what we can glean, very clearly, is that it has made Rachel unhappy. Very unhappy, it seems, and has left her angry and confused. Now, I must assure you, Steph, that you have my confidence. I am here to help Rachel... and you, perhaps?'

'No,' Steph suddenly admitted. 'We don't speak. We haven't spoken in years.' Tears filled her eyes. Mrs Doyle nodded gently and allowed her to talk. Steph wiped her eyes with her hand. 'It's a horrible atmosphere. Our home is not a happy one. I'm unhappy, Rick's unhappy, I suppose. We should have separated years ago, but something... I just couldn't... I didn't... I've been trying to sort things out and I thought I was, but my mother...'

'I am sure you are trying, but Rachel is caught in the middle of it all,' said Mrs Doyle. 'And I believe it is our responsibility here at the Abbey to help our girls as much as we can. We do not wish to interfere in the private lives of parents, but when events are having such a blatant effect on welfare, then, I believe we must step in. Wouldn't you agree?'

'Yes, of course...'

'You see,' continued Mrs Doyle, 'there is something else... the very reason for the fight Rachel was embroiled in. Are you aware what gossip can do to a young girl's self-esteem, Steph?'

Poor Rachel, how humiliating and devastating it must have been for her. With she and Aoife both in the school, of course people knew about Rick and Miriam. And there she was thinking that it was her secret.

'I'll talk to her today.'

Mrs Doyle nodded, not unsympathetically. 'I think that might be a good idea. Girls need leadership, guidance. They cannot be expected to make sense of the adult world all on their own. No one expects you to live a blameless life, but maybe there could be an increase in better communication?'

Steph nodded, fervently. 'Yes, absolutely... And there's another thing,' she said. 'Her grandmother, my mother, is seriously ill. Cancer. She and Rachel have always been close. It's not clear if she's going to be okay.' She stopped talking for a moment, just to try and steady her voice. 'I'm not sure if she'll... make it.' Steph wiped her eyes with her hands just as Mrs Doyle pushed over a box of tissues. 'And Rachel, you see, Rachel must be so worried.'

'And so are you.'

'I am... but I don't think I've helped Rachel at all. Things have been so bad between us. And now things, life, has got worse, just when I thought I might be able to get things under control. My mother and father always looked after Rachel, fussed over her. She loves them so much.'

'And she loves you.'

Steph couldn't speak. If she tried, she knew she would break down completely. She was consumed with the thought of having let Rachel down and not being there for her. No wonder Rachel had been so angry. Steph just hadn't been able to get it together. Sixteen years of living with a man like Rick meant that it was hard to change, to get the strength together to sort it out, even for the sake of the person Steph loved most in the world.

'Thank you for telling me all this, Mrs Doyle,' she said, gathering herself. 'And thank you for looking after Rachel and caring about her.'

Mrs Doyle nodded. 'She's a lovely girl.'

Steph nodded. 'I know,' she whispered.

'I have a teenage daughter. I know what it is like when you have tried to protect them from the truth. It doesn't work. If you would like my advice, which you may not want,' she said, smiling kindly, 'then talk to her. Adults have complicated lives. She can't come up with answers on her own. She can't make this right. And nor should she have to.'

'Yes of course, thank you.' Steph's head was buzzing. She couldn't quite think straight. 'Where's Rachel now?'

Mrs Doyle smiled kindly. 'She's in English at the moment. Listen, I'll have a word with her before she goes home tonight and tell her I've talked to you. It might help.'

'Thank you.' Steph stood up and the two women shook hands.

'I'm here,' said Mrs Doyle. 'The school is here, for so many different reasons. Let me know if I can help again. Anytime.'

'Thank you.' Steph left the office choked with tears and once she was safely in the car, she allowed herself to sob. She texted Rachel.

I love you. I am so sorry. Can we talk tonight? xxxx

She phoned Rick, knowing that this wasn't going to be as easy as firing off a text.

'Busy?' she said.

'Yes,' he answered.

She ignored him. She was fed up with his controlling her, his games. This was more important than either of them. This was about their daughter. 'You need to listen to me,' she said. 'Rachel's unhappy,' she said. 'And it's our fault. She knows, Rick. She knows.'

'I know,' he said, finally. There was regret in his voice. He loved Rachel. What father wouldn't? 'She shouted at me the other night, when you were out...'

'When you...' She meant when he had been drinking and pushed her.

'Yes,' he said, not giving anything away. Steph couldn't gauge how he felt about being reminded about that.

And you took it out on me, she said to herself.

There was silence. 'This is not my fault, Rick, *this* part of it, anyway.'

Silence again.

'You need to take responsibility for your actions.' She took a deep breath. 'You need to move out.'

There, she had said it. The first move in the complicated game of divorce.

'I know,' he said. 'I will.'

'And we will divorce, right?'

'Yes,' he said, neutrally.

'And will you agree to mediation?' she said. 'I don't fancy trying to divorce a lawyer.' She said it half-jokingly but didn't know what his answer would be. But she had to find a way where she would regain some control of this process, the separation. She didn't want abuse and accusations from either side being hurled in the unpretty face of divorce.

'Mediation,' he agreed.

And that was it. The end of her marriage. He was moving out.

For a moment she didn't speak. 'Thank you,' she said. 'Thank you.' She breathed out. This was it, this was her new beginning.

As she slipped her phone back into her bag, it rang. Rachel?

It was Mr Rose, her mother's consultant.

34

EILIS

Her next patient on the health conveyor belt was an old man, looking, as people do in hospital, vulnerable and scared.

'Mr McEntee. I'm Eilis McCarthy.'

He looked at her, this man now felled by age. 'Tom.'

She looked at the notes. 'Right, Tom.'

'Or Macca.' He half-smiled. 'I answer to both.' She'd seen this before. Grown men, scared for their lives, hiding it with their usual banter.

'I'll call you Tom, if that's okay.'

'Fine by me.' His voice was croaky.

'So, Tom,' she said, 'what's the problem?'

'Sick, ill... on the way out. And that suits me grand.'

'We'll see about that. Could you sit up a little bit, Tom?'

He shook his head. 'Me back,' he said. 'It's gone. Can't move.'

'Well, we'll help you.' Eilis called over Becca to help lift him up. She watched as Becca shuffled over to them, looking like she had all the time in the world.

'You know...' he croaked as they lifted him up to sitting, 'I used to scamper up ladders for a living? Scamper! Like a little monkey I was.'

'In the circus were you, Tommo?' asked Becca.

'No,' he said. 'The parks. The council, you know. Out in the cold, every single day of my life. Loved it. Used to complain about it at the time but what I wouldn't give...'

'We'll have you up in no time, won't we Becca?' said Eilis.

'Don't put yourself out, love,' he said. 'I wouldn't bother if I was you.'

'But we want to bother, Tom,' she said. 'That's what we're here for. To bother.'

His watery grey eyes looked defeated.

'Do you have anyone at home, Tom? Anyone to look after you?'

'No. Just me. Never had no one.'

'Never married, Tom, handsome man like you?'

He almost chuckled. 'Never made it that far. The company might have been nice,' he said. 'But...'

'You were too busy scampering up ladders.'

'That's right,' he was smiling now. 'I was.'

They eyed each other, taking the other in. Eilis professional and competent and wearing expensive Italian loafers. Tom with his bare feet, sticking out from his dignity-relieving hospital gown. She felt as she always did that sense of life not ever being fair. Even the ill and the well, it wasn't fair that some people were sick and some were not. She was aware how ridiculous that was, especially for a doctor. She thought of Charlie and what he had said about her giving it up. Could she? What would she do?

When Tom had been given pain relief and she had asked Becca to make him a cup of tea, she went to see the head of the department, Mohit Kapil. The plan was to discharge Tom that afternoon. They needed the bed, he said. They weren't an old folks' home.

'We can't send him home. He has no one to look after him.'

'We have no choice.' He shrugged. 'It's not your decision, I'm afraid.'

'But he's my patient.' Eilis looked steadily at him. 'Surely, that stands for something.'

'Not when there are people who we can save, if only they are given a bed.'

'You are giving up...'

'I wouldn't call it that. But in modern medicine, difficult decisions have to be made. This is not one of them.'

'What?'

'We've done our best. I think it's time for him to go home.'

'But his flat is damp, he told me. He has no money. Here, at least, he is warm and comfortable. We have clean sheets, television, other people...'

'I'm sorry,' said Mohit. 'There is an economic imperative. Not my fault. Not yours. It's the system.'

'The system! Jesus!' It was all so futile, they could only ever do so much and it never felt as though it was enough.

'I want you to sign the discharge today. We'll just make sure he's on the home-care list.' There was nothing more she could do, except accept the situation, however inadequate it was.

Later... she went to find him. 'Good news, you're going home.' She was trying to sound positive.

He looked terrified.

'You'll be fine,' she spoke more in hope than confidence. 'You've improved. And we're always here if it doesn't work out.'

The man needed rest and care. He was old. He'd worked for the council all his life and now we needed him to leave the hospital as quickly as possible so he didn't take up too much space. She felt the frustration rising in her.

She got home at nine o'clock the following morning, exhausted and thinking about climbing into bed and staying there for a week but she was stopped by a yellow post-it stuck on the mirror above the mantelpiece.

> *Eilis,*
> *I'm so sorry for everything.*
> *I love you,*
> *Rob*

What the...? What on earth was happening? What did he mean? Sorry for what? There had been no real change in their relationship. Was he sorry for not going to Greece, he didn't speak to her very much but he'd been like that for months now? What exactly was he sorry for? As she dialled his number, breath short, chest tight.

And then he answered.

'Eilis?'

'Rob?' Silence. 'Are you still there?'

'Yes,' he said, sounding strange and quiet.

'Are you all right? Just tell me if you're all right?'

'I'm all right.'

'So, what's going on?' He was ending them, she knew it. It was over.

'I just need some time alone,' he said. 'I'm sorry Eilis but please don't call me again. I just need to get my head together.'

'What? Just tell me what's going on? Are you leaving me?'

'Yes.' He sounded so anguished, she had never heard him like that, cool, calm Rob. And then she realised he had put the phone down. She called him again but the number wouldn't connect. It kept dropping. She checked the number and called again. Then she dialled it manually, pressing each number in turn. She waited. It dropped again. Had he blocked her number?

She felt rage. She needed to talk to him IMMEDIATELY to tell him what a complete inconsiderate tool he was. And always, if she was totally honest, had been. A post-it indeed.

She thought about phoning a friend of his, someone from the department. What were the names of the people he was going out with lately? Michael someone? Wasn't there a Freddie? She rang his office. It was after eight. His secretary's voice said that they were closed and Eilis was encouraged to leave a message. She declined.

But there was nothing. She tried calling again but the phone wouldn't connect. The next day, she didn't go home but instead drove to one of her favourite places, Mount Usher Gardens. It was an old garden full of the trees and plants and birds and a stream and places for picnics. She often went there on her own to just walk around and clear her head after long shifts at the hospital. It was somewhere that always managed to bring her down to earth again, to make her feel almost normal.

She bought a cup of tea when she arrived and found her favourite spot, a bench in a little clearing of ash trees.

Her peace and contemplation was soon shattered by a group of people, all chatting and being very loud. Sitting up to get a better view and squinting to try and pull them into focus, she thought she recognised one or two of them. They were striking because they were all dressed so colourfully, bright red jumpers, yellow trousers on one of the men, a mauve cardigan, a stripy sun hat and one man at the front in a red and blue checked shirt. Charlie.

Her heart leaped, salmon-like, in her chest. Oh, but she had run away Cinderella-like last time. Would he hate her too? She didn't know what to do.

He was with the gardening group, she realised now. Yes, there was

Pauline and Rosemary. And there was George. They were wending their way along the path, notebooks in hands and all talking excitedly as if they had just returned from a school trip or had been reassured as to the existence of Father Christmas

And then she remembered what it was. At the meeting, Charlie's sister had mentioned the field-trip... it must have been here to Mount Usher.

You would have never thought they were pensioners the lot of them. They were gadding about, practically skipping as they moved along. And then Eilis was struck by a feeling, a thought, a hint, that things were going to be okay. That life didn't have to be about illness and death. It could be full of happiness and excitement. Life, she realised, watching this group of retirees could actually get better. She had never imagined that before. I want to be like them, she thought.

Charlie strode alongside them all, appearing totally contented, as though all he wanted in the world was right here. That was it, Eilis thought as she watched him talking animatedly to Pauline (Rosemary ear-wigging), it seemed that there was nothing else he actually *needed* in life. Happy in his skin, happy to be alive. He was no longer searching.

They came nearer and she thought about hiding. But she had been spotted.

Eilis waved a hand, weakly.

'Ah, look who it is, if it isn't young Eilis!' It was George, bless him.

'Fancy seeing you here. Small world,' said Rosemary.

'It's hardly a coincidence... Dublin is a small city. Practically a large town. It's not exactly Los Angeles or Beijing,' said Pauline.

'Just getting away from it all,' explained Eilis, trying not to look at Charlie and feeling her cheeks grow hot under his gaze. She wished she hadn't run away from him, before. She should have explained about Rob. God, she should have dumped Rob herself and then she wouldn't have made such a fool of herself. 'Relaxing, drinking tea, thinking...'

'Sounds like my perfect day,' said George, kindly.

'We've had no relaxing, have we?' said Rosemary. 'We've been gardening all day. First off, there was the most interesting talk by a charming young man... one of the head gardeners here. My hand is falling off me taking notes.'

'And the questions you asked, Rosemary,' said Pauline. 'I must say, they were a little *entry-level*.'

'And yours, Pauline,' swept in Rosemary, 'if I may pass on some well-meaning feedback, and please, do not take this the wrong way but rather in the spirit of someone who has known you for a very long time, I thought yours were a little bit *irrelevant*. He had to answer them, but surely it was only to be polite.'

Pauline pulled a face at Rosemary. 'Anyway dear,' she said to Eilis, 'will we see you at the next meeting? We need fresh blood in the class. It would be nice to bring the average age down by a few decades.'

'I'm only five years older than you,' said Rosemary. 'She's always going on about it. It's the only thing she's got.'

'Yeah, maybe... I'll try.'

The group moved on but Charlie stayed. 'I'll catch you up,' he called to them. 'So,' he said. 'It's good to see you.'

'You too.'

His face was slightly red from the sun, he looked gloriously relaxed.

'Have you had a good day?'

'Great day,' he said with feeling. 'Nice people, great weather. Beautiful place. It's been fun. And it's good to hang out with older people... you can learn a lot. And they make me feel very young. It's good for my ego.'

She nodded. 'Listen, Charlie,' she said. 'The other day in your office...'

'Don't worry about it, Eilis,' he said. 'My fault entirely. I got the wrong end of the stick. I'm the one who should apologise but I thought it would be better if I kept my distance.'

'It's me,' she said. 'It was my fault.'

He looked at the group who were disappearing round a copse of trees. 'I'd better go...'

'Okay.'

She watched him walk away but then he turned around. 'By the way, I meant those things I said,' he added. 'I just thought you should know.'

He paused. 'He's a lucky man your boyfriend. I hope he looks after you.'

35

STEPH

'Ah, Mrs Fitzpatrick. Sit down, sit down.' Mr Rose motioned grandly to the chair in front of him. She wondered where her parents were and why Mr Rose wanted to see her alone. The back of her throat was dry and she tried to swallow. Please let it be good news, she prayed. Just let Mam be well.

'You said you wanted to see me, straight away.'

'Yes, yes. I'll get to the point. Your mother... Mrs Sheridan.' He paused and looked at Steph. 'She has had two rounds of chemotherapy and she seemed to be responding well. We were pleased with her progress. She's a very determined woman. I've rarely met someone so positive, so strong-minded...'

'Yes, she is, isn't she?' Steph almost laughed. Her mother was the kind of person who would get through anything, even cancer. Good old Nuala. She was going to get through this, sail on to the next adventure.

'Mrs Fitzpatrick,' he said, gravely. 'Despite that early progress, it has halted. Chemotherapy is now not working. She has ceased to respond. In any way.'

'Right...' Steph was trying to think. 'Okay,' she said, still feeling optimistic. They would just have to continue the treatment or consider the other options. 'Shall we...' she said. 'Shall we try something else?'

He looked at her, straight in the eye. 'We have,' he said. 'We have tried different treatments and I am satisfied that we have done all we can medically. But sometimes, it gets away from us and however much chasing we do, we can't get hold of it. And in this case, I am afraid, that is the unfortunate situation we have found ourselves in.'

'What do you mean?' Steph was trying to follow him but she wasn't quite sure if she understood what he had just said. She was thinking of Nuala and of Joe, how Rachel would be.

'The prognosis is not... it's not good,' he said, carefully. 'Not good at all. Now I need you to prepare yourself.' He really wanted her to understand, she knew that. She tried to focus on his words.

'Prepare myself for what exactly?' Please don't let him say the words. Please, just not this.

'Your mother is dying.' He waited for the words to land. The impact was like an explosion in her brain.

'Dying...' she repeated his words. 'She's dying.' It couldn't be true. Where was the plan? Where was the fucking plan that would take them out of this?

'I am sorry, Mrs Fitzpatrick. Very, very sorry.' She looked at him and his eyes met hers. 'We can continue to try – and, of course, we will continue to try – but I am a believer in the family preparing themselves.'

'Are you sure? I mean, a second opinion...?' Had they mixed up the results with some other poor soul who, at this moment, was walking around thinking she was healthy?

'I have spoken with my fellow consultant, Mr Eames, about your mother's results and, I am sorry to say, he is in full agreement. But by all means I can ask him to take another look.'

'Will you do that? Would you ask him again?' Her throat was dry and she had difficulty forming the words.

'Of course.' He gave her a small smile. 'Mrs Fitzpatrick, I wish the news was different, I wish there were miracles we could perform. Cervical cancer,' he said, 'if it is not caught early enough, it can be hard to treat. Very hard to treat.'

Oh God. She felt suddenly as though there was no floor to her world any longer, like if she took a step there would be nothing there, nothing to put her foot on, nothing to catch her if she fell. She felt panicked. What am I going to do? How do I do this? She needed to talk to her mother, she'd know what they were going to do. She would sort it out. But it was her mother who needed the help. If Steph felt like this, what was she going through?

'My mother knows, does she?'

He nodded.

'What about my Dad, have you told him?'

He nodded.

'She's dying...' she repeated. 'Dying?' She hadn't actually considered that this might be a possibility. She just hadn't wanted her mother to be *ill*. She hadn't thought about her *dying*. She knew it was serious but she honestly thought they would get through it, that eventually, they would be a family again and life would be the same. 'How long? How long do we have?' She thought that if they had a few years, then maybe by that time, there would be a new treatment. Or if they only had a few months, there still could be a solution. Things were moving so fast now in cancer research. Maybe a new drug, a new trial?

'Weeks, I would say. Not much more than that.'

'What?' For a moment she thought she was going to faint, her vision went and all she could see what black and white flashes in her eyes, she felt light-headed and sick to her stomach. She held on to the arms of the chair and took a moment, desperately to organise her thoughts. She didn't know in which order she should think. Eventually, she stood up and steadied herself on Mr Rose's desk.

'I am so sorry,' he said, shaking her hand in both of his. 'I wish I could do something.'

'I wish you could too.'

When Steph had taken a moment to compose herself outside Mr Rose's office, she went to find her mother. In her room, Nuala was sitting up in bed, with Joe sitting on a chair right beside her. He was reading out clues from the Irish Times' crossword. It was like their world hadn't changed. Different room, yes, and both looking considerably thinner and paler, but they could have been at home.

Her mother looked up and she and Steph locked eyes, neither saying a word. I love you, thought Steph. I love you and I don't know what I am going to do without you.

Her father stood up. 'Steph,' he said. 'Just the woman to help us – our brains aren't as sharp as they used to be, you see. We are stuck on ten-down. Two words, with a hyphen. Six and seven letters. Beginning with B, ending with D. *A yearning, a loss of love, end of an affair.*'

'I don't know...' she couldn't think straight. 'I'd have to have a look.' She took the paper and pretended to be looking at the clue. After a moment, she gave the paper back to her father and went to her mother and took her hand.

'How are you feeling?' She spoke gently and brought her hand to her lips. Her mother turned their hands around and kissed Steph's. They both had tears in their eyes.

Nuala nodded in Joe's direction. He was bent over the paper, also pretending to be concentrating.

'You know?' said her mother, clearing her throat. 'I'm not bad at all. I had some toast, lovely it was, and tea. The girl who brings it round is so kind. Polish,' she explained. 'She's been keeping the raspberry jam just for me.'

'That's always been your favourite,' said Joe. 'Remember that year when we grew so many you made twenty-four jars. Twenty-four!'

'We were still eating it at Easter.' They both smiled at the memory. 'Remember, Stephanie?'

'Is that the year we all became diabetic?' she said, quietly, trying to play along for their sake, trying to do what she always did, encouraged family jollity.

'Yes, and hyperactive,' said her father. They all tried to laugh. 'You know what we should do?' he said. 'Let's buy some raspberries and make jam. There's nothing like home-made. I don't think it is technically cheating if you buy the fruit.'

'Yes, Joe,' said her mother. 'What a good idea. Raspberry jam.'

'As soon as you're home, you can rest and recover and instruct me how to make it. I'll be your dogsbody.'

'Not my dogsbody. My right hand,' insisted Nuala.

'I don't mind. I like being your dogsbody. Always have.' He smiled at her, but it was a sad smile, one which told a story which stretched all the way back to that dropped ice cream in Kerry, that hot bank holiday weekend. It was a smile of love and longing, of regret and recognition. He loved her, she loved him.

Nuala met his smile with a look of total understanding. 'You're my right hand, my partner, and my best friend. Never my dogsbody,' insisted Nuala, holding out her other hand. He put down the paper and came over, taking her hand and kissing it, holding her one small hand in his two old, safe loving hands.

'Okay so,' he said. 'Whatever it is. I like being it. We need to get you out of hospital and back home.'

'Of course, Joe.'

'And that's not going to be long. Not with doctors like Mr Rose.'

'No, Joe.'

Who was pretending here? wondered Steph. Was Joe pretending for Nuala and was Nuala pretending for Joe? Did he really believe she would come home again and everything would be alright or was this what they needed to do, in order to deal with this? Was this the way they were going to get through it, by behaving as though this was just a bump in the road and before long they would be dog walking and portrait painting all over again?

'And the book clubbers won't stop asking after you,' continued Joe, sitting back down in the chair by the window. 'I met Peggy O'Sullivan in the village yesterday evening. I forgot to tell you. She was asking when you would be getting home. I said should be tomorrow or the day after and she gave me the title of next month's. It's a John Connolly, I think. I wrote it down. It's in here somewhere.' He patted the top pocket of his jacket.

His words were filling this cold and depressing hospital room, with its pink painted walls, its machines and drips, the plastic jug of water on the bedside locker. But his words of love and affection and a lifetime of memories hung in the air above their heads, infusing them all with his spirit.

'Your mother is looking much better, isn't she, Steph?' Joe was on a roll. 'Soon get you out of here, won't we Nuala? Although the nurses are so kind. Especially Jana. She even brings an extra cup of tea for me.'

Steph hadn't spoken yet. She just couldn't get her words straight, or her thoughts in order, or wasn't quite sure this false optimism was the right course of action. 'That's nice, Dad,' she managed. She was still holding her mother's hand. It felt cold and papery. It wasn't the hand of the woman who used to carry her around, who would push her on swings, the hand that would stir the Christmas pudding and lug a giant turkey to the table, the hand that would gently press a plaster onto Steph's grazed knee, the one that brushed and plaited Steph's hair every morning before school. The hand that picked the sweet peas for Steph's wedding bouquet. The hand that dropped the ice cream on that day in Dingle, all those years ago, the day Nuala and Joe met.

Steph suddenly thought of their dog. 'Who's looking after Dingle?' she said.

'He's with Dearbh from across the road,' said Joe. 'Her children love little Dingle. Now, he's one who'll be glad to get you home.'

Nuala smiled and nodded. 'I'm a little fed up of hospitals,' she admitted, with a little laugh, that to Steph felt forced and not like her mother's usual easy, warm chuckles. 'And have a proper pot of tea from my special cup.'

'And bring Dingle for a walk on the hill.'

Nuala nodded. 'I would love that,' she said. 'With all my heart.' She looked at her husband. 'Joe, would you mind going to the shop downstairs and getting some of those mint things. I'm running low.'

'Of course, love. Anything else? Stephanie?'

'No, I'm fine, dad.'

They waited until he had left the room.

'Mum...' Steph let out a wail. The room blurred as her eyes filled with tears. 'Mr Rose said... Mr Rose told me...'

Her mother nodded.

'Is it true? Do you believe him?' Steph hoped her mother would say it was all rubbish and the man was a fool and she was feeling so much better and it was all wrong or a dream, or a nightmare, and that all would be well and they should just go home again. But she didn't.

'I'm sorry, Stephanie,' she said. 'I've known for a week now and I needed some time to take it all in, get used to it. And then I asked Mr Rose to tell you. He offered, actually, says it's the best way to deliver the news. From a third party, apparently, not as shocking.'

'I don't think there's really a way of making it less shocking,' said Steph.

'I know,' said Nuala. 'I'm sorry.'

But hearing it from Nuala made it real, somehow. She hadn't totally believed it before, not completely, but the fact that her mother told her, the one person who had never lied, had never played games, someone who had only ever had her best interests at heart was saying it, meant that it was real. She let out a cry of pain, a yowl of anguish. Steph stood up and went to the window, so Nuala wouldn't see her face and the tears streaming down her face.

'Now, loveen,' said Nuala, trying to sit up. 'Now my sweet, lovely child. There's something important...'

There was no hiding. Steph turned around and went back to sit beside her mother. 'Yes, Mam?' she said softly, looking into her mother's beautiful face.

'Will you promise me something? And Rachel too?'

Steph nodded, wiping her eyes. 'What is it?'

'Get yourself checked. Please. I didn't and maybe... maybe I wouldn't be here now if I had. Promise me.'

Steph began to sob. 'I can't bear the thought of losing you,' she said. 'You not... you not being here.'

'Promise me though. You haven't promised.'

'I promise,' cried Steph. 'Oh Mam.'

'I can't bear not to be with you too,' said Nuala, wiping her own eyes. 'I will miss you so much. And Rachel. The two of you. My angels.'

'So don't go!' She realised that she was like a child, desperate for her mother. Steph tried to wipe away the tears with her sleeve and they smiled at each other, the saddest smile they had ever shared.

'Here. My last tissue.' Nuala gently patted it around Steph's eyes. 'My darling girl,' she said softly.

'I'm sorry, Mum.'

'For what?'

'For being such a mess.'

'What do you mean?' Nuala looked utterly bewildered.

'For being such a failure. Crap marriage, no career, useless parent.' Immediately she felt awful burdening and worrying her mother, something she had never done, and now of all times. She wished she could unsay what she'd said but she was also desperate to tell her mother how she was really feeling, how much she wished things had been different.

'Now listen to me, Stephanie.' For a moment, her mother's old fire and energy was back in her eyes. 'You have been the joy of my life. When I held you in my arms that first time in the maternity hospital and I looked into that little face, I knew that you would bring me such happiness.' She lifted Steph's face up with her small hand. 'And you have. Every single day. You have been my greatest source of pride. Don't ever think you are a failure,' she admonished. 'And don't let anyone tell you otherwise. And, as for Rachel, well! The cherry on my cake.'

'But...'

'No buts. The two of you make my heart leap with happiness every morning. I don't care how highfalutin that sounds, it's the truth. You and Joe, Stephanie, and now Rachel are what have made my life so wonderful.' She smiled at Steph. 'Thank *you* Steph, for what *you* have given me.'

They both fell silent, and held hands, neither wanting to let go.

'I'm scared, Mam. I can't do this without you.' Steph felt her heart was breaking. She couldn't believe after all the conversations, a lifetime of communicating with her mother, they were now talking about the end. She never imagined that they would have to stop.

'You can. I know you can. Okay?'

Steph nodded.

'Promise me something else.' Nuala was looking deep in Steph's eyes, her hand had lost its fragility and her grip was urgent. 'Don't let life frighten you.'

'Will you promise *me* something?' said Steph, who was now using the hem of her skirt to soak up her tears. 'Will you be there with me? Will you be there, somewhere, waiting for me?'

'Always.'

Joe bustled in the door and Steph went to the window while her mother planted a big smile on her face.

'I found it, Nuala,' he said. 'Your book, for the book club. The John Connolly. They had it in the shop downstairs, by the newspapers. That is good news, isn't it? You better get reading. You've never missed a book club yet... and I've worked out the crossword. It came to me while I was in the lift. Broken-hearted. Broken-hearted is the answer.'

His voice and his hands trembled as he placed the book on the table.

36

MELISSA

Melissa decided to go to Nora and Walter's fortieth. She had to see Cormac and Erica for herself. She wanted to wish him well and say a sort of good-bye, for herself if nothing else. She knew he needed space, but she would go, have one drink and wish him bon voyage as he sailed away out of her life.

She was walking up towards Nora and Walter's house, and was just crossing St Stephen's Green, when she saw Rob, with a group of guys. She hadn't seen Eilis for a few weeks, as they'd been away, in Greece.

'Rob!' she shouted, waving madly. 'Rob!' But he didn't turn round. She squinted. She was sure it was him. 'Rob!' she screamed again. People were starting to look at the mad woman who was screeching after a man who obviously, and quite sensibly, wanted nothing to do with her. 'Rob!' she tried one more time.

It can't have been him, she thought. But seeing his doppelganger made her think of Eilis, she promised herself that she would check in with her the next day.

Planting herself on the doormat of Nora and Walter's, bottle in one hand, big smile on face, she was ready to charm and be charmed.

Someone (tall and Teutonic) gave her a glass of Riesling before she had even taken off her coat and Nora proffered a plate. 'Have one of these... pumpernickel... made by Walter... pretty good, if you pretend it's not actu-ally meant to be bread.'

Melissa took a slice which was spread with goat's cheese and just as she bit into it, Axel whacked her with something hard and plastic. She pretended not to wince while carrying on talking to Nora.

'Delicious. Not quite white-sliced, but delicious all the same,' she said.

'You know, you and I are philistines, don't you?' laughed Nora. 'In the eyes of Cormac and Walter, anyway. I secretly prefer sliced white to sourdough or this pumpernickel.'

And there was Cormac. In the corner, in a huddle of people. Melissa was struck how Cormac was always the most handsome man in the room and the only man she ever wanted to talk to.

And then she noticed the woman standing next to him. How had she missed her? She was practically the most beautiful women she had ever seen in real life. Tall with glossy long brown hair, she was laughing at something Cormac had said and showing the kind of teeth only seen in toothpaste ads, and she had a body which wasn't fuelled on crisps and chocolate.

Erica. She looked like a 1990s supermodel.

'So,' she said to Nora, 'so, that's Erica?' She nodded across the room.

Nora looked over. 'Impressive, isn't she?'

Melissa nodded, mutely.

'She's actually really nice. Seriously scary, but only because she's so gorgeous. And confident. But,' continued Nora, 'underneath all that she's really nice.'

Melissa made a non-committal noise.

'I always thought you two would get it together, but, I suppose, if it doesn't happen straight away, it probably never will...'

Another strange noise emanated from Melissa. She didn't trust herself to speak. She might cry or start throwing things around. She had to behave herself. She had to do it for Cormac.

'But, how come you haven't met her? I thought you would be the first person he would want to show her off to.'

Melissa shrugged. 'I don't know...' And then she decided to come clean. 'Cormac seems not very interested in me lately,' she said sadly. 'For some reason. He's... kind of... moving on from me.' And looking at Erica, she understood. Of course, any man would move on from Melissa if Erica was the choice.

'But friendships don't end like that, do they?' asked Nora, puzzled. 'You don't just get tired of someone. Not after years and years, anyway.'

'It seems you do,' said Melissa, sadly, looking over at Cormac and Erica. God, they really did look good together. 'I knew I shouldn't have come.'

'Jesus, Melissa, I had no idea.' Nora was looking at her curiously. 'So, come on, level with me.'

'What do you mean?'

'This is not normal. For friends, for grown-ups to behave like this.'

'Some would say that men and women can't ever be just friends...' As she said the words she realised that she had asked too much. She had asked for intimacy and closeness and time and effort, she had loved him and he had loved her but she would not countenance anything more. And that hadn't been fair on him. Or on her.

'A-ha. Now, we're getting somewhere.'

Melissa didn't speak.

'Go on,' urged Nora.

'Nothing. It's just that...' Melissa trailed off. She loved him. And had always loved him. She had cut off her feelings for him in an act of self-preservation but she had hurt him and herself in the process. How silly she had been.

'It's just that Cormac has been in love with you for years,' said Nora. 'Is that what you are trying to say? And now he's moved on and you miss him?'

'I think he was, oh it sounds awful to say it, but yes he was, and I just couldn't go there. I was so scared. So petrified of everything. Of ruining things, of losing him. I don't know. I thought I might be able to keep him and love him this way, but obviously... obviously I can't,' said Melissa, looking anguished. 'Not anymore. And now... I miss him, but I more than miss him.'

'Holy Jesus, Mother of God.' Nora shook her head. 'Who'd believe it?' Nora's eyes were wide open. 'This is like a film.'

'But it won't end well, like films do.' Melissa spoke as though she was facing the guillotine. 'He looks happy, doesn't he?' she said.

They both glanced over at Cormac and Erica who had been joined by another couple. It looked so cosy, so right. Cormac did look happy, there was no denying it, and there was no spoiling it.

'Nora, have you seen the other corkscrew?' It was Walter with a bottle of wine in each hand and a gang of hollow-eyed guests in his wake. 'It's an emergency.'

'I'll be back,' said Nora, as she went off to find it. Melissa was left standing on her own, lemon-like, not knowing what to do. She glanced over at Cormac and saw Erica whisper something in his ear, and walk away. Melissa made her move, heart thudding, she had to talk to him, even if it meant risking him turning on her and rejecting her. She couldn't just leave him, she had to let him know that they had her blessing, that there were no hard feelings.

'Hi,' she said, shyly. 'How's it going?'

'Fine, you?' He looked surprised to see her.

'Grand,' she said, smiling. 'How's the bakery going?'

'Nearly there. Just finalising things with suppliers now. Writing menus, you know...'

'Great. So exciting.' She sounded like a children's television presenter.

'And you?' he managed. 'Life and stuff?'

'Work's the same. Liam's still crazy. Doesn't like my work anymore... the usual.'

'That Liam,' he said, 'is a total gombeen. Who does he think he is?'

'I like him, actually,' she said. 'Obviously I would never tell him, but he's not the worst.'

Cormac gave a stage-gasp.

'He's got a tough job,' she explained, 'trying to save a dying industry. Anyway, I'm thinking of moving to the Skelligs. Or Tullamore. Or become a nun...'

'Or a priest... I hear they're very short of those, these days.'

'I'd be a good priest. I like wearing black for one thing.'

'You'd be no good at confession though... you wouldn't be able to keep a secret.'

'I'd have reverse confession where they had to listen to my problems all day.'

'Now *that* you'd be good at,' he said.

Melissa laughed again. God, she loved him. They had slipped so easily back into their old camaraderie. Melissa thought about just how much she had missed him, how much she longed for him. She had let him go and the knowledge was so painful but at this moment, them laughing together, sharing their private jokes, she was happy.

'How's Rolo?' she asked. 'Been biting any ankles, making general mayhem. You know, we never did teach him to do a high five. Or play dead.'

He smiled at her. 'No,' he said. 'We never did.'

'I was watching this thing on YouTube,' she said, 'on dog training and it said...'

And then Erica came back. Jesus, up close, she was even better looking. That skin, beautiful white American teeth, lovely dark wavy hair, slim, grey eyes.

She stuck out her hand confidently. 'Hi, I'm Erica...'

'Melissa. Good to meet you Erica. So...'

'I've heard all about you,' said Erica.

'Really?' said Melissa, a panicked smile plastered to her face. 'I bet that didn't take long.' She tried to think of something to say. 'Nora was telling me that you do yoga.' Melissa was never very good at small talk.

'Practice,' said Erica.

'Oh, I'm sure you're very good.'

'No, you say practice... I *practice* yoga.'

'That doesn't make it sound *so* much fun.' She smiled at Erica, hoping that she knew she was just being jokey.

'Well...' Erica glanced away. 'It's not meant to be fun... fun is not the point of it.'

'I wish I could, you know, *practice* yoga,' Melissa said, trying to be friendly, and not daring to look at Cormac. 'I'm just not bendy.'

'Right...' said Erica. 'Yoga's not for everyone, I guess. Some are able to tune in and others... others just aren't. It's a shame because it's about connection... with oneself, the earth, and the unseen energies. It's a profound thing, y'know.'

'And not fun.'

'No, not fun.' Erica looked at Cormac. 'So, you two've known each other for years?'

'Yup.' Melissa still couldn't look at Cormac, she could see out of the corner of her eye that he was standing there, not quite knowing what to say.

'Sweet,' said Erica. 'That's so sweet. God, Dublin is such a small town. Everyone knows everyone.'

'Yes, it's crazy. You can't go anywhere without bumping into an old friend,' agreed Melissa.

'Y'know, I wish I had a male friend like Cormac,' continued Erica. 'You're lucky...'

'But you do, he's right here.' She and Cormac finally made eye contact.

'Yes but we're *sleeping* together, y'know,' she laughed, grabbing his bicep in her vice-like grip. 'You're *not*.'

Was that a warning?

Cormac grimaced. I have to be pleased for him, she thought. I have to be pleased for him, less selfish, a nicer human being...

'Y'know, for me, I can't just be friends with a guy,' Erica was saying, 'It always ends in them falling in love. Y'know? You meet a guy and it's nice and fun and you think, this is great, I've just made a new friend and, before you know it, he's proposing or threatening to kill himself if you don't go out with him, or he turns up on your doorstep after leaving his life behind in San Francisco, or buying you a new car which he has filled with roses. Y'know what I am saying?'

'Not really. I can honestly say no one has filled a car with flowers for me. Or done anything dramatic,' said Melissa laughing. She wondered if Cormac was prepared to throw himself off the Golden Gate Bridge for yoga or start practicing yoga.

'Excuse me,' Erica said. 'I'm just going to grab a bottle, replenish the glasses.'

She slipped away.

'Wow,' said Melissa. 'She's nice. *Fantastisch*.' She put on a fake and terrible German accent, trying to make Cormac laugh. It didn't work. 'So, it's going well, then, is it? You and Eric?' She thought he might laugh, but he had closed up again.

He shrugged. 'It's in its early stages...' he paused. 'But yes, it's going well. Very well, actually.'

'That's nice,' she said. 'I'm really glad for you.' If she kept saying it out loud, she thought, she really would be and, anyway, she would accept anything if it meant that she could have the tiniest bit of Cormac back again. Even Erica and her egregious ego.

'Thank you,' he said.

'Her name's Erica,' he said.

'That's what I said.'

'No you didn't.'

'I did.'

'You said Eric.'

'If you makes you feel better, I will be more formal and call her Erica. Anyway, you used to call Alistair Basil.'

'I did, didn't I?' he said.

'We're obviously not very good at names, are we?' she said and just as they were smiling at each other, Erica returned.

'Y'know,' said Erica, 'I was just thinking. We should set you up with someone. Myself and Cormie...'

Cormie? *Cormie?*

'...will find you a nice guy. Y'know?'

'No, there's no need...' Maybe she should, she was half thinking, move on from Cormac. Moving on was certainly working for him. But how could anyone be better than him? She had spent nearly four decades looking for someone and he'd been by her side the whole time.

'No, there is. Because if there's one thing I know it's that women aren't meant to be alone. We are sociable creatures, we like people. We like men. Am I right? Women need men and men need women. And,' continued Erica, 'I don't want to think of you on your own, watching TV, or comfort eating, or whatever you single gals do on a Saturday night. In America, people go on dates.'

'But I'm not sociable,' said Melissa. 'At all. I don't like people. I only like my cat. And watching Murder She Wrote. And eating ice cream from the tub.'

'What d'you think, Cormie?'

'Uh, I think Melissa is able to...' Cormac began to say.

'No, leave it to me. I've got someone in mind. He works with me, in the bank. He's a great guy. Okay, not totally great, like Cormie, here, but kinda great. Listen, he could lose a few pounds and he's divorced and I think he might be depressed, but he just needs to get out more. Go on a date. Y'know, he's real nice. He's got what you Irish call "a good personality".'

Melissa knew it was time to leave. She had shown Cormac that there were no hard feelings and that she was pleased he was moving on. She could only hope she had conveyed all of that.

'So! I'd better go, another party...' Melissa said. 'I'll see you guys round. Take care.'

She looked behind and saw Erica helping herself to the largest glass of wine she had ever seen. You'd need two hands to support that weight, thought Melissa. And she saw Cormac chatting away about something. He looked happy, didn't he? What straight man wouldn't with a supermodel by his side?

Anyway, none of that mattered. She walked straight out and stood in the cool of the night breathing deeply. Time to move on, she thought. He's someone else's now. It's time to move on.

Goodbye, Cormac, she thought. Goodbye.

37

CORMAC

He watched Melissa leave using only his peripheral vision, like a super-hero, he thought, the kind who can see everything that is going on without having to turn their heads, or show any emotion And it had taken super-hero strength of character not to run after her and go wherever she was going. God, he had missed her. He had seen the look in her eyes when she waved her cheery goodbye and his heart broke for her. And for him. His hands twitched as he longed to reach out and pull her to him and make everything all right.

But, he reminded himself, he was moving on. Remember? Back in the game and all that? And he had the fabulous Erica on his arm and what man wouldn't want someone like that? So he focussed on the beautiful face of Erica.

'Y'know, being single in this country?' Erica was saying.

Was that a question? He didn't know.

'It's a way of life. And even if you are in a relationship, you act like you're single. At an event, people who are married don't spend time together. Men socialise with each other men, women with their friends, y'know?'

'Are you saying we're a nation of outcasts and losers?' he asked.

She laughed. 'Kinda. I suppose. Not you, Cormie. You're a man who likes being with women, y'know? I mean, you and Melissa...'

'Yeah,' he said. 'We've been friends for years. But I do have other friends. Walter. My brothers. I hang out with them.' He managed to think of a few other names to bolster his list. 'So, I would say I fit your category of outcast and loser. I like male company.' He felt it was necessary to distance himself from Melissa. He didn't want any awkward questions from Erica, but there was something Judas-like about his behaviour. Forgive me, Melissa, I know not what I do.

'Yeah, but you and Melissa hang a lot, don't you?'

'Not really,' he said.

'But you do... you said before that you do.' She took a sip of her wine. 'God, this stuff is terrible, she said. 'Walter swore to me that it was a German Kombucha. But this is definitely wine.'

'Is it? Right...' he said vaguely. Oh no. He was going to be rumbled and his chance of happiness with this amazing woman, and probably the only chance he was ever going to get, would disappear. 'Nah,' he said. 'Me and Melissa haven't seen each other for ages.'

'But the two of you seem very comfortable together. You were laughing when I came back. You seemed very friendly. Close.' She was looking at him.

'Yeah, we are. Kind of. But nothing romantic, if that's what you're wondering. Ha! The very idea. The thing is,' he said, 'the thing is that Melissa is gay. She's gay, anyway, so...'

'Really?' Erica looked at him as though she didn't believe him.

'Some more wine?' he said quickly. 'Or shall I see if there is anything like Coke?'

'Coke?' Her eyeballs almost popped out of her head. 'I'll have a water.'

This was worth it, he thought as he went to find a drink for Erica, the lying, the denying, all of it was worth it just to move on with his life. But he kept thinking of Melissa. He hoped she'd got home safely.

38

STEPH

She was sure it was dangerous to drive when your eyes were obscured by tears. She felt like crashing the Mercedes into a wall or speeding along the Rock Road in the bus lane.

What on earth were they going to do without her mother? Life was going to be impossible without her. How was Steph going to cope? Her father? Rachel? It was unimaginable. She kept trying to think but there were no answers

When she arrived home, she called Rick and told him what was going on.

'Mam is dying,' she said, she heard her voice wobble so she cleared her throat. That wasn't actually the point of the conversation and she couldn't allow herself to think about her mother, not right now. She still couldn't and didn't believe it, so she concentrated on Rachel. Something she should have done months ago.

'I'm sorry to hear that,' he said, stiffly. 'If there's anything I can do.' He sounded slightly awkward, as though he was playing a role.

'I'll deal with it,' said Steph. 'But you've got to be more involved with Rachel. We might be splitting up but you are going to have to focus your time. She needs you, Rick. Go and see her play hockey. Okay? She needs her dad... and now with mum...'

'But you've always been so close,' he excused himself. 'I didn't think she needed me as well.' He was being nice to her because of Nuala, she thought. Well, he should have been a bit nicer in the long years of their marriage. Oh well. Just be nice to Rachel, she thought. She's all you have left.

'Of course she does,' she said. 'Girls need their dads and you're her dad.' Talk about stating the obvious but Rick's interpersonal skills weren't impressive and he needed it spelling out. Just up your game, Rick. Okay? She felt like saying but didn't. Up your bloody game. In everything. But she felt braver these days and he seemed distant, as though he didn't feel he had power over anymore. She'd always felt a bit scared of him, and now she felt nothing. She was too busy thinking of Nuala. The thought that she wouldn't be around was horrifying.

'I'm nearly home,' he said. 'I'm on the train, anyway, so I'll see you soon. We can talk about it later.'

Just as she put the phone down, she heard Rachel's key in the door and rushed out to meet her.

'I'm going to my room.' Rachel spoke before Steph could get a word in.

'No,' Steph said. 'No, come and sit down. I need to talk to you.'

She must have looked different or spoke in a way that made Rachel realise something was up.

'Granny?' whispered Rachel, her eyes wide with fear.

Steph nodded, but for a moment she didn't know what to say, or rather, where to even begin. She led Rachel into the kitchen and they sat opposite each other at the table. Steph took Rachel's hand.

'Um... listen, Rach, Granny is...' She stopped and focussed. 'Granny's not going to get better.'

'What? What do you mean?'

'I spoke to her doctor today,' Steph was managing to control herself. 'He said that there is no hope... unfortunately. Do you understand what that means?'

Rachel nodded, blinking back tears, just as Steph herself had done in the hospital talking to Nuala.

'However,' said Steph, trying to stop herself from crying, 'we have time to say goodbye. Lots of people lose their loved ones suddenly and without warning and we... we've got time. Not much but enough to say goodbye properly.'

Rachel began to sob and Steph threw her arms around her.

'Oh Rach! It's the worst, isn't it...? It's the worst thing ever. I know, I know... but we are going to do what we need to do and we are going to get through this. You and me. I promise.'

Eventually, Rachel's heaving sobs began to slow down and calm.

'I think we should go and see her, straight away, what do you think?'

Rachel nodded.

'Now listen, Granddad is pretending it's not true, he's in denial, I think. He's saying that Granny is coming home soon. I mean she is coming home, I think, but to... to die.' The starkness of her own words shocked her.

'Oh no...' Rachel began crying again.

'I'm sorry,' Steph said. 'I don't know how to make this better.'

'You can't,' said Rachel. 'No one can.' Steph looked at her beautiful face, tear-stained, her mascara – which, although it was the least of her worries, she should not have been wearing to school – all smudged.

'Everything else is fixable, isn't it?' said Steph. 'Everything else in your life you can control by decisions you make, but dying, that decision is made for you.'

'Oh Mum...' Rachel sobbed.

'And all those decisions I should have made, I didn't. And now I wish I had the luxury of deciding things and I can't.' She looked at Rachel, meaningfully. 'I made a mistake not protecting you. And I am so, so sorry about that. You dad has made a mistake – and if he knew that he hurt you, then he would be so sorry. He loves you so much. You know that, don't you?'

Rachel shrugged her shoulders.

'Don't you?' said Steph again.

Rachel nodded, reluctantly.

'And you know how much I adore and love you, don't you heart-angel?' Steph used the name she used to called Rachel when she was little. She hadn't called her that for years.

Rachel nodded slowly. She knew.

'Okay. We are going to sort this out, myself and your dad. I promise you. I am not going to be the pathetic weakling you take me for. Time to find my superhero costume. An old leotard will do and a blanket. I'll be right back.' Steph pretended to twirl around and hung a tea towel across her shoulders.

Rachel *almost* laughed. 'Mu-um.'

'What? I'm just showing you that I can be strong. Would you prefer me to be a "doormat" again?' She smiled at Rachel. 'I've let a few things go wrong – eye off the ball and all that – but I'm going to sort them out. I promise.'

'Okay.' Rachel wiped her nose with her sleeve.

'And most importantly, you have to know that whatever happens between me and your dad, you are our priority. We love you more than anything else in the world. Okay?'

'Are you going to get divorced?'

'How would you feel about that?'

'Sad, I guess. But it would be better. Much better than living like this. And you'd be happier, wouldn't you?'

'Yes, I would,' admitted Steph. She pushed Rachel's hair away from her lovely face. As she looked into her eyes, she saw the look of her mother, the same pale grey eyes. Nuala. The thought of her made her stop. 'Okay, Heart-angel? I'm going to be right here, for you. We'll get through this, all of it together. I promise.'

Rachel nodded and squeezed Steph's hand. 'Mum?'

'Yes?'

'Sorry for calling you those names.'

'That's okay. I deserved it.'

'You're not an imbecile.'

'Well, that's good to know.'

I'm going to have to be strong, she thought, for Rachel, for Mam, for me. I am going to have to be super-powered.

They heard Rick coming in the front door. Right, she thought, it's probably not a good idea to talk about the divorce this evening, just as Rachel is reeling from news that her grandmother is dying. We'll talk about it another time. When she's recovered from this shock.

'Rachel?' he called. 'Steph?'

'In here,' Steph replied.

He walked into the kitchen.

'So,' said Rachel, immediately, wiping her eyes with her the back of her hands. 'When are you going to get divorced because sooner might be better than later. I'm dealing with a lot of shit at the moment and it might be better if we just got it done.'

Rick looked at Rachel, amazed at her precocity. 'Yeah,' he said, looking at Steph. 'Your mum and I think it's for the best. That we'd all be happier that way.'

'Good,' said Rachel. 'Because it has been a nightmare.'

Rick said nothing.

'And you know Granny's dying, don't you?' said Rachel, getting angry. 'Which is pretty shit, as well, you know.'

'I know,' he said. Rick was a large man but he seemed smaller somehow with Rachel. He wasn't like that with Steph.

'And you've been having an affair,' she said. With Miriam. That's nice, isn't it? That's nice for Mum. And for me.'

'Your mum and I have talked about this,' he said. 'This is between her and me.'

Rachel raised her eyebrow.

'Let's leave it Rachel,' said Steph. 'Dad's right. It's for us to discuss.'

'Have you said sorry?' said Rachel, ignoring Steph. 'You owe her an apology.'

'I've said I'm sorry.'

'Well, once is not enough, Dad,' said Rachel. 'You had better show you're sorry.'

'I'm sorry, okay?' he said. 'Really, really sorry. Hands up. I'm sorry I let you down, Rach. And sorry Steph. Terrible father, terrible husband. Guilty as charged.' He was looking at Rachel, hoping she might take pity on him.

'So, when are you going?'

'When it suits your mum.' He looked at Steph. 'You know, with your Granny and everything,' he said to Rachel, 'things are complicated.'

Steph nodded. 'We'll get through this, Rach. Dad is going to be really close by, so you can see him all the time.'

'Well, it's not like he's around much anyway, so it'll probably not make much difference,' said Rachel, but she was crying now, tears streaming down her cheeks.

'Oh Rach,' said Steph, who put her arms around her and let her cry.

Rick stood there helplessly, not knowing what to do. He went off to the fridge. He's not getting beer, is he, thought Steph. At a moment like this?

It was a bar of Galaxy chocolate, Rachel's favourite. He pushed it towards her, across the table. At least he was trying. On the pathetic side, but it was at least an attempt at caring. He loves her, thought Steph. And she loves him. We're going to be all right.

'Chocolate?' said Rachel, contemptuously, when she came up for air.

'And that's going to make things better, is it?' She knew, though, that it was his tortured, dysfunctional way of saying that he loved her.

Rick shrugged. 'No... I just thought...'

Rachel picked it up and snapped off a piece and popped it in her mouth.

'Want some?'

Rick took a piece and then so did Steph.

'Life is horrible, isn't it?' said Rachel. 'Is this what growing up is? Life gets horribler and horribler and then you die.'

'No, not at all,' said Steph. 'Life is wonderful, it's just a mixture of everything, you just have to learn how to steer yourself through the horrible parts. It's just sometimes you get the engine caught in weeds and you get a bit stuck.'

'I have no idea what you're saying,' said Rachel. But Steph knew she did.

Steph looked at her watch. 'Come on,' she said. 'Let's go and see Granny. Visiting is over in an hour.'

They left Rick at home and the two ran, hand in hand, to the car to go and see Nuala.

39

MELISSA

Melissa picked Eilis up in the Beetle before Nuala's party and they drove to the pier and walked to the very end, looking out to sea. There were still some decisions to be made about the reunion which was getting closer. They had received most of the RSVPs, but there were a few stragglers who had yet to respond. Melissa and Eilis had taken over the organizing from Steph, as she was so busy with Nuala, and arranging this party.

'Do we do name badges?' wondered Eilis. 'Will everyone be recognizable?'

'I suppose no one changes totally,' said Melissa. 'We'll recognise everyone, I'm sure. We are just older versions of ourselves. Like some Hollywood make-up genius has decorated us with wrinkles and put us in boring clothes.'

'Better than a bottle-green school uniform.'

'Totally. I still can't bring myself to wear anything green.'

There were yachts in the harbour, the hardier sailors, the ones trying to continue the season for as long as possible, were tacking across the bay. She thought of Cormac and the last time she was here was with him.

'Rob's gone,' said Eilis, as they began walking. 'I haven't told anyone because I thought he might come back, but he's gone and he won't talk to me.'

'What? Oh my God.' Another woman? She thought. Not him as well!

'He just left and won't take my calls, nothing. Won't discuss it or explain.'

'What do you think is going on?'

'I don't know. Nervous breakdown? Another woman? Who knows? I can only hazard guesses.'

'What are you going to do?'

'I don't know,' admitted Eilis. 'The house feels strange without him. I keep waiting for him to come back, to hear his key in the door. I keep waiting for my phone to ring... but nothing.'

'Ghosting.'

'What?'

'Ghosting. When people leave someone without a trace. Cut off all contact, like they didn't exist.'

'Well, whatever it is, it's horrible.'

'And how do you feel?'

'Sad, confused... relieved. I know it sounds strange, but it's easier without him. I miss him and hope he's all right, but I feel better without him. We weren't right for each other, I know that. It's just so hard to identify that it's over. You know,' she continued, 'he didn't come to Greece. Well, neither of us went in the end. He told me the day we were meant to go. Refused to go.' She shrugged. 'What could I do? I couldn't force him.'

'Oh you poor thing. You should have told us.'

'I didn't know what to say. I kept waiting for things to become a bit clearer, more understandable. But they got worse.'

'They often do,' said Melissa, smiling at her but half thinking of Cormac. 'In fact, they practically always do. But what if he comes back tomorrow, what will you say?'

Eilis shrugged. 'I'll cross that bridge tomorrow.' She smiled. 'I just hope he's all right.'

'I'm sure he is.' They had reached the lighthouse and they walked up the steps to a bench so they could look out into Dublin Bay and the Irish Sea beyond. It was a sparkling, glittering day.

'It's beautiful here, isn't it,' said Eilis.

'Totally,' said Melissa. 'It makes me think that living around here again wouldn't be the worst.'

'So, how's your mother?' said Eilis. 'How are things between you?'

'Well...' Melissa almost laughed at how outlandish her news was. 'Oh God.'

'What is it?'

'She had... another daughter.' And surprising herself, as well as Eilis, she began to cry. She hadn't realised that the thought of her mother, assaulted, alone, being forced to give up her baby and the long-term damage that went on to have, had affected Melissa. But the sadness of it sometimes took her by surprise. Her poor mother.

'What?' Eilis was immediately jolted back into a story which she decided was infinitely more important that hers. 'Good God...'

'I'm alright,' reassured Melissa. 'Just shocked, you know? And it's just so sad for her, for all of us really. Me and the baby, her other child. Her first daughter.'

'Your poor mother.' Eilis took Melissa's hand and held it.

'She gave her up, though,' said Melissa, who was wiping her eyes with her other hand, using her fingers, to try and keep herself looking unsmudged. 'She was one of those women you read about. She never got over it.' Since she had first been told, she had come to completely sympathise with her mother. She understood that some depths were near impossible to plumb, and this secret may never have been told unless Frankie had written that letter. And she would never have known what lay behind her mother's sadness or desire to drink or depression. It was so crazy to think of it in this day and age where nothing like that could happen. Or it would be just so different. We have moved so far from where we were, she thought. Her mother had lived in an unimaginable time.

Eilis was quiet. 'That's so sad, your poor Mam.'

'I know...' Melissa focussed on a tiny red dinghy bravely battling the swell. 'It is sad,' she said. 'If that isn't the understatement of the century.'

'And does it... does it... explain things for you, give you any answers?'

'I suppose. In some ways it does. It doesn't make it any easier, I guess, but it's part of her story I didn't know before. So, I'm glad I know.'

'And will you meet her? Your sister?'

'Yes, soon. In the next few weeks. I'm feeling nervous already. Mam named her Tara Rose.'

'What a lovely name,' said Eilis.

'It is, isn't it? It's the kind of name someone young, someone innocent would give their child, isn't it.'

They looked at each other and smiled. 'Yeah, exactly.'

'She's Frankie now though.'

'A nice friendly name.'

'Well, I hope she is.'

'What?'

'Friendly. I hope she likes us, you know, wants to be with us. I hope we're not too weird for her.'

'Maybe she'll be too weird for you.'

'Maybe. But I am sure she imagines us to be this amazing family but it's going to be a lot for her, Mam's drinking and her out-and-out strangeness. And then my strangeness. We're not exactly the Obamas.'

Eilis laughed gently. 'You're not strange. At all. Anyway, everyone feels like that.'

'They don't. Look at Steph. Normal, nice family,' said Melissa. 'She is amazed that her life isn't normal. I've no doubt it won't right itself again, like one of those boats. But me? I'm always going to be half-capsized.'

'I'm glad you managed to keep the analogy going.'

'Me too.'

'You're wrong, though. You're not remotely weird or strange. You're amazing. Ask anyone. Ask us, ask your colleagues, ask Cormac.'

Melissa looked down, wishing everything was different but knowing that she had made a mistake and that ship, and that friend, had sailed away. 'But I feel so weird and strange inside.'

'Maybe,' continued Eilis, 'you just *think* you're weird, but it's actually what normal feels like. D'you see what I mean?'

'Clear as mud.'

Eilis laughed. 'What I'm trying to say is that you seem very normal to me. You seem like everyone else I know. Only nicer and saner.'

'But I can't even have a relationship. Look at me. I'm nearly thirty-nine and I don't even have a boyfriend.'

'Well, maybe you are looking at the wrong men. Maybe you only go for the ones you know who'll reject you.'

'But that's deeply screwed up.'

'Yes,' said Eilis, laughing again, 'but entirely normal. Why don't you go for someone who won't reject you?'

'I don't know anyone.'

'Really?' Eilis' eyebrows were so high they almost reached her hairline.

'Well,' she said. 'If you mean Cormac, he's taken now. Has a girlfriend, who looks like some kind of supermodel. You wouldn't want to stand next to her.' She paused and looked again at the little dinghy. The sailors had given up and were heading back into the harbour. At some point, everyone has to give up, she thought. Admit defeat. 'They look good together. You know, happy.'

'But you're gorgeous,' said Eilis. 'Inside *and* out.'

'Shut up,' said Melissa but she was smiling. Not like Erica, she was thinking. *She's* gorgeous. I'm just ordinary, but she was pleased that Eilis was taking the chance to be nice to her. 'I just don't know when it's all going to stop. When life is going to get easier, you know?' She looked at Eilis to see if she understood. 'When will this whirl, this non-stop-ness stop?' She sighed. 'I know I'm not making any sense, but it's just that there's always something around the corner, ready to pounce, you know? I just want some peace.'

'I know exactly what you mean,' said Eilis. 'It's just all so bloody confusing and relentless. Like, when am I going to have all the answers or any answers? Or when will I start to understand things. I'm constantly surprised by things.'

'Yeah,' Melissa laughed. 'It's like where did *that* come from? And *that*?'

'So, to answer your question, I have no idea. But soon, I would hope. But probably never.'

'That's reassuring.'

'Isn't it?' They smiled at each other.

'So, what are you surprised at, then?' asked Melissa.

'Everything... like...' A little dog came along to have a good nose at what they were doing and Eilis stroked his ears. 'Like, when will I wake up and not feel sad about my Mam.'

'Really?'

'I know I should be over it by now. I know I should not give her much thought...'

'Is that how it works? Grieving? Because, although I'm no expert. On anything. I don't think it works like that.'

'I don't know,' said Eilis. 'But all I know is that the day she died I felt sick inside, nauseous. And I still feel exactly the same. I would have thought that would change... wouldn't you?'

Melissa shrugged. 'No, not necessarily. Everyone is different. Everyone processes things in their own way.'

'But I don't seem to have processed it in *any* way.'

'But it was a hugely traumatic event. And the culmination of years of her illness. And then you went straight to do Medicine. And then working. You've never given yourself a break. Never had a chance to get over it.'

'But, and I know this sounds crazy, but I don't want to get over it. I don't want to lose her. I know I have *lost* her. But I can't let go totally. I can't move on, because I don't want to. I don't want to leave her behind.' Eilis fiddled with the hem on her skirt, rolling it up. 'Which sounds certifiable. I'm aware of that.'

Eilis rarely spoke like this, she rarely opened up and, for the first time, Melissa was able to see the real Eilis, the person behind the perfect little face, the super-successful job, the home. She wasn't this super-human, going to medical school in the weeks following my mother's funeral type of person, but she was far lonelier than she could have imagined.

'No, it doesn't. At all,' said Melissa, now taking her hand. 'It sounds the opposite. Sane, in fact. And understandable. But... what if you talked to someone? Like a grief counsellor, someone who might help you talk about her, remember her. You don't, you have never really talked about it, about her, have you? You've kept it to yourself.'

'Yeah, I have, because... it was too painful and I kept waiting and waiting for it not to be but... I still miss her.' She laughed awkwardly, embarrassed. 'Sheesh! What a mess I am.'

'No, you're not. Not remotely. I think you're amazing. You're a survivor.'

'Not anymore. And Charlie hates me now.'

'Charlie?' Melissa spluttered. 'Who's Charlie?'

'I've met someone. Well I haven't. At all. But I have, in a way.'

'What?!' She was one dark horse was Eilis McCarthy, and no mistake.

'No, it's nothing. Much,' said Eilis. 'I just like him. Really like him. But I ruined everything. We kissed and then I ran off in the middle of it all and... I don't know. I just don't know what to do about anything.'

'Join the club. The club for the permanently clueless,' said Melissa. 'So is Charlie the guy with the flowers?'

'Yes, how did you know?'

'I don't know, vibes or whatever. I just sensed something, when you mentioned them. So what's the story?'

'I don't know, I just find myself so... attracted to him. I've never felt like this before, I keep thinking about him. His hands, mainly. But I like talking to him, I just don't want to stop, I want more and more.'

Eilis had never spoken like that about Rob, thought Melissa. She laughed. 'Wow. I've never heard you talk like that before. He sounds wonderful. But hands? Come on! What is he a piano player?'

'No, he's a gardener. But they are all strong and rough and I just like them.'

Melissa nodded, understanding the situation perfectly. 'You fancy the arse off him... or the hands?'

'Both,' admitted Eilis and then she laughed. 'I'm crazy, aren't I?'

'Do you fancy Rob? In the same way? Did you ever?'

Eilis stopped for a moment. 'No,' she admitted. 'Never. Isn't that awful?'

'No.' Melissa shook her head. 'Probably more normal than people might suggest. So... what are you going to do?'

'I don't know. I probably, very likely, won't do anything.'

'And let life happen to you?'

'Yes, isn't that what people do?'

Melissa nodded. 'The very idea of taking charge of my life and actually being a free agent. Ha!'

'It's so much easier,' said Eilis, 'to sweep everything under the carpet and have a nice sit down.'

'And a cup of tea.'

'Of course!'

'You see,' said Melissa. 'I'm in love with someone too. Only I've just realised. And now he's happily in love with a supermodel called Erica and he doesn't want to see me anymore so...'

'Cormac.'

'Yeah, of course, only he's moved on, apparently. We are officially not friends anymore. Well, I've think I've just been demoted to *acquaintance*.'

Eilis shook her head. 'He's been crazy about you forever and you only realise now that he's the best thing since sliced white?'

'He isn't though, anymore. But I love him like you wouldn't believe. I don't know what to do with myself, I miss him so much. I just want to talk to him. And I miss Rolo. I'm dying without them.'

'Jesus Christ,' said Eilis.

'Well, *he's* not been much use.'

'True. Oh Melissa!' Eilis smiled at her, her forehead wrinkled with this new dilemma.

'I'll be alright,' said Melissa, 'I always am, aren't I? The bounce-back kid, woman, whatever I am.'

They got up to walk slowly back to the car, past the boats in the harbour, and the children's sailing club of a flotilla of tiny boats. A seagull skimmed past Eilis' ear, as easy as a paper aeroplane.

'You know,' she said. 'I would give up everything to have my mother back again, or another ten years with her or another five years. Just enough time so she would have seen me grow up a bit more, you know? Just a few more years.'

'I know, you were so young. It was such a tragedy.'

'Yeah, it was, it really was. When I look back on that young girl now, aged seventeen and eighteen nursing my mother and doing my exams. I don't know how I did it, I really don't. I would love to give that girl a hug, you know? Take care of her, a bit.'

'Well, maybe you should.'

'How?'

'Be nice to yourself, don't work so hard. Do things you love. Live the life you deserve.'

And suddenly Eilis had tears in her eyes. She turned around and faced into the wind and she spoke quietly.

'What was that?' said Melissa.

'Do you think my mother would mind if I did that?'

'No, I don't think she would mind if you made a few changes in your life. I don't think she'd mind at all.'

'Thanks Mel.'

'We have spent our entire lives trying to be perfect, you know that? Doing what others wanted, being the good girls but terrified to go after what we want, what might make us happy. I am going to try not being perfect for a while, and see what happens.'

'Imperfect?'

'Exactly.'

'Imperfectly me,' said Melissa. 'Yeah, why not. Want to join me?'

'Why not?'

'Come on.' Melissa had spotted the ice cream van. 'We've still got half an hour before the party. Let's buy that lovely eighteen-year-old an ice cream. Isn't that what she'd like?'

'Yeah,' said Eilis. 'I think she would.'

40

STEPH

It was Nuala's idea to have the party, a get-together of all her friends. 'I haven't seen anyone for ages... it would be so nice to say hello.'

Or goodbye, thought Steph, wiping away the tears that kept falling these days when it was most inconvenient. She would be buying bread and would notice an iced bun and think of Nuala. Or walking past the flower shop and think of the freesias she loved, or just random memories would crowd her mind and then she'd be off again. Like the time Steph saw a beautiful black velvet party dress in a magazine when she was eight, and Nuala made it for her, with the cream lace collar as well. She wore that dress to every party for years and years.

So they phoned around. No one *couldn't* make it to the hello-goodbye party. All of Nuala and Joe's friends were also happy to pretend that this wasn't the end.

And when Nuala appeared in her flowery dress – bought for her ruby wedding anniversary – it hung off her bony shoulders and Steph, who was standing in the hall of the house with Rachel, felt another surge of emotion. Her mother, her lovely, kind, calm, beautiful mother was leaving her, forever. What does one do in that situation? How do you say goodbye, how do you live without someone you love so much?

'Will you tie my scarf, Stephanie?' she said. 'You're always so good at things like that.'

She passed over the pink silk scarf from Rome and Steph went to drape and knot it, but her fingers felt like sausages and she couldn't quite do it. 'I do love this scarf, Stephanie,' said Nuala. 'It's so beautiful. Like you.'

Steph didn't respond, she just carried on trying to make the scarf look good. 'I must have lost my knack,' said Steph. 'I don't know what's wrong with me.'

Nuala took her hands. 'Nothing's wrong with you. Nothing at all.' Steph felt the tears begin but she fought them back.

'Here, I'll do it,' said Rachel. She flipped it over Nuala's shoulders and folded it at the front.

'You look gorgeous, Mum. What do you think, Rachel?'

Rachel had tears in her eyes. She nodded, unable to speak.

'Look at us, what a pair,' Steph said and she reached out and took her daughter's hand and the two of them followed Nuala and Joe into the kitchen. Dingle had a ribbon around his collar and a big bow, also tied by Rachel. He wouldn't let Nuala out of his sight, staying close to her ankles, guarding her, as if he knew.

There was a slight tremble about Joe, as though he was desperately trying to contain something. 'How are you, Dad?' Steph asked.

'Never better,' he said, with a big smile. It was hard to meet his gaze these days. Steph was scared about what she might see there. 'It's great to have your mother home where she belongs. And look at all this food – will it all get eaten, I wonder?'

All the food had been delivered by Nuala's friends throughout the morning, plates covered in cling film, Tupperware boxes filled with fairy cakes and millionaire's shortbreads and brownies. There were offerings from the walking group and others from the art class. Sandwiches – all varieties – were piled high. Peggy O'Sullivan had delivered a cheese and tomato quiche – she was famous for her pastry – and there was a tuna pasta salad from Noreen O'Brien. The pièce de résistance was, of course, by Imelda Cunnane, the self-appointed book club leader. She had made a cake in the shape of a book and its iced title was:

Welcome home wonderful friend!
 Nuala Sheridan

Kick off was at two and it was three minutes to now.

'We're on tea-making duty, okay?' Steph said to Rachel, as the doorbell rang heralding the first guest. And then they spent the afternoon boiling the kettle and pouring cup after cup. Hot drops and fresh cups were the order of the day and the two didn't stop from either washing-up or searching for mugs and refilling the milk jugs.

'Dad was right,' said Steph. 'It *is* like Downton Abbey in this house.'

The noise from the living room was tremendous with all the chatter. Parlourmaids Rachel and Steph handed around cake and sandwiches, which were then balanced on the edge of saucers, while 'Moonlight Serenade' from Joe's collection rose from the record player. And there was Nuala, sitting on an armchair, looking, tired and washed out, and stroking the ears of Dingle, who was curled up on her lap. It was a wake for the living.

Eilis and Melissa were there, being brilliant and chatting to all of Nuala's friends. They were passing around the quiches and sandwiches and the wizened cocktail sausages that someone had bought and the brilliant pineapple and cheese stuck into an orange that someone else had made unironically.

Earlier, that day, before the party, Steph and Rachel had taken Dingle for a walk on Killiney Hill and they began talking – about Nuala and about themselves, what they had both been through and how they had felt.

They were sitting on a bench looking towards Wicklow.

'You and Dad... did you *ever* love each other?' The question was so direct, it was one you couldn't deflect. Rachel seemed fearless these days as though she had tired of the shilly-shallying and life was for getting on with.

'Yes, we did,' said Steph. 'But not enough. We were so young. I was only twenty-one when I met him. But he tried and I tried and because we had you and we both loved you so much we stayed when maybe we shouldn't have. Does that make any kind of sense?'

Rachel nodded. 'I think so.'

'I am sorry that instead of taking action, I let everything go this far.'

'But what are you going to do?'

'We're going to separate, but Dad understands that I can't really do anything while Mam... while Mam is so sick. We will though, and you and I will stay in the house...'

'But we'll be happier,' said Rachel. 'Hopefully.'

'That's the plan.' She smiled at Rachel. 'We were trying to make you happy by staying together. That's the irony.'

'Well, thanks for trying.'

'And failing.'

'Big time!' said Rachel. 'If you set out to make things crap, you couldn't have done any better.' She pulled a face which made them both laugh.

Steph put her head in her hands and groaned. 'It has been crap, hasn't it?'

'Mu-um!' Rachel was shocked.

'Sorry. But it has been. I've been crap.'

'Not all the time. Just some of it. I admire you, actually.'

'What?' Steph was shocked. 'Are you actually saying something nice to me, Rachel Fitzpatrick? Quick, call a photographer. I want to immortalise this moment!'

'Well,' said Rachel, laughing, 'I do. You know, keeping it all to yourself. Trying to protect me, keeping everything going.'

'Thank you,' she said. 'Thank you for saying that. It means a lot. The most. But I was wrong to do it. It didn't help you and it didn't help me... so...'

Rachel nodded. She unclipped Dingle's lead and allowed him to chase off, barking madly.

'It's not going to be the same without her...' said Rachel in a quiet voice.

'I know.' Steph took her hand in hers, it felt so good to hold her hand, to have that casual affection between them restored and renewed. 'I'm going to miss her. So much... so much.'

'Me too.'

They sat quietly for a while watching Dingle playing with some other dogs. Eventually Rachel spoke. 'Granddad is going to be the worst though. What's he going to do? I mean you and me've got each other, but he's got no one.'

'Yes, we've got each other.' Even at this terrible moment Rachel's words were a comfort to Steph. 'But he's got us, hasn't he?' she said. 'We're going to be there for him. And for each other.'

'Maybe he could live with us?' said Rachel.

'Maybe.' Steph had also worried about him. 'We could ask him.' Dingle came up and was sniffing around. 'We'd have to ask Dingle too. Could you cope with that?'

'Definitely.' Rachel stroked him as he remained stock-still, enjoying the moment. 'But Granny, poor Granny.'

Before they set off for home again, Steph took a moment to look towards the mountains again. She realised she had been living in a state of fear for so long, fear of Rick's rages, fear of anyone knowing she was a failure, fear of being caught shoplifting yet unable to stop, fear of everything crumbling, her whole life. She was going to live by the promise she had made to Nuala, not to be frightened by life. She wasn't going to live in the shadows anymore.

And yet here she was facing the worst fear imaginable, facing the death of her own dear mother, but she knew she would survive. She knew she would be okay because of all Nuala had given her. She was strong inside, the rest she could deal with.

I've wasted so much time, she thought. And none of it mattered. It's just me and Rachel now. We are what matters.

She looked over at her daughter who was waiting for her and she smiled. Life doesn't actually frighten me, she thought. Whatever happens, I can cope.

Back in the kitchen, she and Rachel stood together now, sharing a plate of sandwiches.

'I'm glad you are here, Heart-angel,' said Steph.

'Me too, Mum.' Rachel started crying again, which started Steph off again.

'She's not dead yet,' said Steph. 'We can't be doing this, all this crying.'

Rachel wiped her eyes with her sleeve. 'I've never done this before, you know someone dying.'

'Neither have I, actually. We've been lucky.'

'And now we're unlucky.'

'No, we're still lucky. We'll always be lucky. And we are lucky to have had someone like Nuala in our lives. She doesn't disappear because she's dead. We have our memories.'

'How are you feeling?'

'Sad. Really sad.'

'Me too.' They looked at each other, each blurred with tears. 'And there's nothing we can do...'

'Except feel sad,' finished Rachel.

'No...' said Steph. They smiled at each other despite the sadness.

'But we have each other... don't we?'

'We do... we have each other.' Mother and daughter hugged. 'Oh Rachel,' whispered Steph. 'I'm so glad we have each other.'

'Me too, Mum. Me too.'

'Let's go and join the madding crowd.' They went and sat on the two arms of Nuala's chair. Nuala held both their hands in hers.

'My girls,' she said. 'My girls.'

Steph remembered a Christmas Eve when there was a power cut. Joe wasn't home yet and Nuala had padded around the whole house in the pitch-dark, feeling for candles. She must have lit fifteen candles in the sitting room that evening and pulled Steph into her, covered with a rug, and she told her stories of when she was a small girl growing up in Kerry: there were tales of haystack climbing, of picking blackberries, of her little dog Georgie. Steph had forgotten all about the night of power-cut but memories came back to her so distinctly. It had been a magical night, tucked up with her mother. If she closed her eyes, she could still remember what she felt like, under her mother's arm, the scratchiness of the blanket, the flickering of the candles and hearing her voice telling all those stories. She knew for certain, then and there, she had the best mother a little girl could ever have.

Imelda Cunnane was standing up, ominously wielding a large knife.

'Time for speeches now. I'll begin.' She looked around the room. 'Now, I think it was fifteen years ago we began the Dalkey-Killiney Book Club.' The book club members gave a cheer. 'The club is more than a book club, of course. We pride ourselves on always *reading* the books, which, I'm told some rival book clubs don't.'

There were cheers from the room.

'However,' Imelda continued, 'there was one time when none of us could read the book – and if memory serves me right, it was Nuala's choice that week. Can you remember what it was, Nuala?'

Everyone looked over at Nuala who was laughing and nodding. 'I thought we should broaden our horizons,' she said.

The whole room was silent as she spoke.

'And what was it?'

'Ulysses,' said Nuala. 'It was over a thousand pages. None of us got through it.'

'And so,' continued Imelda. 'We have Nuala to thank for derailing the book club.' She paused for the generous laughter. 'But seriously, though, apart from that one misjudged choice, she has been the most wonderful friend to all of us. I know I speak for each member of the book club – and I am sure I speak for everyone in the room – when I say our lives...' her voice faltered and Imelda paused, eyes wide, mouth set, determined not to cry, '...would not be as warm without the friendship of Nuala. Once a month, to sit down with Nuala and talk about books and life, has been a great pleasure in my life over the last fifteen years.'

She stopped again, unable to speak. 'Welcome home, Nuala. We are looking forward to many more years of reading again.' Her voice broke, but everyone seemed determined to pretend that she wasn't dying, that the party was not to say goodbye.

There were 'hear-hears' from the room and teacups were lifted in the direction of Nuala.

The room was full of people who sensed this was a family on the brink of loss. Love was about to change immutably into something else. None of the Sheridan family would ever be the same again, without Nuala. Steph would be motherless, Rachel would not have a grandmother and Joe? How would he be able to live and breathe? Despite the smiles and the chatter, there was the sense of a community bracing itself to help this family through this trauma, the trauma that they were teetering towards.

'Speech, Nuala, speech!' someone said.

Nuala was getting slowly to her feet, leaning on Steph's arm, Dingle jumping to the ground.

'Thank you, everyone, thank you for coming. I am not one for making speeches, but it is such a lovely thing to come home from hospital and see the faces of my friends. I feel blessed to know you all. Thank you from Joe and myself for this lovely party and food. You are all so kind. I do want to say something to Joe, here, for being my best friend since the day we met. He has been the most wonderful companion in my life...' Joe was standing there, leaning at the doorway, tears in his eyes. 'Thank you Joe.'

'It's not over yet, Nuala,' he said. His throat was dry and his voice croaky, but he was trying to laugh. 'We've still got a few years left in us.'

'Of course, we have, Joe,' said Nuala. The room was silent apart from a gulp from Imelda, tears rolling down her face. Around the room, hands were surreptitiously wiping eyes.

'And my daughter and granddaughter, Stephanie and Rachel. They are the stars in my life.'

'We should do this annually, Mum,' said Steph. 'You know, it's the only time you say nice things about us!' Everyone laughed, but Steph and Nuala fixed in each other's gaze. I love you, I'll miss you.

'And my granddaughter,' said Nuala. 'She's the cherry on my cake.'

And then Nuala looked over at Joe and, for a moment, the whole room watched as these two people, who had been in love for over four decades looked at each other, as though there was no one else. It sent a shiver down Steph's spine.

'My Joe,' Nuala managed eventually. 'My Joe.'

And Joe stood there looking at her, not able to move and it was Imelda who broke the tension.

'I have my knife,' she said. 'Cake time?' She began slicing the book and doling out portions onto paper plates.

Steph with the pot, refilling Nuala's cup, who was sitting in the armchair, with Peggy O'Sullivan on one side and Kitty Kenny on the other side. 'How are you doing, Mam?'

'It's been a lovely party,' she said. 'Thanks for all your hard work.'

'You tired?'

'A bit,' Nuala admitted, looking like she was ready to fall down, 'but having everyone here is wonderful.'

'We'll do it next year, Nuala,' said Peggy.

'Only if you make your quiche again. You always did make such good pastry, Peggy. I can never get it that light. What's your secret?'

Peggy smiled enigmatically.

'Go on, I'll bring it to my grave,' said Nuala, winking at Peggy and Kate.

'Mam!'

Nuala laughed. 'Allow me, Stephanie. It's all right. The girls here know me by now, don't you?' Peggy and Kitty nodded.

'Well,' said Peggy, 'I'll tell you. It's bought. I've been buying it for years!'

'What?' Kitty looked aghast. 'But you won that competition last year at the ICA. Your pastry got a first.'

Nuala had begun to laugh. She couldn't stop. 'I don't believe it. Fraud! All these years we've been eating *bought* pastry.'

'I know, I know,' Peggy looked a little ashamed. 'I didn't begin to lie, it just happened. Next thing I know I am famous for my pastry – I couldn't tell everyone then.'

'But the ICA,' said Kitty, 'they have rules.'

'Rules are meant to be broken – and at our age, if we can't break a few of them, what is the point in living?'

41

MELISSA

A few weeks later, Melissa and her mother were sitting in the lounge of Killiney Castle, pot of tea for two in front of them.

They looked at each other, nervously, Mary clutching the handles of her bag tightly, Melissa trying to concentrate on pouring out the tea from a pot which wasn't designed to pour.

They were waiting to meet Tara Rose, aka Frankie, estranged daughter and sister. Frankie and Mary had spoken on the phone twice and they had arranged to meet, here, now. Mary had asked Melissa to come as moral support and Melissa knew that if she didn't come she would go mad in the wondering and thinking about Frankie. She had to be there.

'I haven't had a drink in two weeks,' said Mary, suddenly.

'Really, Mam?' said Melissa, cautiously. A fortnight was definitely the longest Mary had ever managed before, not that she had ever tried particularly hard. 'That's good.'

Mary nodded.

'And how are the meetings going? Helpful?'

'Difficult.'

'But you will keep going, won't you? You promised.'

'I promise, Melissa,' said Mary. 'I promise.'

'Mam, I know it's not easy, I know it must be difficult. But you've got to do the meetings.'

'I will,' she said, taking the cup, it rattling on the saucer. Melissa noticed she looked worse, not better. At least, she thought, let's just get this crazy meeting over with. And let's see what this is like. She couldn't imagine that Frankie was going to be normal in anyway. She hoped that this reunion would not just be a harbinger of the usual chaos and doom and set Mary on a backwards trajectory.

Luckily, Melissa was developing her own support group. As well as Eilis and Steph, she now had a therapist on speed-dial. You had to be prepared these days, she decided. No one can do life totally alone, she thought. I need support. And I need to change.

'So, what did Frankie sound like?' Melissa was trying to be calm. 'Did she sound nice?'

'Very nice, yes,' said Mary.

'And what did she say?' Melissa could feel her hackles rising at the lack of basic information. Keep calm, she told herself. Keep calm. She reminded herself where the door was. Being with her mother was like being on a plane. You always had to know where the emergency exits were. You never knew when you might have to escape. Mary sensed her frustration.

'She lives in Howth and has a boy and girl. Caleb and Cara. Those are nice names, aren't they?'

'Yes...?'

'I... I don't know what else to say, Melissa.'

'And she won't mind me being here?'

'You're her sister. She says she's looking forward to meeting you.'

'*Sister*.' Melissa tried out the word for size. Sister, that magical word. A sister. Her childhood dream. We're quite a pair, thought Melissa. Poor Frankie, what disappointments we're going to be.

Melissa had just put a large shortbread biscuit in her mouth when she realised her mother was standing up to greet a woman in front of them, smiling.

Frankie.

'Come on,' the stranger was saying, 'we should have a hug. It's not every day you meet your mother.'

Melissa had never seen that before: her mother, in the embrace of another. She almost said: See Mum, not so difficult after all. But she managed to keep her mouth shut. She really didn't want to frighten Frankie away.

Although Melissa had expected this woman to be a stranger, she looked just like them. Or specifically, just like Mary, except younger and lighter, brighter. This is what Mam would have looked like if she hadn't been so unhappy, if her tragedy hadn't enveloped her, if she hadn't begun drinking so heavily.

'And you must be Melissa? It's so lovely to meet you.'

They stood there, looking at each other for a moment.

'Hug?' said Frankie.

They laughed.

'Why not?'

Frankie may have been the cut of her mother, but there was a warmth and friendliness that Mary might have had if the circumstances had been different. Frankie was relaxed and was now ordering a fresh pot of tea. How could she be so laid-back when all this was so scary for all of them? But she appeared totally together, smiling, making eye contact. She looked happy.

Oh, wait a minute, not so happy. Frankie's eyes were full of tears.

'Are you okay?' said Melissa.

Frankie was wrestling with a packet of tissues.

'I knew I would need these... it's just, you know, just a little over-whelming to meet you both. I've waited for forty-five years for this.'

'It's just seeing you both here... all I've missed out. A mother... and a sister.'

'Me too,' said Melissa, taking her hand. 'Me too.' She smiled at Frankie. 'Your family... your adopted family. Was it happy?' Mary was listening to every word that Frankie said, but there was something in her eyes when Melissa spoke. What was it? Pride?

'It was normal,' said Frankie. 'We were normally happy. She's been a wonderful mother to me, but I always wondered, you know, about you.' She spoke to Mary, who was still dabbing at her eyes. 'And a sister, too! Well, that has been a shock,' she said turning to Melissa. 'A very nice, amazing, shock. I never imagined it, you. I never thought...'

'It's a shock for me too,' said Melissa, feeling shy all of a sudden. 'A good one.' Maybe curveballs which life sometimes lobbed in your direction could be nice ones.

Mary was looking at her long-lost daughter. 'Your hair,' she said. 'It's so dark.'

'For some reason, I'm not going grey – yet. Was it the same for you?'

'I think so... I don't really remember.'

'Yes, you didn't go grey for ages, Mum,' said Melissa, prompting her. 'And then it went grey overnight, practically.' She smiled at Frankie. 'It's all over for me though, I think. I'm like Gandalf under my hair dye.'

Frankie laughed.

'My beard's pretty Gandalfy too,' said Melissa.

Frankie laughed again.

'Tell us about Caleb and Cara,' said Mary. 'Melissa wants to know all about them. And I do as well,' she said. Melissa realised that her mum was trying to make an effort.

'I have photos.' Frankie delved in her bag and produced pictures of two lovely-looking children, smiling for the camera. Frankie had brought other photographs, too; of her as a child, with her mam and dad, riding a pony, graduating, her wedding day and millions more of Caleb and Cara.

Mary's eyes filled with tears. 'You've had a wonderful life,' she said.

Frankie laughed. 'These are just the highlights. I didn't photograph the ebbs. Or is it the flows? And I didn't choose any photos of me with double chins and a big red face. Or my awkward years. Which lasted some decades.'

This is nice, thought Melissa, surprised how much she liked Frankie. She hadn't wanted to; she had secretly wished that she might be a poorer version of herself, but there was no competition. She wanted to get to know her.

'We should have brought some of our photos, shouldn't we Mam?' she said. Her mother nodded, but Melissa realised that they didn't have those nice family photos of happy moments. She couldn't remember them even owning a camera.

'So, Melissa, tell me about you? Your mother, I mean, Mary... I mean...' She turned to Mary. 'Shall I just call you Mary for the moment? Would that be all right?' Their mother nodded. 'Mary told me you were a journalist and I've been reading your articles online... And you have awards. Wow.'

'Oh... thanks...' For a moment, Melissa didn't know what to say. Mary had never read a single one of her articles. Nothing she did was ever talked about or praised. It was rather strange to be sitting here with someone who was *interested* in her. It was something she could get used to, very used to indeed. 'That's really kind of you... actually, I'm not sure if it's what I want to do anymore... for the rest of my life.'

'Great,' smiled Frankie. 'A new adventure. Taking charge and making a change is one of the most rewarding things a person can do.'

'Really?' said Melissa, 'I feel petrified.'

'You are meant to feel petrified. Or it wouldn't be life.'

The two women smiled at each other. A sister, thought Melissa. A sister. I have a sister. She had so many questions, she wanted to know so much about Frankie, about her life, her upbringing, her happy childhood. She didn't care about their different lives, she was just excited about this new person. There was much to say. But what about Mary? Should she leave them to get to know each other? She couldn't commandeer the meeting. She was only meant to be here for moral support and had to give Mary and Frankie time together. She couldn't hog her.

'I've got to go...' she said. 'It was nice to meet you. Frankie.'

'Thanks for coming,' said Frankie, 'I think I'm going to like having a sister. I've always wanted one.'

'Me too,' said Melissa. 'I really mean that. Thank you for coming to meet us today. It's been brilliant.' She turned to her mother. 'You okay, Mam?'

Her mother nodded and tried to smile. She held out her hand and grasped Melissa's. They smiled at each other. The gesture was affectionate, they were going to move on together. There were tears in Mary's eyes.

'Life is strange, isn't Mam?'

'And wonderful,' said Mary. 'I'll walk you out.'

They stood up and walked away from Frankie, and at the door, they turned to each other. 'Thank you Melissa,' her mother said. 'I don't know what I would have done without you.'

'I'm your daughter, aren't I? This is what we do.' She laughed it off but they grasped each other in a slightly awkward hug. It may have been the only hug of their lives, and the most meaningful one they had ever had, but Melissa was going to make sure it wasn't the last.

'I love you, Mam.'

'Me too,' her mother managed. 'I love you too.'

Melissa quickly walked away and as she put the keys into the ignition, she saw through the windows into the lounge. Her mother was wiping her eyes and Frankie was doing the same. They were both crying again, this time tears of happiness to what the future holds.

42

STEPH

The front door creaked slightly as Steph was leaving the house just before six in the morning. She was going to see Nuala, and relieve the palliative care nurse. She really didn't want Rachel to wake up; she wanted her to sleep. At least when she was asleep, there was the chance of a nice dream.

And then Rick appeared on the stairs, in his dressing gown. He was leaving very soon but Steph hadn't seen much of him, he was working away a lot of the time and she was so busy spending all her time with Nuala.

'How's your mother?' he said, standing in front of her.

'Not great,' she said, trying to sound natural and normal. 'Palliative care nurses are with her every night... we're... we're close to the... end. You know...' she petered out.

'Will you send my best wishes?'

'Your best wishes? She's dying.'

'I know... I know. My wishes, my thoughts, you know.'

'I'll tell her.'

They looked at each other, unsure what to say. Steph had no real interest in what he was going to say anymore. He no longer wielded any power over her. She knew he'd be gone soon forever.

'I'm sorry,' he said. 'That's all. She's a lovely woman. Okay, so she didn't think much of me, but she was very good at hiding it.'

'Anyway... better go...' Steph turned the front door latch.

'Steph?'

She turned back. 'Yes?'

'I'm sorry,' he said. 'I didn't mean to hurt you.'

'Well, you did.'

'I'm sorry.'

'You've said it already.' She shrugged. 'What's done is done.' But then she felt something inside her, a flame light and she relished the feeling of having taken control of her life. It felt good.

'I know I hurt you,' he said. 'With Miriam.' He coughed.

'Yeah,' she said. 'You did. But I'll get over it. It hasn't killed me. This doesn't matter. This doesn't matter to me anymore. We weren't happy. Simple as that. We shouldn't have got married.'

'But then we wouldn't have had Rachel.'

'True.'

'Because I wouldn't change that for anything.'

'Nor me.' She looked at him and saw the face she had been looking at for nearly twenty years and she felt, weirdly, affection. She should hate him, she knew that, but he was just a man with problems and they weren't hers anymore. He could never hurt her again. 'Listen, Rick. Let's be good to each other, okay? Because we haven't been for years and years.'

'I promise. Do you?'

'I do,' she said. 'You know, it's exactly what I need. I promised Mam I would make myself happy. That I would lead my life better. That I would put myself and Rachel first. And this is the first step. Doesn't stop me being terrified though.'

'I'm terrified too,' he said.

'What? The great Patrick Fitzpatrick, master of all he surveys, terrified?' She was teasing and they both smiled at each other. 'Why does life have to be so difficult?' she said.

'Because otherwise it would be boring, I suppose. Listen, I've made some arrangements at the office. I'm going to be working from home on Fridays from now on, so I can have breakfast in some cafe with Rachel before school, if she'd like that, and then go to hockey with her in the afternoon. And then pizza or whatever.'

'That's great.' Steph was amazed.

'She was really pleased when I told her. It made me realise how much I've missed. She's a great girl.'

'She is, she really is.'

'I'm going to get a flat. In Dun Laoghaire. Near home, for Rachel.'

She nodded. 'That sounds... good. Anyway, I'd better go, Mam'll be wondering where I am.' So this is how marriages end, she thought, relieved that this particular union was fading to black so smoothly.

She was late, now, the nurse would be gone and she didn't like Joe having to do everything. She raced up the hill in her Mercedes.

Joe met her at the door. He didn't say anything but she knew by his expression.

'Gone?' she managed. 'She's gone?'

He nodded, blinking at her.

'Oh Dad,' She put her arms around him. 'I don't believe it. 'If only I'd been five minutes earlier.'

'I think she was trying to wait for you...' He was in shock, he couldn't take it in. 'She was holding this, he said, 'when she went.'

He held out a small framed picture of Steph and Rachel. 'Oh Dad!' said Steph, breaking down and falling to her knees. 'And I was nearly here. I was nearly here...'

They went upstairs to see Nuala, to stay at her side and hold her hand for as long as they could. But they would never have long enough, they would never be able to hold her hand ever again.

43

THE GIRLS

'How are you? How are you feeling?' Melissa had called Steph to see how she was. Melissa couldn't stop thinking about her. The funeral had, of course, been an awful occasion, and however much everyone tried to see it as a celebration of life and spirit, there was no getting away from the sight of Steph and Rachel, ashen-faced and clutching each other's hands, and Joe looking more dead than alive, the little dog tucked against his legs, as though searching for comfort or warmth.

'Fine, normal,' said Steph, 'and then I remember and start crying. It's a shock every single time. I wake up in the morning and everything's okay and then I remember it. And it's that horrible feeling all over again. That's the worst; remembering again. It's a bit embarrassing because I keep crying when I'm out and about. And when I dropped Rachel off to school today, she didn't want to go in but I made her – so that made me cry – and then when I was buying milk I saw those biscuits Mam liked, these jam ones, and I started crying again. So,' she said, 'I'm a bit of a mess.'

'You've got to let yourself cry.'

'Apparently. But it is quite inconvenient.'

They were quiet for a moment.

'I'm crying now. Only you can't see it. And everyone is being so nice. So many people at the funeral and then all the cards. You should see what things they said about Mam. About what a great woman she was, funny stories about her. There was even a card from a Brian O'Brien. Apparently went to school with her and always had a soft spot for her. He heard that she had died and he wanted to say how sorry he was. He said she was the most beautiful girl he had ever seen. She used to have a yellow dress that he thought made her look like a film star.'

'How lovely...'

'You see, it's started me off again. I miss her. I just miss her. And as for Dad... he doesn't know what to do with himself. He's taken to going for incredibly long walks with Dingle. I don't think he likes being in the house without her.'

She thought about her father. She'd seen him that morning. She was making tea for the two of them and when she passed him the cup, he said, 'There's no funny side to this, is there, Stephanie? We'll never find a funny side to this.'

'No, Dad,' she said. 'We won't.'

He was looking at the painting that Nuala had done with Joe, the one with the blue nose. They both stood there for a moment and looked at it.

'She was a wonderful woman, your mam,' he said. 'I've never known such a whirlwind. Meeting her was the most miraculous thing. We almost never met and things would have been very different.'

'Yes, Dad. She was our miracle.'

'It must be so hard...' said Melissa.

'Yes...' Steph sighed.

'What about Rick?' said Melissa. 'Where's he now?'

'He moved out last week. Asked me if it was too soon after the funeral, but I said no, that we should keep moving forwards. It's what Mam would have wanted. And it's what I want.'

'Where's he living?'

'In a posh flat in Dun Laoghaire. Nice view of the marina. Black leather sofa. Nespresso machine. The full bachelor works. It suits him, he says, near the train for going into town, and he can see Rachel easily.'

'Would you like me and Eilis to come round tonight? We could bring wine, tea, take-away for you? Maybe Joe would come down too?'

'He's been invited to the book club by Imelda Cunnane. She wouldn't take no for an answer. It might be good for him to get out but he keeps crying too. But I think Imelda is one of those women who can take it in her stride.' Everyone was rallying around, it had to be said. Everyone was there for them... except for the one person they needed most.

'Poor Joe.'

'About losing his wife or having to spend the evening with Imelda Cunnane?'

'Both.' They shared a small laugh together and for Steph it felt strange to be laughing, almost as though she shouldn't be. But she thought of Nuala, someone who spent her life laughing and she knew it would make her happy.

'What about Rachel?' said Melissa.

'It's her night with Rick. He watches her play hockey and then they go for pizza.'

'How's it going?'

'Fine,' she said carefully. 'So far. Let's see if he can keep it up'

'Apparently, he never had that trouble before,' said Melissa.

Steph managed to laugh. 'I'm so glad you rang, Mel,' she said. 'You've made me feel a *tiny* bit better.'

'Tiny is better than nothing.' Melissa paused. 'As Miriam probably said to Rick.' Steph laughed openly now. She couldn't believe she would ever have laughed at something which once had given her so much pain.

That night, Eilis and Melissa turned up with a selection of food. Melissa had picked up some sushi on the way over and Eilis carried in a cool bag in which she had put six lasagnes ('for the freezer,' she said, 'for you and Rachel and Joe'), along with nice bread and cheese, to keep them going.

And Melissa had made a lemon drizzle cake. 'Didn't you say this was Rachel's favourite?' she said.

None of them felt like drinking so they made tea and ate the sushi and Steph brought them up to date on everything.

'Dad is... well, he's doing his best,' she said. 'But the house feels so awful. Every time you walk in, it's like there is something missing. Well, there is...'

'Do you think he'll stay there?'

'He says he wants to... and the thought of packing everything up and selling the house is not something any of us wants to contemplate, but I was thinking that maybe he could move in here for a while. I don't know, we can see.'

Steph suddenly noticed Eilis was trying to find a tissue to wipe away her own tears.

'Are you all right Eilis?' she said.

'Yes, of course, I'm sorry Steph,' said Eilis.

'There's no need to be sorry,' said Steph, gently.

'It's bringing a few things to the surface, you see,' said Eilis. 'My mother... I didn't know at the time how to grieve... I wanted to get on with things and be a success... and I never grieved properly. I told Melissa about it the other day.'

'I wish we could have helped you better at the time,' said Melissa.

'But we were all eighteen,' said Eilis. 'None of us knew how to cope with anything, never mind Mam dying. You did used to try and get me to come out with you all the time when I was in the middle of exams. I remember that much!' Eilis cleared her throat. 'And Rob's gone, left. And he won't tell me where or why. Melissa knows all of it.'

'You were so caught up with the funeral and everything,' explained Melissa.

'Jesus Christ Eils,' said Steph. 'What's going on?'

Eilis shrugged. 'You know, after he wouldn't go to Greece, I knew something was seriously wrong, like a breakdown, or something.'

'He didn't go to Greece?' said Steph.

'No,' said Eilis, shaking her head. 'He refused to go. I know, nice of him, wasn't it?'

'Very nice,' said Steph. 'Is he depressed?'

'I have no idea. And is he okay?'

'Yes, because he's going into work every day. I rang his office and his secretary told me he was there. But it's just me, he doesn't want to see *me*.'

Melissa and Steph made eye contact. What was going on? Another woman, had to be. But why couldn't he just be upfront about it?

'Anyway,' said Eilis, 'I'm just getting on with things...'

'But that is so difficult,' said Steph, 'not knowing. It's really not fair.'

'No,' said Eilis, 'it's not fair.'

'Anyway, don't you have other things on your mind?' teased Melissa. 'Don't they say that the way to get one man off your mind is to get another...?'

'What's that?' said Steph.

'Oh, just some crush of Eilis,' said Melissa. 'A cross between Poldark and Jesus, it seems. Perfect man.'

They all laughed, even Eilis.

'No, that is definitely *not* my perfect man,' she said. 'Oh, I don't know...'

'I know something for sure, anyway,' said Melissa. 'You need some of my cake. I'll put the kettle on again.'

Steph got up to clear the plates and just as she was walking into the kitchen, Rachel came home.

'Did you have a good time?' she asked.

'Yeah, it was nice. We won our match and then we went for pizza but I got tired and wanted to come home.'

'Well, you're just in time for lemon drizzle cake. Come and have a slice.'

And so tea was made and Rachel joined her mum, Melissa and Eilis and they chatted about their own memories of school.

'Your mother,' said Melissa, 'once handed out condoms to all the girls in Sixth Year.'

'What?' Rachel looked shocked.

'They weren't to *use*,' Steph said quickly, 'We were all still good girls. It was a *political* act.'

'Oh, is that what it was?'

'Well, to be honest,' said Steph, 'If I remember right, I didn't really know what they were for, but they were giving them out at the students' union when I went for the open day and when I told them I was at the Abbey, one of the women there, gave me a box and told me to distribute them. I knew the nuns would go mad.'

'And they did!'

'But they never would have believed it was your mother,' said Eilis. 'She was far too goody-goody. They never did get to the bottom of it.'

'I remember being terrified my parents would find it and so I threw it in the bin on my way home from school,' said Steph.

Rachel was laughing. 'So you weren't very rebellious then?'

'We tried to be,' said Steph.

'And another time,' said Melissa, 'your mother was caught bringing vodka into the school-leavers' disco.'

'Immediately confiscated and no questions asked,' said Steph. 'Those nuns could smell alcohol from miles away.'

'And don't think they threw it away. They had their own party later, once we had gone home,' said Eilis.

'More cake Rachel?' said Melissa.

'No, I'm fine,' she said. 'I think I'll head up to bed.' She stood up. 'Night everyone.'

'Good night, Rachel, sleep well,' they all said.

'I'll be up in a minute,' said Steph.

At the door, Rachel stopped. 'It was really nice meeting you all properly.'

'You too,' they beamed at her.

And once she was gone, Steph started crying again. 'Look at me,' she said. 'I'm a mess.'

'You guys are going to get through this, you really are,' said Melissa. 'Look at you two already. You're both amazing.'

44

STEPH

The house was quiet, Rachel still asleep and without Rick there, Steph was the only one up. She was making a cup of tea for herself, when from somewhere outside she heard a scream and some raised voices.

And then, 'OH MY GOD!' Rachel shouted from upstairs. 'Mum, come up here!' Steph ran upstairs and into Rachel's room, where Rachel was standing at the window. From there they had a perfect view of next door's front garden.

Miriam was standing on the lawn in a black silk nightdress (the kind of thing Alexis from Dynasty would have worn) surrounded by a suitcase and clothes scattered around her. A window opened and Hugh threw more clothes out on top of her. He shouted something and disappeared while Miriam howled and sobbed. Black mascara smudged, hair on end. If it was the King's Road, circa 1979, it might have worked. Here, now, no.

Hugh was at the window again and this time lobbed out two pink floral wellies which boinged off the ground, just beside Miriam's bare feet.

'Just go and be gone!' Hugh roared. 'I never want to see you again! You black-hearted bitch!' All of Miriam's make-up (all that Chanel, that Estee Lauder, the Laura bloody Mercier) rained down on her. She darted around, trying to dodge them. It was like some Japanese gameshow.

Steph and Rachel looked at each other, their mouths open. Nice Hugh gone all Shakespearean and mad. This is what lying and cheating does to all of us, thought Steph. Turns us insane.

'So Aoife's gone and done it, Mum,' said Rachel. 'Gone and told Hugh. She said she was going to.'

Steph nodded. 'She had to, she couldn't keep that secret any longer, poor thing. Grown-ups are so stupid, aren't they?' she said to Rachel. 'We are embarrassing. I can only aplogised for my own kind.'

Another load of clothes was tossed out onto the lawn. Hugh was bright red in the face and yelling more obscenities. 'You sour-souled, two-faced, lying cheating, marriage-wrecking doom-mongerer!' He was really getting into his stride now.

'Poor Aoife, Mum, look.'

They peered out and Aoife was now on the lawn with her mum, trying to pull her indoors. The look on her face was stricken. It was horrible to see.

'We have to do something, Mum.'

They could hear Miriam's racking sobs, and Aoife's increasingly hysterical pleadings, and Miriam was shouting, 'I'm sorry okay! It was a mistake! Come on, Hughie, please?!'

At that moment, the window was pulled open and Hugh's furious face appeared and a leopard-skin bra and matching knickers floated featherlike to the ground while the words 'bloody tart!' echoed around the Sunday morning quiet.

'My *Agent Provocateur*,' said Miriam, in a whisper, who was now on Steph's path. 'I only bought them the other day.'

And then Miriam noticed that a little crowd of neighbours had gathered and curtains on Kish Road were twitching. She tried to pull down her black silk nightdress and smoothed her hair back and braced herself, while Aoife stared, eyes like saucers, worried. However, Steph couldn't help noticing – hell, the whole street couldn't help noticing – that Miriam's breasts looked perky, defying not only age but gravity as well. Surely not. They were literally *unreal*. However bedraggled Miriam was, she still looked sexy, like a batty Brigitte Bardot.

And then the last anguished shout from Hugh. 'You have broken my heart,' he half wailed, half keened across the street, before he slammed the window shut.

Steph went downstairs, with Rachel on her heels, and opened the front door. There was palpable excitement from the neighbours, a frisson rippled through the air, they all knew the whole story, obviously. What would Steph say to the woman who shagged her husband? She began walking towards Miriam. Even, Hugh, she could see, was peering out from the upstairs window, waiting to see what would unfold.

'Miriam?'

Miriam looked at her, tear-streaked and beaten. 'Yes?' she said in a small voice. She looked wary and anxious.

'Do you...' Steph looked at her. 'Do you want to come in and have some tea? You and Aoife. It looks like you need a cup. The kettle's on.'

Miriam stared back. 'Tea?'

'Yes, come on,' she said. 'You can't stay outside in your nightdress. Come on.' She looked at Aoife whose eyes had welled up, and then quickly she ran down their path, through their gate and over to Rachel. The two girls hung on to each other, both crying. They ran indoors, and straight upstairs to Rachel's room.

It was just Miriam and Steph left.

If this was a soap opera, they would have been rolling around on the lawn, dragging clumps of hair out, screaming at each other over some stupid fucking man. But she looked at Miriam's skinny body, the bird's nest hair and Alice Cooper make-up, and all she could see was a lonely woman. Welcome to the club, Miriam. Welcome to the club. But she had a feeling that Miriam wouldn't be lonely for long. The curtain-twitching was getting frenzied. You could sense that whole families were peering out, phone calls and texts were being made, the energy in the road was fizzing with gossip.

'Look, Miriam, I know,' she said. 'I know everything. But, as Rachel might say, whatever. I'm over it. Rick has moved out and I'm moving on. I don't quite know how, yet, but I am.' She looked at the neighbours who were practically taking pictures for the Dalkey Newsletter. 'I think,' she said, 'we should have a cup of tea inside.'

Miriam nodded quickly and made her way to Steph's garden. 'Thank you!' Miriam called out. 'Thank you for watching. The next performance will be the matinee.' She smiled her big smile. 'Come back then!'

Steph had to marvel at how quickly Miriam was making a return. She was never going to be down and out for long.

In the kitchen, Steph put on the kettle and began to dig out cups, milk, teabags, while Miriam sat on her only armchair, shivering and feeling sorry for herself. Steph pulled over one of the kitchen chairs and sat beside her and waited to see what Miriam would say.

Miriam had begun to cry. 'I'm so sorry,' she said. 'I am so sorry.' Great huge sobs choked her throat, her mascara even more smudged. 'It's over, anyway. Whatever it was... it's over. All of it. I – I – we...' Miriam gave up. And she began to cry again. 'He was seeing someone else, Steph, did you know? It wasn't just me.' She was actually trying to make Steph an ally, that they were both wronged by Rick, as though Steph was just another woman. But Steph didn't move a muscle, just gazed back at her. 'I knew he wasn't interested in me anymore,' continued Miriam. 'I could tell before we went to Rome, you know? I could just tell.'

Steph remained silent.

'I know you must be simply furious with me, I would be,' said Miriam, trying to charm her. 'He told me you and he were over years ago. So I didn't think it was so bad.' She looked at Steph beseechingly. 'And I thought now he had moved out that maybe... maybe... we would... oh, I don't know.' She was hard to understand through the sobbing. 'But anyway,' went on Miriam, 'last week I saw him out with some girl in town and I confronted him... and he...' she began to wail again, 'he told me to go away and said I was drunk and embarrassing. Which, it has to be said, is true. But...'

'But not the point,' said Steph, a little too helpfully. I am the wronged one, she had to remind herself. Not Miriam. Focus, Steph.

Miriam was losing it now. 'And then, and he tried to walk away and I grabbed him and threatened to tell everyone and ruin him. But he just walked away from me. Went off with that woman.'

'So,' she said carefully, 'how did Hugh find out?'

'Aoife told him last night. She had to, poor lamb. She had known for ages as well. And it wasn't fair on her. So...'

'Well, it's probably for the best that everyone knows. No secrets. They eat people up.'

Miriam nodded miserably.

'Let's just try and deal with this, the best we can, and let's just think of our daughters. We have to put them first, don't we?' She stood up. 'Now, would you like sugar in your tea? Six spoons?'

Miriam drank the tea in one – she mustn't have had sugar in years, but she did look a million times better when she placed the mug on the table.

45

MELISSA

'Meeting?' It was Liam. 'Could you honour us?'

'Coming,' Melissa called and stood up, breathing in the stale office air. I used to love this place, she thought, this horrible air. I used to feel my heart lift, my soul soar in this building. And now? Now, I feel as though I'm going to go quite mad if I stayed another second.

'Melissa!' Liam said, as she reached his office. 'My favourite woman.'

'I never know if you are being sarcastic or what,' she said, sitting herself down.

'With you, Melissa, always sincere. With others, it all depends.'

'On what?'

'What I need from them,' he said, raising just the one eyebrow. 'Anyway, 'I've got a lunch appointment so we won't be long,' he said. 'But I was wondering...' He smiled annoyingly, '...if you had any thoughts about your editorial for this week?'

'Um...'

'I mean, are you ready to have F-U-N-N spells fun?'

'It doesn't.'

He laughed.

'Liam ...' Melissa thought about the years she had spent at this paper, the hours sweating over her copy, the excitement of seeing it in print and reading and rereading it again and again. She'd had fun, but it wasn't the kind that Liam wanted from her. Telling the stories of the dispossessed had been, if not actually fun, exciting, a blast. She had felt she was doing something important and that had been a wonderful ride. But it was over.

'Well, actually, Liam' she said smiling sweetly, 'I'm leaving. This is me handing in my notice. From now.'

'What?' His grin faded as quickly as a shaken Etch A Sketch.

'I've had fun. But I don't want to have the kind of fun you want. I don't want to interview celebrities, or ask people about their sex lives. Or dogs with over-large testicles or cats with one leg or a woman who has grown the largest tomato in the northern hemisphere.'

'Those are good ideas,' he said. 'What are you saying? You're not doing them or you are?'

'Liam,' she said. 'Let me spell it out for you...'

'I-T,' he said, laughing at his own joke. 'You said let me spell it out for you... never mind. Melissa Murphy... is you *resigning*? Because there is no way you are.'

'I am,' she said. 'And this is what it sounds like. 'I'm resigning. Goodbye Liam, goodbye Standard, goodbye computers which never work, printers that never print and the worst coffee I have ever tasted. Goodbye windows that need cleaning and farewell stained carpet tiles.'

He looked at her. 'Why?'

'Liam! I've already told you. I can't write the kind of features you want and I don't want to be squeezed on page fifteen below the personal ads and the horoscope. I'm going to write but not here, not like this. Not anymore.'

'But I thought you were being your usual humorous self.' He looked stunned. 'Melissa, wait a moment. Take some time off. We can arrange something. We'll come up with something. Okay? I know these changes have been difficult, I know my style can be a little abrasive...'

Melissa stood up and shook his hand. 'I don't need to think about it. I'm just not the journalist for you.'

'Let's keep this conversation going? Let's keep talking. Okay?'

'I have to go. I have stuff going on... I can't be here anymore. This is it. I'm going to take some holiday... and then I'm gone.'

'If you change your mind...'

'I won't,' she said. 'It's time to go. Sorry Liam.'

He looked at her, thinking, doing his usual plotting and planning. 'Listen,' he said, 'my pal Peter Carberry is looking for freelancers at the Times. I'll give him your number. Keep the wolf from your door.'

'That'd be great. Thanks Liam.'

'They might be right up your street. They don't do "craic" over there.'

'Suits me, so.'

'What are you going to do... now you're free-range?'

'I don't know exactly. Sort some stuff out. Sort me out. Begin a novel... Perhaps. Perhaps not. Have some F-U-N-N.'

'You take care of yourself, okay. And join us for Christmas drinks on the 19th. Fallons. Promise?'

'I'll be there. Promise.' She wasn't sure she would.

'I never did give you one of my bollockings, did I?'

'No... I thought I'd get out before you did. They were legendary.'

'You know, Mel? The place will be a lot quieter without you... and not as much fun.'

'Now there's an irony.'

Melissa could still hear Liam laughing as she said goodbye.

As she walked out, Lulu was hovering and wearing a dress so tight and short that only the very young or the very optimistic could wear it. She had boots that reached to mid-thigh leaving a gap of flesh.

'Going somewhere nice?'

'Business meeting,' coughed Lulu. 'With Liam, I mean Mr Connolly.'

'Right...' said Melissa, the penny dropping. 'Well, I'll see you Lulu around. I'm moving on.'

'Really?'

'Yeah. Good luck with everything. You're a good writer, keep on doing it.'

Lulu blushed. 'Thanks Melissa. From you that means the world.'

Melissa held out her arms and hugged her. 'I expect to see you win some awards. Or the Pulitzer Prize one day.' She winked at her as she walked away.

I hope she likes Bananarama, thought Melissa. Hope her eighties music is up to scratch. Somehow she doubted it was. She walked straight into Jimbo who was carrying a packet of Hula Hoops.

'How's it going?' he said. 'Haven't seen ye for a while?' He was looking at her, curiously, he knew something was going on. That's the problem with journalists, thought Melissa, they always wanted to know what was going on.

'Jimbo,' she said. 'I'm leaving.'

He said nothing, just looked at her. 'As in fecking off?' he said after a moment.

'Yes, for good. I've just told Liam.'

'And what did he say? Did he bollock you? Is that why you're off?'

'No, it's just that there's no place for me here anymore. I don't fit in.'

'That's a bit drastic,' he said. 'Why didn't you just bollock him instead?'

'Because I want a change. I want to move on with my life. I don't know what's out there for me, but there's got to be something.'

'Aye,' he said, after a moment. 'There will be. Smart girl like you. You'll be fine.'

She smiled at him. 'Let's stay in touch, all right?'

'You do that, give me a call.'

'And you can fill me in on the romance between Lulu and Liam.'

'Never!' He whistled.

Melissa shook her head. 'And you call yourself a bloodhound.'

'I'll never understand women,' he said. 'That eejit. And I was hoping to make my Hula Hoop mobile. I thought I'd give you the first bite.'

'Well, sorry Jimbo. You'll have to try it yourself.'

'Right.' He looked disappointed.

'It's just that my life needs a reboot,' she tried to explain. 'A change, a challenge, an adventure. You know?'

'Aye,' he said, nodding. 'We all need that from time to time. Good luck with it. I'll see ye around.'

'See you Jimbo.'

She wondered if they were going to hug but they didn't. They stood there for a moment and then Jimbo turned away and walked down the corridor.

Just as he was about to disappear, he turned around. 'You're the only person I have ever been able to stand,' he said. 'In an office situation.'

Melissa almost fainted at the compliment. 'I'll miss you too,' she called, but he didn't turn around again.

She raced down the steps, all the way to the ground floor, this time thinking of her mother, Mary, and wondered what their future held. They had Frankie now... and, she supposed, Caleb and Cara. In fact, Frankie had called her and just she and Melissa were going to meet up, once Christmas was out of the way, and spend some time together at Frankie's house and she'd meet Caleb and Cara then.

But there was Cormac, of course.

She had discovered life without Cormac was a soul-withering and spirit-depleting situation but she had no choice except to get on with it and strike out anew.

She should have felt terrified but there was something that kept her walking out of the door of the building. No, it definitely wasn't fear that was fuelling her, it was something else, a sense of her own power, a sense that she could control her own destiny. That she didn't need to be scared of anything ever again. She was sure she was doing the right thing. I am never going back, from now on, she thought, from now on I only go forwards.

She began scrolling through her phone. When she had found Cormac's number, she pressed Delete Contact on her phone. That's it, Cormac gone, job gone. She was going to start again.

46

EILIS

Eilis was waiting for the delivery of a new sofa. She had gone to Ikea and had chosen the softest, squishiest and most comfortable sofa in the shop. She had practised the various positions she might be in: the full recline when watching TV, the cross-legged perch when eating tea and toast and, of course, the relaxed, casual normal sitting-on-a-sofa pose. It had passed all the tests with flying colours. She had just waved off the Rob's old one which she was giving away to a good home. An architect couple turned up to collect it, delighted with their new sofa.

Eilis had even bought some cushions for it, adding to the one Steph had bought her. And a rug. Immediately the house seemed more like somewhere she felt she belonged.

A knock on the door. She wondered who it was. The architect couple returning the sofa saying that they had changed their minds and it was way too uncomfortable.

Standing there, with a full hipster beard, was Rob. 'Hi,' he said. Eilis gaped at him in shock.

Eilis mouthed an inaudible response and looked at him with wide eyes. It was like seeing a ghost. She had heard nothing from him in months.

'Where have you been?' she managed.

'Staying with friends.' He looked awkward.

'But...'

'Eilis?'

She looked at him.

'Eilis, I'm here to say sorry.'

'Okay... so you've said it. I've heard you. And that's all grand.' She went to close the door but he pushed it open.

'Eilis... look, I'm so, so sorry. But I had no choice.'

'No choice? It seems very clear that you *chose* to leave.'

'Can I come in? Please? I want to explain.'

She stood back and let him pass. She'd begun the process of moving on but she did deserve an explanation, she figured. She was still curious what happened. Rob walked into the kitchen, looking around at his old house, taking in the changes.

'It's nice to be back.'

She glared at him. He wasn't coming back, if that's what he thought. She had just begun thinking that she was moving on, making the place her own. 'What do you want Rob?'

He looked at her, sadly. 'Listen... I... it's just... I don't know how to explain this, any of it.'

'Just try,' she said. 'If you want to tell me.'

He cleared his throat. 'Eilis, you have always been my best friend, since we met, it was great. I love you, I loved our life together but...'

'But what? You met someone else, someone more attractive than me? Someone better?'

'Kind of.'

She didn't expect him to say that, so for a moment she felt winded. She turned slowly to look at him. And there was Rob, totally disarmed, so unlike the smooth, in-control Rob she knew. For a moment, she saw the young boy from Ennis she had met more than two decades ago. He was still there, he'd never gone away... he'd just been hidden.

Eilis broke the silence: 'So, who is she?'

'He.'

'He?'

'Yes, he.' Rob looked at her, imploring her to understand.

She looked confused. 'He?' she said again.

'He.' He coughed, trying to clear his throat. 'I'm gay. Always have been. Just hoped I wasn't. And then I met you and, at first, for ages, I thought I was straight and I was just so relieved. But I hadn't stopped being gay because I met you. I was. I am. And I can't deny it any longer. It's been killing me.'

'You're gay?' she said, trying to take it in. 'As in gay?'

He nodded. 'I thought I could just pretend I wasn't, that sex wasn't important. I thought I could ignore it and everything would be okay. But I couldn't.' He stopped. 'May I have a drink of water, please?'

She reached for a glass. This was something she hadn't even considered for a moment. She realised she had been stupid to have missed all the signs. Of course! But why hadn't he told her, it could have saved years of her life. She turned on the tap and handed the glass over

'Thank you.' He drank it down. 'About four years ago, I actually realised I couldn't live like this. I wanted to be seen, to be real. I wanted the world to know who I was. I wanted to be visible, not hiding away. It's the most basic of feelings. I want the world to know who I truly am. But the thought of hurting you, of... coming out, of being me, was horrifying.' He stopped. 'But I knew I had to do it. I just didn't make a very good job of it.'

'No, you didn't. It was quite brutal.'

'I'm sorry,' he said. 'I thought I was going to either crack up.' He stopped unable to speak anymore.

'So...' Eilis prompted.

'So, I began going online... to different sites and talking to people. Men.' He sipped his tea. 'Men like me. Men in marriages, men in denial, unhappy, lonely men, like me.'

'So, you decided to do all of this without breathing a single word to the woman with whom you shared your life and home. Why didn't you tell me twenty-one years ago? My whole life! My whole adult life has been dominated by this relationship, which I now discover was entirely a lie. Your selfishness, your need for secrecy has meant that I've wasted two whole decades!'

'I am so sorry. I really am.'

'Jesus Christ, Rob! How could you?'

'I'm sorry.' He looked down.

'So, where've you been staying?' She spoke more gently now, as she realised how sad he was. It wasn't easy, obviously, to admit his true self.

'With Michael.'

'Is he gay too?' she said softly.

Rob nodded.

'Right,' she said. 'Are you two... you know? Are you together?'

He nodded again. Eilis wondered about protocol in situations like this, should she throw something? One of his silly angular mugs, perhaps. Or boil the remote-controlled kettle dry?

'So why are you here now?'

'To collect my things... and to explain to you.'

'In that order?'

'No. Not, in that order. Please Eilis, come on...'

'Why should I?'

'Because... because I am sorry. I made a mistake.'

He was right, it had been a mistake, their whole life together had been fake and unreal. Theirs hadn't been a relationship, it was barely companionship. She liked him and he liked her but not enough, never enough, to blend their lives, to marry, to have a child, all of those things she had never allowed herself to dream of but she had wanted. And now it was probably too late for her.

'A child would have been nice,' she said looking out of the window... She felt as though her heart was being constricted, squeezed into a tiny ball. It was a physical pain.

'It's not too late.'

'Easy for you to say, Rob,' she said, feeling her voice break. 'Off for your new life. It's so easy. You change your mind. I've decided I'm gay, sorry everyone!' Her voice was rising to a pitch now. 'But you don't have a biological bloody clock, do you. Convenient that! I do though. I'm nearly thirty-nine, Rob. I have given up so much for you – so fucking much.' She looked at him meaningfully and he looked down at his lap. 'And this! This is how you repay me.'

And breathe. She calmed herself. If only she had paid more attention at the yoga class she took years ago, she might have been able to do alternate nostril breathing or whatever it was, and not lost her equilibrium in the first place.

But she suddenly realised she felt relieved. All the uncertainty was over. She didn't have to think about Rob ever again, if she didn't want to. She always knew, deep down, that they weren't right for each other. Now, she could move forward. The photo of her mother was on the windowsill. She wondered what she would make of it or what she would say. Brigid was a woman who always gave people the benefit of the doubt, who was forgiving and loving. Brigid would have seen the good in Rob, she thought. It must have been so difficult for him to keep the pretence going all these years. But he'd done it now, better later than never.

'Sorry,' he said again and this time she shrugged. What was done was done.

'I forgive you,' she said.

'What?'

'I forgive you.' She felt free. It was a wonderful feeling, not scary at all. 'You are an eejit, though. You might have saved me years of trouble had you bothered to come out before.'

'Tell me about it.' He placed his hand over hers and squeezed it.

'I'm seeing someone too.'

'Really?'

'Well, a counsellor,' Eilis laughed. 'You know my mum... I never did quite talk about it enough...' she trailed off.

'That sounds like a good idea. You're very brave, Eilis. That was one of the things I most loved about you.'

'Loved?'

'Love.' He smiled at her.

'*Loved* is better. But thank you for trying to save my feelings.'

'Listen, may I have a cup of tea? Please? I'm gasping.'

She stood up and began filling the kettle.

'By the way,' she said. 'Make sure you take your kettle with you when you go. I'm going out to buy a new one this afternoon. One that doesn't require a gadget just to have a cup of tea.'

47

STEPH

It was to be the first Christmas without Nuala, the first time Steph wouldn't be buying her a present. A festive frenzy had descended on Dublin, madness was in the air, and it was the seemingly small things that stopped Steph in her tracks these days. It seemed so wrong not to buy Nuala something. She left Grafton Street and began walking down Nassau Street. At the National Gallery she paused and looked through the big doors. She used to love this place, spend all her time here, going for lectures, sketching some of her favourite paintings, meeting friends in the café. She hadn't been here for years. And to think that for all this time, it had been here and she had forsaken it.

She pushed open the doors. At last, here was somewhere she could breathe. The high ceilings, the quiet hush, it was soothing and reassuring after the bedlam of outside. She walked straight upstairs and found the Caravaggio and it was there, sitting on a bench, she began to cry. She had kept everything together for so long, desperate to help Rachel through this tumultuous time in their lives that she hadn't taken enough time to cry for herself. For Nuala, for Joe, for her marriage, for Rachel. For herself.

Quiet and semi-dark, after the crazy cacophony of Grafton Street, it was like being in church. The painting's beauty and the sense of awe it always inspired in her never failed to work its magic but never before had it made her cry and, for a long time, she sat there sobbing and sobbing. The silent security guard shuffled around discretely, ignoring her, as though a woman crying in front of a painting was an entirely normal part of his day. She wondered if The National Gallery was a popular place for people in the throes of a breakdown.

A couple of visitors neared the bench and quickly veered away. Eventually, Steph's tears became snivels and she realised she had created an invisible exclusion zone in which tourists and art lovers avoided her. I can't believe I have basically prevented all these people from seeing the Caravaggio, she thought, realizing she would never be able to return. There was nothing to do except sneak out, burglar-like.

'And now, in this room we have the jewel in the collection...' a loud voice was saying as a group of Japanese tourists all wearing earpieces shuffled into the room.

Oh no, thought Steph, hiding her face, tear-streaked, puffy and red.

'The great Italian painter Caravaggio painted this in Rome 1602. How the painting found its way to the National Gallery is an interesting story...' The voice went on, echoing around the room.

Steph lifted herself off the bench and began to tiptoe to the door.

'It was discovered, dusty and forgotten in the home of...' the commanding voice dropped to an insistent whisper, ridiculously audible through the microphone. 'Steph? Steph Sheridan?'

Steph looked at the tour guide through puffy pinpricks of eyes. 'It's me Eileen. Jesus Christ! I don't believe it!' She was still speaking through the microphone. All the tourists were looking at the two of them, totally ignoring the Caravaggio. Eileen! Eileen, her friend from college.

'One moment ladies and gentlemen...' said Eileen, and then to Steph. 'Don't you dare move or I will kill you... okay?' She gave Steph a delighted thumbs-up before smoothly returning to her tour-guide voice.

'So here in this painting... we have the interplay between light and darkness...' Eileen continued, speaking far too quickly for the foreigners, unused to her accent, to follow. And then never had a tour been wrapped up to so quickly ('andthat'sitfortodayfeelfreetowanderandthanksforcoming!') before Steph and Eileen were hugging each other.

'I can't believe it's you. I thought you were in the West!' said Steph.

'Was. Then London. Got married but now here, newly divorced – I ditched the Italian – Salvatore – what was I thinking? I may as well have married a Martian. Oh My God, it's *such* a relief to be home, with *normal* people again. It's great to see you. Do you know, I was just thinking of you and Pippa the other day, remember that time in Achill?'

'Achill. Oh God, yes. That was crazy. I haven't touched tequila since.' They looked at each other.

'And Rome!'

'Yes, Rome,' said Steph, weakly, thinking that she had ruined Rome forever, after her last doomed trip.

'So, elephant in the gallery,' said Eileen. 'You look like you've been crying.'

Steph nodded, feeling the tears welling up again. 'It's nothing... I mean... well apart from divorce for me too and death... my mother...' She began to cry again.

Eileen linked her arm through Steph's. 'Let's go to the cafe for some tea.'

Downstairs, Steph told Eileen everything.

'Snap,' said Eileen. 'My Mam too... five years ago...'

'I'm so sorry, I didn't hear.'

Eileen shrugged. 'It's okay... She had dementia in the end... but I try to remember her when she was young. And funny. And my Mam.'

Eileen topped up their cups from the pot.

'It's just it's all so raw, still, you know?' said Steph.

Eileen nodded. 'Give yourself time, okay? It's not a competition about who can get over huge life changes the fastest. Death, divorce. They're the biggies.'

'I know,' said Steph. 'It was nice just coming here. Time on my own. I have the chance for a new start, but I haven't quite started yet.'

'Time enough. Stay in limbo for as long as you need. You'll know when you're ready to brave real life again.'

And then Steph told her about Rick.

'We've never been happy, actually, if I'm honest. And it's not my fault – or his. He was horrible, and then it became the worst mess imaginable. We stayed for Rachel but ended up making everything worse, to be honest. My job now is to make it up to her.'

'Salvatore and I never... we didn't have a child... made it easier to leave, I suppose. So every cloud... I would have liked a mini-Eileen though, or even a mini-Salvie. I would have called it some fiendish Irish name, though, to annoy his family. Something they couldn't spell.'

They looked at each other, grinning.

'It's good to see you, Eileen.'

'You too, Steph. You know, despite your *annus horribilis*, you're looking good.'

'I'm not, I look terrible.'

'No, you were always gorgeous. Haven't lost it, you know.'

Steph blushed. Eileen was always good for making you feel better.

'So,' said Eileen. 'Are you working?'

'Gave it all up when I was married. I know, I know...' she said in response to Eileen's quizzical eyebrow. 'Haven't worked since. I've missed it. A lot.'

'Well, I've an idea. They need someone to do tours here. I'm only filling in – maternity leave, before I start teaching. What about it? Four days a week, tours every two hours. And there's other work too, cataloguing. Might be worth thinking about? It's a start.'

'Oh God. I don't know anything anymore.' But the very thought, the very idea, suddenly filled her with possibilities and excitement. Could she?

'Maybe you could start refreshing your memory. Do you still have your Gombrich?'

'Of course.'

'Well, dust it down. Blow off the cobwebs and give it a go. There is a training course starting next week. You need an art history degree, which you have. And the ability to talk to the public. Which I know you have too.'

'I have to say yes, don't I?' The idea was growing and growing on her. This was a chance for her to do something. This was a second chance.

'Yes, yes you do. I'm going to put your name down for the course. It takes two weeks. I think you'd be brilliant. I'm your sponsor or whatever it is. Say yes.'

'Okay, yes, then.'

'Good.' Eileen was smiling at her.

Steph could feel a tingling, like her phoenix feathers were sprouting. I'm doing it, Mam, she thought. Look! I'm doing it.

48

MELISSA

Melissa already had two freelance commissions and was working on her contacts. She'd really let them go in the last few years, but it was time to reignite her career. It was so frightening to be on her own but liberating too. She didn't dare to feel excited, but there was some unnamable feeling inside her that if she didn't know any better she might just have labelled it excitement. And she had started sketching ideas for a novel... it was going to be about a young girl in the late 1960s who found herself unmarried and pregnant...

She had even bought a small Christmas tree for her flat. It was a symbol that she was celebrating and embracing her new life. She toasted it with a glass of sparkling apple juice. Her new business cards were ready from the printers, so she took the bus into town and battled the people and traffic of George's Street, when she saw someone she recognised.

A woman was striding along the street, dressed in a long camel overcoat. While everyone else was in unflattering woolly hats, she wore her brown hair down her back and she wore long boots and a fur scarf.

Erica.

Melissa didn't know whether to smile and wave or to duck down and keep walking. Erica looked her usual gorgeous self. She didn't even seem bothered by the abysmally-dismal weather. Melissa wondered about Erica and Cormie's first Christmas together. Would they be roasting a goose or a turkey? Organic, obviously. Or maybe some kind of Gwyneth

Paltrow-inspired nut roast, all chia seeds and baobab (whatever that was).

'Melissa!' She had been spotted. Immediately she felt awful for skulking around. It wasn't Erica's fault that she and Cormie had met and fallen in love. She was blameless. It was she, Melissa, who had brought all this misery on herself.

'Erica!' She smiled, faking her surprise delight.

'I thought it was you, buttoned up. It's so hard to tell what people look like in this weather.'

'Yes, it's total pants, isn't it?'

Erica looked puzzled.

'It's pretty bad, that's what I meant,' Melissa explained. She was dying to ask how Cormac was... was he okay? Was he eating? Was he still beautiful? Was he still alive? She hadn't seen him since Nora and Walter's party. It had seemed so strange to carry on with life without him, and all the things that had happened to her since them. She lost a job and gained a sister. Not bad going.

'Yeah, y'know,' Erica was saying. 'I don't think I can do another Irish winter. It's not the cold, it's the constant drizzle. It's so not good for my body, y'know?'

'It's not good for mine, either,' agreed Melissa. 'It's not good for anyone's. That's why they invented the Aran sweater. It's the only thing you should wear in Ireland. And a tweed cap. You should get one.'

Erica looked confused and then tried to laugh. 'Oh, you're joking again. Cormie always said you had a great sense of humour.'

'Right...' said Melissa, wondering how to end the encounter and not wishing to know about Eric and Cormie's life together.

'So...' Erica took charge of the conversation. 'I'm heading back to the States. Better weather, for one. Nicer food and I think... I think it's a good move. Professionally and personally. I'm leaving tomorrow.'

Melissa quickly put aside her indignation of the casual assassination of her nation and desperately thought of Cormac. He was leaving? But what about the bakery? And Rolo? He would never survive quarantine... he wasn't... no, he wasn't going to give him to the pound? Not Rolo. Thoughts of poor Rolo locked in the cage, desperately seeking a new owner were interrupted by Erica, saying: 'You didn't know about me and Cormie?'

'No...' said Melissa, miserably, as the drizzle segued into rain. And

Cormac on the other side of the Atlantic, time zones away.

'Well,' she said. 'It wasn't working. He's super nice and everything but he doesn't have the drive of guys from the US? He's easy-going, too easy-going.'

'He's not going with you?' Melissa dared to hope.

'We've broken up,' said Erica. 'No, he would never leave Ireland anyway. He's a home boy.'

'And of course Rolo.' Melissa almost punched the air. Of course Cormac would never leave Ireland. He loved the rain too much.

'That dog! Don't talk to me about that dog. It was always scratching at his fleas.'

'I don't think Rolo has fleas,' said Melissa stiffly, thinking that Erica could slag off Ireland if she wanted to, it was, after all a free would, but criticising Rolo was going too far. 'He's pristine. He's a dog who takes his personal hygiene very seriously.'

'Yeah, right.' Erica was sceptical. 'Anyway,' she looked away for a moment. 'I think Cormie is in love with someone else?'

Melissa was again plunged into the depths of despair. What fresh hell is this? Who was this new rival?

'Really? Who is it?' she asked, weakly.

'Just someone he can't get out of his head. Someone he's been in love with forever.'

Melissa racked her brain. It wasn't... it couldn't be...

'Someone who might just love him back,' said Erica.

'Who?' croaked Melissa. 'Who?'

'You.'

Tears filled Melissa's eyes. 'Me?' she managed. 'He loves me?'

'Y'know, he tried to tell me that you were gay. And it was then I knew exactly what was going on. Call me Jessica Fletcher if you like, but as soon as he said that I knew the truth.'

'But I'm not gay...'

'Exactly.' Erica looked at her watch. 'Listen, there's a gathering at the bakery tonight. It's already started. Why don't you get yourself down there and see what happens? You never know, y'know.'

'No,' said Melissa, 'No you don't.'

'So, what are you waiting for?'

'I'll go, I'm going... oh, thank you Erica.' Melissa suddenly wanted to hug Erica, months of bad feeling and resentment melted away as she realised Erica was not just a pretty face, she had a very beautiful soul too.

Erica was smiling at her. 'If I am not going to have a Christmas romance, then someone else might as well. And, anyway, I like playing cupid.'

'But you don't mind?'

'No, I'll just find myself a new guy back in the States. It won't take me long.'

'I don't doubt it.'

'See you, Melissa. I hope I get to hear how it turns out.'

Melissa began to run towards the Dart station and turned to shout to Erica. 'Thank you! And happy Christmas!'

Erica gave her a wave and turned back, gliding effortlessly through the bedlam of the city centre.

What a woman! If Melissa actually was gay then there might be a different ending to this story, but she wasn't and so she ran through town, zig-zagging around shoppers, dodging buses and taxis, almost coming a cropper with a child on a scooter and avoiding gangs of lads in Christmas jumpers. She took the short cut through Trinity College, colliding with students and tourists and, finally, arrived on the Dart platform gasping for breath.

On the train, she urged it forward, heading towards her destiny. I am not afraid, she wanted to shout out for everyone to hear. I am not scared! But she was. Was Erica telling the truth? Would he want to see her? Would she embarrass herself? She didn't care, all she needed was to give this one last chance and this was it.

She disembarked at the station in Dalkey and ran down to Church Street, festive lights swaying in the dark and whirling wet of a winter night. It was no winter wonderland but she didn't care about the weather, she was right where she wanted to be.

Outside The Daily Bread, where the blinds had been pulled down, making the figures in the shop look like shadow puppets, she could hear music and voices and laughing. She paused at the realisation that Cormac was on the other side of the door and so was, perhaps, her destiny. She gulped a breath of freezing air. Come on, Melissa. Take charge of your life. Stop hiding and being scared. You can do this. She knocked on the door.

No answer.

She knocked again, louder, knowing that she still had time to walk away. No one would ever know. She may yet survive this night without making a fool of herself.

Too late, the chance had passed and someone was unlocking the door.

It was Cormac's mum, Meenie Cullen. 'Melissa, loveen! I was wondering where you were. Cormac said you were far too busy. That's not like our Melissa, I said. Always there. Part of the family.' She called to the room behind her. 'Melissa has arrived. Finally!'

And then she turned again to Melissa. 'Come on in.' They hugged hello.

'I just wanted to pop in and say Happy Christmas,' said Melissa to Meenie. 'You know, see you all and everything.' She had known Meenie Cullen for so long now but, for the very first time, Melissa felt awkward. I'm in love with your son, she wanted to say. So in love with him you wouldn't believe. I can't breathe when I think I might have lost him, and I needed to see if he could, perhaps, maybe, love me.

Suddenly she was nearly knocked off her feet by a ball of fur. Rolo! A tartan ribbon around his neck, he was licking and jumping up. 'Hello boy!' she said, grabbing him and kissing him. Even if things don't go to plan, she thought, she was glad to have seen Rolo and who couldn't love this little bundle of joy. Well, obviously Erica couldn't but *she* did. She wondered would her reunion with Cormac be so exuberant. Somehow, she didn't think it would.

The bakery was decorated beautifully and bathed in candlelight. There was a tree with decorations made out of dough in star and heart shapes tied on with neon ribbon. The room was crowded with people. There were Nora and Walter, the new baby with a pair of reindeer horns on his head, Axel hitting someone with his sword.

And there was Cormac, standing at the back, talking to his dad and brother, Ciaran, holding a bottle of red and a bottle of white in each hand. Melissa put up her hand and gave an arthritic wave. But Cormac seemed to be frozen to the spot.

Oh no, thought Melissa, this has been a mistake. He doesn't want to see me. This was a bad idea, thought Melissa, beginning to plan her escape.

Cormac handed each bottle to his dad and stepped towards her.

'I'll go and get you a glass of something...' Meenie disappeared in search of refreshments.

'Hi,' he said.

'Hi.' They stood there for a moment. 'So,' she said, 'the shop looks amazing.'

'Thanks.'

'So... Anyway,' Melissa said, 'I just wanted to say Happy Christmas.'

'Melissa... it was... what I said before... I...' he began.

'No, don't say it. I want to talk. I have something to say...' she began stuttering a bit. 'Um.' She gulped some air. 'Right.' Here we go, she thought. Come on Melissa, this is your chance. Come on, girl.

'I've missed you, Cormac Cullen,' she said, letting the words rush over themselves. 'Appallingly, in fact. I've missed every single thing about you. Every single thing. I've missed being in the same room as you, breathing the same air as you. I've missed knowing you and being with you. I just want to tell you that. I want to say that you are the most important person – thing – in my life and I am really miserable without you. And I am sorry, I am really, really sorry that I took you for granted and I was so selfish. And all I was consumed with was me and my life. And I'm sorry. And I have missed you so, so much. I don't want to do life without you, I don't not want to see you all the time...'

She stood awkwardly as her words sunk in. She felt raw and exposed.

'I... I... I want... I want you, she continued, trying to fill the silence. 'I want to be with you. That's all I have to say. I want you, simple as that. I want you. I love you. But if you don't want me, that is fine. And I will go and I promise, promise, promise, never to call around again and make a holy show of myself. And I've missed Rolo, terribly. I didn't think you could miss dogs but it turns out you can. And their owners. I've missed the whole package, you and Rolo.' There. She had said it.

'Right,' he said.

'So...' she said. Of course he doesn't feel the same. Of course he doesn't. She'd got it all wrong. As had Erica, obviously. 'Anyway...'

Should she crawl away now or wait for Meenie to come back with the drink? She had never worked out the protocol for awkward situations.

'I know someone who has been equally miserable,' he said.

'Who?' Melissa didn't dare to hope.

'Himself there.' Cormac pointed to Rolo looking up at them with his brown eyes. 'He's been pining for you.' Rolo had pushed himself against Melissa's legs and had sat down on her shoes.

'Have you, sweetheart, have you?' Melissa bent down and stroked his ears. It gave her something to do. It was obvious that Cormac didn't feel the same. If he had once, then he didn't any longer. Erica had been wrong. Well, at least she had tried. At least she had Rolo's affections. 'Okay, so...' she stood up again.

'Well... there's someone else too... Someone else who's been pining for you.'

'Who?' She sounded like she had laryngitis.

He coughed. 'Me. I hate life without you too. It's been the worst time of my life. I really wanted to invite you tonight. It seems so wrong to have something like this and not have you here, but I thought you wouldn't come after how I'd treated you. I treated you terribly. I hurt you, I pushed you away. And I'm sorry, so sorry.'

Meenie bustled up. 'Red or white? Melissa? I know you like a drop!' She had a bottle in each hand and a glass precariously sticking out from between her fingers.

'Neither, thank you Meenie. Do you have juice or something?' She was giving alcohol a wide berth these days. She sometimes wondered if she would ever drink again.

'I'll have a look through the minerals, for you now, loveen. Stay right there,' said Meenie, 'I think we have some of that Seven Up... on my way.'

Cormac and Melissa stood looking at each other, both of them grinning. Melissa felt like she was exploding with happiness. Was it this easy? she thought. Is it this easy to be happy? Was it here all the time and I never knew?

Cormac reached across and took her hand and brought it to his lips.

'You are the brightest and best person I have ever met,' he said. 'Oh my God, life is just so boring without you. Everything I do, everything I have ever done is to impress you. I can't move for wondering what you would say. You'd drive a man to poetry.'

'Please don't,' said Melissa, laughing.

'No, wait,' he said, it's coming to me. What rhymes with Melissa?'

'I don't know,' she said, delighted, holding his hand and thinking how gorgeous he was and loving the feeling inside, the warmth, the happiness spreading through her body. And, of course, the warmth on her feet of Rolo.

'There was a young woman called Melissa,' he began. 'And when she was away I would miss her. She turned up one night, and try as I might, I couldn't get the courage to kiss her.'

But then he did. Right on the lips and Melissa thought that she couldn't feel any happier or more right.

'But you did,' she said, 'you did get the courage.'

'You were the brave one,' he said. 'I was the coward, running away.'

'No, I get it,' she said. 'It was both of us. We nearly missed each other.'

He looked at her. 'Thank you,' he said, 'for coming here tonight. You have made my life.'

'And you mine,' she said, grinning at him.

'Here we go.' Meenie was back with a brimming glass. 'It's a great man Seven Up. Great for all sorts of sicknesses.'

'What about lovesick? Does it cure that?' said Melissa, looking at Cormac who was squeezing her hand tightly.

'I'll leave you two alone, so I will,' said Meenie, bustling off, smiling broadly.

Melissa and Cormac gazed into each other's eyes.

'I love you,' he said quietly, into her ear. 'Always have.'

'And I love you,' answered Melissa. 'Always have.'

'Always will,' he said.

'Always will,' she echoed.

And then they realised that the whole room had gone silent, everyone had been listening in and watching. And then there were cheers and yelling and shouting. 'About time!' called Ciaran. 'We've been waiting for far too long for ye to get it together!'

Cormac and Melissa laughed. She could feel his strong arms pulling her into him and as she did, she realised that all the other relationships may not have failed because there was something wrong with her, that they may have failed because they weren't the right man. They weren't Cormac.

'I'm never letting you go again,' he whispered into her ear. 'Never.'

'Promise me?'

'I promise.'

And they kissed and kissed to the sound of cheers. And it was as wonderful as she could ever have dared to imagine.

49

EILIS

After Rob had left, Eilis stood in the kitchen thinking. Suddenly, it felt as though life was kicking in. Her flickering excitement about life's potential kept getting stronger and stronger. She was totally utterly free, unencumbered, she had only herself to worry about. Brigid, she was sure, would have agreed.

She almost felt giddy. It could all go wrong but she didn't care. The feeling of being alive was intoxicating. She had been toying with a business idea for a while now but it would involve making room in her professional life. There was no time like the present and she thought she had better send an email before she stopped feeling giddy and began feeling sensible and normal.

'Dear Mohit,' she wrote. 'I am writing to tender my resignation from the hospital... I have spent many rewarding and happy years there but have decided to pursue other interests...'

She pressed send.

She would work out her notice and then... who knew what would happen? She was stepping off the cliff and she wondered what parachute – if any – would open; it was now or never. Rob had freed her. Maybe she should thank him.

But there was someone else, someone she wanted to see and talk to and explain everything to. Someone who she couldn't shake from her mind, someone who had sparked something inside her and had made her entirely revaluate her life. Charlie. But would he understand? There was only one way to find out.

It was the evening and dark out but she got in the car, the roads lit by flashing Santas and fairy lights, and drove to O'Malley's Garden Centre.

The shop was closed. There was a silver birch in a pot decorated with lights, old-fashioned baubles hung in the window. Pressing her face against the window, she saw a lamp glowing in the office. She knocked on the glass. She waited and then a face appeared, looking out. Charlie.

Her heart began thudding. Part of her hadn't expected him to be here. She waved at him, wondering what he would do. She felt butterflies in her stomach; she felt the joy of being alive, of taking risks and being in love. Finally, she could admit it.

And then he smiled and stood there for a moment looking at her. He pulled a key out of his pocket and unlocked the door.

'What brings you here on this dark night?' he said. 'Slug pellets?'

She laughed. 'No, something else...'

'Really?'

'Can I come in?'

'Of course... of course. Come in... it's only slightly warmer in here. I've got the stove on in the office.'

He was looking so sexy, so handsome... she just wanted to touch him, to kiss him again. In fact, she thought that if she didn't, she might go mad.

'It's over between me and Rob,' she said quickly. 'He left ages ago and then he came round today and came out...'

'Came out?'

'He's gay,' she said.

'Gay? He kept that quiet, didn't he?'

'Yes,' she laughed. 'But it doesn't matter. We'd become just friends anyway. And so I'm sorry for running away that time and acting so strangely...'

'But I like strange,' he said. 'I thought you knew that. Especially your kind, the normal-strange.' He smiled at her and she was suddenly aware of the devastating effect he had on her; his blue eyes, the sheer, unbridled sexiness of the man. She was being born anew.

'So,' she said, breathing in deeply, 'I just thought I'd ask you something, you having a garden shop and all...'

'Yes,' he said, raising an eyebrow.'

'I wonder if you have any mistletoe.'

'I do as a matter of fact. Great big bunches of it.' He wasn't smiling anymore; he was looking at her intently. 'Why do you want it?'

'Well, there's a tradition,' she said. 'You might have heard of it? Where you ask someone you really like if...'

'If they want to kiss?' he said.

'You've heard it too?'

'I might have.' He was still looking at her, his whole body rigid with intensity. 'And I want to ask you... as the person I most want to kiss in the whole wide world, if, maybe, you would like to kiss me?'

'I would,' she said and they fell into each other's arms and kissed deeply for a long time, far longer than tradition would have expected them to, far longer, in fact, than was actually necessary. But traditions are meant to be improved upon.

This is what it is meant to be, she thought, ages later when they had finished and she was wrapped in his arms. This is what it is meant to feel like; this is what the fuss is all about.

'Come here, you gorgeous, sexy woman,' he said. 'You're coming home with me.'

And she did, and much to her delight he had one of the comfiest sofas she had ever sat on. It was the sign, she now believed, of the kind of person she wanted to be with. And what was more, the kettle was a normal one, no remote control in sight.

50

STEPH

'Can everyone hear me?' Steph adjusted her headset.

There were nods and smiles from the group. Steph had spent the last fortnight planning this, her very first tour at the National Gallery, Representations of Jesus, it was called. The visit would swoop around the gallery looking at ten paintings in all, Jesus featuring in each one. She had thought it a nice one to start, especially as it was practically Christmas.

And there in the crowd was her favourite face in the world, smiling and giving a thumbs up. Rachel. She winked back. She and her daughter had already come such a long way together, and they still have further to go but the new arrangements with Rick now moved out, had helped all of them. They all seemed happier. Everything is going to work out, she thought. Well, everything is going to be a lot better for all of us.

Suddenly, she thought of Mrs Long, her old employer and mentor. She wondered what she would make of Steph's return to the art world. She reckoned she'd be pleased. Would she say, I told you so? Probably.

As the tour group progressed around the gallery, stopping at painting after painting, it seemed to be going well. Well-ish. She got lost a couple of times, brought everyone down the wrong corridor and then got a few dates mixed up and couldn't remember the name of Jesus' mother and someone had to prompt her, but she put it all down to nerves. And, incredibly, she even managed to make her group laugh a few times.

I could get to enjoy this, she thought, feeling giddy with self-confidence and trying to remind herself not to get carried away. And then, finally, it was all over. She felt drenched with sweat and high on adrenaline.

'Mum, you were brilliant,' Rachel came up to her beaming, and she hugged her.

'That might be overstating it a bit,' said Steph, thinking how nice it was to hear her daughter say this. 'I got through it though and that's the most important thing. And I didn't trip. Or swear. So not all bad.'

'I thought it was so interesting,' said Rachel. 'I never knew half that stuff. I might do Art History next year.'

'If you want, you should,' said Steph, smiling at her. 'Anyway, what are you doing in town?'

'Half-day... that talk thing was cancelled so I thought I'd come in and see how you were getting on.'

'Okay, why don't we go and do a bit of shopping... I thought we'd put the decorations up tonight.'

Christmas was inexorable. Even if you didn't fancy it much, it always crept in.

'Looking forward to Christmas?' she asked Rachel.

'A little bit, yes. I didn't think I was going to, but I can't help it. It's still Christmas.'

'We'll have a nice time,' said Steph. 'It'll be quiet and a bit strange...'

'Well, maybe we could still have it with Dad?' said Rachel. 'He could come round for the day?'

Oh God, thought Steph. Could we? Okay, so he wasn't always a good husband (make that never), she didn't want Rachel to miss out on her father.

'Why not?' said Steph. 'The more the merrier!' After all, it was only one day and from the look on Rachel's face, it meant the world to her.

'Mum, do you mean it?' Rachel looked delighted. 'I was so worried about him on his own in that flat.'

'Let's ask him. He would hate to be away from you.'

'And Grandad, as well.'

'Of course.'

Joe was doing okay, actually, thought Steph. Better than she might have imagined. He was keeping to a routine, walking Dingle every day and the entire neighbourhood had taken it upon itself to pop in to keep him company. There was always someone there, either arriving or leaving.

Steph had suggested to him he moved in with herself and Rachel but he had told her he was happy in the house where he shared his life with Nuala.

'By the way,' Rachel said, 'Aoife's house is up for sale. The sign went up this morning. She's really upset. But there is no other way, apparently. Hugh's moved out and Miriam's renting somewhere.'

'That was quick. I'm so sorry, Rach, I'm so sorry for you and Aoife. But I'm sure they will do the best for Aoife. Hugh is steady. He'll make sure she's alright.'

'I hope so.' Rachel linked her arm into Steph's and it felt so right and natural. And so nice.

'Listen,' said Steph. 'I was thinking, would you like to come to Rome with me? Just the two of us? Next month, perhaps. At the end of January. We could go shopping, look round the galleries, eat pizza, it'll be cold but beautiful. Just wander around... what do you think? You've never been...'

Rachel looked delighted. 'I would love to! Cool! As long as we don't go to any churches.'

'That's impossible in Rome...'

'Just one, then.'

'Two?'

'Deal.'

Steph was already looking forward to it, to rekindling her love with Rome and her biggest love, her daughter.

Just then a motorbike roared past them. Steph thought she recognised the blonde woman clinging onto the driver, dressed in tight black leathers.

'Was that...?'

'Miriam?'

'Yes. Was it?'

'It looked like her, didn't it?'

They stood there speechless looking after the bike. The figure turned around and waved at them. Miriam.

'Okay?' she said to Rachel. 'What's wrong?'

'I don't know... it's just that... it's just that she doesn't seem to feel bad about any of it. She's just carrying on as though nothing happened. And all of it was her fault.'

Steph shrugged. 'It wasn't though. It might seem it, but it's not. She was just part of the story. I was responsible too. I should have acted earlier. But things happen, in life, things go wrong and sometimes people don't deal with them well enough and then things get worse. Being grown-up is all about learning. You never stop, it seems.'

They watched as the motorbike pulled up outside the Merrion Hotel and Miriam dismounted, shaking her hair out of the helmet and adjusting her leather trousers as though she was hoiking up a pair of tights. She looked up and for a moment; Steph and Miriam's eyes met.

The driver took his helmet off, pursing his lips for a kiss. He looked old enough to be her father, certainly pushing seventy. Miriam hesitated and then leaned in to acquiesce. The man grabbed her bottom and gave it a hard pinch. His strength was impressive for a man of older years. She winced in pain.

Steph and Rachel looked at each other and laughed.

'Oh my God, Mum! Did you see that?'

'I almost... not quite, but I almost – almost – feel sorry for her.'

They turned to go.

'Come on, I fancy a jumper, something with sequins on.'

'Me too.' And the two of them went off to TopShop in search of sartorial cheer... which Steph paid for. A new leaf, a new start, she thought. A new beginning. This time, this year, I'm in charge. It felt good.

51

MELISSA

'We should get up,' said Melissa. 'It's practically the afternoon.'

'I have been up...' said Cormac. 'Working...'

'And got back in again.'

'It's cold outside. At least Rolo's had his walk. And you need feeding.'

'It is nice in here... with you,' she said, thinking how easy it was with him, how perfectly they and their lives slotted together. 'Let's never get up again. We could direct all operations from bed. Like John and Yoko.'

'Or Morecambe and Wise,' he said. 'Except they wore pyjamas.'

'So not like Morecambe and Wise, then.'

'Nothing like them. I was wrong, utterly wrong. For one thing, as far as I know, they didn't want to do this...' He kissed her on her lips. 'Or this...'

'I love you, Cormac,' she whispered.

'I love you, Melissa.' He stopped and looked over to Rolo. 'Strange. What's that on your collar? Come here, boy.'

Rolo jumped onto the bed. There was a square box, tied to his collar.

'What is it?' Melissa asked.

Cormac untied it and handed it over. 'Uh... I think this is for you.'

She opened it up, fingers trembling. It was a simple gold ring with two tiny diamonds embedded in the band.

'It's beautiful,' she said, heart thumping, suddenly overcome with emotion.

'Melissa Murphy,' said Cormac, 'will you marry me?'

'Cormac Cullen, I thought you'd never ask!'

'And I've been waiting for *you* to ask *me* all these years!'

'Yes, I will,' she said. 'It would be the best thing ever.' She slipped it on and tears filled her eyes. 'I love it.'

'Now, come back to bed, Yoko,' he said. 'You're letting all the heat out.'

For a moment Melissa was speechless. This is happiness, she thought. This is happiness. She closed her eyes.

'I love you,' Cormac said. 'Always have done, always will. You're not an easy woman to forget, Melissa Murphy, but you're exceptionally easy to love.'

'Thank you for loving me and not giving up.'

'Never,' he said. 'Never, ever, ever.'

He was the kind of person who made the world go round, she thought. There weren't many like that, but Cormac was one of them. She'd always known it but she'd never believed she might be the kind of woman who deserved someone so good, someone like Cormac.

But she did. She really did. She just had to get used to the idea.

52

THE GIRLS

The Christmas decorations were up in the Horseshoe Bar in the Shelbourne and parties in all their forms were milling and spilling. Celebration was in the air. It was the night of the school reunion and Eilis went straight to the bar where the girls had arranged to meet.

There were the stragglers of various office parties and things were getting messy. One girl was crying in the corner, make-up dislodged, her two friends talking animatedly beside her, oblivious to her misery. A man was slumped on the table, head lying on an empty packet of crisps, while two others kissed passionately. There was a moral here... sometimes you *can* start the party too early.

Pointlessly perusing the menu and already knowing she would have a posh gin and tonic, and a bowl of fancy peanuts (why not? It *was* Christmas), Eilis perched, waiting for Steph and Melissa.

She drank with unbecoming speed, feeling something quite, quite new. Excitement. Her business was to be called, she had decided, Greenfingers. She was going to call out to everyone locally who grew beautiful garden flowers and she was going to create a delivery business. It could, she thought, include other plants, seedlings, vegetables and fruit. But it would start with flowers. Local, beautiful flowers grown by the green-fingered, such as Rosemary, Pauline and Frank... and Charlie, and none of those flown-in, perfect specimens from far-flung climes. Greenfingers could, she thought, take off. She was going to meet with her bank manager at the beginning of January and until then she was working on her business plan. Greenfingers wouldn't pay very much at first but there was the offer of consultancy work from Mohit, so life would be on her terms. She was going to be in charge.

Earlier that day she had received a wedding invitation. Bogdan and Becca from the hospital were getting married on New Year's Eve and did she want to join them? She had declined, ever so politely, because she had a much better invitation. Charlie wanted to try out his new fire pit and they were going to sit in the garden, round the blazing flames, rugs over their knees, drinking champagne. And thinking about the New Year and their new relationship. She *couldn't* wait.

She and Charlie had spent the last two weeks talking and talking. She had no idea that she could feel like this, so happy and so excited. They were half in each other's houses, spending every moment with each other. There was just so much to say. And she had begun sleeping, something she hadn't done for years. Deep, slumberous sleeps where she would wake feeling rested. Only that morning, Charlie brought her up a cup of tea and a croissant in bed. Rob wasn't one for eating in bed. He was always worried about crumbs. Charlie was a man after her own heart and believed in the pleasure of breakfast in bed. And everything else that could be done in bed.

Rob had sent her a card for Christmas. It was a picture of their old college in Trinity, covered in snow. There was a bicycle leaning against the front of the building which looked exactly like her old Raleigh. She almost cried when she opened it. Inside he had written: 'thank you for the memories'. One day, they might even be friends, she thought. You never knew what was around the corner.

She couldn't stop grinning these days. She popped a peanut into her mouth and wondered if she should order another drink. But then, in a bundle of scarves and gloves, and kisses and hugs and ordering of more drinks, Steph and Melissa appeared. They appraised each other. All of them dressed up and looking fabulous.

'Heels, Eilis?' said Melissa, with mock-shock. 'Where are the comfortable shoes?'

'In my bag, give these things half an hour and then the loafers are coming out. But I've bought new ones... green suede. I'm in love with them.'

'They are not going to go with the dress.'

'And I'm not going to care,' she said. Looking forward to going back home at the end of the night where Charlie would be waiting for her in bed.

'Now,' said Melissa. 'Have you got your narrative all sorted?' said Melissa.

'What do you mean?' said Steph.

'You know, when you get asked what have you been doing for the last twenty years, you have something snappy and cool to say, such as working on a crocodile farm in Australia, training bats in Romania, or dedicating yourself to the word of God. Whatever. You can't actually go into detail. Just be wafty and enigmatic. That's the done thing at reunions.'

'I'll work on it,' said Steph. She had decided to turn up, after some deliberation. She wasn't quite ready to start partying, but it was Rachel who had persuaded her.

'Go on, Mum,' she had said. 'Granny would want you to.'

And Rachel had done her make-up and had made a really good job of it. Maybe a bit too much sparkle but she felt good.

Melissa was sitting there, smiling beatifically. 'My story is I've been working in the diamond mines of Peru,' she said. 'And cattle rustling in Mongolia.'

'Outer or inner?' asked Steph.

'Both.'

There was something most definitely different about Melissa. She assumed the glow of someone with *news*.

'You look... different, Melissa. Like you're happy?' Eilis accused.

'Might be...' Melissa giggled. (Giggled? That was a first.) She didn't quite know how to put it. 'Cormac and I... we've...'

'Yes... yes?' Eilis and Steph clutched each other. 'You haven't, have you? At long last?'

'We've... we've fallen in love. Have been for years. We just didn't know it. Or just didn't sort it out. I don't know. But we are now. And it's amazing.' She beamed at them.

Eilis and Steph actually laughed out loud.

'Talk about slow train coming!' said Steph. 'We've known for years.'

'Why'd you wait so long?' said Eilis. 'Men like Cormac are thin on the ground. No, endangered. He should be cloned.'

'I've been a fool, I know that,' said Melissa. 'I wasn't ready, I suppose. I didn't trust myself with him. You know, not to spoil it.'

Eilis and Steph nodded. They knew, they understood.

'And there's this.' She held up her ring. 'I almost forgot!'

They all squealed.

'We should order champagne!' said Eilis.

'Not for me,' said Melissa. 'I've decided to lay of the sauce for as long as... maybe forever. I just don't want to be like... you know...'

Mary hadn't drunk in two months now and was diligently going to A.A. She and Frankie had met up again and Mary was fretting about what to buy Cara and Caleb for Christmas. Melissa had suggested some books she thought they might like. And something plasticky to off-set the books.

'Anyway,' said, Steph. 'I'm so glad for you. You are perfect for each other.' She had tears in her eyes.

'Do you really think?' Melissa was enjoying the corroboration of her own feelings. It was so lovely to let go and... bask. This was a *nice* feeling.

'Yes, I do. Really.'

'Thanks Steph,' said Melissa. They smiled at each other. 'And how are you... how's it all going?' They were all suddenly thinking of Nuala.

'Grand, so. Kind of. You know. One day at a time,' she tried to smile. 'Dad's taking it hardest, but he's with us most days, me and Rachel. We're getting him through it, which is helping us. And with Rick...'

'With a silent P,' said Melissa, sipping her Elderflower spritzy-thing.

'Indeed, Mr Silent-P is gone... and it's so wonderful to wake up and know that the day is mine to be in charge of.' She shrugged knowing that no one could hurt her ever again, knowing that she and Rachel could look forward to a calm future. She was never going to relinquish control over her life as easily as she had done before. Who ever thought living alone could be empowering? 'I can do whatever I like,' she said. 'No eggshells, no atmosphere. No Miriam.'

'You mean Mrs Mad McMad,' said Melissa.

Steph actually thought she was going to laugh. Surely not? This was *not* a laughing matter. She should have been crying into her glass, planning elaborate revenges or dreading the lonely hinterland of the peri-menopause. Instead, she was drinking a glass of Prosecco with her friends and was feeling her mouth twitch into something resembling a smile.

She held up her glass, feeling suddenly unburdened by it all. It didn't have to be terrible. The thought of Nuala not being here was awful but her mother was the most life-giving person she had ever met. She would want her to *live*. 'Here's to adultery,' she said, the idea slowly spreading. 'Thank God for adultery! The escape route for the non-proactive, unhappy wife!'

'To adultery!' the other two chorused, clinking and slightly spilling their drinks. 'And to inaction! And apathy!' Others in the bar were looking over at them. They all laughed.

'So Eils, what about you? Any news?' said Steph, waiting for Eilis to do her usual and not say much. But Eilis cleared her throat.

'Um…' she began. How to put it all into words? 'Well, Rob's gay and I have embarked on a sordid and immensely satisfying affair with a man who is the handsomest thing ever to walk the planet and brings me out in a cold sweat every time I think of him.'

Steph and Melissa gaped for a moment trying to take it all in, and then the three of them burst into laughter, the kind of gasping for air, flappy-hands, choking laughter which, to all the fellow drinkers in the bar, looked as though they had lost their minds.

In fact, it was just the opposite. It may have taken more than four decades, but minds had been found, never to be lost again.

'It's been quite a year, hasn't it?' said Eilis.

'Yes,' said Steph, 'It's been one of the most roller-coasty of my life. I am looking for less drama next year. I don't think I could go through another year like this.'

'To us and our continued adventures,' said Melissa. 'Together.'

They clinked, all of them with tears in their eyes.

'You know,' said Steph. 'I didn't realise how lonely I was without you both. I mean, I was just getting on with things, but not to have you, people I could talk to, was awful. It made everything worse.'

'Me too,' said Eilis. 'I missed you both.'

'Well, let's make sure it never happens again, okay?' said Melissa. 'We've got plenty of years left to go. And things will happen to us. The remarkable, the unremarkable. But this time, we'll do it together.'

'Okay, gang,' said Steph.

'I'm in,' said Eilis.

'Jesus Christ!' Melissa looked at the time on her phone. 'It's time! Are you ready to face your past?' Melissa said.

The reunion was starting.

'Let's go!' said Eilis. And in they walked, the three of them, arm in arm. Life, they had discovered, worked so much better when they were together. They were the perfect fit. The DJ was playing tunes from the 1990s.

Steph looked at her friends on either side. 'I couldn't have done any of this without you,' she said.

'I'd be in a crumbling heap,' said Melissa, grinning, giddy on love and life. 'Weeping in the gutter without you two.'

Eilis grinned at them. 'Friends like you,' she said. 'I don't know what I'd do if you two hadn't walked back into my life.'

'Friends like us,' said Steph.

'Jesus!' said Melissa. 'I've just seen Sister Attracta. She's waving to us. We'll have to go over and be nice.'

And they did. They could have been eighteen again, meeting their past selves and lives. But what about the future? Life was better, it was obvious, the future brighter when they had each other.

MORE FROM SIÂN O'GORMAN

We hope you enjoyed reading *Friends Like Us*. If you did, please leave a review.

If you'd like to gift a copy, this book is also available as an ebook, digital audio download and audiobook CD.

Sign up to Siân O'Gorman's mailing list for news, competitions and updates on future books.

https://bit.ly/SianOGormannewsletter

ABOUT THE AUTHOR

Sian O'Gorman was born in Galway on the West Coast of Ireland, grew up in the lovely city of Cardiff, and has found her way back to Ireland and now lives on the east of the country, in the village of Dalkey, just along the coast from Dublin. She works as a radio producer for RTE.

Follow Sian on social media:

- facebook.com/sian.ogorman.7
- twitter.com/msogorman
- instagram.com/msogorman
- bookbub.com/authors/sian-o-gorman

ABOUT BOLDWOOD BOOKS

Boldwood Books is a fiction publishing company seeking out the best stories from around the world.

Find out more at www.boldwoodbooks.com

Sign up to the Book and Tonic newsletter for news, offers and competitions from Boldwood Books!

http://www.bit.ly/bookandtonic

We'd love to hear from you, follow us on social media:

[f] facebook.com/BookandTonic

[🐦] twitter.com/BoldwoodBooks

[📷] instagram.com/BookandTonic

ACKNOWLEDGMENTS

Thank you to my agent Ger Nichol and my editor Caroline Ridding. And to my daughter Ruby... quite simply, the nicest and loveliest person I have ever met. Thank you for being you.

ACKNOWLEDGMENTS